SLOW HORSES

MICK HERRON

ISIS
LARGE PRINT
Oxford

First published in Great Britain 2010
by
Constable
An imprint of Constable & Robinson

Published in Large Print 2010 by ISIS Publishing Ltd.,
7 Centremead, Osney Mead, Oxford OX2 0ES
by arrangement with
Constable & Robinson Ltd.

British Library Cataloguing in Publication Data
Herron, Mick.
   Slow horses.
   1. Intelligence service - - Fiction.
   2. Kidnapping - - Fiction.
   3. Suspense fiction.
   4. Large type books.
   I. Title
   823.9'2–dc22

ISBN 978–0–7531–8694–7 (hb)
ISBN 978–0–7531–8695–4 (pb)

Printed and bound in Great Britain by
T. J. International Ltd., Padstow, Cornwall

i.m.

DA, SC, AJ & RL

a sourcing
whom my lost candle like the firefly loves
John Berryman

This is how River Cartwright slipped off the fast track and joined the slow horses.

Eight twenty Tuesday morning, and King's Cross crammed with what the O.B. called *other people*: "Non-combatants, River. Perfectly honourable occupation in peacetime." He had a codicil. "We've not been at peace since September '14."

The O.B.'s delivery turning this to Roman numerals in River's head. MCMXIV.

Stopping, he pretended to check his watch; a manoeuvre indistinguishable from actually checking his watch. Commuters washed round him like water round a rock, their irritation evident in clicking of tongues and expulsions of breath. At the nearest exit — a bright space through which weak January daylight splashed — two of the black-clad achievers stood like statues, their heavy weaponry unremarked by non-combatants, who'd come a long way since 1914.

The achievers — so called because they got the job done — were keeping well back, as per instructions.

Twenty yards ahead was the target. "White tee under a blue shirt," River repeated under his breath. Adding details, now, to Spider's skeleton outline: young, male, Middle Eastern looking; the blue shirt's sleeves rolled up; the black jeans stiff and new. Would you buy new trousers for a jaunt like this? He stuffed the information away; a question to be asked later.

A rucksack on the target's right shoulder listed, suggesting weight. The wire coiled into his ear, like River's own, might have been an iPod.

"Confirm visual."

River, touching his left ear with his left hand, spoke quietly into what looked like a button on his cuff. "Confirmed."

A gaggle of tourists crowded the concourse, their distribution of luggage suggesting they were circling the wagons. River skirted them without taking his eyes off the target, who was heading for the annexe platforms; those which waved off trains towards Cambridge, and points east.

Trains generally less packed than the northbound HSTs.

Unbidden images arrived: of twisted metal scattered along miles of broken rails. Of trackside bushes lit with flame, and hung with scraps of meat.

"What you have to bear in mind" — the O.B.'s words — "is that worst sometimes does come to worst."

The worst had increased exponentially over the last few years.

Two transport cops by a ticket barrier ignored the target but studied River. Don't approach, he warned silently. Don't come anywhere near me. It was the small details on which enterprises foundered. Last thing he wanted was an audible altercation; anything that startled the target.

The cops went back to their conversation.

River paused, and mentally regrouped.

He was of average height, this young man River Cartwright; was fair-haired and pale-skinned, with grey eyes that often seemed inward-looking, a sharpish nose and a small mole on his upper lip. When he concentrated, his brow furrowed in a way that led some to suspect him of puzzlement. Today he wore blue jeans and a dark jacket. But if you'd asked him that morning about his appearance, he'd have mentioned his hair. Lately, he'd favoured a Turkish barber, where they go in close with the scissors, then apply a naked flame to the ears. They give no warning that this is about to happen. River emerged from the chair scoured and scalded like a doorstep. Even now, his scalp tingled in a draught.

Without taking his eyes off the target, now forty yards ahead — without, specifically, taking his eyes off the rucksack — River spoke again into his button. "Follow. But give him room."

If the worst was a detonation on a train, next worst was one on a platform. Recent history showed that people on their way to work were at their most vulnerable. Not because they were weaker. But because there were a lot of them, packed in enclosed spaces.

He didn't look round, trusting that the black-clad achievers were not far behind.

To River's left were sandwich outlets and coffee bars; a pub; a pie stall. To his right, a long train lingered. At intervals along the platform travellers negotiated suitcases through its doors, while pigeons noisily changed rafters overhead. A tannoy issued instructions, and the crowd on the concourse behind River swelled, as individuals broke away.

Always, in railway stations, there was this sense of pent-up movement. A crowd was an explosion waiting to happen. People were fragments. They just didn't know it yet.

The target disappeared behind a huddle of travellers.

River shifted left, and the target appeared again.

He passed one of the coffee bars, and a sitting couple triggered a memory. This time yesterday River had been in Islington. His upgrading assessment involved compiling a dossier on a public figure: River had been allocated a Shadow Cabinet Minister who'd promptly had two small strokes, and was in a private ward in Hertfordshire. There seemed no process for nominating a substitute, so River had picked one off his own bat, and had followed Lady Di two days straight without being spotted — office/gym/office/wine bar/office/home/coffee bar/office/gym . . . This place's logo sparked that memory. Inside his head, the O.B. barked a reprimand: "Mind. Job. Same place, good idea?"

Good idea.

The target bore left.

"Potterville," River muttered to himself.

He passed under the bridge, and turned left too.

A brief glimpse of overhead sky — grey and damp as a dishcloth — and River was entering the mini-concourse that housed platforms 9, 10 and 11. From its outside wall half a luggage trolley protruded:

platform 9 ¾ was where the Hogwarts Express docked. River passed inside. The target was already heading down Platform 10.

Everything speeded up.

There weren't many people around — the next train wasn't due to leave for fifteen minutes. A man on a bench was reading a paper, and that was about it. River picked up his pace, closing the gap. From behind him came a shift in the quality of the noise — from all-over babble to focused murmur — and he knew the achievers were drawing comment.

But the target didn't look back. The target kept moving, as if his intention was to climb into the furthest carriage: white tee, blue shirt, rucksack and all.

River spoke into his button again. Said the words — *Take him* — and began to run.

"Everybody down!"

The man on the bench rose to his feet, and was knocked off them by a figure in black.

"Down!"

Up ahead, two more men dropped from the train's roof into the target's path. Who turned to see River, arm outstretched, waving him to the floor with the flat of his hand.

The achievers were shouting commands:

The bag!

Drop the bag!

"Put the bag on the ground," River said. "And get to your knees."

"But I don't —"

"Drop the bag!"

The target dropped the bag. A hand scooped it up. Other hands grabbed at limbs: the target was flattened, spreadeagled, wiped on the tiles, while the rucksack was passed to River. Who set it carefully on the now vacant bench, and unzipped it.

Overhead, an automated message unspooled around the rafters. *Would Inspector Samms please report to the operations room.*

Books, an A4 notepad, a pencil tin.

Would Inspector Samms

A Tupperware box holding a cheese sandwich and an apple.

please report to

River looked up. His lip twitched. He said, quite calmly —

the operations room

"Search him."

"Don't hurt me!" The boy's voice was muffled: he had a faceful of floor, and guns pointing at his head.

Target, River reminded himself. Not *boy*. Target.

Would Inspector Samms

"*Search* him!" He turned back to the rucksack. The pencil tin held three biros and a paperclip.

please report to

"He's clean."

River dropped the tin to the bench and upended the sack. Books, notepad, a stray pencil, a pocket-sized pack of tissues.

the operations room

They scattered on the floor. He shook the rucksack. Nothing in its pockets.

6

"Check him again."

"He's clean."

Would Inspector Samms

"Will somebody turn that bloody thing off?"

Catching his own note of panic, he clamped his mouth shut.

"He's clean. Sir."

please report to

River again shook the rucksack like a rat, then let it drop.

the operations room

One of the achievers began speaking, quietly but urgently, into a collar-mic.

River became aware of someone staring at him through the window of the waiting train. Ignoring her, he began to trot down the platform.

"Sir?"

There was a certain sarcasm to that.

Would Inspector Samms please report to the operations room.

Blue shirt, white tee, River thought.

White shirt, blue tee?

He picked up speed. A transport policeman stepped forward as he reached the ticket bay but River looped round him, shouted an incoherent instruction, then ran full pelt back to the main concourse.

Would Inspector Samms — and the recorded announcement, a coded message to staff that a security alert was taking place, switched off. A human voice took its place:

"Due to a security incident, this station is being evacuated. Please make your way to the nearest exit."

He had three minutes tops before the Dogs arrived.

River's feet had a direction of their own, propelling him towards the concourse while he still had room to move. But all around, people were getting off trains, onboard announcements having brought sudden halts to journeys that hadn't yet begun, and panic was only a heartbeat away — mass panic was never deep beneath the surface, not in railways stations and airports. The phlegmatic cool of the British crowd was oft-remarked, and frequently absent.

Static burst in his ear.

The tannoy said: "Please make your way calmly to the nearest exit. This station is now closed."

"River?"

He shouted into his button. "Spider? You idiot, you called the wrong colours!"

"What the hell's happening? There are crowds coming out of every —"

"White tee under a blue shirt. That's what you said."

"No, I said blue tee under —"

"Fuck you, Spider." River yanked his earpiece out.

He'd reached the stairs, where the crowd sucks into the underground. Now, it was streaming out. Irritation was its main emotion, but it carried other whispers: fear, suppressed panic. Most of us hold that some things only happen to other people. Many of us hold that one such thing is death. The tannoy's words chipped away at this belief.

"The station is now closed. Please make your way to the nearest exit."

The tube was the city's heartbeat, thought River. Not an east-bound platform. The tube.

He pushed into the evacuating crowd, ignoring its hostility. *Let me through.* This had minimal impact. *Security. Let me through.* That was better. No path opened, but people stopped pushing him back.

Two minutes before the Dogs. Less.

The corridor widened at the foot of the stairs. River raced round the corner, where a broader space waited — ticket machines against walls; ticket windows with blinds drawn down; their recent queues absorbed into the mass of people heading elsewhere. Already, the crowd had thinned. Escalators had been halted; tape strung across to keep fools off. The platforms below were emptying of passengers.

River was stopped by a transport cop.

"Station's being cleared. Can't you hear the bloody tannoy?"

"I'm with intelligence. Are the platforms clear?"

"Intelli —?"

"Are the platforms clear?"

"They're being evacuated."

"You're sure?"

"It's what I've been —"

"You have CC?"

"Well of course we —"

"Show me."

The surrounding noises grew rounder; echoes of departing travellers swam across the ceilings. But other sounds were approaching: quick footsteps, heavy on the tiled floor. The Dogs. River had little time to put this right.

"Now."

The cop blinked, but caught River's urgency — could hardly miss it — and pointed over his own shoulder at a door marked *No Access*. River was through it before the footsteps' owner appeared.

The small windowless room smelled of bacon, and looked like a voyeur's den. A swivel chair faced a bank of TV monitors. Each blinked regularly, shifting focus on the same repeated scene: a deserted underground platform. It was like a dull science fiction film.

A draught told him the cop had come in.

"Which platforms are which?"

The cop pointed: groups of four. "Northern. Piccadilly. Victoria."

River scanned them. Every two seconds, another blink.

From underfoot came a distant rumble.

"What's that?"

The cop stared.

"*What?*"

"That would be a tube train."

"They're running?"

"Station's closed," the cop said, as if to an idiot. "But the lines are open."

"All of them?"

"Yes. But the trains won't stop."

They wouldn't need to.

"What's next?"

"What's —?"

"Next train, damn it. Which platform?"

"Victoria. Northbound."

River was out of the door.

At the top of the shallow flight of stairs, barring the way back to the mainline station, a short dark man stood, talking into a headset. His tone changed abruptly when he saw River.

"He's here."

But River wasn't. He'd leaped the barrier and was at the top of the nearest escalator; snapping back the security tape; heading down the motionless staircase, two deep steps at a time.

At the bottom, it was eerily empty. That sci-fi vibe again.

Tube trains pass closed stations at a crawl. River reached the deserted platform as the train pulled into it like a big slow animal, with eyes for him alone. And it had plenty of eyes. River felt all of them, all those pairs of eyes trapped in the belly of the beast; intent on him as he stared down the platform, at someone who'd just appeared from an exit at the far end.

White shirt. Blue tee.

River ran.

Behind him someone else ran too, calling his name, but that didn't matter. River was racing a train. Racing it and winning — drawing level with it, outpacing it; he could hear its slow motion noise; a grinding mechanical feedback underpinned by the terror growing within. He could hear thumping on windows. Was aware that the driver was looking at him in horror, thinking he was about to hurl himself on to the tracks. But River couldn't help what anyone thought — River could only do what he was doing, which was run down the platform at exactly this speed.

Up ahead — blue tee, white shirt — someone else was also doing the only thing he could do.

River didn't have breath to shout. He barely had breath to push himself onwards, but he managed . . .

Almost managed. Almost managed to be fast enough.

Behind him, his name was shouted again. Behind him, the tube train was picking up pace.

He was aware of the driver's cabin overhauling him, five yards from the target.

Because this was the target. This had always been the target. And the swiftly narrowing distance between them showed him for the youngster he was: eighteen? Nineteen? Black hair. Brown skin. And a blue tee under a white shirt — *fuck you, Spider* — that he was unbuttoning to reveal a belt packed tight with . . .

The train pulled level with the target.

River stretched out an arm, as if he could bring the finishing line closer.

The footsteps behind him slowed and stopped. Someone swore.

River was almost on the target — was half a second away.

But close wasn't nearly enough.

The target pulled a cord on his belt.

And that was that.

Part One

Slough House

Let us be clear about this much at least: Slough House is not in Slough, nor is it a house. Its front door lurks in a dusty recess between commercial premises in the Borough of Finsbury, a stone's throw from Barbican Station. To its left is a former newsagent's, now a newsagent's/grocer's/off-licence, with DVD rental a blooming sideline; to its right, the New Empire Chinese restaurant, whose windows are constantly obscured by a thick red curtain. A typewritten menu propped against the glass has yellowed with age but is never replaced; is merely amended with marker pen. If diversification has been the key to the newsagent's survival, retrenchment has been the long-term strategy of the New Empire, with dishes regularly struck from its menu like numbers off a bingo card. It is one of Jackson Lamb's core beliefs that eventually all the New Empire will offer will be egg-fried rice and sweet-and-sour pork. All served behind thick red curtains, as if paucity of choice were a national secret.

The front door, as stated, lurks in a recess. Its ancient black paintwork is spattered with roadsplash, and the shallow pane of glass above its jamb betrays no light within. An empty milk bottle has stood in its shadow so long, city lichen has bonded it to the pavement. There is no doorbell, and the letterbox has healed like a childhood wound: any mail — and there's never any mail — would push at its flap without achieving entry. It's as if the door were a dummy, its only reason for existing being to provide a buffer zone between shop and restaurant. Indeed, you could sit at the bus stop opposite for days on end, and never see anyone use it. Except that, if you sat at the bus stop opposite for long, you'd find interest being taken in your presence. A thickset man, probably chewing gum, might sit next to you. His presence discourages. He wears an air of repressed violence, of a grudge carried long enough that it's ceased to matter to him where he lays it down, and he'll watch you until you're out of sight.

Meanwhile, the stream in and out of the newsagent's is more or less constant. And there's always pavement business occurring; always people heading one way or the other. A kerbside sweeper trundles past, its revolving brushes shuffling cigarette ends and splinters of glass and bottle tops into its maw. Two men, heading in opposite directions, perform that little avoidance dance, each one's manoeuvre mirrored by the other's, but manage to pass without colliding. A woman, talking on a mobile phone, checks her reflection in the window as she walks. Way overhead a helicopter buzzes, reporting on roadworks for a radio station.

And throughout all this, which happens every day, the door remains closed. Above the New Empire and the newsagent's, Slough House's windows rise four storeys into Finsbury's unwelcoming October skies, and are flaked and grimy, but not opaque. To the upstairs rider on a passing bus, delayed for any length of time — which can easily happen; a combination of traffic lights, near-constant roadworks, and the celebrated inertia of London buses — they offer views of first-floor rooms that are mostly yellow and grey. Old yellow, and old grey. The yellows are the walls, or what can be seen of the walls behind grey filing cabinets and grey, institutional bookcases, on which are ranged out-of-date reference volumes; some lying on their backs; others leaning against their companions for support; a few still upright, the lettering on their spines rendered ghostly by a daily wash of electric light. Elsewhere, lever arch files have been higgledy-piggled into spaces too small; piles of them jammed vertically between shelves, leaving the uppermost squeezed outwards, threatening to fall. The ceilings are yellowed too, an unhealthy shade smeared here and there with cobweb. And the desks and chairs in these first-storey rooms are of the same functional metal as the bookshelves, and possibly commandeered from the same institutional source: a decommissioned barracks, or a prison administration block. These are not chairs to sit back in, gazing thoughtfully into space. Nor are they desks to treat as an extension of one's personality, and decorate with photographs and mascots. Which facts in themselves convey a certain information: that those who labour here are not so well regarded that their comfort is deemed as being of account. They're meant to sit and perform their tasks with the minimum of distraction. And then to leave by a back door, un-observed by kerbside sweepers, or women with mobile phones.

The bus's upper deck offers less of a view of the next storey, though glimpses of the same nicotine-stained ceilings are available. But even a three-decker bus wouldn't cast much light: the offices on the second floor are distressingly similar to those below. And besides, the information picked out in gold lettering on their windows says enough to dull interest. *W W Henderson*, it reads. *Solicitor and Commissioner for Oaths*. Occasionally, from behind the serifed flamboyance of this long-redundant logo, a figure will appear, and regard the street below as if he's looking at something else altogether. But whatever that is, it won't hold his attention long. In a moment or two, he'll be gone.

No such entertainment is promised by the uppermost storey, whose windows have blinds drawn over them. Whoever inhabits this level is evidently disinclined to be reminded of a world outside, or to have accidental rays of sunshine pierce his gloom. But this too is a clue, since it indicates that whoever haunts this floor has the freedom to choose darkness, and freedom of choice is generally limited to those in charge. Slough House, then — a name which appears on no official documentation, nameplate or headed notepaper; no utility bill or deed of leasehold; no business card or phone book or estate agent's listing; which is not this building's name at all, in any but the most colloquial of senses — is evidently run from the top down, though judging by the uniformly miserable decor, the hierarchy is of a restricted character. You're either at the top or you're not. And only Jackson Lamb is at the top.

At length, the traffic lights change. The bus coughs into movement, and trundles on its way to St Paul's. And in her last few seconds of viewing, our upstairs passenger might wonder what it's like, working in these offices; might even conjure a brief fantasy in which the building, instead of a faltering legal practice, becomes an overhead dungeon to which the failures of some larger service are consigned as punishment: for crimes of drugs and drunkenness and lechery; of politics and betrayal; of unhappiness and doubt; and of the unforgivable carelessness of allowing a man on a tube platform to detonate himself, killing or maiming an estimated 120 people and causing £30m worth of actual damage, along with a projected £2.5 billion in lost tourist revenue — becomes, in effect, an administrative oubliette where, alongside a pre-digital overflow of paperwork, a post-useful crew of misfits can be stored and left to gather dust.

Such a fancy won't survive the time it takes the bus to pass beneath the nearby pedestrian bridge, of course. But one inkling might last a while longer: that the yellows and greys that dominate the colour scheme aren't what they first appear — that the yellow isn't yellow at all, but white exhausted by stale breath and tobacco, by pot-noodle fumes and overcoats left to dry on radiators; and that the grey isn't grey but black with the stuffing knocked out of it. But this thought too will

19

quickly fade, because few things associated with Slough House stick in the mind; its name alone having proved durable, born years ago, in a casual exchange between spooks:

Lamb's been banished.

Where've they sent him? Somewhere awful?

Bad as it gets.

God, not Slough?

Might as well be.

Which, in a world of secrets and legends, was all it took to give a name to Jackson Lamb's new kingdom: a place of yellows and greys, where once all was black and white.

Just after 7 a.m. a light went on at the second-storey window, and a figure appeared behind *W W Henderson, Solicitor and Commissioner for Oaths.* On the street below, a milk float rattled past. The figure hovered a moment, as if expecting the float to turn dangerous, but withdrew once it passed from sight. Inside, he resumed the business at hand, up-ending a soaking black rubbish sack on to a newspaper spread across the worn and faded carpet.

The air was immediately polluted.

Rubber-gloved, wrinkle-nosed, he got to his knees and began picking through the mess.

Eggshells, vegetable ends, coffee grounds in melting paper filters, parchment-coloured teabags, a sliver of soap, labels from jars, a plastic squeezy bottle, florets of stained kitchen towels, torn brown envelopes, corks, bottle tops, the coiled spring and cardboard back of a spiral-notepad, some bits of broken crockery which didn't fit together, tin trays from takeaway meals, scrunched-up Post-its, a pizza box, a wrung-out tube of toothpaste, two juice cartons, an empty tin of shoe polish, a plastic scoop, and seven carefully bundled parcels made from pages of *Searchlight*.

And much else that wasn't immediately identifiable. All of it sopping wet and glistening, sluglike, in the light of the overhead bulb.

He sat back on his haunches. Picked up the first of the *Searchlight* parcels, and unwrapped it as carefully as he could.

The contents of an ashtray fell on to the carpet.

He shook his head, and dropped the rotting newspaper back on the pile.

A sound made its way up the back stairs, and he paused, but it didn't repeat. All entrances and exits from Slough House came via a back yard with mildewed, slimy walls, and everyone who came in made a large, unfriendly noise doing so, because the door stuck and — like most of the people using it — needed a good kicking. But this sound had been nothing like that, so he shook his head and decided it had been the building waking up; flexing its lintels or whatever old buildings did in the morning, after a night of rain. Rain he'd been out in, collecting the journalist's rubbish.

Eggshells, vegetable ends, coffee grounds in melting paper filters . . .

He picked another of the paper parcels, its scrunched-up headline a denunciation of a recent BNP demo, and sniffed it tentatively. Didn't smell like an ashtray.

"A sense of humour can be a real bastard," Jackson Lamb said.

River dropped the parcel.

Lamb was leaning in the doorway, his cheeks glistening slightly as they tended to after exertion. Climbing stairs counted, though he'd not made a squeak on them. River could barely manage such stealth himself, and he wasn't carrying Lamb's weight: most of it gathered round his middle, like a pregnancy. A shabby grey raincoat shrouded it now, while the umbrella hooked over his arm dripped on to the floor.

River, trying to hide the fact that his heart had just punched him in the ribs, said, "You think he's calling us Nazis?"

"Well, yes. Obviously he's calling us Nazis. But I meant you doing this on Sid's half of the room."

River picked up the fallen bundle but it gave way as he did so, the paper too wet to contain its contents, spilling a stew of small bones and scraped-away skin — for a nasty moment, evidence of a brutal, baby-sized murder. And then the shape of a chicken asserted itself from the collection; a misshapen chicken — all legs and wings — but recognizably a former bird. Lamb snorted. River rubbed his gloved hands together, smearing sodden lumps of newspaper into balls, then shaking them into the pile. The black and red inks wouldn't lose their grip so easily. The once-yellow gloves turned the colour of miners' fingers.

Lamb said, "That wasn't too clever."

Thank you for that, River thought. Thanks for pointing that out.

The previous night he'd lurked outside the journo's past midnight, wresting what shelter he could from the slight overhang of the building opposite while rain belted down like Noah's nightmare. Most of the neighbours had done their civic duty, black sacks lined up like sitting pigs, or council-supplied wheelie bins standing sentry by doors. But nothing outside the journo's. Cold rain tracked down River's neck, mapping a course to the crack of his arse, and he knew it didn't matter how long he stood there, he was going to have no joy.

"Don't get caught," Lamb had said.

Of course I won't get bloody caught, he'd thought. "I'll try not to."

And: "Residents' parking," Lamb had added, as if sharing some arcane password.

Residents' parking. So what?

So he couldn't sit in his car, he'd belatedly realized. Couldn't cosy down, rain bouncing off a waterproof roof, and wait for the bags to appear. The chances of a parking revenue attendant — or whatever they were called today — doing the rounds after midnight were slim, but not non-existent.

It was all he'd need — a parking ticket. On-the-spot fine. His name in a book.

Don't get caught.

So it was the slight overhang in the pouring rain. Worse than that, it was the flickering light behind the thin curtains of the journo's street-level apartment; it was the way a shadow kept appearing behind them. As if the hack inside, dry as toast, was busting a gut at the thought of River in the rain, waiting for him to put his rubbish bag out so he could whip it away for covert study. As if the journo knew all this.

Not long after midnight, the thought occurred to River: maybe he did.

That was how it had been for the past eight months. Every so often, he'd take the bigger picture and give it a shake, like it was a loose jigsaw. Sometimes the pieces came together differently; sometimes they didn't fit at all. Why did Jackson Lamb want this journo's rubbish, enough to give River his first out-of-the-office job since he'd been assigned to Slough House? Maybe the point wasn't getting the rubbish. Maybe the point was River standing in the rain for hours on end, while the hack laughed with Lamb about it over the phone.

This rain had been forecast. Hell, it had been raining when Lamb had given him the op.

Residents' parking, he'd said.

Don't get caught.

Ten more minutes, and River decided enough was enough. There was going to be no bag of rubbish, or if there was, it wasn't going to mean anything, other than that he'd been sent on an idiot's errand . . . He'd walked back the way he'd come, collecting a random rubbish sack on the way; had flung it into the boot of the car he'd parked by the nearest meter. Had driven home. Had gone to bed.

Where he'd lain for two hours, watching the jigsaw reassemble itself. Jackson Lamb's *Don't get caught* might have meant just that: that River had been given an important task, and mustn't get caught. Not crucially important — if so, Lamb would have sent Sid, or possibly Moody — but important enough that it had to be done.

Or else it was a test. A test to discover whether River was capable of going out in the rain and bringing back a bag of rubbish.

He went out again not long after, abandoning the random sack of rubbish in the first litter bin he passed. Cruising slowly past the journo's, he could hardly believe it was there, slumped against the wall below the window: a knotted black bag . . .

The same bag's contents were now strewn across the floor in front of him.

Lamb said, "I'll leave you to clear that, right?"

River said, "What am I looking for precisely?"

But Lamb was already gone; audible on the stairs, this time — every creak and complaint echoing — and River was alone in Sid's half of the office; still surrounded by unsweet-smelling crap, and still weighed down by the faint but unmistakable sensation of being Jackson Lamb's punchbag.

The tables were always packed too close in Max's, in optimistic preparation for a rush of custom that wasn't going to happen. Max's wasn't popular because it wasn't very good; they re-used the coffee beans, and the croissants were stale. Repeat trade was the exception, not the rule. But there was one regular, and the moment he stepped through the door each morning,

newspapers under his arm, the body on the counter
would start pouring his cup. It didn't matter how often
the staff turned over: his details were passed down
along with instructions about the cappuccino machine.
*Beige raincoat. Thinning, brownish hair. Permanently
irritated*. And, of course, those newspapers.

This morning, the windows were a fogged-over
drizzle. His raincoat dripped on to the chessboard lino.
If his newspapers hadn't been in a plastic bag, they'd
have been a papier-mâché sculpture waiting to happen.

"Good morning."

"It's a lousy morning."

"But it's always good to see you, sir."

This was the morning's Max, a name they all shared
as far as Robert Hobden was concerned. If they wanted
him to tell them apart, they shouldn't all work the same
counter.

He settled in his usual corner. A redhead, one of only
three other customers, was at the next table, facing the
window: a black raincoat hung from the back of her
chair. She wore a collarless white shirt and black
leggings cut off at the ankle. He noticed this because
her feet were hooked round her chair legs, the way a
child might sit. A baby-sized laptop sat in front of her.
She didn't look up.

Max delivered his latte. Grunting acknowledgement,
Hobden placed keys, mobile and wallet on the table in
front of him, like always. He hated sitting with lumps in
his pockets. His pen and notebook joined them. The
pen was a thin-nibbed black felt-tip; the keyring a
memory stick. And the newspapers were the quality

dailies, plus the *Mail*. Piled up, they made a four-inch stack, of which he would read about an inch and a half; significantly less on Mondays, when there was more sports coverage. Today was Tuesday, shortly after seven. It was raining again. Had rained all night.

. . . *Telegraph, Times, Mail, Independent, Guardian*.

At one time or another, he'd written for all of these. That wasn't so much a thought that occurred to him as an awareness that nudged him most mornings, round about now: cub reporter — ridiculous term — in Peterborough, then the inevitable shift to London, and the varied tempos of the major beats, crime and politics, before he ascended, aged forty-eight, to his due: the weekly column. Two, in fact. Sundays and Wednesdays. Regular appearances on *Question Time*. From firebrand to the acceptable face of dissent; an admittedly long trajectory in his case, but that made arrival all the sweeter. If he could have freeze-framed life back then, he'd have had little to complain about.

These days, he no longer wrote for newspapers. And when cab drivers recognized him, it was for the wrong reasons.

Beige raincoat discarded for the moment; the thinning, brownish hair a permanent accessory — as was the irritated look — Robert Hobden uncapped his pen, took a sip of his latte, and settled to work.

There'd been lights in the windows. Ho knew before opening the door that Slough House was occupied. But he'd have been able to tell anyway — damp footprints

27

in the stairwell; the taste of rain in the air. Once in a harvest moon, Jackson Lamb would arrive before Ho; random pre-dawn appearances that were purely territorial. You can haunt this place all you like, Lamb was telling him. But when they pull down the walls and count the bones, it'll be mine they find on top. There were many good reasons for not liking Jackson Lamb, and that was one of Ho's favourites.

But this wasn't Lamb, or not Lamb alone. There was someone else up there.

Could be Jed Moody, but only if you were dreaming. Nine thirty was a good start for Moody, and it was generally eleven before he was ready for anything more complicated than a hot drink. Roderick Ho didn't like Jed Moody, but that wasn't a problem: Moody didn't expect to be liked. Even before he'd been assigned to Slough House, he'd probably had fewer friends than fists. So Ho and Moody got on okay, sharing an office: neither liking the other, and neither caring the other knew. But there was no way Moody was here before him. It was barely seven.

Catherine Standish was more likely. Ho couldn't remember Catherine Standish ever arriving first, which meant it had never happened, but she was usually next in. He'd hear the door's agonized opening, and then her soft creak on the stairs, and then nothing. She was two floors above — in the small room next to Lamb's — and out of sight, she was easy to forget. Actually, standing in front of you, she was easy to forget. The chances of sensing her presence weren't good. So it wasn't her.

That suited Ho. Ho didn't like Standish.

He made his way up to the first floor. In his office he hung his raincoat on a hook, turned his computer on, then went into the kitchen. An odd smell was drifting down the stairs. Something rotten had replaced the taste of rain.

So here were the suspects: Min Harper, who was a nervous idiot, constantly patting his pockets to check he'd not lost anything; Louisa Guy, who Ho couldn't look at without thinking of a pressure cooker, steam coming out of her ears; Struan Loy, the office joker — Ho didn't like any of them, but he especially didn't like Loy: office jokers were a crime in progress — and Kay White, who used to be on the top floor, sharing with Catherine, but had been banished downstairs for being "too damn noisy": thanks, Lamb. Thanks for letting the rest of us suffer. If you can't stand her chatter, why not pack her back to Regent's Park? Except none of them were going back to Regent's Park, because all of them had left a little bit of history over there; an ungainly smudge on the annals of the Service.

And Ho knew the shape and colour of each and every smudge: the crimes of drugs, drunkenness, lechery, politics and betrayal — Slough House was full of secrets, and Ho knew the size and depth of each and every one of them, excepting two.

Which brought him to Sid. It could be Sid up there.

And here was the thing about Sid Baker: Ho didn't know what crime Sid was being punished for. It was one of two secrets that eluded him.

That was probably the reason he didn't like Sid.

As the kettle boiled, Ho picked over some of Slough House's secrets; thought about the nervous idiot Min Harper, who'd left a classified disk on a train. He might have got away with this if the disk's pouch hadn't been bright red, and stamped *Top Secret*. And also if the woman who'd found it hadn't handed it in to the BBC. Some things were too good to be true, unless you were the one they were happening to: for Min Harper, the episode had been too awful to believe, but had happened anyway. Which was why Min had spent the last two years of a once-promising career in charge of the first-floor shredder.

Steam billowed from the kettle's lip. The kitchen was poorly ventilated, and plaster frequently flaked from the ceiling. Give it a while, the whole lot would come down. Ho poured water into a teabagged mug. The days were diced and sliced into segments like this; divided into moments spent pouring cups of tea or fetching sandwiches, and further mentally subdivided by rehearsing Slough House's secrets, all but two . . . The rest of the time Ho would be at his monitor; ostensibly inputting data from long-closed incidents, but most of the time searching for the second secret, the one that ate away at him, and never slept.

With a spoon he fished the teabag out, and dropped it into the sink; a thought striking him as he did so: I know who's upstairs. It's River Cartwright. Has to be.

There wasn't a single reason he could think of why Cartwright might be here this time of the morning, but still: place your bets. Ho bet Cartwright. That's who was upstairs right now.

That figured. Ho *really* didn't like River Cartwright.

He carried his mug back to his desk, where his monitor had swum into life.

Hobden put the *Telegraph* aside, its front-page photo a gurning Peter Judd. He'd made a few notes on the upcoming by-election — the Shadow Culture Minister had handed his cards in, last January's strokes wrapping up his career — but nothing more. When politicians voluntarily shrugged off the mantle it was worth a closer look, but Robert Hobden was a veteran at parsing a story. He still read copy as if it were Braille; bumps in the language letting him know when D-notices were an issue; when the Regent's Park mob had left their fingerprints on the facts. This was most likely what it seemed to be: a politician heading back to the sticks after a health scare. And Robert Hobden trusted his instincts. You didn't stop being a journalist just because you were no longer in print. Especially when you knew you had a story, and were waiting for its fin to show above the waves of the everyday news. It would break surface sooner or later. And when it did, he would recognize it for what it was.

Meanwhile, he'd continue his daily trawl through this sea of print. It wasn't as if much else troubled his time. Hobden wasn't as connected as he used to be.

Face it, Hobden was a pariah.

And this, too, was down to Regent's Park: at one time or another, he'd written for all these newspapers, but the spooks had put paid to that. So now he spent his mornings in Max's, hunting down his scoop . . .

This was what happened when you were close to a story: you worried everyone else was on it too. That your scoop was under threat. Which went double when spooks were involved. Hobden wasn't an idiot. His notebook contained nothing that wasn't public domain; when he typed his notes up, with added speculations, he saved them to his memory stick to keep his hard drive clean. And he kept a dummy, in case anyone tried to get clever. He wasn't paranoid, but he wasn't an idiot. Last night, prowling his flat, unsettled by the sense of something left undone, he'd run through unexpected encounters he'd had recently, strangers who had started conversations, but couldn't come up with any. Then he'd run through other recent encounters, with his ex-wife, with his children, with former colleagues and friends, and couldn't come up with any of them either. Outside of Max's, no one wished him good morning . . . The thing left undone had been putting the rubbish out, but he'd remembered eventually.

"Excuse me?"

It was the pretty redhead at the next table.

"I said, excuse me?"

It turned out she was talking to him.

Fish bits. The last of the *Searchlight* parcels contained fish bits: not the bones and heads that would indicate that the journo fancied himself in the kitchen, but the hardened edges of batter and skin, and lumps of charcoaled chip that suggested his local takeaway wasn't the best.

River had graded most of the crap, and none of it amounted to a clue. Even the Post-its, carefully uncrumpled, yielded nothing more than shopping lists: eggs, teabags, juice, toothpaste — the original ideas on which this mess was based. And the cardboard backing of the spiral-notepad was just that; no pages survived. He'd brushed a fingertip across the board, in case any scrawling was embedded there, but found nothing.

From the ceiling above came a thump. Lamb's favourite summons.

They were no longer the only ones here. It was coming on for eight; the door had opened twice, and the stairs creaked their usual greeting. The noises that had ended on the floor below belonged to Roderick Ho. Ho was usually first in, often last out, and how he spent the hours between was a mystery to River. Though the cola cans and pizza boxes surrounding his desk suggested he was building a fort.

The other footsteps had passed River's floor, so must have belonged to Catherine. He had to delve for her surname: Catherine Standish. Havisham would have suited her better. River didn't know about wedding gowns, but she might as well have walked round draped in cobweb.

Another thump from the ceiling. If he'd had a broom handy, he'd have thumped back.

The mess had migrated. It had started off contained within the newspaper island he'd laid out; now it had spread, covering much of Sid's half of the floor. The smell, more democratic, occupied the whole room.

A twist of orange peel, unreadable as a doctor's signature, lay curled under the desk.

Another thump.

Without removing his rubber gloves, River stood and headed for the door.

He was fifty-six years old. Pretty young redheads didn't speak to him. But when Robert Hobden sent an enquiring glance her way she was smiling, nodding; signalling all the openness one animal offers another when something is wanted or needed.

"Can I help you?"

"I'm supposed to be working? On this assignment?"

He hated that upward inflection. How did the young let each other know when an answer was required? But she had a light dusting of freckles, and her shirt was unbuttoned enough that he could see they reached as far as her breasts. A locket on a thin silver chain hung there. Her ring finger was bare. He continued to notice such details long after they'd ceased to have relevance.

"Yes?"

"Only I couldn't help noticing the headline? On your paper? One of your papers . . ."

She reached across to tap his copy of the *Guardian*, offering a better view of those freckles, that locket. It wasn't a headline she meant, though. It was a teaser above the masthead: an interview with Russell T. Davies in the supplement.

"My dissertation is on media heroes?"

"Of course it is."

"I'm sorry?"

"Be my guest."

He slid *G2* from its mother-paper, and handed it to her.

She smiled prettily and thanked him, and he noticed her pretty blue-green eyes, and a slight swelling on her pretty lower lip.

But sitting back, she must have misjudged her pretty limbs, because next moment there was cappuccino everywhere, and her language had become unlady-like —

"Oh shit I'm so sorry —"

"Max!"

"I must have —"

"Can we have a cloth over here?"

For Catherine Standish, Slough House was Pincher Martin's rock: damp, unlovely, achingly familiar, and something to cling to when the waves began to crash. But opening the door was a struggle. This should have been an easy fix, but Slough House being what it was, you couldn't have a carpenter drop round: you had to fill out a property maintenance form; make a revenue disbursement request; arrange a clearance pass for an approved handyman — outsourcing was "fiscally appropriate", standing instructions explained, but the sums spent on background vetting put the lie to that. And once you'd filled out the forms, you had to dispatch them to Regent's Park, where they'd be read, initialled, rubber-stamped and ignored. So every morning she had to go through this, pushing against the door, umbrella in one hand, key in the other, shoulder hunched to keep her bag from slipping to the ground. All the while hoping she'd maintain balance when the door deigned to open. Pincher Martin had it easy. No doors on his Atlantic rock. Though it rained there too.

The door gave at last with its usual groan. She paused to shake excess water from her umbrella. Glanced up at the sky. Still grey, still heavy. One last shake, then she tucked the umbrella under her arm. There was a rack in the hall, but that was a good way of never seeing an umbrella again. On the first landing, through a half-open door, she glimpsed Ho at his desk. He didn't look up, though she knew he'd seen her. She in her turn pretended she hadn't seen him, or that's what it must have looked like. Actually, she was pretending he was a piece of furniture, which required less effort.

Next landing up, both office doors were closed, but there was a light under River and Sid's. A rank smell tainted the air: old fish and rotting vegetation.

In her own office, on the top floor, she hung her raincoat on a hanger, opened her umbrella so it would dry properly, and asked Jackson Lamb's shut door if it wanted tea. There was no answer. She rinsed the kettle, filled it with fresh water, and left it to boil. Back in her office she booted up, then fixed her lipstick and brushed her hair.

The Catherine in her compact was always ten years older than the one she was expecting. But that was her fault and nobody else's.

Her hair was still blonde, but only when you got close, and nobody got close. From a distance it was grey, though still full, still wavy; her eyes were the same colour, giving the impression that she was fading to monochrome. She moved quietly, and dressed like an illustration in a pre-war children's novel; usually a hat; never jeans or trousers — nor even skirts, but always dresses, their sleeves lacy at the cuff. When she held the compact closer to her face, she could trace damage under the skin; see the lines through which her youth had leaked. A process accelerated by unwise choices, though it was striking how often, in retrospect, choices seemed not to have been choices at all, but simply a matter of taking one step after the other. She'd be fifty next year. That was quite a lot of steps, one after the other.

The kettle boiled. She poured a cup of tea. Back at her desk — in a space she shared with no one, thank God; not since Kay White had been banished downstairs on Lamb's orders — she picked up where she'd left off yesterday, a report on real estate purchases for the past three years in the Leeds/Bradford area, cross-referenced against immigration records for the same period. Names appearing under both headings were checked against Regent's Park's watch-list. Catherine had yet to find a name to set alarms ringing, but ran searches on each anyway, then listed the results by country of origin, Pakistan at the top. Depending on how you viewed the results, they were either evidence of random population movement and property investment, or a graph from which a pattern would eventually arise, readable only by those higher up the intelligence-gathering chain than Catherine. Last month, she'd produced a similar report for Greater Manchester. Next would be Birmingham, or Nottingham. Her reports would be couriered over to Regent's Park, where she hoped the Queens of the Database would pay it more attention than they paid her maintenance requests.

After half an hour she paused, and brushed her hair again.

Five minutes later River Cartwright came upstairs, and entered Lamb's room without knocking.

The girl was on her feet, using the newspaper as a sort of funnel to direct cappuccino away from her laptop, and for a second Hobden felt a twinge of proprietorial annoyance — that was his paper she was rendering unreadable — but it didn't last, and anyway, they needed a cloth.

"Max!"

Hobden hated scenes. Why were people so clumsy?

He stood and headed for the counter, only to be met by Max, cloth in hand, saving his smile for the redhead, who was still ineffectually applying the *Guardian*. "It's no problem, no problem," he told her.

Well, it was a bit of a problem actually, Robert Hobden thought. It was a bit of a problem that there was all this fuss going on, and coffee everywhere, when all he wanted was to be left in peace to trawl through the morning's press.

"I'm so sorry about this," the girl said.

"It's quite all right," he lied.

Max said, "There. All done."

"Thank you," the girl said.

"I'll bring you a refill."

"No, I can pay —"

But this too was no problem. The redhead settled back at the table, gesturing apologetically at the coffee-sodden newspaper. "Shall I fetch you another —"

"No."

"But I —"

"No. It's of no importance."

Hobden knew he didn't handle such moments with grace or ease. Maybe he should take lessons from Max, who was back again, bearing fresh cups for both of them. He grunted a thanks. The redhead trilled sweetness, but that was an act. She was deadly embarrassed; would rather have packed up her laptop and hit the road.

He finished his first cup; put it to one side. Took a sip from the second.

Bent to *The Times*.

River said, "You thumped?"

Looking at Lamb, sprawled at his desk, it was hard to imagine him getting work done; hard to imagine him standing up even, or opening a window.

"Nice Marigolds," Lamb replied.

The ceiling sloped with the camber of the roof. A dormer window was cut into this, over which a blind was permanently drawn. And Lamb didn't like overhead lighting, so it was dim; a lamp on a pile of telephone directories was the main light-source. It looked less like an office than a lair. A heavy clock ticked smugly on a corner of the desk. A corkboard on the wall was smothered with what appeared to be money-off coupons; some so yellow and curling, they couldn't possibly be valid.

He thought about peeling the rubber gloves off, but that would be a sticky business, involving pinching each finger end then tugging, so decided not. "Dirty work," he said instead.

Unexpectedly, Lamb blew a raspberry.

The desk hid Lamb's paunch, though hiding it wasn't enough. Lamb could be behind a closed door, and his paunch would remain evident. Because it was there in his voice, let alone his face or his eyes. It was there in the way he blew a raspberry. He resembled, someone had once remarked, Timothy Spall gone to seed, which left open the question of what Timothy Spall not gone to seed might look like, but painted an accurate picture nevertheless. Spall aside, that stomach, the unshaved jowls, the hair — a dirty blond slick combed back from a high forehead, which broke into a curl as it touched his collar — made him a ringer, River thought, for Jack Falstaff. A role Timothy Spall should consider.

"Good point," he said. "Well made."

"Thought there might be a veiled criticism in there," Jackson Lamb said.

"Wouldn't have occurred to me."

"No. Well. Occurred to you to do this dirty work over Sid's side of the office."

River said, "It's difficult to keep a bagful of rubbish all in one place. Experts call it garbage-creep."

"You're not a big fan of Sid's, are you?"

He didn't reply.

"Well, Sid's not your biggest admirer either," said Lamb. "But then, competition for that role's not fierce. Found anything interesting?"

"Define interesting."

"Let's pretend for the moment I'm your boss."

"It's about as interesting as a bagful of household rubbish gets. Sir."

"Elaborate, why don't you?"

"He empties his ashtray into a sheet of newspaper. Wraps it up like a present."

"Sounds like a loony."

"Stops his bin from smelling."

"Bins are supposed to smell. That's how you know they're bins."

"What was the point of this?"

"Thought you wanted to get out the office. Didn't I hear you say you wanted to get out the office? Like, three times a day every day for months?"

"Sure. On Her Majesty's, etc etc. So now I'm going through bins like a dumpster diver. What am I even looking for?"

"Who says you're looking for anything?"

River thought about it. "You mean, we just want him to know he's being looked at?"

"What do you mean we, paleface? You don't want anything. You only want what I tell you to want. No old notebooks? Torn-up letters?"

"Part of a notebook. Spiral-bound. But no pages. Just the cardboard backing."

"Evidence of drug use?"

"Empty box of paracetamol."

"Condoms?"

"I imagine he flushes them," River said. "Should the occasion arise."

"They come in little foil packets."

"So I recall. No. None of those."

"Empty booze bottles?"

"In his recycling bin, I expect."

"Beer cans?"

"Ditto."

"God," said Jackson Lamb. "Is it me, or did all the fun go out of everything round about 1979?"

River wasn't going to pretend he cared about that. "I thought our job involved preserving democracy," he said. "How does harassing a journalist help?"

"Are you serious? It ought to be one of our key performance indicators."

Lamb pronounced this phrase as if it had been on a form he'd lately binned.

"This particular example, then."

"Try not to think of him as a journalist. And more as a potential danger to the integrity of the body politic."

"Is that what he is?"

"I don't know. Anything in his rubbish suggest he might be?"

"Well, he smokes. But that's not actually been upgraded to security threat."

"Yet," said Lamb, who'd been known to light up in his office. He thought for a moment. Then said, "Okay. Write it up."

"Write it up," River repeated. Not quite making it a question.

"You have a problem, Cartwright?"

"I feel like I'm working for a tabloid."

"You should be so lucky. Know what those bastards earn?"

"Do you want me to put him under surveillance?"

Lamb laughed.

River waited. It took a while. Lamb's laugh wasn't a genuine surrender to amusement; more of a temporary derangement. Not a laugh you'd want to hear from anyone holding a stick.

When he stopped, it was as abrupt as if he'd never started. "If that's what I wanted, you think I'd pick you?"

"I could do it."

"Really?"

"I could do it," he repeated.

"Let me rephrase," said Jackson Lamb. "Supposing I wanted it done without dozens of innocent bystanders getting killed. Think you could manage that?"

River didn't reply.

"Cartwright?"

Screw you, he wanted to say. He settled for "I could do it," again; though repetition made it sound an admission of defeat. He could do it. Could he really? "No one would get hurt," he said.

"Nice to have your input," Lamb told him. "But that's not what happened last time."

Min Harper was next to arrive, with Louisa Guy on his heels. They chatted in the kitchen, both trying too hard. They'd shared a moment a week ago, in the pub across the road, which was a hellhole: an unwindowed nightmare, strictly for the lager and tequila crowd. But they'd gone anyway, both suffering the need for a drink within sixty seconds of leaving Slough House, a margin too thin to allow for reaching anywhere nicer.

Their conversation had been focused at first (Jackson Lamb is a bastard), then becoming speculative (what makes Jackson Lamb such a bastard?) before drifting into the sentimental (wouldn't it be sweet if Jackson Lamb fell under a threshing machine?). Crossing back to the tube afterwards, there'd been an awkward parting — what had that been about? Just a drink after work, except no one in Slough House went for a drink after work — but they'd muddled through by pretending they'd not actually been together, and found their separate platforms without words. But since then they'd not positively avoided each other, which was unusual. In Slough House, there was almost never more than one person in the kitchen at a time.

Mugs were rinsed. The kettle switched on.

"Is it me, or is there a strange smell somewhere?"

Upstairs, a door slammed. Downstairs, one opened.

"If I said it was you, how upset would you be?"

And they exchanged glances and smiles both turned off at exactly the same moment.

44

★ ★ ★

It took no effort for River to remember the most significant conversation he'd had with Jackson Lamb. It had happened eight months ago, and had started with River asking when he was going to get something proper to do.

"When the dust settles."

"Which will be when?"

Lamb had sighed, grieving his role as answerer of stupid questions. "The only reason there's dust is your connections, Cartwright. If not for grandad, we wouldn't be discussing dust. We'd be talking glaciers. We'd be talking about when glaciers melt. Except we wouldn't be talking at all, because you'd be a distant memory. Someone to reminisce about occasionally, to take Moody's mind off his fuck-ups, or Standish's off the bottle."

River had measured the distance between Lamb's chair and the window. That blind wasn't going to offer resistance. If River got the leverage right, Lamb would be a pizza-shaped stain on the pavement instead of drawing another breath; saying:

"But no, you've got a grandfather. Congratu-fuckinglations. You've still got a job. But the downside is, it's not one you're going to enjoy. Now or ever." He beat out a tattoo on his desk with two fingers. "Orders from above, Cartwright. Sorry, they're not my rules."

The yellow-toothed smile accompanying this held nothing of sorrow at all.

River said, "This is bullshit."

"No, I'll tell you what's bullshit. One hundred and twenty people dead or maimed. Thirty million pounds' worth of actual damage. Two point five billion quid in tourist revenue down the drain. And all of it your fault. Now *that* — that's bullshit."

River Cartwright said, "It didn't happen."

"You think? There's CC footage of the kid pulling the cord. They're still playing it over at Regent's Park. You know, to remind themselves how messy things get if they don't do their jobs properly."

"It was a training exercise."

"Which you turned into a circus. You crashed King's Cross."

"Twenty minutes. It was up and running again in twenty minutes."

"You crashed King's Cross, Cartwright. In rush hour. You turned your upgrade assessment into a circus."

River had the distinct impression Lamb found this amusing.

"No one was killed," he said.

"One stroke. One broken leg. Three —"

"He'd have stroked anyway. He was an old man."

"He was sixty-two."

"I'm glad we agree."

"The mayor wanted your head on a plate."

"The mayor was delighted. He gets to talk about oversight committees and the need for airtight security processes. Makes him look like a serious politician."

"And that's a good idea?"

"Can't hurt. Given he's an idiot."

46

Lamb said, "Let's try for a little focus. You think it's a good idea you turned the Service into a political football by being, what would you call it? Colour-deaf?"

Blue shirt, white tee.

White shirt, blue tee . . .

River said, "I heard what I heard."

"I don't give a ferret's arse what you heard. You screwed up. So now you're here instead of Regent's Park, and what might have been a glittering career is — guess what? A miserable clerk's job, specifically tailored to make you save everyone a lot of grief and jack it in. And you only got that much courtesy of grandpa." Another flash of yellow teeth. "You know why they call this Slough House?" Lamb went on.

"Yes."

"Because it might as well be in —"

"In Slough. Yes. And I know what they call us, too."

"They call us slow horses," Lamb said, exactly as if River had kept his mouth shut. "Slough House. Slow horse. Clever?"

"I suppose it depends on your definition of —"

"You asked when you were going to get something proper to do."

River shut up.

"Well, that would be when everyone's forgotten you crashed King's Cross."

River didn't reply.

"It would be when everyone's forgotten you've joined the slow horses."

River didn't reply.

"Which is going to be a very fucking long time from now," Lamb said, as if this might somehow have gone misunderstood.

River turned to leave. But there was something he had to know first. "Three what?" he asked.

"Three what what?"

"There were three somethings, you said. At King's Cross. You didn't say what they were."

"Panic attacks," said Lamb. "There were three panic attacks."

River nodded.

"Not including yours," Lamb said.

And that had been the most significant conversation River had had with Jackson Lamb.

Until today.

Jed Moody would turn up eventually. A couple of hours after everyone else, but nobody made an issue out of this because nobody cared, and anyway, nobody wanted to get on the wrong side of Moody, and most sides of Moody were the wrong one. A good day for Moody was when some character took up residence at the bus stop over the road, or sat too long in one of the garden patches in the Barbican complex opposite. When this happened, out Moody would go, even though it was never serious — was always kids from the stage school down the road, or someone homeless, looking for a sit-down. But whoever it was, out Moody would slope, chewing gum, and sit next to them: never engaging in conversation — he just sat chewing gum. Which was all it took. And when he came back in he was a little lighter of step for five minutes: not enough to make him good company, but enough that you could pass him on the stairs without worrying he'd hook a foot round your ankle.

He made no secret: he hated being among the slow horses. Once he'd been one of the Dogs, but everyone knew Jed Moody's screw-up: he'd let a desk-jockey clean his clock before making tracks with about a squillion quid. Not a great career move for a Dog — the Service's internal security division — even without the subsequent messy ending. So now Moody turned up late and dared anyone to give him bullshit. Which nobody did. Because nobody cared.

But meanwhile Moody wasn't here yet, and River Cartwright was still upstairs with Jackson Lamb.

Who leant back in his chair, folding his arms. There'd been nothing audible, but it became apparent he'd farted. He shook his head sadly, as if attributing this to River, and said, "You don't even know who he is, do you?"

River, half his mind still at King's Cross, said, "Hobden?"

"You were probably still at school when he was successful."

"I dimly remember him. Didn't he use to be a Communist?"

"That generation were all Communists. Learn some history."

"You're about the same age, aren't you?"

Lamb ignored that. "The Cold War had its upside, you know. There's something to be said for getting teenage disaffection out your system by carrying a card instead of a knife. Attending interminable meetings in the back rooms of pubs. Marching for causes nobody else would get out of bed for."

"Sorry I missed that. Is it available on DVD?"

Instead of replying, Lamb looked away, beyond River, indicating they weren't alone. River turned. A woman stood in the doorway. She had red hair, and a light dusting of freckles across her face, and her black raincoat — still glistening from the morning rain — hung open, showing the collarless white shirt beneath. A locket on a silver chain hung at her breast. A faint smile hovered on her lips.

Under one arm she held a laptop, the size of an exercise book.

Lamb said, "Success?"

She nodded.

"Nice one, Sid," he told her.

Sidonie Baker put the laptop on Lamb's desk. Without looking at River she said, "There's been some kind of accident. Downstairs."

"Does it involve rubbish?" Lamb asked.

"Yes."

"Then relax. It wasn't an accident."

River said, "Whose is that?"

"Whose is what?" Sid asked.

"The laptop."

Sid Baker might have walked out of a commercial. It didn't matter for what product. She was all clean lines and fresh air; even her freckles seemed carefully graded. Underneath her scent, River detected the whiff of fresh laundry.

Lamb said, "It's okay. You can rub it in."

It was all the clue River needed. "That's Hobden's?"

She nodded.

"You stole his laptop?"

She shook her head. "I stole his files."

River turned to Lamb. "Would they be more or less important than his rubbish?"

Lamb ignored him. "Did he notice?" he asked.

"No," Sidonie said.

51

"Sure?"

"Pretty sure."

Lamb raised his voice. "Catherine."

She appeared in the doorway like a creepy butler.

"Flash-box."

She disappeared.

River said, "Let me guess. Feminine wiles?"

"Are you calling me a honey trap?"

"If the cliché fits."

Catherine Standish returned with a flash-box she placed on Lamb's desk next to his clock. She waited, but Lamb said nothing. "You're welcome," she told him, and left.

Once she'd gone, Lamb said: "Tell him."

"His key-fob's a memory stick," Sid said.

"A flash drive," River said.

"That's right."

"And he keeps his back-up files on it?"

"Seems a reasonable conclusion. Given that he carries it everywhere."

"Well, you would, wouldn't you? If it's attached to your keys."

"There's certainly something on it. A couple of megabytes' worth."

"Maybe he's writing a novel," River said.

"Maybe he is. You didn't find a draft in his rubbish, did you?"

He was going to lose this conversation if he wasn't careful. "So you picked his pocket?"

"He's a man of habit. Same café, every morning. Same latte. And he piles his pocket contents on the table before he sits." Sidonie produced a barrette from her pocket. River thought that was what it was called. A barrette. "I swapped his stick for a dummy while his attention was elsewhere."

Which meant she'd had a dummy with her, which meant she'd had Hobden under surveillance. How else would she have had an identical memory stick?

"And then I copied its contents on to the laptop."

She slotted the barrette behind her left ear, making a science-fiction shape of her hair. There was no way she could know what it looked like, River thought. Which made it all the stranger that the shape appeared intentional.

"And then I swapped it back."

"While his attention was elsewhere."

"That's right," Sid said, smiling brightly.

Lamb was bored now. He picked up the flash-box. The size of an A4 box-file, it was self-locking, and any attempt to open it without its series key would produce a smallish bonfire. He reached for the laptop. "Was he still there when you left?"

"No. I waited him out."

"Good." Lamb fitted the computer into the box. "Stick?"

"There's nothing on it."

"Did I ask?"

Sidonie produced the stick, a twin to the one on Hobden's key-ring. Lamb dropped it into the flash-box, then snapped the lid shut.

"Abracadabra," he said.

Neither quite knew what to say to that.

"And now I have a call to make," he said. "If the pair of you wouldn't mind, you know." He waggled a hand in the direction of the door. "Fucking off."

From the landing, River could see Catherine at her desk in the adjoining office; absorbed in paperwork with the absolute concentration of someone who knows they're being observed.

Sid said something over her shoulder, but he didn't catch what.

In his office, Lamb made his phone call. "You owe me. Yes, it's done. All his files, or everything on his stick, anyway. No, the rubbish was clean. As it were. Yeah, okay. This morning. I'll send Baker." He yawned, scratched at the back of his neck, then examined his fingernails. "Oh, and another thing? Next time you want errands running, use your own boys. Not like Regent's Park is running out of bodies."

After he hung up, he leant back and closed his eyes. It looked for all the world like he was taking a nap.

Downstairs, River and Sid surveyed the scattered rubbish. River had the uncomfortable feeling that this joke wasn't funny any more, and even if it had been, he was as much its butt as Sid. It wasn't like the smell had kept to her side of the room. But any possible apology died in the face of what had just happened. For a couple of minutes last night, standing under an overhang in the pouring rain, he'd convinced himself he was doing something important; that he was on the first rung of a ladder back into the light. Even if that feeling had survived the downpour, and the rummaging through the rubbish this morning, it wouldn't have survived this. He didn't want to look at Sid. Didn't want to know the shape of the smile on her lips when she spoke. But did want to know what she'd been up to.

"How long have you been playing Hobden?" he said.

"I haven't been playing him."

"You've been doing breakfast."

"Just often enough to clock his habits."

"Uh-huh."

"Are you going to clear this mess up?"

River said, "When'd you ever hear of a joe being sent out solo? Domestic, I mean. Middle of London."

This amused her. "So now I'm a joe?"

"And how come Lamb's running an op off his own bat?"

"You'd have to ask him. I'm going for coffee."

"You've already had coffee."

"Okay then. I'm going somewhere else until you've got rid of all this crap."

"I haven't written it up yet."

"Then I'll be gone a while. The gloves suit you, by the way."

"Are you taking the piss?"

"I wouldn't know where to start."

Unhooking her bag from her chair, she left.

River kicked a tin can which might have been put there for that purpose. It bounced off the wall, leaving a bright red contact wound, and dropped to the floor.

Peeling off his rubber gloves, he added them to the sack. When he opened the window a cold blast of London air filtered through, adding traffic fumes to the mix. Then a familiar thumping on the ceiling set the lampshade wobbling.

He picked up the phone, tapped out Lamb's extension. A moment later, he heard it ring upstairs. It felt like he had an offstage role in someone else's drama.

"Where's Sid?" Lamb asked.

"Gone for coffee."

"When will she be back?"

There was an office code, of course. You didn't dob a colleague in.

He said, "Quite a while were her exact words. I think."

Lamb paused. Then said, "Get up here."

River was listening to the dial tone before he could ask why. He took a breath, counted to five, then headed back upstairs.

Lamb said, "All cleaned up?"

"More or less."

"Good. Here." He tapped the flash-box in front of him with a fat finger. "Deliver this."

"Deliver it?"

"Is there an echo in here?"

"Deliver it where?"

"Is there an echo in here?" Lamb repeated, then laughed: he'd made a joke. "Where do you think? Regent's Park."

Regent's Park was the light at the top of the ladder. It was where River would be now, if he hadn't crashed King's Cross.

He said, "So this Hobden thing, it's Regent's Park?"

"Of course it bloody is. We don't run ops from Slough House. Thought you'd worked out that much."

"So how come Sid got the real job? And I'm left collecting the rubbish?"

"Tell you what," said Lamb. "You have a good long think about that, and see if you can come up with the answer all by yourself."

"And why would the Park want us anyway? They've no shortage of talent, surely."

"I hope that's not a sexist remark, Cartwright."

"You know perfectly well what I mean."

Lamb looked at him blankly, and River had the sense he was thinking deep thoughts, or else wanted River to think he was thinking deep thoughts. But when he answered, it was only to shrug.

"And why do they want me to deliver it?"

"They don't," Lamb said. "They want Sid. But Sid's not here. So I'm sending you."

River picked up the flash-box, and its contents slid from one end to the other. "Who do I deliver it to?"

Lamb said, "Name's Webb. Isn't he an old mate of yours?"

And River's stomach slid sideways too.

Flash-box under one arm, he cut through the estate to the row of shops beyond: supermarket, newsagent's, stationer's, barber's, Italian restaurant. Fifteen minutes later, he was at Moorgate. From there he caught a tube part way, then walked across the park. The rain had stopped at last, but large puddles swamped the footpaths. The sky was still grey, and the air smelled of grass. Joggers loped past, trackies plastered to their legs.

He didn't like it that Lamb had sent him on this errand. Liked even less knowing that Lamb knew that, and knew he knew it too.

In the weeks after King's Cross, River grew accustomed to a scraped-out feeling, as if that desperate dash along the platform — his last-second, doomed attempt to put things right — had left permanent scars. Somewhere in his stomach it was always four in the morning, he'd drunk too much, and his lover had left. There'd been an inquiry — you didn't crash King's Cross without people noticing — the upshot of which was, River had made sixteen basic errors inside eight minutes. It was bullshit. It was Health and Safety. It was like when a fire breaks out in the office, and afterwards everyone's ordered to unplug the kettle when it's not in use, even though it wasn't the kettle started the fire in the first place. You couldn't count a plugged-in kettle as an error. Everyone did it. Almost no one ever died.

We've run the numbers, he'd been told.

Running the numbers happened a lot at Regent's Park. Pixellating, too; River had heard that lately — *we've pixellated this*, meaning we've run it through some software. We've got screenshots. It sounded too techie to catch on as a Service word. He couldn't see the O.B. being impressed.

All of this was background static; his mind throwing up a curtain, because he didn't want to hear the numbers.

But the numbers, it turned out, were inescapable. He heard them whispered in corridors his last morning. One hundred and twenty people killed or maimed; £30m worth of damage. A further £2.5 billion in lost tourist revenue.

It didn't matter that none of these numbers were real, that they had simply been conjured up by those who took special pleasure in concocting worst-case scenarios. What mattered was that they'd been committed to paper and passed round committees. That they'd ended up on Taverner's desk. Which was not a desk you wanted your mistakes to end up on if you had hopes of them being forgotten.

But no, you've got a grandfather, Lamb had told him. *Congratufuckinglations. You've still got a job.*

Much as River hated to admit it, that had been true. If not for the O.B., even Slough House would have been out of reach.

But the downside is, it's not one you're going to enjoy. Now or ever.

A career of shuffling paper. Of transcribing snatched mobile phone conversations. Of combing through page after page on long-ago operations, looking for parallels with the here and now . . .

Half of the future is buried in the past. That was the prevailing Service culture. Hence the obsessive sifting of twice-ploughed ground, attempting to understand history before it came round again. The modern realities of men, women, children, wandering into city centres with explosives strapped to their chests had shattered lives but not moulds. Or that was the operating wisdom, to the dismay of many.

Taverner, for instance. He'd heard Taverner was desperate to alter the rules of the game; not so much change the pieces on the board as throw the board away and design a new one. But Taverner was Second Desk, not First, and even if she'd been in charge, there were Boards to answer to these days. No Service Head had been given free rein since Charles Partner: the first to die in office and the last to run the show. But then, Partner had been a Cold War warrior from his fur-lined collar to his fingerless gloves, and the Cold War had been simpler. Back then, it had been easier to pretend it was a matter of us and them.

All before River's time, of course. Such fragments, he'd gleaned from the O.B. His grandfather was the soul of discretion, or so he liked to think; imagining that a lifetime's sealed lips had left him close with a secret. This belief persevered despite the evident truth that he liked nothing better than Service gossip. Maybe this was what age did, thought River. Confirmed you in your image of yourself even while it unpicked the reality, leaving you the tattered remnant of the person you'd once been.

His hand hurt. He hoped it didn't look too obvious. But there was nothing he could do about it now. He was minutes from Regent's Park, and it wouldn't look good if he was late.

★ ★ ★

In the lobby, a middle-aged woman with the face of a traffic warden made him wait ten minutes before issuing his visitor's pass. The laptop, snug in its padded envelope, was passed through an X-ray machine, which left River wondering if its contents had been wiped. If he'd been Sid, would he have been kept waiting? Or had James Webb left instructions that River be kept hanging about until the obvious was hammered home: that a visitor's pass was the best he'd ever get?

Where Spider was concerned, River easily got paranoid.

That ordeal over, he was allowed through the large wooden doors, where there was another desk, this one manned by a balding red-cheeked type who'd pass for an Oxford porter but was doubtless an ex-cop. He motioned River to a bench. Sore hand in pocket, River sat. He put the envelope next to him. There was a clock on the facing wall. It was depressing to watch the second-hand crawl round, but difficult not to.

Behind the desk, a staircase curved upwards. It wasn't quite large enough to choreograph a dance sequence on, but it wasn't far off. For one inexplicable moment, River had a vision of Sid coming down those stairs, heels clacking off the marble so loudly, everyone in earshot would stop and look.

When he blinked, the image vanished. The footsteps echoed for a moment, but they were made by other people.

He'd thought, first time he'd come into this building, that it resembled a gentlemen's club. Now it occurred to him that the truth might be the other way round:

that gentlemen's clubs were like the Service, the way the Service used to be. Back when what it did was known as the Great Game.

At length another ex-cop showed up.

"That's for Webb?"

One proprietorial hand on the envelope, River nodded.

"I'll make sure he gets it."

"I'm supposed to give it to him myself."

There was never going to be any doubt about this. He had a visitor's pass and everything.

To give him credit, his new friend didn't fight it. "This way, then."

River said, "That's okay. I know my way round," but only to get a rise.

He didn't get one.

River was led, not up the stairs, but through a set of doors to the left of the desk, and into a corridor he'd not been in before. The padded envelope felt like a present he was bringing Spider, though that was an unlikely scenario.

White tee under a blue shirt. That's what you said.

No, I said blue tee under —

Fuck you, Spider.

"What was that?"

"I didn't say anything," River assured him.

At the end of the corridor, a set of fire doors opened on to a stairwell. Through a window, River saw a car turning down the ramp into the underground car park. He followed his guide up a flight of stairs, then another.

On each landing a camera blinked, but he resisted the temptation to wave.

They went through another set of fire doors.

"Are we nearly there yet?"

His guide offered him a sardonic look. Halfway along the corridor, he stopped and rapped twice on a door.

And River, all of a sudden, wished he'd left the parcel at reception. He'd not seen James Webb in eight months. For the year preceding that, they'd been all but inseparable. What made it a good idea to see him now?

White tee under a blue shirt. That's what you said.

Apart from anything else, the urge to deck the bastard might prove overwhelming.

From inside the room a voice called a welcome.

"In you go, sir."

In he went.

It wasn't as large as the office River shared with Sid, but it was a whole lot nicer. The wall to the right was book-shelved floor to ceiling, lined with colour-coded folders, while in front of him was a big wooden desk, which might have been carved from the hull of a ship. A pair of friendly-looking visitors' chairs were placed in front of this, while behind it loomed a tall window that gave a view of the park, which was mostly muted browns right now, but would be glorious in spring and summer. Also behind it, in front of the view, sat James Webb; inevitably Spider.

. . . First time in eight months, though for the year preceding that they'd been all but inseparable. Friends wasn't the word — it was both too big and too small. A friend was someone you'd go for a drink with; hang out with; share laughs. He'd done those things with Spider, but not because Spider was his first choice for doing them with; more because he'd spent days with Spider doing assault courses on Dartmoor, which had felt like it was going to be the most difficult part of training, until the days spent learning torture resistance techniques somewhere on the Welsh borders. Resistance techniques were taught slowly. Things had to be broken down before being built up again. Breaking down happened best in darkness. When you'd been through that, you wanted to be near others who'd been through it too. Not because you needed to talk about it, but because you needed your need not to talk about it to be shared by those you were with.

Friendship, anyway, was best conducted on level ground. Without the competitive undercurrent generated by the knowledge that they were in line for the same promotion.

White tee under a blue shirt. That's what you said.

Fuck you, Spider.

So here he was, eight months later: no bigger, no wider, no different.

"River!" he said, getting to his feet, thrusting out a hand.

They were of an age, River Cartwright and James Webb, and similar sizes: both slim, with good bones. But Webb was dark to River's sandy lightness, and Webb favoured smart suits and polished shoes, and looked like he'd stepped off a billboard. River suspected that for Spider, the worst parts of those assault courses had been staying muddy for days on end. Today he wore a charcoal two-piece with a faint chalk stripe and a grey shirt with a button-down collar, the obligatory splash of colour hanging round his neck. There was an expensive haircut not long in his past, and River wouldn't be surprised to learn he'd stopped for a shave on his way in — paid someone else to do it, with a warm towel and flattering banter.

Someone who'd pretend to be a friend for as long as the moment lasted.

River ignored the outstretched hand. "Someone threw up on your tie," he said.

"It's a Karl Unger. Peasant."

"How have things been, Spider?"

"Not bad. Not bad."

River waited.

"Takes getting used to, but —"

"I was only being polite."

Spider eased back into his chair. "Are you going to make this difficult?"

"It's already difficult. Nothing I do'll make a difference." He surveyed the room, his gaze lingering on the bookshelf. "You keep a lot of hard copy. Why's that?"

"Don't play games."

"No, seriously. What comes in hard copy?" River looked from the shelves to the sleek, paperback-thin computer on the desk, then back. Then said: "Oh, no. Jesus. Don't tell me."

"It's above your pay grade, River."

"Are they job applications? They are, aren't they? You're doing applications."

"I'm not just doing applications. Have you any idea how much paperwork an organization the size of —"

"Jesus, Spider. You're HR. Congratulations."

Spider Webb licked his lips. "I've had two meetings with the Minister this month already. How's your career looking?"

"Well, I don't have an arse two inches in front of my nose, so my view beats yours."

"The laptop, River."

River sat in one of the visitors' chairs, and passed Webb the padded envelope. Webb produced a rubber stamp, and carefully affixed its mark.

"Do you do it every morning?"

"What?"

"Change the date on your stamp."

Webb said, "When I remember."

"The responsibilities of rank, eh?"

"How's the delightful Sidonie?"

River recognized an attempt to regain the high ground. "Not sure. She went swanning off this morning almost before she'd arrived. Didn't show much dedication."

"She's a bright officer."

"I can't believe you just said that."

"She is."

"Maybe so. But Christ, Spider — *bright officer*? You're not back at Eton, you know."

Webb opened his mouth — to point out, River knew, that he hadn't been at Eton — but came to his senses in time. "Did you have breakfast? We have a canteen."

"I remember the canteen, Spider. I even remember where it is."

"I don't get called that any more."

"Not in your hearing, possibly. But face it — everybody calls you that."

"This is schoolboy stuff, River."

"Nyah nah-nah nyaah nyaah."

Webb opened his mouth and closed it again. The padded envelope lay in front of him. He drummed his fingers upon it briefly.

River said, "My office is bigger than yours."

"Real estate's cheaper that end of town."

"I thought the action took place upstairs. On the hub."

"I'm there a lot. Lady Di —"

"She lets you call her that?"

"You're a laugh a minute, River. Lady Di — Taverner, she keeps me busy."

River waggled an eyebrow.

"I don't know why I'm even bothering."

River said, "You ever going to admit you made a mistake?"

Webb laughed. "You still on that?"

"He was wearing a white tee under a blue shirt. That's what you told me. Except he wasn't, was he? He was wearing a blue tee under a —"

"The guy was wearing what I said he was wearing, River. I mean, what, I get the colours the wrong way round and there just *happens* to be someone there, that exact moment, wearing what I said? Same general profile as the target? What are the odds?"

67

"And the tape not working. Don't forget the tape not working. What are the odds on that?"

"EFU, River. Happens all the time."

"Enlighten me."

"Equipment fuck-up. You think they dish out state-of-the-art gear for assessment ops? We're up against budgetary constraints, River. You don't want to get Taverner started on that — oh, but hang on, you won't, will you? On account of you're in Slough House, and the closest you'll get to the inner circle is reading someone's memoirs."

"There isn't an acronym for that? RSM?"

"You know something, River? You need to grow up."

"And you need to admit that the mistake was yours."

"Mistake?" Webb showed his teeth. "I prefer to call it a fiasco."

"If I was you, and smirked like that, I'd have someone watching my back."

"Oh, I play London rules. I don't need anyone watching my back but me."

"I wouldn't bet on it."

"Time to go."

"Should I shout for a guide? Or have you pressed a secret button?"

But Webb was shaking his head: not in response, but in reaction to River's presence, which had tired him, because he had important things to get on with.

And nothing River said would get Webb to admit it was him who'd screwed up, not River. Besides, what difference would it make? It had been River on that platform, a star on CCTV. When you got to boardroom level, playing fair wasn't even a bullet point. Who'd screwed up didn't matter; who'd been visible during the screw-up did. Webb could put his hands up right now, and Diana Taverner wouldn't care.

The only reason you're still here is your connections, Cartwright. If not for grandad, you'd be a distant memory.

River stood, hoping an exit line would occur before he got to the door. Something to make him feel less like he'd been dismissed: by Spider bloody Webb.

Who said, "Didn't Lamb have a flash-box?"

"A what?"

"A flash-box, River." He tapped the padded envelope. "The kind you can't open without a key. Unless you want a magnesium flash."

"I've heard of those. But at Slough House, frankly, I'm amazed we've got jiffy bags."

River's need for an exit line evaporated. Scorched hand wrapped tightly round the memory stick in his pocket, he left.

When lovely woman stoops to folly, all bets are off. Was that how it went? Didn't matter. When lovely woman stoops to folly, something's got to give.

Such thoughts were pitilessly regular; as familiar as the sound of her footsteps clickety-clacking up the stairs of her apartment block. Lovely woman stoops to folly. This evening's earworm, picked up from an ad on the tube.

When lovely woman stoops to folly, the shit has hit the fan.

Catherine Standish, forty-eight a memory, knew all bets were off. Last thing she needed was her subconscious reminding her.

And she had been lovely once. Many had said so. One man in particular: *You're lovely*, he'd told her. *But you look like you've had some scary moments.* Even now she thought he'd meant it as a compliment.

But there was nobody to tell her she was lovely any more, and it was doubtful they'd say so if there were. The scary moments had won. Which sounded like a definition of ageing, to Catherine. The scary moments had won.

At the door to her flat she put her shopping on the floor and hunted out her key. Found it. Entered. The hall light was on, because it was on a timer. Catherine didn't like stepping into the dark, not even for the second it would take to flip a switch. In the kitchen, she unpacked the shopping; coffee in a cupboard, salad in the fridge. Then she took the toothpaste into the bathroom, where the light was on the same timer. There was a reason for that too.

Her worst scary moment had been the morning she'd turned up at her boss's flat to find him dead in his bathroom. He'd used a gun. Sat in the tub to do it, as if he didn't want to make a mess.

You had a key to his house? she'd been asked. *You had a key? Since when?*

That had been the Dogs, of course. Or one Dog in particular: Sam Chapman, who they called Bad Sam. He was a dark difficult man, and knew damn well she'd had a key to Charles Partner's house, because everyone knew she'd had a key to Charles Partner's house. And knew it hadn't been because of an affair, but simply because Charles Partner had been hopeless about taking care of himself — ostensibly simple things like remembering to buy food, remembering to cook it, then remembering to throw it away when he'd forgotten to eat it. Charles had been twenty years older than Catherine, but it hadn't been a father/daughter thing either. That was a convenient label, but the reality had been this: she had worked for Charles Partner, cared for him, shopped for him, and had found him dead in his bathroom once he'd shot himself. Bad Sam

71

could growl all he liked, but he'd only been going through the motions, because Catherine had been the one to find the body.

Funny how swiftly that happened; how swiftly you went from being Charles Partner — not a man whose name was known to the public at large, true, but a man whose decisions dictated whether significant numbers of them would live or die, which had to count for something — to being "the body". All it had taken was one calculated moment in a bathtub. He didn't want to make a mess, but what mess he'd made was for others to clean up. Funny.

Less funny was how quickly the scary moments accumulated.

Because she was in the bathroom, and because the light was already on, it was hard for Catherine not to catch herself in the mirror. It held no surprises. Yes, the scary moments accumulated, but that was the least of it. Some damage was gifted by your genes. Some you discovered for yourself. Her nose grew red-tipped in the cold, as did her cheekbones. This made her look witchy and raw. Nothing she could do about that. But the rest of it — the spidery tracing of broken veins; the gaunt stretching of the skin across the skull — they told a different story, one she'd written herself.

My name is Catherine and I am an alcoholic.

By the time she'd got around to formulating that sentence, alcohol was a problem. Prior to that, it had seemed like a solution. No, that was too glib: rather, it hadn't seemed like anything at all; it had simply been what one did. Perhaps a tad self-dramatic (a bottle for solace was such a time-worn trope, it felt like you weren't doing heartbreak properly without a glass in your hand) but more often, just the normal backdrop. It was the obvious adjunct to an evening alone with the box, and absolutely de rigueur for an evening out with girlfriends. And then there were dates, which Catherine often had in those days, and you couldn't have a date without a drink. A meal meant a drink; the cinema meant a drink afterwards. And if you were plucking up courage to ask him back for coffee, a drink was necessary, and ultimately . . . Ultimately, if you needed somebody there, because you didn't want to wake in the middle of the night knowing you were alone, you were going to have to fuck somebody, and sooner or later you were going to have to fuck anybody, and that demanded a drink if anything did.

There was a phrase: the slippery slope. Slippery implied speed and blurriness, and the ever-present threat of losing your feet. You'd end up flat on your back, breathing splinters. But Catherine's journey had been more moving staircase than slippery slope; a slow downwards progression; a bore rather than a shock. Looking across at the people heading upwards, and wondering if that was a better idea. But somehow knowing she'd have to reach the bottom before she could change direction.

It had been Charles Partner who'd been there when that happened. Not literally, thank God; not actually present when she'd woken in a stranger's flat with a broken cheekbone, finger-shaped bruises on her thighs. But there to make sure the pieces were gathered together. Catherine had spent time in a facility that was beyond anything she'd have been able to afford had she been paying. Her treatment had been thorough. It had involved counselling. All this, she was told, was in line with Service protocol (*Do you think you're the first?* she'd been asked. *Do you think you're the only one it gets to in the end?*) but there'd been more to it than that, she was sure. Because after the retreat, after the drying-out, after the first six everlasting months of sober living, she'd turned up at Regent's Park expecting to be assigned to the outer limits, but no: it was back to regular duties as Charles's doorkeeper.

Most things, at that time in her life, had made her want to weep, but this seemed more warranted than most. It wasn't as if they'd been close. Sometimes he'd called her Moneypenny, but that was it. And even afterwards they were hardly friends, though it did not escape her that he never called her Moneypenny again. Nor did they discuss what had happened, beyond his asking, that first morning, if she was "back to her old self". She'd given him the answer he'd wanted, but knew that her old self was long gone. And from there, they'd continued as before.

But he had cared for her when it mattered, and so she cared for him in return. They were together another three years, and before the first was out she was playing a role in his non-working life. He was unmarried. She'd long registered his threadbare aura. It wasn't that he was seedy, but seediness was a possibility, and poor diet an ongoing fact. He needed looking after. And she needed something. She didn't need to wake up next to more strangers, but she needed something. Partner turned out to be it.

So she kept his freezer full, and arranged for a weekly cleaner; took his diary in hand and made sure he had the odd day off. She became a barrier against the worst of his underlings — the atrocious Diana Taverner, for a start. And did all this while remaining part of the wallpaper: there was never physical contact, and nor did he acknowledge that she was anything other than secretary. But she cared for him.

Though not enough to recognize that he needed more help than she could give him.

She tilted her head to one side now, allowing her hair to fall across her face. She wondered if she should tint it, bring the blonde out, but who for? And would anyone notice? Apart from the odious Jackson Lamb, who'd ridicule her.

She could accept, Charles Partner being dead, that there was no place for her at Regent's Park. But Slough House felt like a deferred punishment for a crime she'd already atoned for. Sometimes she wondered if there were more to that crime than her own wine-dark past; if she were held responsible in some way for Charles's suicide. For not knowing it was going to happen. But how could she have known that? Charles Partner had spent a lifetime dealing in other people's secrets, and if there was one thing he'd learned, it was how to keep his own. *You had a key to his house?* she'd been asked. And: *You were expecting this to happen?* Of course she hadn't. But she wondered now if anyone had ever believed her.

75

Ancient history. Charles Partner was bones, but she still thought about him most days.

Back to the mirror. Back to her own life. Lovely woman had stooped to folly, and this was where it had left her.

My name is Catherine and I am an alcoholic.

She hadn't had a drink in ten years. But still.

My name is Catherine and I am an alcoholic.

She turned off the bathroom light, and went to make supper.

Min Harper spent a chunk of the evening on the phone to his boys: nine and eleven. A year ago, this would have left him knowing more than he needed to about computer games and TV shows, but it seemed both had crossed a line at the same time, and now it was like trying to have a conversation with a pair of refrigerators. How had that happened? Change should come with a warning, and besides, shouldn't there have been a breathing space where his nine-year-old was concerned? More childhood to negotiate before adolescence crept in? But prising information from him was like scratching at a rock. By the time his ex-wife was on the line Min was ready to take it out on her, though she was having none of it:

"It's a phase. They're the same with me. Except all the time they're grunting and saying nothing, I'm cooking their meals and washing up. So don't tell me you're having problems with it, right?"

"At least you get to see them."

"You know where we are. Would it kill you to get round more than once a week?"

He could have fought a rearguard action — the hours he worked; the distance involved — but marriage had taught him that once the battle lines were drawn, defeat was only a matter of time.

Afterwards, he couldn't settle. It was hard, after such calls, not to end up thinking about the trajectory his life had taken; a free fall he could pin down to one specific moment. Prior to that brainless second, he'd had a marriage, a family and a career, along with all the accompanying paraphernalia — dentist's appointments and mortgage worries and direct debit arrangements. Some of which still happened, of course, but its relevance, the evidence it supplied that he was building a life that worked, had been washed away by the Stupid Moment; the one in which he'd left a computer disk on a tube train. And hadn't known he'd done so until the following morning.

He supposed few people had had their careers dismantled via Radio 4. The memory hurt. Not the abject belly-panic as it sank in that the object under discussion was supposed to be in his keeping, but the moments before that, when he'd been enjoying a peaceful shave, thinking: *I'm glad I'm not the pitiful bastard responsible for that.* That was what hurt; the notion that all over the country other people were having exactly the same thought, and he was the only one who didn't deserve to.

Other, more drawn-out painful moments had followed. Interviews with the Dogs. Comedy riffs on

TV shows about secret service idiots. People on the street didn't know Min was the butt of these sketches, but they were laughing at him all the same.

Worst of all was the assumption that incompetence had caused the screw-up. Nobody had suggested treachery; that leaving a report outlining gaps in Terminal 5's security procedures on the Piccadilly Line had been a bungled dead-letter drop. That would have been to accord Min Harper a measure of respect. He could have been in the grip of misguided idealism, or lured by wealth, or at the very least making a conscious decision, but no: even the Dogs had written him off as an idiot. Any other year, he'd have been out of the door, but a combination of hiring freeze and budget tightening meant that if Min had gone, his job would have left with him, and it proved politic to keep him on the books until his departure would allow for a replacement.

Regent's Park, though, was in his past.

Min checked his pockets, reminded himself not to, then poured a drink and tuned the radio to the sports channel. As ball-by-ball commentary on an overseas Test Match filled the room, a rewritten history swarmed through his head; a more amenable version of his life, in which he was halfway on to the platform at Gloucester Road when he turned and saw the disk on the seat and went back and collected it, feeling the hot chill of near-disaster tickle his nape — a sensation he'd feel again later that evening, as he helped put the boys to bed, and then forget about entirely as his career and life continued on their even tenor: marriage, family, career; dentist's appointments, mortgage; direct debit arrangements.

As so frequently when he was trying not to have such thoughts Min startled himself by groaning aloud, but nobody heard. He was alone. There was only the radio. And as for the phone: once he'd spoken to his uncommunicative children and rowed with his ex, well: he didn't have anyone else to talk to. So he turned it off.

Louisa Guy went home to her rented studio flat: examined its four walls — what she could see of them behind stuff in the way: piles of CDs, books, damp laundry on collapsible racks — and almost went straight out again, but couldn't face the choices that would entail. She microwaved a lasagne and watched a property programme instead. House prices were in freefall, if you owned one. They remained laughably lunar to the rent-bound.

Her phone stayed silent. That wasn't unusual, but still: you'd think somebody would have found time to dial a number. Ask how Louisa was. If she'd done anything interesting lately.

She left her plate to soak. Changed channel. Encountered someone telling her that pink placebos were more effective than blue ones. Could that be right? Was the brain that easily bamboozled?

Her own felt bamboozled constantly; not so much tricked as stifled into submission. When she closed her eyes at night, illegible data scrolled down her eyelids. Sleep was repeatedly yanked from her by a sensed error, the feeling that something was out of sequence for a reason she'd nearly grasped, and grasping would have rehabilitated her career. But it was always gone and she'd be stone awake once more, her unsleeping head on a pillow too thin and too warm, no matter how cold the rest of her bed was.

Jesus, she'd think, each time. Could she get a break? Could she get a decent night's sleep? Please?

And in the morning, she'd do it all over again.

It was screen-watching. Which wasn't what she'd joined the Service for, but what she'd ended up doing. And it felt like ending up, too; felt like she had no future other than the one that waited every morning behind the flaking back door of Slough House, and stretched out minute by endless minute until the door shut behind her when she left. And the time in between was spent fuming at the injustice of it all.

She should quit. That's what she should do. She should just quit.

But if she quit, that would make her a quitter. She hadn't joined the Service to be a quitter, either.

The screen-watching was virtual surveillance, trolling among the mutant hillbillies of the blogosphere. Some of the websites she covered were Trojan horses, Service-designed to attract the disaffected; others might have belonged to other branches of the State — she sometimes wondered if she were lurking in chatrooms peopled entirely by spooks; the undercover equivalent of teen-sites populated entirely by middle-aged men. Genuine or not, the sites covered a range of mood, from the in-your-face (how to make your own bomb) to the apparently educational ("the true meaning of Islam") to the free-for-all forums where argument spat like a boiling chip pan, and rage brooked no grammar.

To pass for real in the world of the web she'd had to forget everything she'd ever known about grammar, wit, spelling, manners and literary criticism.

It felt pointless. Worse, it felt undoable . . . How could you know when something worse than words was meant, when all you had to go on were the words? And when the words were always the same: angry, vicious, murderous? Several times she'd decided that a particular voice rang darker than the rest, and had passed the information upstream. Where, presumably, it was acted upon: ISP addresses hunted down; angry young men tracked to their suburban bedrooms. But perhaps she was kidding herself. Maybe all the potential terrorists she ever identified were as ghostly as herself; other spooks in other offices, who were sending her own webname upstream even as she was sending theirs. It wouldn't be the only aspect of the War on Terror that turned out to be a circle jerk. She should be out on the street, doing actual work. But she'd tried that already, and had screwed it up.

Every time she thought about this — which was a lot — her teeth clamped together. Sometimes she found herself thinking about it without realizing that's what she was doing, and the clue was the grinding of teeth, and an ache in her jaw.

Her first field op, a tracking job: the first time she'd done it for real. Following a boy. Not the first time she'd done that for real, but the first time she'd done it like this: at a distance, keeping him in sight at all times, but not so close he'd sense her presence.

Tracking jobs were done in threes, minimum. That day there'd been five: two ahead, three behind. The three behind kept changing places, as if engaged in a country dance. But it all took place on city streets.

The boy they were following — a black youth as far from the tabloid image as you could get: he wore a pinstripe and plastic-rimmed corrective glasses — was point man in a gun drop. A cache of decommissioned handguns had been hijacked the previous week, en route to a furnace. "Decommissioned" was like "single" or "married": a status liable to abrupt change. The handguns hadn't been hijacked because they'd make nice paperweights. They'd been hijacked to be retooled, and released into the community.

"Three? Take point."

An instruction through an earpiece, propelling her to the front of the queue.

The agent who'd had the target's heels peeled away: he'd hover by a newspaper stand for a while, then rejoin the procession. Meanwhile, she had the wheel. The target was maintaining an unbroken pace. This either meant he had no idea he was under surveillance, or was so used to it that it didn't faze him.

But she remembered thinking: *He has no idea.*

He has no idea. He has no idea. Repeated enough, any phrase ceases to have meaning. *He has no idea.*

Less than a minute later, the target stepped into a clothes shop.

This wasn't necessarily significant. He liked his threads: you could tell. But shops made good meeting places. There were queues, occasional crowds. There were changing rooms. There were opportunities. He stepped into the shop, and she followed.

And lost him immediately.

In the follow-up, which began later that day and went on for weeks, the unspoken accusation was of racism. That she could not tell one black youth from another. This was not true. She had had a firm mental picture of the target, and retained it even now: the slight dint in his jaw; his razor-sharp hairline. It was just that there were at least six other young men in the shop — same size, same colour, same suit, same hair — and they'd all been put in play.

Afterwards, it became clear he'd spent less than three minutes in the shop. Into a changing room, out of his suit. When he walked back on to the street, he was dressed like he belonged there: shades, a floppy grey top, baggy jeans. He'd walked straight past Two, who was heading inside to back Louisa up, and passed One, Four and Five unnoticed. Louisa — Three — was just starting to feel the panic. Not a good day at the office.

It got worse when the guns started turning up: in bank raids, in hold-ups, in street corner shootings . . .

Among the casualties was Louisa Guy's career.

She thought about pouring another drink, then decided to turn the TV off and get to bed instead. It would bring the morning sooner, but at least there'd be oblivion between now and then.

It was a while coming, though. For at least an hour she lay in the dark, stray thoughts nipping and nagging at her.

She wondered what Min Harper was doing.

Jed Moody edged his way past the crowd by the door and bagged a pavement table where he smoked three cigarettes with his first pint. The shops opposite were a High Street palindrome — Korean grocery, courier service, letting agents, courier service, Korean grocery — and buses passed with noisy frequency. When he'd finished his pint he went back in for a second, but this time carried it upstairs, where tables lined along an internal balcony allowed a view of the stewing masses below. He was halfway through it when Nick Duffy joined him. "Jed."

"Nick."

Duffy sat.

Nick Duffy, late forties, had been an exact contemporary of Moody's: they'd finished training at the same time, both winding up in the Service's internal security system — the Dogs — a dozen years later. The Dogs were kennelled at Regent's Park, but had licence to roam. The furthest Moody had ranged was Marseilles — a junior operative had been knifed to death by a transsexual prostitute in what turned out to be a case of mistaken identity — but Duffy had made it as far as DC. He had close-cropped grey hair these days and, like Moody, wore a jacket but no tie. They must have resembled a pair of off-duty whatever, Moody thought. Accountants, estate agents, bookies;

perhaps, to the more astute observer, cops. Maybe one in a million would have guessed Five. And Moody would want a background check on that particular bastard.

"Keeping busy?" he asked.

"You know."

Meaning he didn't. And wasn't allowed to.

"I'm not after classified, Nick. I'm asking how things are."

Duffy tilted his head to the bar below. "Far end. Check it out."

He'd been followed, was Moody's first thought. His second was: Oh. Okay. At the far end of the bar sat two women whose skirts, combined, would have made a decent lens cloth.

One was wearing red underwear.

Duffy was waiting.

He said, "Jesus, you're kidding, aren't you?"

"Feeling old?"

"I didn't ask you out on the pull."

"Why is that not a surprise?"

"And if I had, I wouldn't trawl this place. Not without penicillin."

"You're a laugh a minute, Jed." As if testing this assertion, Duffy checked his watch, then took a long steady pull on his pint.

So Moody cut to the chase. "You have much to do with Taverner?"

Duffy realigned his beer mat, and set his glass upon it.

"Is she approachable?"

Duffy said, "You want to talk approachable? That blonde's sending out smoke signals."

"Nick."

"You really want to do this?"

And that was it, before they'd even started. Six words, and Duffy had told him he might as well shut up now.

"I just need a chance, Nick. One small chance. I won't screw up again."

"I hardly ever see her, Jed."

"You get ten times as close as I do."

"Whatever you want from her —"

"I don't want *from* her —"

"— it's not going to happen."

Moody stopped flat.

Duffy went on: "After that mess last year, they needed someone to throw to the wolves. Sam Chapman handed his hat in, and that was a start, but they wanted an unwilling victim. That would be you."

"But they didn't kick me out."

"You reckon you're in?"

Moody didn't reply.

Duffy, because it was his job, put the boot in. "Slough House is not *in*, Jed. Regent's Park, that's the centre of the world. The Dogs — well, you know. We roam the passageways. Sniff whoever we like. We make sure everybody's doing what they're supposed to be doing, and nobody's doing what they're not. And if they're not, we bite them. That's why they call us the Dogs."

Throughout this, he kept his voice light and breezy. Anyone watching would think he was telling a joke.

"Whereas over at Slough House, you get to — what is it you get to do again, Jed? You get to frighten people if they lurk at the bus stop too long. You make sure nobody steals any paper clips. You hang around the coffee machine listening to the other screw-ups. And that. Is. It."

Moody said nothing.

Duffy said, "Nobody followed me. I know that, because I'm the one says who follows who. And nobody followed you, because nobody cares. Trust me. Nobody's keeping an eye on you, Jed. The boss made a mark on a piece of paper, and forgot you ever lived. End of story."

Moody said nothing.

"And if that's still bothering you, try another line of work. When cops get the boot, they pick up security jobs. Given that any thought, Jed? You'd get a uniform and everything. Nice view of a car park. Move on with your life."

"I wasn't given the boot."

"No, but they figured you'd quit. Have you not worked that out yet?"

Moody scowled and reached into his pocket for his cigarettes, before contemporary reality kicked in. When was the last time he'd enjoyed a smoke in a pub? Then again, when was the last time he'd had a drink with a colleague, and joked about the job? Or the last time he'd felt okay about being Jed Moody? Inside his pocket, his hand curled into a fist. He loosened it, stretched his fingers, laid both hands on the table in front of him.

"He's up to something," he said.

"Who is?"

"Jackson Lamb."

Duffy said, "Last time Jackson Lamb stirred himself to do anything more strenuous than break wind, Geoffrey Boycott was opening for England."

"He sent Sid Baker on an op."

"Right."

"A real one."

"Jed, we know, okay? We know. You think Lamb farts without permission?" He raised his glass to his lips again, but it was empty. He put it down. "I've got to go. Early meeting in the morning. You know how it is."

"Something to do with a journo." Moody tried to keep desperation out of his voice. To keep it on a level Duffy would understand: that if an op was being run from Slough House, Moody should be part of it. Christ knows, he had more experience than the rest of them put together. Sid Baker was barely out of a training bra, Cartwright had melted King's Cross, Ho was a webhead, and the others were fucking fridge magnets. Moody alone had kicked down doors in earnest. And don't tell him it wasn't about kicking down doors. He knew it wasn't about kicking down doors. But when you were running an op you wanted someone who could kick down doors, because sooner or later that's what it would be about after all.

Duffy said, "Jed, a word of advice. Jackson Lamb's got the authority of a lollipop lady. You're three rungs below that. We know what Baker was doing, and only a rank amateur would call it an op. It was an errand. Get the difference? An errand. You think we'd trust him with anything bigger?"

Before he'd finished speaking he was getting to his feet.

"I'll put one behind the bar. No hard feelings, okay? If anything comes up, I'll let you know. But nothing's going to come up."

Moody watched as Duffy vanished down the stairs then reappeared in the bar below, gave money to the barman, pointed a thumb in Moody's direction. The barman glanced up, nodded, and fed the till.

On his way out Duffy paused by the short-skirted blonde. Whatever he said caused her to open her eyes wide and give a little scream of laughter. Before Duffy left she was huddling up, passing his words on to her friend. A little ripple of friendly filth; just another hit-and-run on a weekday evening.

Jed Moody drained his pint and leant back in his seat. Okay, you son of a bitch, he thought. You know everything, I know nothing. And I'm stuck in the wilderness while you're having early meetings and deciding who follows who. I got the shitty stick. You got the whole of the moon.

But if you're so clever, how come you think Sid Baker's a man?

He didn't bother collecting the pint Duffy had paid for. It was a small victory, but they added up.

Years ago — and he wouldn't thank you for reminding him — Roderick Ho had worked out what his Service nickname would be. More than that, he'd settled on his possible responses first time it was used. *Yeah, make my day,* he'd say. Or *Feeling lucky, punk?* That's what you said when people called you Clint.

Roderick Ho = Westward Ho = Eastward Ho = Clint.

But nobody had ever called him Clint. Perhaps political correctness wouldn't allow them to make the oriental elision from Westward to Eastwood.

Or perhaps he was giving them too much credit. Perhaps they'd never heard of *Westward Ho!*

Actually, bunch of morons. He worked with a bunch of morons. Couldn't make a pun with a dictionary and a Scrabble board.

Like Louisa Guy, like Min Harper, Ho was at home this evening, though his home was his own, and a house not a flat. It was an odd house, though that was none of his doing: it had been odd when he'd bought it. Its oddness lay in its upstairs conservatory; a glass-roofed, tiled-floor mezzanine. The estate agent had made much of this feature, pointing out the array of plants that created a micro-climate there; *natural* and *green* and *eco*-whatever peppering her spiel. Ho had nodded like he cared, calculating how many electronics he could fit into here once this eco-shit was off the premises. Quite a lot had been his estimate. This turned out to be the precise exact amount.

So now he sat surrounded by quite a lot of electronics, some quietly awaiting his touch; others humming pleasantly in response to pre-set commands; and one blasting out death metal at a volume that threatened to make the genre literal.

He was too old for this music, and he knew it. He was too old for this volume, and knew that too. But it was his music, his house, and the neighbours were students. If he didn't make his own noise, he'd have to listen to theirs.

Currently, he was virtually crawling through Home Office personnel files. Not looking for anything in particular. Just looking because he could.

Ho's parents had left Hong Kong ten years before handover, and Ho — who obsessed about what-ifs; who'd devoured you-make-the-decisions books as a teenager, when not playing Dungeons and Dragons relentlessly, unsleepingly — often wondered how he'd have turned out if they'd stayed. Odds on he'd have been a webhead in a more commercial area, software design or SFX, or lackeying for some vast faceless corporation whose tendrils touched every corner of the known world. Odds on he'd be pulling down more money than he was now. But he wouldn't have these opportunities.

The previous evening he'd been on a date with a woman he'd met on the tube that morning. They hadn't spoken. First dates were like that.

She'd been mousy blonde, and wore a regulation City outfit — charcoal jacket and skirt, white blouse — but what attracted Ho was her building pass, which dangled on a chain round her neck. Strap-hanging eight inches away, he had no trouble reading her name; ten minutes after reaching Slough House, he'd established her address and marital status (single); her credit history (pretty good); her medical records (usual female stuff); and was wandering through her e-mails. Work. Spam. A bit of flirting with a colleague, which was going nowhere. Plus, she was looking to buy a second-hand car, and had responded to an ad in her local free press. The owner hadn't replied.

So Ho gave him a call, and established that he'd already sold the car but hadn't bothered informing the unlucky enquirers. That was fine Ho assured him before calling the woman himself, to see if she was still interested in a six-year-old Saab. She was, so they arranged to meet that evening in a wine bar. Ho, established in a corner before she turned up, had watched her grow visibly more frustrated over the following hour; had even thought of approaching her; sitting her down and explaining that you couldn't be too careful — that you could not. Be. Too. Careful. A security pass on a chain round her neck? Why not sport a badge reading *Rape My Life*? Financial details, favourite websites, numbers dialled, calls received. All it took was a name, and one other bite: place of work did fine. Tax codes, criminal records, loyalty cards, travel passes. It wasn't simply that these things could be found, along with everything else. It was that they could be changed. So you leave home one morning, security pass like a cowbell round your neck, and by the time you reach work your life's not your own any more.

Roderick Ho was here to tell this woman that.

But hadn't, of course. He'd watched until she'd given up and left in a storm of silent fury, and then finished his alcohol-free lager, and walked home satisfied that he'd had her in the palm of his hand.

His secret.

One among many.

So now he sat in front of his screen, not hearing the music blasting through his room; not even blinking. A Home Office flunkey might as well be standing by his monitor, ushering him in; leading him to the filing cabinets. Offering him a key. Would sir like an alcohol-free lager while he prowled? Why, yes. Sir would.

Ho plucked the can from the holder screwed to his desk.

Thank you, flunkey.

He contemplated swapping the birth dates of some of the higher-ranking apparatchiks, which would mess up a pension plan or two, but was distracted by a link to an external site, which led him to another, and then another. It was surprising how quickly time passed: next time he looked up it was midnight, and he was miles from the Home Office; was navigating his way round a small-time plastics factory with deep-cover links to the MoD. More secrets. This was the playground he'd been born to run around in: didn't matter where his parents ended up. This was his element, and he'd dig in it until time healed over; like a miser sifting heaps of dust, in search of the nugget of gold.

And all of it was practice, nothing more. None of his trawling had brought him anywhere near uncovering the mystery that really tormented him.

Roderick Ho knew exactly what sins had brought his colleagues to Slough House; the precise nature of the gaffes and blunders that had condemned them to the twilight of the second-rate. He had calibrated their wrongdoings to the minutest detail, knew the dates and places where they'd fallen, and understood the consequences of their screw-ups better than they did themselves, because he'd read the arse-covering e-mails their superiors had subsequently penned. He knew exactly whose hand had given the thumbs-down in every instance. He could quote chapter and verse, chapter and verse.

For every sin but two.

One was Sid Baker's, and he was starting to have his suspicions about that.

As for the other, it remained as elusive as that hidden nugget.

Ho raised the can once more, but it was empty. Without looking behind, he tossed it over his shoulder; had forgotten about it by the time it hit the wall.

Kept his eyes glued to his screen.

Every sin but two.

The days when he'd been a creature of instinct were in Jackson Lamb's past. They belonged to a slimmer, smoother version of himself. But previous lives never really disappear. The skins we slough, we hang in wardrobes: emergency wear, just in case.

Approaching his house, he became aware of a figure lurking in the shadow of the adjoining lane.

A shortlist of suspects wouldn't have been hard to draw up. Lamb had made enemies over the years. Lamb, to be frank, had made enemies over the days — it never took him long. So he rolled his *Standard* into a baton as he neared the junction; rotated it hand to hand, as if conducting music in his head. He must have looked oblivious to the world. He must have looked an easy target.

He must have looked a lot less friendly two seconds later.

His arms knew the movement. Like falling off a bike.

"Jesus mister —"

And then the voice was cut off by the *Standard*: a brief taste of the thrills you could expect if you poked a sleeping beast with too short a stick.

A light went on nearby. It wasn't a neighbourhood where anyone was likely to step outside to question events, but it wasn't unusual for residents to want a closer look.

In the brief yellow glow before a curtain was drawn, Lamb saw he'd netted a kid; just another teenage hustler. His face so dappled with acne, someone might have carved him with a knife.

Slowly, he removed the newspaper from the boy's mouth. The boy promptly threw up.

Lamb could walk away. It wasn't like the boy would follow, seeking vengeance. But on the other hand, he didn't have far to walk. The kid would see which house he went into. Lamb's life was built up of moments in which he decided who should know what. In this particular instance, he decided he didn't want this kid learning anything new. So he waited, right hand clutching the kid's collar. The left had discarded the *Standard*, which had reached its use-by date even more swiftly than usual.

At length, the kid said: "Jesus *Christ* —"

Lamb let him go.

"I was mindin me own business."

Lamb was interested to find that he was only mildly out of breath.

"You some kind of fuckin lunatic?"

Except that, now he thought about it, his heart was racing, and he could feel a strangely unpleasant heat pulsing at his forehead, and through his cheeks.

The kid was still speaking. "Not doin any harm."

There was a self-pitying twang to this assertion, as if it were a temporary victory.

Lamb rode over his body's complaints. He said, "So what are you doing?"

"Hangin."

"Why here?"

A sniff. "Everybody's gotta be somewhere."

"Not you," Lamb said. "You go be nowhere, somewhere else." He found a coin in his pocket: two quid, two pee; he didn't know and didn't care. He tossed it over the kid's shoulder. "Okay?"

When the kid had disappeared from view, he waited a few minutes more.

His heart slowed to its normal rate. The sweat on his forehead cooled.

Then Jackson Lamb went home.

Not everyone was so lucky that night.

He was nineteen years old. He was very frightened. His name didn't matter.

You think we give a toss who you are?

He'd parked the car two streets away, because that was as close as you could get. This area of Leeds was slowly overcrowding — too many immigrants, his father had laughed; too many Poles and East Europeans, coming over here, "taking our jobs": ha ha, dad — and as he'd walked back he'd been working on a riff about how it was a funny thing with cars: there wasn't anything else you owned which you'd leave overnight two streets away and expect to find in the morning. There was something there, he knew. Throw in a two-beat pause . . .

"Mind you, round our way, that's gunna happen."

The thing about punchlines, they had to slide into the socket. No room for ambiguity. And never use two words when one will do, but that one word had to do its job. *That's gunna happen.* By which he meant: of course, round our way, if you leave your car out overnight, it'll get stolen. Would an audience pick that up straight off? It was all in the delivery.

"Mind you, round our way, *that's* gunna happen."

Pause.

"Round our way, you leave your *house* on the street overnight —"

And then the first shape appeared, and he'd known he was in trouble.

He was in the back lane. He shouldn't have taken the shortcut, but that was what happened when he was riffing: his feet took over while his brain went AWOL. Creativity was like being drunk, when you got down to it. He should make a note of that, but there was no time now because the first shape had stepped out of a garage doorway where he could have been taking a leak, or lighting up, or doing anything essentially innocent except for this one detail: he wore a stocking over his head.

Fight or flight? Never in question.

"If you ever find yourself in trouble . . . street hassle?" Something his father had once said to him.

"Dad, don't even try."

"Aggro?"

"Dad —"

"A rumble?"

"I know what you're trying to say, dad. Use your own words to say it, okay?"

"Run like hell," his father had said simply.

Words to live by.

But there was nowhere to run, because the first shape was just that: the first. When he turned there was a second. Also a third. They too wore stocking masks. The rest of their wardrobes faded into insignificance.

Run like hell.

Trust this: he tried.

He got three yards before they put him on the ground.

Next time he opened his eyes, he was in the back of a van. A foul taste in his mouth, and the memory of cotton wool. They'd drugged him? The van's bouncing went on forever. His limbs were heavy. His head hurt. He slept again.

Next time he opened his eyes, there was a bag on his head and his hands were tied. He was naked, except for his boxers. The air was damp and chill. A cellar. He didn't have to see it to know. Or hear the voice to know he wasn't alone.

"You're gunna be good, now."

It wasn't a question.

"You're not gunna make any problems, and you're not gunna try to escape." A pause. "No fuckin chance of that anyway."

He tried to speak, but all that came out was a whimper.

"You need to piss, there's a bucket."

And this time he managed to find a voice. "Wh — where?"

His reply was a tinny kick over to his left. "Hear that?"

He nodded.

"That's where you piss. Shit. Whatever."

Then something was dragged across the floor; something he couldn't see but which sounded monstrous and punitive; a device they'd strap him to before applying sharp tools to his softer parts . . .

"And here's a chair."

A *chair?*

"And that's your lot."

And then he was alone again. Footsteps receding. A door shutting. A lock being thrown: that was the verb, *thrown*, as if any chance of opening that door had been heaved out of reach.

His hands, tightly bound, were at least in front of him. He raised them to his head and pulled the sack off, nearly throttling himself in the process, but managing it. That was one small victory at least. He threw it to the floor, as if it were responsible for all that had happened these last — what? Hours?

How long since they took him in the lane?

Where was he now?

And *why?* What was this about? Who were they, and why was he here?

He kicked at the rag on the floor. Tears were running down his cheeks: how long had he been crying? Had he started before the voice left the room? Had the voice heard him crying?

He was nineteen years old, and very frightened, and more than an audience — more than a roomful of people laughing at his routines — what he wanted was his mother.

There was a chair in front of him, an ordinary dining room chair, and with one swift kick he laid it flat on the floor.

And there was a bucket in the corner, exactly as promised. He might have kicked that too, if the phrase didn't have disturbing connotations.

Wh — where?

He hated himself that he'd said that. "Where's the bucket?" As if he'd been asking about the amenities in a guest-house. As if he'd been grateful.

Who were these people? And what did they want? And why him?

That's where you piss. Shit. Whatever.

They were going to keep him here long enough he'd need to take a crap?

100

The thought buckled him at the knees. Crying took it out of you. He sank to the cold stone floor.

If he hadn't kicked the chair over, he'd have sat on it. But the task of putting it back on its legs was beyond him.

What do they want from me?

He'd not spoken aloud. But the words crawled back to him anyway, from the edges of the room.

What do they want?

There were no answers handy.

A single lightbulb lit the cellar. It dangled, shadeless, three feet or so above him, and he became aware of it now mostly because it went out. For a few seconds, its glow hung in the air, and then it too went wherever ghosts go in the dark.

He thought he'd felt panic before, but that was nothing to what he felt now.

For the next moments he was entirely inside his own head, and it was the scariest place he'd been. Unspeakable horrors hid there, feeding on childhood nightmares. A clock struck, but not a real one. It was a clock he'd woken to once aged three or four, that had kept him awake the rest of the night, terrified that its tick-tick-ticking was the approach of a spindly-legged beast. That if he slept, it would have him.

But he'd never be three or four again. Calling for his parents would have no effect. It was dark, but he'd been in the dark before. He was frightened but —

He was frightened but alive, and angry, and this might be a trick; a rag-week stunt pulled by the cooler kids on campus.

Angry. That was the thing to hold on to. He was angry.

"Okay, guys," he said out loud. "You've had your fun. But I'm tired of pretending to be scared."

There was a tremor in his voice, but not much of one. Considering.

"Guys? I said I'm tired of pretending."

It was a prank. A *Big Brother*-influenced routine he'd been made the butt of.

"Guys? You're pretty cool, okay. You think. But you know what?"

He couldn't see his own tied hands as he raised them to the level of his face, and extended both middle fingers.

"Sit and spin, guys. Sit. And. Spin."

And then he set the chair on its feet once more, and sat, hoping that his shoulders didn't betray how ragged his breathing was.

It was important that he get himself under control.

The thing to do was not lose his head.

Earlier that evening, River had joined the commuter shuffle from London Bridge; by eight, he'd been on the outskirts of Tonbridge. A phone call on the move had been the only notice he gave, but there was no sense he'd caught the O.B. on the hop: supper was a pasta bake, and a big salad that hadn't come from a bag.

"You were wondering if you'd find me with a tin of beans in front of the telly."

"Never."

"I'm all right, you know, River. At my age, you're either alone or dead. Either way, you get used to it."

River's grandmother had died four years ago. Now the Old Bastard, as River's mother called him, rattled around the four-bedroomed house on his own.

"He should sell the place, darling," she'd said to River on one of her vanishingly rare visitations. "Get himself a nice little bungalow. Or move into one of those residential complexes."

"I can see him going for that."

"It's not all daytime TV and abuse these day. They have," and she'd waved her hand airily; her standard semaphore for trivial detail, "*regulations.*"

"They could have Commandments," River told her. "It wouldn't tear him from his garden. Is it his money you're after?"

"No, darling. I just want him to be unhappy."

That might have been a joke.

After they'd eaten, River and his grandfather retreated to the study, the room where spirits were drunk. Protestations to the contrary notwithstanding, the O.B. clung to the pattern his wife had designed for their lives.

Glenmorangie in hand, firelight dancing in the corners, River had asked, "Do you know Robert Hobden?"

"That toad? What's your interest?"

He'd tried to sound bored, but a glint in his eye betrayed him.

River said, "Casual. My interest in him's casual."

"He's a spent force."

"We specialize in them. At Slough House."

His grandfather studied him over the top of his spectacles. The ability to do this was a fine argument for wearing glasses. "They won't keep you there forever, you know."

"I was given the impression they might," River said.

"That's the point. If you knew it was only for six months, it wouldn't hurt."

It had already been more than six months, but they both knew that, so River said nothing.

"You do your time. Whatever grunt work Jackson Lamb throws your way. Then you head back to Regent's Park, sins forgiven. Fresh start."

"What was Lamb's sin?"

The O.B. pretended not to hear. "Hobden was a star in his day. His time on the *Telegraph* especially. He was their crime reporter, and did a series on the drug trade in Manchester which opened a lot of eyes. Up until then drugs were an American problem, most people thought. He was the real deal all right."

"I didn't know he'd been a reporter. I thought he was a columnist."

"Eventually. Back then, most of them had been reporters. These days, all you need is a media studies degree and an uncle on staff. But don't get me started on how degraded that profession's become."

"Good idea," River said. "I'm only here for the evening."

"You're welcome to stay."

"Better not. Wasn't he a member of the Communist Party?"

"Probably."

"That didn't raise eyebrows?"

"Things aren't always black and white, River. A wise man once said he wouldn't trust anyone who hadn't been a radical in his youth, and Communism was the radicalism of choice back then. What's wrong with your hand?"

"Kitchen mishap."

"Playing with fire." His expression changed. "A hand up?"

River helped him to his feet. "Are you okay?"

"Damn waterworks," he said. "Don't ever get old, River."

105

He shuffled out. A moment later, the door to the downstairs bathroom closed.

River sat, his chair's leather soft as a diary's binding. The study ticked pleasantly as he swirled the liquid in his glass.

The O.B. had spent his working life in the service of his country, at a time when the battle lines were drawn less crookedly than now, but the first time River had seen him he'd been on his knees at a flowerbed, and couldn't have looked less like a fighter in secret wars. He wore an umpire's hat not broad enough to keep the sweat from trickling down his brow, and his face shone like a cheese. At River's approach, he rocked back on his haunches, trowel in hand, speechless. River, seven years old, had arrived a quarter of an hour earlier, deposited by his mother and the man currently keeping his mother company. They'd left him on the doorstep with careless kisses and a curt nod respectively. Until that morning, he hadn't known he'd had grandparents.

"They'll be delighted to have you," his mother had told him, throwing random articles of his clothing into a suitcase.

"Why? They don't even know who I am!"

"Don't be silly. I've sent them photographs."

"When? When did you ever —?"

"River. I've told you. Mummy has to go away. It's important. You want Mummy to be happy, don't you?"

He didn't answer. He didn't want Mummy to be happy. He wanted Mummy to be there. *That* was important.

"Well then. It won't be for long. And when I come back — well." She dropped a badly folded shirt into the case and turned to him. "Maybe I'll have a surprise for you."

"I don't want a surprise!"

"Not even a new daddy?"

"I hate him," River said, "and I hate you too."

They were the last words he'd say to her for two years.

His grandmother had been first shocked, then kind, and fussed over him in the kitchen. As soon as her back was turned, he'd slipped out the back door to flee, but here was this man on his knees by a flowerbed; who for the longest time said nothing, but whose silence held River rooted. And in his memory, they at length had the following conversation, though in truth it might have happened at a different time, or possibly never, and was simply one of those episodes the mind constructs to retrospectively explain events that would otherwise remain haphazard.

His grandfather said, "You must be River."

River didn't reply.

"Damned silly name. Still. Could have been worse."

River's experiences at a number of schools suggested that the old man was wrong about this.

"You mustn't think badly of her."

Not knowing whether *yes* or *no* was required, River didn't answer that either.

"Blame myself. Don't blame her. Least of all blame her mother. That would be your grandmother. The lady in the kitchen. She's never spoken about us, has she?"

That definitely didn't need a reply.

After a while his grandfather pursed his lips, and examined the patch of earth he was tending. River didn't know what he was doing: planting flowers or digging up weeds — River had spent his life in flats. Flowers arrived in colourful wrapping, or sprouted in parks. If he could magic himself back to one of those flats now he'd do so, but magic was unavailable. The grandparents he'd encountered in stories were sometimes, not always, benign. There remained the possibility of murderous intent.

"It's easier with dogs," his grandfather continued.

River didn't like dogs, but decided to keep this information to himself, until he knew which way the wind was blowing.

"You look at their paws. Did you know that?"

This time, it seemed an answer was required.

"No," River had said, after a gap of maybe three minutes.

"No what?"

"I didn't know that."

"Didn't know what?"

"What you said. About dogs."

"You look at their paws. If you want to know how big they're going to get." He began trowelling again, satisfied with River's contribution. "Dogs grow into their feet. Children don't. Their feet grow with them."

River watched soil dribble down the trowel's edge. Something red and grey and squirming happened, briefly. A flick of the tool, and it was gone.

"I don't mean your mother grew bigger than we'd expected."

It had been a worm. It had been a worm, and now — if what River had heard was true — it was two worms, in two separate places. He wondered if the worm remembered being just one worm, and if that had been twice as good, or only half. There was no way you could answer such questions. You could learn biology, but that was all.

"I meant we couldn't know she was a bolter."

More trowelling.

"Made a lot of bad decisions, your mother. Your name was the least of them. And you know what the worst thing is?"

This too required a response, but the best River could manage was a shake of the head.

"She hasn't noticed yet." He was trowelling harder, as if there were something in the soil to be brought into the light. "We all make mistakes, River. Made a couple myself, and some have hurt other people. They're the ones you shouldn't get over. The ones you're meant to learn from. But that's not your mother's way. She seems intent on making the same mistake over and over again, and that doesn't help anyone. Least of all you." He gazed up at River. "But you mustn't think badly of her. What I'm saying is, it's in her nature."

It was in her nature, River thought now, as he waited for his grandfather to return from the bathroom. That was undeniable, at this point in time. She'd been making the same mistakes ever since, and showed little sign of slowing down.

109

As for the old man: when River thought back on scenes like that — on the umpire's hat and the jumper holed at the elbow; at the trowel and the rivulets of sweat creasing his round country face — it was hard not to see it as an act. The props were certainly to hand: big house with wrap-around garden; horses within spitting distance. English country gentleman down to the vocabulary: "bolter" was a word from early twentieth-century novels; from a world where Waughs and Mitfords played card games on tables designed for the purpose.

Except that acts could shade into reality. When River remembered his childhood in this house, it was always bright summer, and never a cloud in the sky. So perhaps it had worked, the game the O.B. played; and all the clichés he espoused, or pretended to espouse, had left their mark on River. Sunshine in England, and fields stretching into the distance. When he'd become old enough to learn what his grandfather had really done with his life, and determined to do the same himself, those were the scenes he was thinking about, real or not. And the O.B. would have had an answer for that, too: *Doesn't matter if it's not real. It's the idea you have to defend.*

"Am I going to live here now?" he had asked that morning.

"Yes. Can't think what else to do with you."

And now he came back into the room, more sprightly than the way he'd left it. It was on the tip of River's tongue to ask if he was all right, but he put that tongue to better use, and sipped whisky instead.

His grandfather settled back in his armchair. "If Hobden's on your radar, it's political."

"I heard his name. Can't remember the context. It rang a bell, that's all."

"In your line of work, lying can be a matter of life and death. You're going to have to practise, River. Speaking of which, what did you really do to your hand?"

"Opened a flash-box without the code."

"Idiot activity. What was that about?"

"I wanted to see if I could do it without getting burnt."

"Got your answer, didn't you? Had it seen to?"

It was River's left hand. If he'd used his right he'd have been quicker and perhaps not burnt himself at all, but he'd taken the pragmatic approach: if the box went off like a grenade, he'd rather lose the hand he didn't favour. As it was, he'd doused the brief flame with bottled water. The box's contents got wet, but were undamaged. He'd copied the computer's files on to a new memory stick, then slid the laptop into the jiffy bag which, like the stick, he'd bought at the stationer's near Slough House. All this on a bench by a children's playground.

The hand wasn't too bad; a bit red, a bit raw. If you wanted to carry a moral from the exercise, it would be that flash-boxes weren't much cop. Though Spider had been only too happy to believe that Slough House lacked even that degree of technology.

If you wanted another moral, it would be to work out what you're doing before you do it. The whole episode

111

had been generated by his own slow-burning resentment: at having been sent on an idiot's errand while Sid went out on an actual op; most of all, at being made Spider Webb's errand boy . . . He hadn't examined the stick's contents yet. Just having the damn thing was an imprisonable offence.

"It's okay," he said to his grandfather. "A bit scorched. Nothing to worry about."

"There's something on your mind, though."

"You know what I've been doing for the past month?"

"Whatever it is, I doubt you're supposed to tell me about it."

"I think you can be trusted. I've been reading mobile phone conversations."

"And this is beneath your talents."

"It's a waste of time. They're hoovered up from high-interest areas, mostly from near the more radical mosques, and the transcripts are generated by voice-recognition software. I've only been given those in English, but still, there are thousands of them. The software renders a lot of them gibberish but they've all got to be read, and graded as to levels of suspicion. One to ten. Ten being very suspicious. As of this afternoon, I've read eight hundred and forty-two of them. You know how many I've graded above one?"

His grandfather reached for the bottle.

River made a zero sign with finger and thumb.

His grandfather said, "I hope you're not planning anything foolish, River."

"It's beneath my abilities."

"It's a hoop they're making you jump through."

"I've jumped. I've jumped over and over again."

"They won't keep you there forever."

"You think? What about, I don't know, Catherine Standish? You think she's a temporary assignment? Or Min Harper? He left a disk on a train. They've a whole club at the MoD of Hooray Henries who've left classified disks in taxis without having their lunch privileges revoked. But Harper's never going back to Regent's Park, is he? And neither am I."

"I don't know these people, River."

"No. No." He brushed his brow with his hand, and the smell of ointment stung his nostrils. "Sorry. Frustrated, that's all."

The O.B. refilled his glass. More whisky was the last thing River needed, but he didn't demur. He was aware that none of this was easy for his grandfather; suspected that what Jackson Lamb had told him months ago was true: that River would have been out on his ear if not for the O.B. Without this connection, River wouldn't have been a slow horse, he'd have been melted down for glue. And maybe Lamb was right, too, that this dull, grinding scut-work was intended to make him give up and walk away — and would that be such a bad thing? He wasn't yet thirty. Time enough to pick up the pieces and have a career that might even, who knows, earn some money.

Except even while that thought was forming, it was packing its bags and heading west. If River had inherited anything from the man sitting with him, it was this obstinate sense that you should see the course you'd chosen to its end.

His grandfather now said, "Hobden. You're not running a game on him, are you?"

"No," River said. "His name came up, that's all."

"He used to have pull. He was never an asset, nothing like that — too damn fond of blowing his trumpet — but he had the ear of some important people."

River said something forgettable about the mighty having fallen.

"There's a reason that got to be a cliché. When a Robert Hobden pisses on his chips in public, it doesn't get forgotten." The O.B. didn't often descend to crudity. He meant River to pay attention. "The kind of club he belonged to can't be seen to change its mind about kicking you out. But remember this, River. Hobden wasn't excommunicated because of his beliefs. It was because there are certain beliefs you're supposed to keep under wraps if you want to dine at High Table."

"Meaning what he believed in came as no surprise to those around him."

"Of course it didn't." River's grandfather leant back in his chair for the first time since his bathroom excursion. A distant look filmed his eyes, and River had the impression he was looking into the past, when he'd fished in similar waters. "So you be careful if you're thinking about going off reservation. The company Hobden kept before his fall from grace is a lot less savoury than the type he's mixed with since."

114

"I'm not running a game. I'm not going off reservation." Did every occupation come with its own language? "And Hobden's of no interest. Don't worry, old man. I'm not heading for trouble."

"Call me that again and you will be." Sensing a natural end to the conversation, River started making the movements you make when you're ready to leave, but his grandfather hadn't finished. "And I don't worry. Well, I do, but there's precious little point in it. You'll do what you're going to do, and nothing I say'll steer you on to any other course."

River felt a pang. "You know I always listen —"

"It's not a complaint, River. You're your mother's son, that's all." He gave a low chuckle at whatever expression washed across River's face. "You think you get it from me, don't you? I wish I could claim the credit."

"You raised me," River said. "You and Rose."

"But she had you till you were seven. She could have taught the Jesuits a thing or two. Heard from her lately?"

This last thrown in casually, as if they were discussing a former colleague.

River said, "Couple of months ago. She called from Barcelona to remind me I'd missed her birthday."

The O.B. threw his head back, and laughed with genuine amusement. "There you go, boy. That's how you do it. Set your own agenda."

"I'll be careful," River told him.

The old man caught his elbow as River bent to kiss his cheek goodbye. "Be more than careful, lad. You

115

don't deserve Slough House. But make a mess trying to break out, and nothing anyone says will save your career."

Which was as close as his grandfather had ever come to admitting he'd put a word in after the King's Cross fiasco.

"I'll be careful," he repeated, and left to catch his train.

He was still thinking about that the following morning. *I'll be careful.* How many times did you hear that, immediately before somebody had an accident? *I'll be careful.* But there was nothing careful about the memory stick in his pocket; nothing accidental about its being in his possession. The only careful thing he'd done so far was not look at it.

Doing that would make him privy to information closed to Sid Baker; probably even to Spider Webb. It would give him an edge, make him feel a full-fledged spook again. But it could also get him banged up. What was the word the O.B. had used? Excommunicated . . . *There are certain beliefs you should keep under wraps if you want to dine at High Table.* River was a long way from High Table, but there was further to fall. And if he got caught with the stick in his possession, he'd fall all right.

Though if that happened, everyone would assume he'd read what was on the stick anyway . . .

His thoughts chased backwards and forwards. A guilty conscience was the worst thing to be wearing. Climbing the stairs at Slough House, he had to fix his expression into whatever it usually was, this time of the morning: *When you need to act natural, don't think about what you're doing.* An old lesson. *Think about anything else. Think about the last book you read.* He couldn't remember the last book he'd read. But whether the effort of trying to do so made him look less or more natural he never found out, because no one was interested in River's state of mind that morning.

Roderick Ho's office door was open, so River saw from the landing that everyone was gathered there: an unprecedented event. But at least they weren't talking to each other. Instead, all were staring at Ho's monitor, the largest in the building. "What is it?" River asked, but hardly needed to. Stepping inside he could make out, over Ho's shoulder, a badly lit cellar, an orange-clad figure on a chair with a hood over its head. Gloved hands held up an English newspaper, which was shaking. This made sense. Nobody ever sat in a badly lit cellar holding the day's newspaper for a camera without feeling fear.

"Hostage," said Sid Baker, without looking away from the screen.

River stopped himself from saying *I can see that.* "Who is it? Who are they?"

"We don't know."

"What *do* we know?"

Sid said, "They're going to cut his head off."

Not everyone had been in Ho's office when River got there. How had he failed to register Jackson Lamb's absence? Before long this was rectified: a heavy thump on the stair; a loud growling noise which could only have emanated from a stomach. Lamb could move quietly when he wanted, but when he didn't, you knew he was coming. And now he didn't so much enter Ho's office as take possession of it; breathing heavily, saying nothing. On the monitor, the same absence of event: a gloved, hooded boy in an orange jumpsuit, holding the English newspaper with its back page showing. It took a moment for River to register that he'd reached that conclusion — that the figure was a boy.

A thought interrupted by Lamb. "It's not nine o'clock and you're watching torture porn?"

Struan Loy said, "When would be a good time to watch —"

"Shut up," Sid Baker told him.

Lamb nodded. "That's a plan. Shut up, Loy. This live?"

"Coming over as a live feed," Ho said.

"There's a difference?"

"Do you really want to hear about it?"

118

"Good point. But that's today's paper." Lamb nodded again, approving his own deductive brilliance. "So if it's not live, it's not far off. How'd you pick it up?"

"From the blogs," Sid said. "It appeared about four."

"Any prologue?"

"They say they're going to cut his head off."

"They?"

She shrugged. "Don't know yet. Grabs the attention, though."

"Have they said what they want?"

Sid said, "They want to cut his head off."

"When?"

"Forty-eight hours."

"Why forty-eight?" asked Lamb. "Why not seventy-two? Three days, is that so much to ask?"

Nobody dared ask what his problem was. He told them anyway.

"It's always one day or three. You get twenty-four hours, or seventy-two. Not forty-eight. You know what I already hate about these tossers?"

"They can't count?" River suggested.

"They've no sense of tradition," Lamb said. "I don't suppose they've said who the little blind mouse is, either?"

Roderick Ho said, "The beheading threat came over the blogs, along with the link. And the deadline. No other info. And there's no volume on the feed."

Through all of this, none of them had taken their eyes off the screen.

"Why so shy?" Lamb wondered. "If you're cutting somebody's head off, you're making a point. But if you don't tell anybody why you're doing it, it's not going to help your cause, is it?"

"Cutting heads off doesn't help anyone's cause," Sid objected.

"It does if your cause involves chopping people's heads off. Then you're preaching right at your niche market."

Ho said, "What difference does it make who they are? They're Al Qaeda, whatever they call themselves. Sons of the Desert. Sword of Allah. Wrath of the Book. They're all Al Qaeda."

There was another late entry: Jed Moody, his coat still on. "You've heard?"

"We're watching it now."

Kay White started to say something, but changed her mind. In a more cruel mood, everyone present would have marked this down as a first.

River said, "So what do we do?"

Lamb said, "Do?"

"Yes. What do we do?"

"We get on with our jobs. What did you think we did?"

"For Christ's sake, we can't just act like this isn't happening —"

"No?"

The short, sharp word punctured River's balloon.

Lamb's voice became flat and unimaginative. The boy on the monitor, the hood on his head, the newspaper he held — it might have been a screensaver.

He said, "Did you think the Batphone was about to go off, Lady Di shouting all hands on deck? No, we'll watch it on telly like everyone else. But we won't *do* anything. That's for the big boys, and you lot don't play with the big boys. Or had you forgotten?"

Nobody said anything.

"Now, you've got papers to shuffle. Why are we all in this room?"

So one by one everybody left, except Ho and Moody, whose room it was. Moody hung his raincoat on the back of the door. He didn't speak, and Ho wouldn't have answered if he had.

Lamb stood a moment longer. His upper lip was flecked with an almond croissant's sugary dust, and as he watched the computer monitor, on which nothing happened that hadn't been happening for the past several minutes, his tongue discovered this seam of sweetness and gathered it in. But his eyes remained oblivious of what his tongue was doing, and if Ho or Moody had turned his way, what they saw might have startled them.

For a short while, the overweight, greasy has-been burned with cold hard anger.

Then he turned, and plodded upstairs to his office.

In his own room River booted up, then sat silently cursing the time his computer took to flicker into life. He was barely aware of Sid Baker arriving, and jumped when she spoke:

"Do you think —"

"*Jesus!*"

Sid recovered first. "Well, sorry! Christ! It's my office too, you know."

"I know, I know. I was . . . concentrating."

"Of course. Turning your PC on, that's a tricky business. I can see it would take all your attention."

"Sid, I didn't realize you'd come in. That's all. What do you want?"

"Forget it."

She sat at her desk. River's monitor, meanwhile, enjoyed its usual fake awakening; swimming into blue then reverting to black. Waiting, he glanced at Sid. She wore her hair tied back and seemed paler than usual, which might have been her black cashmere V-neck, or might have been the ten minutes she'd just spent watching a young man with a hood on his head, who'd apparently been condemned to death.

And she wasn't wearing her silver locket. If he'd been asked if this was unusual he'd have said he had no idea, but the fact was Sid wore the locket about half the time, from which he drew the inference that it held no special emotional significance for her. But nobody was likely to ask him.

His computer emitted that high-pitched beep that always sounded impatient, as if he'd been keeping it waiting rather than the other way round.

He said, only half aware he was about to do so, "About yesterday. I'm sorry. It was stupid."

"It was."

"It felt like it might be funny at the time."

"Stupid things often do," Sid said.

"Clearing it up was no fun, if it makes you feel any better."

"It would make me feel better if you'd done a proper job of it. There were still eggshells under my desk this morning."

But she was half-smiling, so that probably drew a line under the episode.

Though the question of why Sid had been sent on an op in the first place continued to rankle.

His computer was awake now but in a familiarly human sort of way, which meant it would be another few minutes before it was up to speed. He clicked on the browser.

Sid spoke again: "You think Ho's right? They're Al Qaeda?"

About to make a smart remark, River bit it back. What was the point? He said, "What else? It's not like we've not seen this before."

Both fell silent, remembering similar broadcasts a few years earlier; of a hostage beheaded for the crime of being Western.

"They'll be on the radar," Sid said.

River nodded.

"All this stuff we do, here and Regent's Park, GCHQ — the lid's on pretty tight. Once they establish who the kid is, and where it's happening, they'll run up a shortlist of suspects. Won't they?"

He was online at last. "What was that link?"

"Sec."

A moment later an e-mail winked on to his screen. He clicked on the link it held, and the browser changed

123

from a bland civil service logo to the now-familiar boy, hood, cellar.

Nothing had changed in the minutes since they'd left Ho's room.

Again they sat in silence, but a different silence to the one that usually prevailed in their office. It was shared, rather than dictated by awkwardness.

But if either were hoping it would be broken by a voice from that cellar, they were disappointed.

At last, River said, "There's a lot of time, effort and money been spent on covering extremist groups."

Sid had forgotten she'd asked the question.

"But there's not a whole lot of live intel out there."

"Assets," she said.

Any other day, River might have scoffed. "Assets," he agreed. "Infiltrating extremist groups used to be an easier business."

"You sound like you know about this."

"I grew up with the stories."

"Your grandfather," she said. "He was David Cartwright, wasn't he?"

"He still is."

"I didn't mean —"

"He's still alive. Very much so." He glanced round. She had pushed her chair from her desk, and was watching him rather than the screen. "And it's not like he told me State secrets as bedtime stories."

"I wasn't going to suggest that."

"But the first bedtime story he ever did read me was *Kim*." River could tell she recognized the title, so didn't elaborate. "After that, well, Conrad, Greene. Somerset Maugham."

"*Ashenden*."

"You get the picture. For my twelfth birthday, he bought me le Carré's collected works. I can still remember what he said about them."

They're made up. But that doesn't mean they're not true.

River returned to the screen. The newspaper the boy held trembled. Why was he holding it with the back page showing, though? *England triumph* — last night's World Cup qualifier.

"The BBC," he said out loud, thinking of the link Sid had sent him.

"A blog on their news pages. The link was posted there, along with the beheading threat. Then it mushroomed. It'll be everywhere now."

River had a sudden image of darkened rooms all over the country, all over the world; heads bent over monitors, studying iPhones, watching nothing happening, slowly. In some of the hearts of those watching would be the same sick dread he felt now; and in others, there'd be unholy joy.

"Can we trace the link?" Sid asked. "The IPS, I mean? Where it's being broadcast from?"

He said, "Depends. If they're clever, no. If they're stupid . . ."

But both knew that this wasn't going to end as swiftly and satisfactorily as that.

Sid said, "He pissed you off, didn't he? More than usual, I mean?"

River didn't need to ask. She meant Jackson Lamb.

He said, "How long have you been here now?"

"Just a few months."

"I meant exactly."

"I don't know exactly. Since August sometime."

About two months.

He said, "I've been here eight months, two weeks and four days."

Sid Baker was quiet a few moments, then said, "Okay. But hardly worth a long-service medal."

"You don't get it, do you? Being here means I have to sit watching this like everybody else. That's not what I joined the Service for."

"Maybe we'll be needed."

"No. That's what being in Slough House means. It means not being needed."

"If you hate it so much, why don't you quit?"

"And do what?"

"Well, I don't know. Whatever you like."

"Banking?" he said. "Insurance?"

She fell silent.

"The law? Property sales?"

"Now you're taking the piss."

"This is what I'm for," he said. He pointed at the screen, on which a hooded boy sat on a chair in a cellar. "To make things like this not happen. Or when they happen, make them stop. That's what it is, Sidonie. I don't want to do anything else."

He couldn't remember he'd ever called her that before.

She said, "I'm sorry."

"What for?"

She turned away. Then shook her head. "Sorry you feel that way. But one mistake doesn't mean your career's over. You'll get another chance."

"What did you do?" he asked.

"Do?"

"To deserve Slough House."

Sid said, "What we're doing is useful. It has to be done."

"And could be done by a bunch of trained monkeys."

"Thanks a lot."

"It's true."

"Yesterday morning? Taking Hobden's files?"

"Yeah, okay, you got to —"

"I'm not rubbing it in. I'm simply pointing out, maybe things are changing. Maybe Slough House isn't such a dead end. I did something real. You went out too —"

"To bring the rubbish in."

"Okay. A monkey could have done that."

River laughed. Then shook his head. On his monitor, nothing had changed. The laugh turned sour in the air.

"This poor sod needs more than monkeys on his side," he said.

Sid nodded.

River's hand dropped to his thigh, and he felt the hard nub of the memory stick in his trouser pocket.

She meant well, he supposed, but her predecessor here had quit the Service, ground into submission by routine tasks. As had his own; a man called Black, who

127

had lasted only six months, and left before River arrived. That was the true purpose of Slough House. It was a way of losing people without having to get rid of them, sidestepping legal hassle and tribunal threats. And it occurred to him that maybe that was the point of Sid's presence: that her youth and freshness were meant as a counterpoint to the slow horses' failure, rendering it more pungent. He could smell it now. Looking at this hooded boy on his screen, River could smell failure on his own skin. He couldn't help this kid. Whatever the Service did, it would do without River's assistance.

"What is it?"

He turned back to Sid. "What's what?"

"You look like something occurred to you."

He shook his head. "No. Nothing."

On his desk was a fresh pile of transcripts. Catherine Standish must have delivered them before the news broke. He picked up the topmost, then dropped it. That small slapping noise was as much impact as it would ever have; he could spend the next hour writing a report on another chunk of chattering from another supposed hot spot, and all it would earn would be a cursory once-over from Regent's Park. Sid said something else, River didn't catch what. Instead, he locked his eyes on the computer screen; on the boy in the hood who was going to be executed for some reason, or no reason at all, in less than forty-eight hours, and if the newspaper he held was to be believed, this was happening here in the UK.

Bombs on trains were bad enough. Something like this, the press would go intercontinental.

Whatever it was Sidonie Baker had said, she now said again. Something about gloves. "Why do you think he's wearing gloves?"

"I don't know." It was a good question. But River had no answer.

What he mostly knew was that he needed to do something real, something useful. Something more than paper-shuffling.

He felt the hard nub of the memory stick once more.

Whatever it held, it was in River's pocket. Was the fruit of a real-live op.

If viewing its contents was crossing a line, River was ready to cross it.

At Max's, the coffee was bad and the papers dull. Robert Hobden leafed through *The Times* without troubling his notebook, and was contemplating today's front-page blonde on the *Telegraph* when he became aware of background mutter. He looked up. Max was at the counter with a customer, both staring at the TV on its corner plinth. Usually, Hobden insisted they lower the volume. Today he turned the world upside down, and insisted they raise it.

". . . has yet claimed responsibility, and nor has anyone appeared onscreen other than the young man pictured, but according to an anonymous post that appeared on the BBC's current affairs blog at four o'clock this morning, the young man you're watching is to be executed within forty-eight hours . . ."

Max said, "Do you believe this shit?"

The customer said, "They're monsters. Plain monsters. They want shooting, the lot of them."

But Hobden was barely hearing it.

Sometimes you knew you had a story, and were just waiting for its fin to show above the waves of the everyday news.

And here it was. Breaking surface.

Max said again, "Do you believe this?"

But Hobden was back at his table, gathering up keys, mobile, wallet, pen and notebook; tucking everything into his bag, except the newspapers.

Those, he left where they lay.

It wasn't long after nine. A watery sunshine spilt over London; a hint of good weather to come, if you were in an optimistic mood.

On a large white building near Regent's Park, it fell like a promise that this was as good as things might get.

Diana Taverner had a top-floor office. Once she'd enjoyed an expensive view, but post-7/7, senior staff had been moved away from external walls, and her only window now was the large pane of glass through which she could keep an eye on her team, and through which they in their turn could cast glances her way, keeping an eye on her keeping an eye on them. There were no windows on the hub either, but the light that rained on it was gentle and blue and, according to some report or other — it would be on file; labelled and archived and retrievable on request — was the closest electricity could come to natural sunlight.

Taverner approved. She didn't begrudge a younger generation the prizes her own had won for them. There was no sense fighting the same battles twice.

Her apprenticeship had been served in the fag-end of the Cold War, and it sometimes felt like that was the easy part. The Service had a long and honourable tradition of women dying behind enemy lines, but was less enthusiastic about placing them behind important desks. Taverner — Lady Di everywhere but to her face — had done her best to shake that particular tree, and if she'd been told ten years ago that a woman would be running the Service within the decade, she'd have assumed she'd be the woman in question.

History, though, had a way of throwing spanners in every direction. With Charles Partner's death had come a feeling that new winds were blowing down the Service's corridors; that a fresh outlook was required. "Troubled times" was the recurring phrase. A safe pair of hands was needed, which turned out to belong to Ingrid Tearney. The fact that Tearney was a woman would have been a soothing balm to Taverner, if it hadn't been a severe irritant instead.

Still, it was progress. It would have felt more like progress if it hadn't involved someone else, but it was progress. And she, Taverner, was Second Desk, even if the new dispensation involved there being several Second Desks; and her team had spring-sunshine lighting and ergonomic chairs, and that was fine too. Because they also had young men with rucksack-bombs on tube trains. Anything that helped them do their jobs was fine by Taverner.

This morning, they also had an execution in progress.

The link had appeared on a BBC blog around 4a.m., its accompanying message brief but effective: *we cut his head off forty-eight hours*. Unpunctuated. Short. Radical groups, especially your religious types, tended to sermonize: spawn of Satan, eternal fire, et cetera. That this wasn't the case made it more disturbing. A hoax would have had claptrap attached.

And now, like all successful media events, it was playing on every screen in sight. Would be playing on every screen in the country, in fact: in homes and offices; above treadmills in gyms; on palm-pilots and iPhones; on the back seats of black cabs. And all round the globe, people would be catching up with it at the different times of their day, and their first reaction would be the same as that of the team on the hub: that *this couldn't be happening in Britain*. Other parts of the world boasted outlaw lands aplenty. Tell your average Western citizen that they played polo with human heads in Kazakhstan, and you'd get a nod. *Yeah, I heard about that*. But even on the wildest of Britain's inner city estates, they weren't chopping heads off. Or not on the BBC, anyway.

And it wasn't going to happen, Taverner told herself. This was not going to happen. Stopping it was going to be the highlight of her career, and would call time on a lousy era for the Service, years of dodgy dossiers, suspicious deaths. It was going to get them out of the doghouse: herself, her superiors, and all the boys and girls on the hub; the hardworking, underpaid guardians of the State who were first in line when duty called, and last to be celebrated when things went right . . . It wasn't twelve months since her team had rolled up a terrorist cell that had mapped out a full-scale assault on the capital, and the arrests, the captured weaponry, had made for a two-day wonder. But at the trial, the main question was: how come the cell had thrived for so long? How come it had so nearly achieved its objective?

The anniversaries of failure were marked on the streets, with crowds emerging from offices to observe a silence for the innocent dead. Successes were lost in the wash; swept from the front pages by celebrity scandal and economic gloom.

Taverner checked her watch. There was a lot of paper heading her way: the first sit-rep was due on her desk any minute; there'd be a Crash Room meeting thirty seconds later; a briefing for the Minister before the hour was out; then Limitations. The press would want a statement of intent. Ingrid Tearney being in DC, Diana Taverner would deliver that too. Tearney would be relieved, actually. She'd want Taverner's fingerprints on this in case it went tits up, and a citizen had his head cut off on live TV.

And before any of that happened there was someone at the door: Nick Duffy, Head Dog.

It didn't matter which rung of the ladder you were on: when the Dogs appeared uninvited, your first reaction was guilt.

"What is it?"

"Something I thought you should know."

"I'm busy."

"Don't doubt it for a minute, boss."

"Spit it out."

"I had a drink with an ex last night. Moody. Jed Moody."

She said, "He got the boot after the Miro Weiss business. Isn't he at Slough House?"

"Yes. And not liking it."

The door opened. A kid called Tom put a manila folder on Taverner's desk. The first sit-rep. It looked implausibly thin.

Taverner nodded, and Tom left without speaking.

She said to Duffy, "I'm somewhere else in thirty seconds."

"Moody was talking about an op."

"He's covered by the Act." She scooped up the folder. "If he's running off about his glory days, bring him in and slap him round. Or get a tame policeman to do it. Am I really telling you how to do your job?"

"He wasn't talking about the past. He says Jackson Lamb's running an op."

She paused. Then said, "They don't run ops from Slough House."

"Which is why I thought you should know."

She stared past him for a second, through the glass at the crew on the hub. Then her focus shifted, and she was looking at her own image. She was forty-nine years old. Stress, hard work and Father bloody Time had done their worst, but still: she was heir to good bones, and blessed with a figure. She knew how to make the most of both, and today wore a dark suit over a pale pink blouse, the former picking up the colour of her shoulder-length hair. She was fine. A bit of maintenance between meetings, and she might make it to nightfall without looking like something dragged round a barnyard by pigs.

Provided she didn't get many unexpected moments.

She said, "What shape did this op take?"

"Someone I thought at the time was a bloke, but —"

"Sidonie Baker," Taverner said. Her voice could have cut glass. "Jackson Lamb sicced her on a journalist. Robert Hobden."

Nick Duffy nodded, but she'd put a hole in his morning. It was one thing to bring a bone to the boss. Another to find she'd buried it in the first place. He said, "Right. Sure. It was just —"

She gave him a steely look, but give him credit: he didn't back down.

"Well, you said yourself. They don't run ops from Slough House."

"It wasn't an op. It was an errand."

Which was so nearly what Duffy had told Jed Moody that it startled him for a moment.

Taverner said: "Our slow horses, they push pens, when they're not folding paper. But they can be trusted with petty theft. We're stretched, Duffy. These are difficult times."

"All hands on deck," he found himself saying.

"That would cover it, yes. Anything else?"

He shook his head. "Sorry to bother you."

"Not a bother. Everyone has to be on the ball."

Duffy turned to go. He was at the door when she spoke again.

"Oh, and Nick?"

He turned.

"There are those who'd take it badly if they knew I'd been sub-contracting. They might think it shows lack of faith."

"Sure, boss."

"Whereas it's simply a sensible use of resources."

"My ears only, boss," he said. And left.

Diana Taverner wasn't one to make marks on paper when she could avoid it. Jed Moody: that wasn't much to remember.

On the wall-mounted TV, coverage continued: the orange-clad, hooded boy. For tens of thousands around the globe, he'd be the object of pity and prayer by now, and of massive speculation. For Diana Taverner, he was a figure on a board. Had to be. She couldn't do what she needed to do, the end result of which would be his safe return home, if she allowed herself to be distracted by emotional considerations. She would do her job. Her team would do theirs. The kid would live. End of story.

She rose, gathered her paperwork, and got halfway to the door before returning to her desk, opening a drawer, and locking inside it the memory stick James Webb had given her the previous afternoon. A copy of Hobden's own memory stick, he'd told her, made by Sid Baker. Safely delivered. Unlooked at. The interim laptop wiped. She'd believed him. If she'd thought he'd look at it, she'd have had a higher opinion of him, but wouldn't have set him this task.

On the TV, the hooded boy sat in silence, newspaper fluttering. He'd live, she told herself.

Though even Diana Taverner had to admit, he must be scared.

Fear lives in the guts. That's where it makes its home. It moves in, shifts stuff around; empties a space for itself — it likes the echoes its wingbeats make. It likes the smell of its own farts.

His bravado had lasted about ten minutes by his reckoning, and less than three in reality. Once that was done, his fear rearranged the furniture. He'd voided his bowels into the bucket in the corner; had clenched and unclenched until his guts ached, and long before he'd finished he'd known this wasn't rag week. Didn't matter how edgy these bastards thought they were, this was way past playtime. This was where policemen became involved. *We were only kidding* didn't play in court.

He didn't know whether it was day or night. How long had he been in the van? The filming might have been yesterday, or might have been two hours ago. Hell, it might have been tomorrow, and that newspaper a fake, crammed with news that hadn't happened yet . . .

Concentrate. Keep a grip. Don't let Larry, Moe and Curly smash his mind to pieces.

Which was what he was calling them: Larry, Moe and Curly. Because there were three of them, and that's what his dad called customers who came in threes. When they came in pairs, they were Laurel and Hardy.

That had once been so lame: the names, and the fact that his dad used them two or three times a week. Larry, Moe and Curly this; Laurel and Hardy that. Get a fresh script, dad. But now his father's words were a comfort. He could even hear the voice. *Right bunch of comedians you've got yourself mixed up with.* Not my fault, dad. Not my fault. He'd simply been walking down a lane at the wrong time.

But walking and daydreaming, he reminded himself. His mind playing its usual games, working up a piece of shtick; a comedy riff which distracted him long enough for these goons to get the drop on him . . . Except that was a laugh too, wasn't it? A trio of twelve-year-olds could have "got the drop on him". He wasn't Action Man.

But they'd taken him, and doped him, and stripped him to his shorts and dumped him in this cellar; had left him for an hour or two, or three, or a fortnight, until he'd grown so used to the dark that the sudden light was like the sky ripping open.

Larry, Moe and Curly. Rough hands, big loud voices.

God, you dirty bastard —

The stink in here —

And then they were thrusting his new uniform at him, an orange jumpsuit and a hood for his head. Gloves for his hands.

"Why are you —?"

"Shut up."

"I'm nobody. I'm just —"

"You think we give a toss who you are?"

They'd slapped him down on the chair. Thrust a newspaper into his hands. From noises they made, words they said, he suspected they were setting up a camera. He was crying, he realized. He hadn't known this could happen to adults: that they could cry without knowing they'd started.

"Stop moving."

Impossible advice. Like *stop itching*.

"Keep still."

Keep still . . .

He kept still, tears rolling under his hood. Nobody spoke, but there was a hum that might have been their camera; a scratching it took a while to identify: it was the newspaper's pages, rustling as he shook. And he thought: that's not enough noise. He should scream. He should swear his head off, let these bastards know he wasn't scared, not of lowlife chickenshits like them; he should shout, scream and swear, but didn't. Because there was part of him saying *If you swear they might not like you. They'll think you're a bad person. And if they think that, who knows what they'll do?* Advice this little voice kept squeaking while newspaper rustled and camera hummed, until at last one of the comedians said, "Okay," and the humming stopped. The newspaper was snatched from his hands. He was pushed from the chair.

On landing he bit through his lip, and that might have been the moment he let fly. But before he could make a sound there was a heavy head next to his, breathing a filthy message into his ear that arrived with the hot stink of onions, blasting its meaning deep inside his brain, and then the men were gone and he was swallowed by the dark. And the little voice in his head breathed its last, for it had arrived at a true understanding of what was happening, and that it didn't matter what kind of person they thought he was, or whether he swore or meekly followed orders, because everything that he could be to them had slotted into place long ago. The colour of his skin was enough. That he didn't share their religion. That they resented his presence, his very existence; that he was an affront to them — he could swear, or get down on his knees and give each of them a blow job: it didn't matter. His crime was who he was. His punishment was what they'd already decided it would be.

We're going to cut your head off.

That's what the voice had said.

We're going to show it on the web.

That's what it said.

You fucking Paki.

Hassan wept.

The dreadful pub across the road served food of sorts, and its sprawl promised undisturbed nooks. River's lunch break was early enough to qualify as a late breakfast, but Slough House was absorbed by the morning's news, and he didn't suppose anyone would notice. He needed to do something which didn't involve paperwork; he wanted a taste of what Spider Webb might be doing. He booted up his laptop and plugged in the memory stick. This was technically a criminal act, but River was pissed off. There are always moments in a young man's life when that seems reason enough.

Ten minutes later, it seemed a lot less than that.

The bacon baguette he'd ordered sat ignored; the coffee was undrinkable filth. Cup to one side, plate to the other, laptop in the middle, he was working through the files Sid had stolen from Hobden. Except she couldn't have, River decided. She couldn't have, unless —

"What you doing?"

River couldn't have looked more guilty if he'd been caught with kiddie porn.

"Working," he said.

Sid Baker sat down opposite. "We have an office for that."

"I was hungry."

"So I see." She eyed his untouched baguette.

"What do you want, Sid?"

"I thought you might be getting drunk."

"And?"

"And I didn't think that was a clever move."

Closing the laptop, he said, "What's happening?"

"Ho says it's a loop."

"I didn't spot that."

"You're not Ho. He says it's running at thirty-something minutes, seven or eight."

"Not live, then."

"But this morning. Because of —"

"Because of the newspaper, yeah, I got that. What about a location?"

"Ho says not. They've bounced the transmission off PCs stretching halfway round the globe. By the time you've traced the next in the chain, it's thirty machines ahead of you. This is Ho, mind. GCHQ might have a better shot."

"Too complicated to be a hoax?"

Sid said, "Until we know who the kid is, and who's got him, nobody's ruling anything out. But with the whole world watching, we've got to treat it as real."

He leant back. "That was rousing. We?"

She flushed. "You know what I mean. And none of that answers my question, anyway. What are you doing here?"

"Missing a pep-talk, apparently."

"Do you ever give a straight answer?"

"Do you?"

"Try me."

"How much research did you do on Hobden?"

Her eyes changed. "Not much."

"But enough to find out where he has breakfast."

"That's not tricky, River."

"You don't usually call me River."

"I don't usually call anyone River. It's not an everyday name."

"Blame my mother. She had a hippy phase. Did Lamb tell you to keep the job quiet?"

"No, he told me to blog it. It's on bloody stupid questions, dot gov, dot UK. My go. How much do you know about Hobden?"

"Hotshot reporter back in the day. Firebrand leftie, moved right as he got older. Ended up doing why-oh-why columns for the little-England press, explaining why the country's problems are all down to immigration, the welfare state and some bloke called Roy Jenkins."

"Labour Home Secretary in the sixties," Sid said sweetly.

"History GCSE?"

"Google."

"Fair enough. Anyway, it's all standard retired-colonel stuff, except he had a few national newspapers to sound off in. The occasional pitch on *Question Time*."

"Beats holding forth at the vicar's garden party," she said. "So that's Robert Hobden, then. Angry young man to irritated old fogey in twenty years."

"A common trajectory."

"Except his was more severe than most. And when it turned out he was a fully paid-up member of the British Patriotic Party, that was his career shot to pieces."

"The nation's last defence, as their website has it."

"Made up of those who thought the BNP had gone soft."

River found he was enjoying this. "And who weren't going to let a newfangled thing like political correctness get in the way of the old-time virtues."

"The direct approach, I think they called it," Sid said.

"Paki-bashing is what they called it," River said.

"You'd have thought he'd try to keep that quiet."

"Hard to do when the membership list turns up on the internet."

And now they shared a smile.

River said, "And that was the end of an almost-glorious career." He remembered his grandfather's words. "Not because of his beliefs. But because there are some beliefs you're supposed to keep under wraps if you don't want to be excommunicated."

All of this from an hour's web-research, on getting home last night.

"Did the Service really leak the list?"

River shrugged. "Probably. Didn't Lamb give any hint?"

"I'm not supposed to discuss it."

"You're not *supposed* to be in the pub."

"He gave no hint. No."

"You'd say that anyway."

"I'm sure that must be frustrating for you. You know, this is the longest conversation we've ever had?"

A record they'd broken twice today.

"Did you really read *Ashenden*?" he asked.

"As in, the whole thing?"

"That answers that."

"I do pub quizzes. I know the titles of a lot of books I've never read." Her focus shifted to his laptop. "What are you doing, anyway? Still on those transcripts?"

Before he could answer she'd reached out and turned the computer, opening its screen. The page of numbers he'd been staring at stared right back at her.

"Pie," she said.

"You'll have to ask at the bar."

"Funny ha ha. *Pi*."

"I know."

She scrolled down. "To what looks like a million places."

"I know."

He turned the laptop back round, and closed the file. There were fifteen on the memory stick, and he'd only opened seven, but all contained nothing but pi. To what looked like a million places.

He'd bet his uneaten bacon sandwich that the remaining eight were the same.

Sid was waiting. She raised an eyebrow.

"What?"

"So what are you doing? Memorizing it?"

"Nothing."

"Right," she said. "Nothing."

He folded the laptop shut.

"Do you usually spend your lunchtimes in the pub?" she asked.

"Only when I want privacy."

She shook her head. "Pub stands for public. Clue's in the name." She checked her watch. "Well, you're still among the living. I'd better get back."

"Did you really copy Hobden's files?"

It was something the O.B. had told him. *A lot of questions go unanswered because nobody thinks to ask.*

"We've been through that."

"Tell me again."

She sighed. "He's a man of habit. He has coffee at the same café every morning. First thing he does is empty the contents of his pocket on to the table. Which includes his memory stick." She waited, but he said nothing. "I caused a fuss by spilling some coffee. When he went off to fetch a cloth, I swapped his stick for a dummy and loaded it on to my own laptop. Later, I swapped it back." She paused. "The laptop's the one you delivered to Regent's Park."

"Did you look at the files?"

"Of course not."

There were ways of telling when someone was lying. The direction their eyes were pointing, for instance: left for memory, right for creation. But Sid's eyes were directed straight at River's. Which meant she wasn't lying, or else was very good at it. They'd done the same courses, after all.

"Okay, so —"

But she'd gone.

He shook his head, then returned to his laptop. It only took five minutes to confirm that all the files were the same; eternal strings of figures mapping one endless circle. Unless Hobden had taken pi places it had never been before, it seemed unlikely that this was what Regent's Park had been after. So either Hobden was the kind of total paranoid who flaunted dummy back-ups of his real secrets, or Sid herself had pulled a fast one.

146

Or something else was going on, and River was in the dark.

That sounded plausible. That sounded entirely likely ... Abandoning his sandwich, he headed back to Slough House.

Where there was communal activity again. When he reached the landing, Louisa Guy and Min Harper called him into Ho's office, as if waiting for someone else to share the news with. "They're showing a new film."

"A new one?"

"A new one." This was Ho, in front of his monitor. The others were gathered around him, Sid among them. "The first was a loop," Ho said. There was no definite inflection to these words, but everyone caught the hidden meaning: the first had been a loop, which he had noticed and nobody else had. "Now there's a new one. Also a loop."

Stepping to one side, looking round the bodies clustered in his way, River got his first look at the screen.

"And," Struan Loy said, "you're not gunna believe this."

But River was already believing it, because there it was on Ho's monitor: same set-up as before, except this time the kid wasn't wearing a hood. His face was plain to see, and it wasn't a face they'd been expecting.

Somebody said, "It doesn't mean it's not Islamists. Who've got him, I mean."

"Depends on who the kid is."

"He'll turn out to be a squaddie — a Muslim squaddie. Exactly the kind of victim they're looking for."

Sid Baker said, "He doesn't look like a squaddie."

He didn't, it was true. He looked soft and dreamy. And scared stiff, and even a squaddie can be scared stiff, but it went deeper than that: his features had that untested gloss which is one of the first things squaddies get kicked out of them.

"That's why they had him wearing gloves," Sid said. "They were hiding his colour."

"How long's the loop?" River asked.

"Twelve minutes. Twelve and a bit," Ho said.

"Why are they doing that?"

"A continuous feed would be easier to trace. Less impossible, anyway." Ho sighed. He liked people knowing he knew this stuff, but hated having to explain it. "You'd get little breaks in transmission every time they switched computer. If their network's limited to a set number of proxies, that might give us an edge in tracking them."

"What's that in the background?" Catherine Standish said. River hadn't noticed she was there.

"What's what?"

"Over his left shoulder."

Something leant against the wall a couple of yards behind the boy.

"A piece of wood."

"A handle of some sort."

"I think it's an axe," Catherine said.

"Jesus . . ."

Loy was still worrying away at the kid's identity. "If he's not a squaddie, maybe he's a name. Wonder who his parents are?"

"Anyone missing on the diplomats' list?"

148

"Well, there might be. But it's not like we'll be told. Besides, if the kid was a name, the kidnappers would have said. Ups the box-office value."

Sid said, "Okay, say he's not a squaddie or an embassy snatch. Who is he?"

"One of their own who they think's been turned."

"Or they caught him with a tart."

"Or a half of bitter and a jazz mag," Loy put in.

River said, "Unless he's not."

"Meaning what?"

"Unless he's some random kid who happened to be the right colour."

Ho said, "He look the right colour to you?"

Sid said, "Depends on who's got him. That's your point, right?"

River nodded.

Ho said, "Didn't we cover this? Swords of the Desert, Wrath of Allah. Doesn't matter what they call themselves. They're Al Qaeda."

"Unless they're not," River said.

Without fanfare, Jackson Lamb appeared among them. He stared at the screen a full fifteen seconds, then said, "He's Pakistani."

Sid said, "Or Indian or Sri Lankan or —"

Lamb said, flatly, "He's Pakistani."

"Do we have a name?" River asked.

"Fuck should I know? But it's not Al Qaeda's got him, is it?"

That he'd been about to say something similar didn't stop River from countering this. "Doesn't rule it out."

"Besides," Ho said. "Who else? Chopping a kid's head off on prime-time? Nobody does that except —"

"Idiots," said Lamb. "You're all idiots."

His slow gaze took them all in: River, Sid and Ho; Min Harper and Louisa Guy; Struan Loy and Kay White; Catherine Standish, on whom he seemed to focus with particular disdain. "It's on the table now. Don't you get it? They cut heads off, so can we. That's the masterplan behind this piece of theatre. Somebody somewhere will be using the words *fight fire with fire*. Some other dickhead'll be saying that what works in Karachi works just as well in Birmingham." He caught Loy's mouth about to open. "*Or wherever.*" Loy closed it. "Trust me, he's Pakistani, because that's the average numpty's shorthand for Muslim. And whoever's strapped him to that chair's not Al Qaeda. They've strapped him to that chair because *he's* Al Qaeda, or'll do nicely until the real thing comes along. These aren't Islamic fuckwits waging war on Satan's poodle. They're home-grown fuckwits who think they're taking it back to the enemy."

Nobody spoke.

"I'm disappointed. Nobody think I'm off the wall?"

River would have pulled his own tongue out sooner than tell him he'd had the same thoughts. "If you're right, why haven't they said so? Why mask him until now?"

"That's the way I'd do it," Lamb said. "If I wanted maximum attention. I'd start off letting everybody think they knew what was happening. So by the time I got around to explaining the real deal, everyone would already have an opinion."

And he was right, thought River. The fat bastard was probably right. Everywhere, everybody would be doing what Lamb had said: reconfiguring their earlier position that this was Islamist extremism. And he wondered how many of them would experience a brief hiccup before civilized outrage reasserted itself; a moment in which the thought would intrude that this foul threat, if neither fair nor just, was at least some kind of balancing.

Catherine said, "I've had enough of this," and left.

Lamb said, "Speaking of which, I assume this little gathering means you've all finished your current assignments? Because I want hard-copy updates by three. Along with a ten-bullet explanation of precisely why it's crucial we get a six-month extension on each of them." He looked round. Nobody blinked. "Good. Because we don't want to end up credit-crunched for looking like a bunch of useless tossers, do we?"

On Ho's monitor, the slightest of flickers indicated that the loop had come to an end and the reel was beginning again. The boy's face was still soft and glossy, but his eyes were shafts into the dark.

"Where's Moody, anyway?" Lamb asked.

But nobody knew, or nobody said.

A shag was making its way up and down the Thames, carving out a stretch of river between Hungerford Bridge and Canary Wharf. She didn't know much about the behaviour of birds — wasn't one hundred per cent this was a shag — but she suspected that if another turned up there'd be trouble; feathers would fly, and the loser would end up downriver, looking for a quiet life. That was what happened when territory was at stake.

Take this space here: a bench where you could sit with your back to the Globe. Streams of tourists passed every hour, and in either direction fire-jugglers, buskers and itinerant poets jealously guarded their patches; fistfights, even stabbings, resulting from encroachment on another's turf. Income was at stake. For the shag, food was the prize; for the hustler, tourist silver. But none of them knew the real value of the estate, which was that it was a blank spot. The bench on which Diana Taverner sat was in a twelve-yard corridor of CCTV limbo. It was a small safe cupboard in the open air, and had been reserved for her alone by a foul-looking splash of birdshit running most of its length; a revolting mess ensuring that even the weariest tourist would look elsewhere to rest his bones, though it was, in fact, a plastic transfer.

Unregarded, then, and off the leash, she lit a cigarette, and dragged a lungful of sweet poison into her system. Like most pleasures, this one diminished the more you indulged it. In normal circumstances Lady Di could let a pack last a month, but today, she suspected, she might be setting records.

A weak light fell upon the river. On both banks, the usual noises obtained: the rattle and honk of city traffic; the constant buzz of a million conversations. Way overhead, airliners were stacking up for Heathrow, while nearer to ground level a helicopter discovered a new shortcut between one side of London and the other.

Taverner breathed out smoke which hung in the air two seconds, then broke apart like a daydream. A passing jogger altered course to avoid the drift. Smoking was almost as good a guarantor of privacy as fake birdshit. Though give it another year or two, and it would probably be an arrestable offence.

Her current need for nicotine lay in the fact that she wasn't long out of the day's third meeting: this one with Limitations, formerly Steering & Oversight. It wasn't clear whether a sense of humour lay beneath the rebranding. Limitations was a cross between an Oxbridge MCR and a railway platform: a collection of chinless wonders, with a sprinkling of field-hardened veterans. You had more chance of reaching a consensus with a vox pop on Marmite. The suits hated operations because operations cost money; the field guys loved

153

them, because the best produced pure gold. To outward appearances Taverner was a suit, but her heart belonged with the field guys, the handlers. Besides, if you removed operations from the curriculum, security didn't amount to more than putting on a peaked cap and a shiny badge. As far as the war on terror went, you might as well start digging trenches, and handing out tin hats.

The folders she'd brought to this particular meeting were all the same buff-colour; had all been time-stamped fifteen minutes previously; were all logo-ed Mozart, this year's Grade-A classification. They'd made their way round the table even faster than the pastries.

For a few moments there was near-silence.

At length, a suit piped up. "You're quite sure about this?"

"Of course."

"Humint?"

A snort. The vets loved it when the footlights crowd slipped in a tradecraft term.

"Human intelligence," she said. "Yes."

"And this Albion crew —"

Somebody else said, "Could we do this by the numbers, please?"

General clearing of throats, shuffling of papers.

Tradition decreed that Limitations gatherings were minuted, regardless of whether the session was designated open, and thus recorded, or closed, and thus officially not recorded. So by the numbers it was: date, time, those attending. In the chair, Leonard Bradley of

Westminster Parish. In the hot seat, Lady Di. Not that anyone called her that.

"For those who don't know, Ms Tearney, Ingrid, is in Washington this week, or would of course be here. We're grateful to Diana for stepping into her shoes, but then we all know how capable a Second she is. Diana."

"Thank you, Leonard. Good morning, everyone." Replies were murmured. She tapped her folder. "The first anyone knew of this, it popped up on a BBC blog at 4.22 a.m."

"I hate to interrupt," a suit said.

The almost audible rolling of multiple pairs of eyes suggested that this wasn't entirely true.

"Can't such entries be traced via, ah, I believe they're called —"

Diana Taverner said: "If we had a trace, we wouldn't need this meeting. We'd have wrapped the whole thing up before *Today* aired."

Bradley made a hand gesture that would have looked more complete if he'd been brandishing a pipe. "Perhaps we could let Diana finish. Or even start."

She said: "Hassan Ahmed. Born Birmingham, 1990. His grandparents arrived from Islamabad in the early seventies. His grandfather ran a soft furnishings business which his father took over when the old man retired. Hassan is the youngest of four, in his second year at Leeds University. Business Studies. Shares a flat with three other students, but by all accounts, he's a shy kid. No girlfriend known, or boyfriend either. His tutor couldn't pick him out from a crowd. He belongs to a student society calls itself the Last Laugh, for budding stand-up comedians, but nobody there has much to say about him. He's clearly not lighting fires."

She paused to take a sip of water.

"He's Muslim, but only nominally. Before university, he was a regular attender at his local mosque, which is not — and never has been — on a watch list. But his homelife is secular, and his father in particular seems to regard the mosque as a networking opportunity. They don't use Urdu at home, and it's not clear Hassan speaks it. There's no record of his having contact with extreme influences, nor has he been clocked on demos or marches. His name popped up on a petition objecting to the 21/7 convictions, but it's possible it was hijacked. And even if it wasn't, it might just mean he happened to be there when the petition went round."

When she replaced the glass on its coaster, she took care to position it dead centre.

"It's a brief profile, and we all know that moderate backgrounds can produce blazing extremists, but there's absolutely nothing on Hassan to suggest that he's anything other than what he seems to be. A British Asian studying for a degree. Either way, we do know he was taken late last night on his way home from the comedy club. He was snatched in a back lane not far from his flat, taking a shortcut from where he'd parked his car. The snatchers —"

"He drives a car?" somebody asked.

"It was a present from his father," Taverner said.

She waited, but that seemed to satisfy him.

"The snatchers call themselves the Voice of Albion."

Now Leonard Bradley leant forward, his face creasing into that mask of perplexity he liked to wear when about to pick holes in somebody's case. "You'll forgive me —"

She waved him ahead, like a driver might a friendly bus.

"I thought there'd been no actual contact with these *snatchers*. But you've identified them already? That's smart work. Very smart."

One or two murmurs of assent met this.

Diana Taverner said, "There's been no contact, no. That's to say, they've not made any demands or identified themselves in relation to this particular, ah, episode."

"But you've been keeping tabs on them."

"That's well within our remit, I think you'd agree."

"Absolutely. Absolutely. Couldn't agree more."

Down the table, Roger Barrowby made a clucking noise with his tongue.

Barrowby was usually called the Barrowboy, a nickname he detested and pretended to revel in. He had thinning sandy hair, a prominent chin, and a habit of pressing the tip of a finger to its central dimple, as if trying to encourage it back into his jaw. But he appeared to have done something about his dandruff.

"Roger!" Leonard Bradley's tone couldn't have sounded heartier at a barbecue. "You have an interjection? An objection?" You could have cut the bonhomie with a knife. Taverner wondered why they hated each other.

"An observation, Len. Merely an observation."

157

"Care to share?"

Barrowby said, "Bloody lucky, that's all. We have a watching brief on a bunch of original thinkers, just as they're attempting a coup? I mean, how often does that happen?"

Despite herself, Taverner smiled at "original thinkers".

Bradley said, "We could argue about gift horses and dental plans. But perhaps Diana has a view?"

"Watching brief is pitching it high," Diana said. "They're one of seventeen groups on the radar right now, which is also a bit high, but there've been murmurs something like this was on the horizon. And —"

"Excuse me?"

Barrowby again.

"*Murmurs?*"

She'd have answered, but knew there was no way this was getting past the assembled ex-handlers, who provided a chorus:

"Not our remit, Roger."

"Not even close."

"Intelligence gathering's outside the sphere of this committee."

"Of course," Barrowby agreed. "But if we're paying for supper, we get to glance at the menu, surely?"

"We'll check the books when the financial year closes," somebody else said. "But how Operations shells out the booty is their game."

Bradley was nodding. "We get to taste the sausages, Roger," he said, "if you'll allow me to pursue your metaphor. But we don't get to watch them being made."

Barrowby raised his hands in mock surrender. "Diana. Forgive me. You heard *murmurs*. You allocated resources. Fair enough. It looks like you, or perhaps Ms Tearney, made a wise, *operational*, decision."

Leaving unaddressed the degree to which Ingrid Tearney had been involved, Diana went on: "Like I say, not a watching brief. That is, we weren't actually keeping them under surveillance, otherwise this caper wouldn't have got off the ground. And that, I'd agree, would have been *bloody* lucky. As it is, I'm confident we can roll this up in short order."

"Before they chop young Hassan's head off," Leonard Bradley said.

"Precisely."

"Well, there's no need to spell out the public relations aspect, is there? The half of the country that's not watching this yet will be glued to it by suppertime." He glanced at the papers in front of him. "Voice of Albion, eh? I'd be more impressed if there was any chance these halfwits had actually read Blake."

Silence greeted this.

He said, "Our friends in blue?"

"We haven't released the details, the Voice of Albion connection," Taverner said. "We will if necessary, but I'm confident that by this time tomorrow, we'll be able to present them with the whole package."

"The boy was snatched in Leeds city centre?" someone piped up.

"Not quite the centre. Headingley."

"Don't they have CCTV? I was rather under the impression one couldn't cross the road without being a reality TV star."

"It appears that the traffic monitoring system was off air for six hours last night, from a little before midnight until a short while ago. Routine maintenance, we're told."

"Bit of a coincidence."

"We're looking into it. Or the police are. But I don't think Albion have that sort of reach. You'll find a printout of their homepage in the folder, if you want an idea of the clout they wield."

There was a general rustling of pages.

Bradley glanced up. " 'Natoinal purity'," he noted with distaste. It wasn't clear whether it was the concept or the spelling which pained him.

"We're not dealing with the sharpest pencils in the box," Taverner agreed.

"Can't you trace them through the site?" Barrowby asked.

She said, "Now, there they have shown nous. The proxy's in Sweden, where they treat client privilege very seriously. Getting their details will take a while. More than the deadline allows. But let me repeat, I have every confidence that this crew will be under wraps before the deadline becomes an issue."

Then Bradley did that thing with his hand again, and said, "Let me say on all our behalf — behalves? — that we're grateful to Diana for a remarkably full picture drawn in a remarkably short time. And that we'll be equally grateful for hourly updates, leading to a swift and happy conclusion."

There was a knock on the door, and Tom entered, a folded sheet of paper in his hand. Without a word, he handed it to Diana Taverner, and left.

Taverner unfolded it, and read it in silence. Her expression betrayed not the slightest clue as to whether the information it contained was new to her, confirmation of something already suspected, or an out-of date report on weather happening elsewhere. But when she looked up, the atmosphere shifted.

"This is fresh. There'll be copies in a moment."

Bradley said, "Perhaps you might . . ."

She might. She did.

"People, it would appear this isn't the random snatch we'd thought."

New information demanded at least as much action as discussion. It was Diana Taverner's role to leave to see about the action, and everybody else's to get the discussion under way. Or almost everybody's. She was halfway to the lift when the Barrowboy caught her — almost literally: she turned to find him reaching for her arm. The look she bestowed upon him would have stuck six inches out the back of a more sensitive man.

"Not a good time, Roger."

"When is it ever? Diana, this new information."

"You know as much as I do."

"I doubt that. But either way, it doesn't change anything, does it?"

"You think? Not even a little?"

"What I meant was, you seemed confident enough before this apparent bombshell went off. Who he is doesn't make your job harder."

"'Apparent'?"

Each vowel was its own icicle.

"Poor choice of word. All I meant was, you've an asset in place, yes? You don't get Mozart-grade info from random phone-grabs or lists of dodgy loan applications."

"It's nice to hear from an expert, Roger. Remind me, where was your finest hour? Beirut? Baghdad? Or the bar at the Frontline Club?"

But it washed off him. "I only meant, that's the stuff they do over at Slough House." He barked a self-appreciative laugh. "Hoping to bore the deadweights into jumping ship. This is higher grade. So. You have an asset."

She jabbed the lift button with an index finger. "Yes, Roger. We have an asset. That's how intelligence gathering works."

"But he didn't know this latest twist?"

"If he knew everything he wouldn't just be an asset, Roger. He'd be Wikipedia."

"So how close to the action is he?"

"Pretty close."

"Handy."

"Some might say so. Others call it foresight."

"Well, there's foresight and foresight, isn't there? Not much credit in reading the runes if you laid them out in the first place."

"That's right up there with *apparent*, Roger. Are you trying to tell me something?"

The lift arrived. Before its doors were fully open she was inside; pressing the button for floor level. Pressing it three times, in fact. Someday they'd invent a button which made things happen faster the more you pressed it.

"Nothing really, Diana. Just that it might be an idea to be careful."

The doors didn't quite cut off his coda:

"Swimming with sharks, that kind of thing."

Swimming with sharks, she thought now, crushing her cigarette underheel. She checked her watch. It was fifteen seconds short of one o'clock.

He approached from the east, and even if she hadn't pulled up his records earlier, before making the call, she'd have recognized him. At Regent's Park they called them slow horses, and half the fun had been letting the slow horses know it. So it became self-fulfilling: when Slough House met Regent's Park, it was always clear who was wearing the boots. And here he came, approaching her with a slow horse's determination, as if reaching the finishing line meant the battle was won. When, as anyone with breeding knows, coming first is the only result that matters.

At the bench, he treated her to a look half aggressive, half defensive, like a wronged lover, and then curled his lip at the bench itself.

She said, "It's not real and it's quite dry."

He seemed dubious.

"For God's sake. This is a useful bench. You think we'd let a gull crap on it?"

Jed Moody sat.

Out on the water the shag was halfway through another circuit, while near Bankside Pier a street-preacher had staked out an imaginary pulpit, and was haranguing passers-by. Everything normal, in other words.

Taverner said, "I'm told you reached out last night."

"Nick's an old friend," Moody said.

"Shut up. You told him Jackson Lamb was running an op, that he'd sent one of your junior colleagues on a data-snatch. That this wasn't anything Slough House does, and that if it was, it should be you doing it."

"It's true. I spent six years —"

"Shut up. What I want to know is, how did you find out about it?"

"About what, ma'am?"

She'd been focused on the buildings on the far bank, but now turned to face him. "Don't for a moment imagine we're having a conversation. When I ask for information, you give it. You don't pretend you don't know what I'm talking about, and you don't dream about telling anything but the truth. Or you'll find there are colder, deeper things than this river, and I'll take pleasure in burying you in one of them. Clear?"

"So far."

"Good. Now, I gave Lamb a specific instruction about a specific job. I don't remember telling him to let you know about it. So, how did you find out?"

He said, "There's a bug."

"There's. A. Bug."

It wasn't exactly a question. So Moody didn't exactly answer. He just swallowed, hard.

"Are you seriously telling me you planted a *bug* in Jackson Lamb's office?"

"Yes."

"Sweet Jesus." She threw back her head and laughed. Then stopped. "Sweet Jesus," she said again.

"It wasn't . . ."

"Wasn't what? Wasn't something that could get you, what, thirty years? Given the climate?"

"Have you any idea what it's like?"

But she was shaking her head: not interested in his prepared outburst. He might be frustrated, thwarted, feel he'd been made to carry the can for a Service balls-up. But the fact was, he'd never have made it out of his current pay grade. If you needed a walking definition of foot soldier, a glance at Jed Moody's file would do it.

"I don't care. All I want to know is, how come the sweeps didn't pick it up? Oh, no. Don't tell me."

So he didn't.

"You do the sweeping."

He nodded.

"Set a thief to catch a . . . Christ. What else do you lot get up to over there? No, don't even start. I don't want to know."

True to her earlier forebodings, Diana Taverner fished her cigarettes out again. She offered the pack to Moody. He'd already produced a lighter, and with one big hand shielding the flame, lit them both. For a brief

165

moment, membership of the twenty-first century pariahs' club united them.

He said, "I wasn't eavesdropping. Well, I was. But not for anybody else. I used to be one of the Dogs. Lamb's got me running background checks when they get a new waiter next door. Not because he thinks anyone's about to post an asset there. He's just taking the piss, and doesn't care if I know it."

"So why not quit?"

"Because it's what I do."

"But you're not happy."

"Nobody's happy at Slough House."

Taverner concentrated on her cigarette, or pretended to, but had good peripheral vision, and was studying Jed Moody. He'd probably been handy once, but the drink and the smoking had put paid to that, and it was a safe bet that exile had sealed the downward spiral. These days, he probably guilt-splurged at the gym; seven-hour workouts making up for lost weekends. He'd keep kidding himself this was working. Whenever the truth looked like breaking in, he'd have another drink, and light another smoke.

"Not even Lamb?" she asked.

Rather to her surprise, he gave her a straight answer: "He's a burn-out. A fat, lazy bastard."

"You ever wonder why he's at Slough House?"

"What good would he be anywhere else?"

That wasn't quite so straight. The one self-evident fact about Lamb being allowed to run his own little kingdom — even from a crackpot palace like Slough House — was that he must know where bodies were buried. Moody didn't want to raise that with Diana Taverner. Which meant, she surmised, that Moody was treading round her with caution. Which was exactly how she preferred it.

Moody's cigarette had burned to the filter. He let it fall from his fingers, and it rolled into the crack between two paving stones.

When he looked up, she fixed him with a stare that left no doubt who was in charge. "Here's what's going to happen," she said. "You're going to do one or two favours for me. Off the books."

"Illegal."

"Yes. Which means that if for any reason things go even slightly wrong, and you end up in a small room being questioned by angry men, there's no possibility I'll pretend to have heard of you. Are we clear on that?"

Moody said, "Yes."

"And are we happy about it?"

Moody said, "Yes" again, and she could tell this was the truth. Like other slow horses before him, he wanted to be back in the game.

From her bag, she produced a mobile phone, and handed it to him. "Incoming only," she said.

He nodded.

"And dump the bug. Slough House may be a dead end, but it's a branch of the Service. It gets out it's been compromised, and your former mates from Internal Investigations'll take you apart, bone by bone."

She stood, but instead of moving straight off, she hovered a moment.

"Oh, and Moody? Word of warning. Lamb's a burn-out for a reason."

"Meaning?"

"Meaning when he was in the field, he had more to worry about than his expenses. Things like being caught, tortured and shot. He survived. You might want to bear that in mind."

She left him sitting there, an asset bought and paid for. Some were cheaper than others. And she already knew to what use she could put him.

From the window River gazed down on the traffic backed up along Aldersgate, victims of the roadworks that had plagued the street forever. Sid was at her desk, her monitor still unreeling the twelve-minute loop of the boy in the cellar; the actual twelve minutes long swallowed by the passing day, but each loop nevertheless chopping away at the time left to him.

"A far-right group," River said, and though it was a while since either had spoken, Sid Baker picked up the tune without missing a beat:

"There's more than one of them."

He turned. "I'm aware of that. You want me to run through some of the more obscure —"

"River —"

"— nutjob circuses, in case any have slipped your mind?"

"Don't assume it's Hobden's crew. That's all I'm saying."

"Because it's more likely to be coincidence that he pops on to Five's radar the day before this happens?"

"He popped on to *yours* the day before this happened. I expect he's been on Five's a lot longer."

River's grandfather would have recognized the stubborn look on his face. Sid Baker pressed on regardless.

"The British Patriotic Party are the usual bunch of shallow-enders, blaming their lack of prospects on the nearest victim group. Get them lagered up, and they'll break windows and beat up a shopkeeper, sure. But this is out of their league."

"You don't think Hobden's got the nous to put this together?"

"Nous, yes. But why would he want to? Besides, if Five thought he was behind this, you think they'd be stealing his files? They'd have him answering questions in a basement."

River said, "Maybe. Or maybe he's got enough friends in high places that he can't be tossed into a van without people getting upset."

"You think? He's spent the last couple of years being strung up in print by the rags he used to write for."

"Because they can't afford to look like they support him."

"Oh, for Christ's sake. They've strung him up because he deserves it. There's no sympathy for views like his in the mainstream. Twenty years ago, perhaps. But times have changed."

"And keep changing. There's a recession on, did you notice? Attitudes have hardened. But we're off the point, anyway. What this is, we've a far-right group performing a terrorist act the same day we pull a data-theft on the highest-profile right-wing nutcase in the country. No way is that just one of those things."

Sid turned back to her monitor. "You're always saying we do nothing important here at Slough House. How does that fit in with us suddenly being on point for the whole damn Service? If Hobden's behind this, and Five were checking him out, we wouldn't know about it, would we?"

He had no answer for that.

"He'll be found. It's not going to happen, River. This boy is not going to get his head chopped off on camera. Not tomorrow, not any other day."

"I hope you're right. But —"

He bit the rest of his sentence off.

"But what?"

"Nothing."

"You were about to say something. Don't pretend you weren't."

But I saw what you took from Hobden's laptop, and it was gibberish. Whatever you were trying to steal, you didn't get. Which means if he is involved in this, he's at least one step ahead of Five, which means it's not looking good for that kid right now . . .

"Is this about what you were looking at in the pub?"

"No."

"You're lying."

"Okay, I'm lying. Thanks."

"Give me a break. I'd lie too if I'd come into possession of knowledge I shouldn't have. I mean, given we're spies and all."

She was trying to get him to laugh, he realized. That was an odd feeling. He couldn't recall the last time a woman had tried to get him to even smile.

Wasn't going to work though. "It was nothing," he repeated. "Just some corrupted files."

"Weird form of corruption, translating everything into pi."

"Wasn't it?"

"Sounds more like some kind of security scrambling."

"Look, Sid, it was nothing important. And even if it was, it's none of your business."

Judging by the look on her face, it would be a while before she attempted to put a smile on his again.

"Fine," she said at last. "Fine. Excuse me for breathing." She stood abruptly, and her chair toppled backwards. "And speaking of breathing, this room still stinks. Open a bloody window, can't you?"

She left.

Instead of opening the window, River looked out of it again. The traffic hadn't noticeably shifted. He could stand here the rest of the day, and that sentence wouldn't need changing.

It's not going to happen, River. That boy is not going to get his head chopped off on camera. Not tomorrow, not any other day.

He hoped she was right. But he wasn't banking on it.

But the police found Hassan safe and sound.

It turned out there'd been a partial witness to the abduction; from her bedroom window, a woman had seen some lads "rough-housing" — her word — at the end of the lane opposite, then they'd all bundled into the back of a white van, a Ford, and headed east. She'd thought nothing of it at the time, but the news reports stirred her memory, so she took her snippet of information to the local cops. There were traffic lights in the direction the van had gone; overhanging cameras monitored the junction. A partial number plate had been captured. This fragment was swiftly disseminated the length and breadth of the country; every force in the land matched it against recorded sightings of white Ford vans on motorways, in city centres, on garage forecourts. After that, it was only a matter of time. But it was a peculiar stroke of luck that broke the case wide open and brought armed-response cops bursting into Hassan's cellar; it seemed that a local homeless man had . . .

Hassan opened his eyes. Darkness stared back. He closed them again. Armed-response cops burst in. He opened them. No they didn't.

He hadn't known time could crawl so slowly.

And hadn't known this, either: that fear could take you away from yourself. Not simply out of time, but out of your body. Sitting in a hood and jumpsuit, like a patient in a surrealist's waiting room, his grasp on the here-and-now slipped away, and that shrill voice at the back of his mind popped up, the one that delivered all his best riffs. Shaky, but recognizably his own, and trying to pretend none of this was happening; or that it had happened, but was now safely over; was now, moreover, material for the most scrotum-tightening stand-up routine ever. All those other hostages — the

172

ones who'd spent years chained to radiators — they wrote their books, they made their documentaries, they hosted radio shows. But how many of them took it open-mic?

"Let me tell you about my hood."

Pause.

"No, really. My *hood*."

And then they'd get it, his audience; they'd get that he meant *hood*, the thing they'd put on his head. Not his 'hood, where you couldn't leave your car out overnight.

But that was as far as the shrill voice got. Because it wasn't over. The stink was too foul for it to be over: the vomit, the shit, the piss; everything that fear had shifted out of its way when making space inside him. He was here. He didn't have an audience. He'd never had an audience; every open-mic night at the Student U he'd been there, head full of material, stomach full of knots, but he'd never dared take the stage.

Funny thing was, he'd thought that had been fear. His dread of making a tit of himself in front of beered-up fellow students — he'd thought that had been fear. Like stubbing your toe on a railway sleeper, and hopping on the spot with the pain. Not seeing the train bearing down on you.

One minute, walking home. Next, bunged into a cellar, holding a newspaper for the camera.

Now that was fear.

And this, too was fear: *We're going to cut your head off and show it on the web.*

He liked the internet. He liked the way it brought people closer. His generation had thrown its arms around the globe, tweeting and blogging to its heart's content, and when you were chatting online with a user called PartyDog, you didn't know if they were a boy or a girl let alone black or white, Muslim or atheist, young or old, and that had to be a good thing, didn't it? . . .

Except that Hassan had once read about some toerag who'd seen a woman collapse in the street, and instead of trying to help, like a normal person — or hurrying past, like a normal person — he'd *pissed* on her, actually pissed on her, and filmed himself on his phone doing it, then posted it on the web for other toerags to laugh at. It was as if the internet validated certain actions . . . For a tiny moment it felt good to have something to blame for all this, even if what he was blaming was the internet, which could never be made to care.

And then that tiny moment too became another chip knocked off a block that was rapidly growing smaller; and the awareness that the moment had passed occupied the moment that followed it, and also the moment after that, and in neither of those moments, nor in any of those that came after it, did armed-response cops burst into the cellar, and find Hassan safe and sound.

The kitchen wasn't anywhere you'd want to cook a meal. On the other hand, it wasn't anywhere a meal had been cooked; its surfaces piled with takeaway containers and plastic cutlery, with greasy brown paper bags and pizza boxes, with empty soft drink bottles and discarded cigarette packets. Ashtrays had been made of anything that didn't move. The lino curled at the corners, and a blackened patch by the back door suggested a small fire in the past.

In the centre of the room sat a formica-topped kitchen table, its red surface scarred with circular burns and razor-straight slashes. A laptop computer occupied the centre of this table, its lid currently closed. An assortment of cables snaked on top of it like electrical spaghetti, and next to these lay a folded tripod and a digicam about the size of a wallet. Once upon a time, you'd needed a building's worth of hardware to reach the world, but "once upon a time" was another way of saying the old days. Arranged around the table were four mismatched chairs, three of them occupied. The fourth was tilting at a crazy angle, held upright only by the pair of booted feet that were alternately pushing it away then hauling it back. Every other second it seemed the chair would topple, but it never did.

The feet's owner was saying, "We should webcam it."

". . . Why?"

"Stick it on the intranet. 'Stead of those clips. Let the whole world watch him crap himself start to finish."

The other two shared a glance.

They were bulldog males, the three of them; different shapes and sizes, but with this much in common: they were bulldog males. You wouldn't put your hand out to any of them and feel sure you'd get it back. Below them, in the cellar, Hassan Ahmed was calling them

Larry, Curly and Moe, and if they'd formed a line-up for him, this was how it would have shaken down:

Larry was tallest, and had the most hair, though this wasn't a fierce contest: where the other two were shaved to the bone, a mild fuzz covered Larry's skull, somehow conferring on him an air of authority, as if he were wearing a hat in a room full of bareheaded men. He was thin-faced with restless eyes, which kept checking door and window, as if either might burst open at any moment. His white shirt had the sleeves rolled up; he wore black jeans and brand-new trainers. Moe, meanwhile, was the middleman in every sense: shorter than one, taller than the other, and with a belly a black tee-shirt did nothing to minimize. Unwisely he sported a goatee he stroked constantly, as if checking it remained attached.

As for Curly — the owner of the feet — he seemed to be the stupid one.

Larry told him, "We don't want a webcam."

"Why not?"

"We just don't."

"He's stinking that room out like a rat inna trap. We should let the world see what they're like. When they're not clambering on to buses with rucksacks loaded with Semtex."

Moe, his tone of voice suggesting this wasn't the first time they'd had this conversation, said, "We set up a webcam, we double the chances of getting caught."

"We're already putting the video clips out there."

You could spend all day trying to drum simple stuff into Curly's head, Larry thought, but sooner or later you were going to have to give up. If you wanted him to understand anything more complicated than a two-horse race, you'd either have to draw him a picture or just give him a cigarette and hope he'd forget about it.

But Moe persevered. "This stuff on the web, people are going to be trying to find where it's coming from. There's ways of hiding our tracks, and we've done all that. But we go live — we put a webcam down there, and it'll be easier for them to trace us."

"And it's the internet," Larry said. "By the way."

"What?"

"Internet. Intranet's something's else."

"Same difference."

Larry looked at Moe again, and an unspoken thought passed between them.

"Anyway," Curly said. "Think he's scared now? He'll be a steaming pile of chickenshit this time tomorrow."

This with an air of finality, as if it were the final step in a careful argument.

"I'm going for a crap," he added.

Both chairs hit the floor when he stood.

When he'd gone, Larry lit a cigarette, then tossed the pack to Moe. "Do you think he's up to this?"

"He's not as stupid as he pretends to be."

"No, well. Cunt can walk and breathe at the same time, he's obviously not as stupid as he looks."

"I said pretends."

"I heard."

On the other side of the kitchen door Curly listened without moving a muscle, until satisfied they'd finished. And then he moved like smoke down the hallway and up the stairs, where he locked himself in the bathroom, and made a quiet call with a phone he shouldn't have had.

Lamb was at his desk with a folder in front of him — an analysis of congestion charge anomalies, or Twitter feeds, or cash-in-hand real estate purchases in Beeston — but his attention seemed focused on the corkboard on his wall, on which an array of money-off tokens were pinned: the local takeaway pizza place; Costcutter's price promise on Ginster's sausage rolls. Catherine watched from the doorway. She'd intended to walk in, add her own report to his pile and leave, but something had snagged her. Lamb didn't look like the Lamb they all knew and hated. There was something there that hadn't been there before.

The funny thing was, Catherine Standish had once been keen on meeting Jackson Lamb. It had been Charles Partner's fault. Lamb had been one of Partner's joes, back in the Middle Ages. He'd turned up one day in the modern world; was Partner's 10a.m. *He's one of a kind, Jackson Lamb,* Partner had said. *You'll like him.* And given the source, she'd thought she would.

At the time, Lamb had been in transition; making the jump from foreign holidays — as the joes all called them — to tending the home fires. This was in that blissful break when the world seemed a safer place, between the end of the cold war and about ten minutes later. And she'd known he'd spent time behind the Curtain. You couldn't know a detail like that without it colouring your expectations. You didn't expect glamour, but you understood the bravery involved.

So he was unexpected, this overweight, dishevelled man who'd stumbled into her office an hour and twenty minutes late, hungover, or still drunk. Partner was in another meeting by then, and if he'd been surprised by Lamb's no-show he hid it well. *When he turns up, give him coffee.* So she'd given Lamb coffee and put him in the visitor's chair, which he'd occupied the way a sloth occupies a branch. He'd fallen asleep, or pretended to. Every time she looked his eyes were closed and a bubble was forming at his lips, but still: she felt watched all the time he was there.

A couple of years later, the world was upside down. Partner was dead; Slough House was up and running; and Jackson Lamb was king.

And for some reason, Catherine Standish was beside him. Lamb had asked for her specifically, she discovered, but he never gave her one hint why. And she'd never asked him. If he'd had designs on her, he was years too late; there'd been a time when she'd have slept with him without giving it much thought, or remembering it afterwards, but since drying out she'd been more particular, and had slept with precisely no one. And if that ever changed, it wasn't going to be for Jackson Lamb.

But now here he was, and there was something about him that hadn't been there before. Anger, perhaps, but anger with the brakes on; held in check by the same impotence that curbed everyone else in Slough House. Lamb had spent the best part of his working life behind enemy lines, and now here the enemy was, and there was bugger all Lamb could do but sit and watch. Weirdly, this had the effect of making Catherine want to say something comforting. Something like: "We'll get them."

We'll get them. People were saying this in offices up and down the country; in pubs, in classrooms, on street corners. *Can't happen here. We'll get them*; and by *we* they all meant the same thing: those in jobs like her own and Jackson Lamb's; those who worked, one way or the other, for the security services. Those who didn't allow things like this to happen, even if they generally didn't succeed in stopping it until the fifty-eighth minute. And it occurred to Catherine that if anyone thinking these thoughts ever got a look around Slough House, they might re-evaluate their position sharpish. *That kid in the cellar? Doesn't have a prayer.*

So she backed away from the door and returned to her room, her report still tucked under her arm.

There wasn't much of a moon, but that hardly mattered. River was opposite Robert Hobden's flat again. Less than forty-eight hours ago rain had been falling in torrents, and River had been on the pavement, stealing shelter from an overhanging window. Tonight it wasn't raining, and he was in the car — if a warden came, he'd move. From behind Hobden's curtain, a thin light shone. Every so often, a shadow fell across it. Hobden was a prowler, unable to sit still for long. Much as River hated to admit anything in common with him, they shared that much. Neither could rest quietly in their own skin for long.

And now River almost jumped out of his: *what the* —

Just a tap on the glass, but he hadn't seen anyone approaching.

Whoever it was bent, and peered into the car.

"River?" she mouthed.

Jesus, he thought. Sid Baker.

He opened the door. She slid inside, pulled it shut, then shook her head free of her hood. She was carrying a pair of take-out coffees.

"Sid? What the hell are you doing?"

"I could ask you the same thing."

"Have you been following me?"

"You'd better hope not, hadn't you?" She handed him one of the coffees, and he was helpless to do anything but accept it. Peeling the polystyrene lid from her own released a gust of steam. "Because that would mean I'd tracked you halfway across London without you noticing." She blew softly on the liquid's surface, and the steam flurried. "On foot. Which would make me pretty special."

Opening his own cup involved splashing hot coffee on to his thighs. She handed him a napkin. He fumbled with it, trying to mop himself dry without spilling more. "So what, you guessed I'd be here?"

"It wasn't that difficult."

Great, he thought. Nothing like being transparent. "And you thought I might want company?"

"I can honestly say I've never thought that, no." She looked past him. "Which one's Hobden?"

River pointed.

"And he's alone?"

"Far as I know. So why are you here?"

She said, "Look. You're probably wrong. If Hobden's got anything to do with Hassan —"

"They've released his name?"

"Not officially. But Five have got it, and Ho picked it up a couple of hours ago. That boy's slick. It's a good job he's working for us."

"So who is he?"

"Hassan Ahmed. Ho's probably got his shoe size by now, but that's all he had when I left. Anyway, if

Hobden's involved, he'd hardly still be loose. Five would have brought him in."

River said, "That had occurred to me."

"And?"

He shrugged. "I know he's up to something."

"That stuff you were looking at in the pub. Ready to tell me what that was about?"

He might as well. It wasn't like he could convince her he wasn't up to anything. "They were Hobden's," he said. "The files you stole the other day."

"They were *what*?"

He told her what he'd done, as briefly as he could.

When he'd finished, Sid was silent for a full minute. He was glad about that. She could easily have launched into a catalogue of exactly what an idiot he was; explained that theft of government property was one thing, and theft of classified information another. Even if that information turned out to be useless. He didn't need to know any of that. And nor did she mention that merely hearing what he'd told her put her in the same situation as him. If River wound up in the dock, she'd be by his side. Unless she left the car now. And called the Dogs.

Instead, when the minute was up, she said, "So what's with pi? Code?"

"I don't think so. I think his back-up's a dummy. I think he's the kind of paranoid who expects someone to lift his files, and wants to be sure they don't get anything. No, more than that. Wants them to know he was expecting it. He wants to have the last laugh."

River remembered something else: that Hobden used copies of *Searchlight*, the anti-fascist newspaper, to wrap his kitchen leavings in; an up-yours to anyone who rifled his dustbins. *You think he's calling us Nazis?* he'd asked Lamb. *Well, yes,* Lamb had said. *Obviously. Obviously he's calling us Nazis.*

"Well, you can't say he's wrong," said Sid. "I mean, I lifted his files. You went through his rubbish."

"And that list didn't get on the web by accident," River said. "Let's face it, the Service screwed him good and proper."

"And his revenge involves setting up some kid for execution? You know what kind of backlash there'll be if it actually happens?"

"I can imagine." His coffee was still too hot. He placed the cup on the dashboard. "Islamic communities taking to the streets. Oh, there'll be plenty of sympathy from the liberal left, why wouldn't there be? An innocent kid killed on camera. But it won't just be demonstrators waving placards and demanding respect. It'll be about revenge. There'll be stabbings and God knows what. You name it."

"That's what I meant. He might be a raving idiot, but he's a patriot, for what that's worth. You really think he wants chaos in the streets?"

"Yep. Because after the chaos comes the clampdown, and that's what he's after. Not the backlash but what follows, when everything gets harsh. Because nobody wants kids executed on TV, but they want riots on their doorstep even less."

Sid said, "I hate conspiracy theories."

184

"It's not a theory once it's proved. After that, it's just a conspiracy."

"And sitting outside Hobden's flat helps how?"

"Let me get back to you in the morning."

"You're seriously planning on sitting here all night?"

"I hadn't got as far as making it a plan."

She shook her head, then sipped from her cup. "If nothing happens, you're buying breakfast."

He didn't know what to say to that, but before it became obvious, another thought occurred to her.

"River?"

"What?"

"You know you're an idiot, don't you?"

He smiled but turned away first, so she wouldn't notice.

That was at ten. For the next hour, it seemed breakfast was on River; there was almost no movement on the street, and none involving Hobden. The light at his window remained steady. An occasional shadow on the curtain proved he was still in there, or that someone was — perhaps River should knock on his door. That might provoke a reaction.

But provocation was a no-no. *It distorts the data.* Spider Webb, speaking up during a seminar: *It distorts the data to provoke the target into a course of action he might not otherwise adopt.* No doubt Spider had been parroting somebody who knew what he was talking about. On the other hand, if Spider was against it, River was for it.

185

An argument he'd had with himself five times now, and wasn't close to resolving.

He stretched his legs as best he could, trying not to make it obvious. He was wearing everyday gear: blue jeans, a white collarless top under a grey V-neck. Sid wore black jeans and hooded sweater. Tradecraft, but she looked good in it. She'd pushed the car seat back and was mostly in shadow, but every so often her eyes picked up light from a nearby streetlamp and threw it in his direction. She was thinking about him. When a woman was thinking about you, it was always either a good thing or a bad thing. River had no idea which in this case.

To put an end to it, he said, "So what made you sign up?"

Now she held his gaze. "What else? The glamour."

"You've seen the show. Now live the life."

"I'm not stupid, you know."

"Didn't think you were."

"I took a first in Oriental Languages."

"That's got to be a comfort."

She rolled her eyes. "It'd be a greater one if you'd shut up."

So he shut up.

On the street the pavements stayed empty, and there was little traffic.

Prowling his apartment . . . Hobden could be issuing orders on his mobile, or e-mailing confederates. But River didn't think so. He didn't think Hobden would be doing anything that rendered him vulnerable to electronic eavesdropping. He was just prowling like a cat in a cage; waiting for something to happen.

River could relate to that.

Sid said, "You're Service family."

He nodded.

Once, it hadn't been uncommon; the same way some families go in for police or plumbing. Even now, you'd encounter third- or even fourth-generation spooks; roles in life handed down like family silver. With a grandfather a Service legend, River had never stood a chance. But this was Sid's story, so he said nothing.

"I don't have your pedigree. Never gave the Civil Service a thought, let alone this branch. I was heading for banking. Mum's a barrister. I was going to be an even higher-paid banker. That's how you measure success, isn't it? Earning more than your parents."

He nodded again, though the thought of his mother earning money was quite funny.

"But I was still at uni when the bombs went off."

And this was no surprise either. No one had joined the Service since the bombs without the bombs being part of the reason.

He listened without looking at her. People talked about that day in different ways. Either it was a story about them in which bombs happened, or it was a story about the bombs, and they'd just happened to be there. Whichever this turned out to be, it would be easier for her if he wasn't watching.

"I was temping at a bank in the City. It was a holiday job, and I was pretty new, and I didn't know you should wear trainers for the commute. And keep a pair of shoes in the office, you know? So anyway, I was coming out of Aldgate, and I heard it happen. It wasn't just a noise, it was a . . . a sort of swelling. Like when you open a vacuum-packed jar, that release of air you get? Only bigger. And I knew what had happened — everyone knew what had happened. As if we'd all spent three and a half years waiting for it. And hadn't realized it until that moment."

A car appeared at the far end of the road, its headlights pinning them into their seats.

"The funny thing was, there was little panic. On the street, I mean. It was as if everyone knew this was a time for good behaviour. For not indulging in fake heroics . . . Letting the professionals do their job. And all the while, stories were spreading about other bombs, and buses blowing up, and something about a helicopter crashing into Buckingham Palace — I don't know where that one came from."

There'd been other rumours too, spun at the speed of the web. For all the sangfroid on show, it had been a day on which you could peer through the fabric of the city itself, and see how fragile its underpinnings were.

"Anyway, my office was being evacuated by the time I got there. We'd rehearsed for this. We used to gather outside, and everybody would look grim and check their watches while fire marshals counted heads. But I never even got inside the building that morning. You could see their point. That would have been a hell of a good time to rob a bank."

Her voice had settled into that pattern people fall into when they know they'll not be interrupted; when a tale they've rehearsed in their head is finding an audience. If they were anywhere but in a car, River thought, he could sneak quietly away, and Sid would keep talking.

She said, "Anyway. I keep saying that, don't I? Anyway. Anyway, I walked home. A lot of Londoners did that on the seventh of July. It was walk home from work day. And by the time I got home, my feet were in ribbons . . . I'd been wearing heels for work. Because I was new, and because I wanted to look smart and feel sexy, because this was the City, after all . . . And because nobody told me that my second week on the job, a bunch of murderers were going to take their lunatic grievances into the underground, kill fifty-six people and close London for half a day." She blinked. "I got home and put my shoes in a cupboard and that's where they've been ever since. Everybody's got their own memorial, haven't they? Mine's a pair of ruined shoes in a cupboard. Every time I look at them, I think about that day." Now she looked at River. "I'm not being very clear, am I?"

"You were there." It came out a croak. He cleared his throat. "It's your memory. It doesn't have to be clear."

"What about you?"

Where'd he been when the bombs went off, she meant.

As it happened he'd been on leave; a make-or-break Italian jaunt with his last serious girlfriend, a civilian. So he'd watched the day unfurl on CNN, when not frantically altering his flight home. "His" flight, because she'd stayed. He wasn't certain she'd ever returned.

Sometimes, River Cartwright felt like a career soldier who'd never seen action.

Instead of answering, he said, "So that's why you joined. To stop anything like that happening again."

"Makes me sound naive, doesn't it?"

"No. It's part of the job."

Sidonie said, "What I thought was, even if I'm only filing cards. Trawling through websites. Even if I'm just making cups of tea for the people who are stopping it happening again, that'll be enough. Just to be part of it."

"You are part of it."

"So are you."

But making cups of tea is not enough, he didn't say.

Down the road, another car turned off the main drag and almost immediately pulled into a space. For a moment it sat, lights on, and River could make out the purr of its engine. Then it died.

"River . . ."

"What is it?"

"You wanted to know why I was assigned to Slough House."

River said, "Don't worry about it."

"I have been."

He shook his head. "I don't need the details." Because when you got down to it, it didn't take a genius. Sid must have embarrassed the wrong person, either by not sleeping with him — or her — or by sleeping with him or her, and still being there in the morning. She didn't belong in Slough House. But that wasn't a reason to make her tell him about it. He said, "I've messed up plenty myself."

190

Bombs on underground trains had propelled Sid into the Service. A non-existent bomb on an underground platform had all but propelled River out of it. One day he might be able to say something like that out loud, and hear her laugh; hear himself laugh, even. But not yet.

"I didn't mess up, River."

River's view of the newly parked car was mostly blocked by the car in front, but he could tell nobody had got out of it.

"I mean, there's a reason I'm there."

Could be making a phone call. Or waiting for someone. Maybe here was a rare example of someone who'd pull up near a friend's house after dark, and refrain from blowing their horn to announce their presence.

"River?"

He didn't want to hear it. Might as well come clean; he didn't want to hear about Sid's sexual history. Months of pretending she barely existed; it had been a way of guarding against rejection, because Christ knew, he was already a reject. The whole world knew about him crashing King's Cross. The footage was used for training purposes.

"Christ . . ."

There might have been movement down the road. Did one shadow leave the parked car, and join the larger shadows on the pavement? He couldn't tell. But if it had, it had been too clean to be an accident.

"Will you pay afuckingttention?"

"I'm listening," he said. "So what's the reason? For you being at Slough House?"

"You are."

And now he did pay afuckingttention. Sid, half her face in shadow, the other half white as a plate, said, "I was put there to keep an eye on you, River."

"You're kidding, right?"

She shook her head.

"You're kidding."

The one eye he could see gazed steadily back. He'd known good liars, and maybe Sid was one. But she wasn't lying now.

"Why?"

"You're not supposed to know about this."

"But you're telling me. Right? You're telling me."

This choking feeling was nothing new. He felt it every morning, familiar as an alarm clock. It was what dragged him out of sleep. *White shirt. Blue tee. Blue shirt. White tee . . .* Some days he couldn't remember which way round Spider had said it, and which way round the guy was dressed; all he knew for certain was that Spider had set him up, but underlying that was a layer of puzzlement. Spider had screwed him to clear his own career path? It wasn't that he didn't think Spider that kind of bastard. Spider was exactly that kind of bastard. But Spider wasn't a clever enough bastard. If he had been, he wouldn't have had to do it. He'd have had the edge over River to start with.

And now here was Sid telling him someone else had been responsible — that someone had been pulling River's strings. Sid had been put in Slough House to keep an eye on him. And who could have done that, except whoever had put River there to start with?

"Sid —"

And now her eyes were widening and she was pointing over his shoulder. "River? What's that?"

He turned in time to glimpse a black shape disappearing over the five-foot wall to the right of Hobden's window.

"Sid?"

"Looked like —" Her eyes widened. "One of the achievers?"

Black-clad. Heavy weaponry. So called because they got the job done.

River was out of the car before she'd finished. "Watch the door. I'll take the wall."

But pretty much hit the wall, in fact, misjudging his vault. He had to back up and try again. An undignified scramble dropped him into a garden: mostly lawn, trimmed by a narrow flowerbed. Plastic furniture here and there; a table with a forlorn, dripping umbrella. And nobody in sight.

How long since that shape had appeared? Fifteen seconds? Twenty?

The building had a shared lobby round the back. This had a double-fronted, glass-panelled door, which hung open. Down the corridor to River's left another door closed as he stepped into the lobby, cutting in two a noise that had barely begun. Half a syllable. A note of shock.

River's boots click-clacked on the lobby's tiles.

There were two doors to choose from, but if his mental map was accurate, Hobden's was on the left. He guessed the man in black had gone straight in — skeleton key or pick. But was this really an achiever? And if it was, what did River think he was doing . . . But it was too late, time was happening too fast; he was here and now, bracing himself against the corridor wall. The same boot that had click-clacked across the lobby hit the door with a splintering thud, and the door broke open, and River was inside the flat.

A short corridor, more doors to either side, both ajar, bathroom and bedroom. The corridor ended in a sitting room, on the far side of which was the front door he'd been watching from across the road; the rest of the room was books, papers, portable TV, shabby sofa, table strewn with leftover takeaway, curtained window through which he'd watched Hobden's shadow prowling, prowling; a restless movement suggesting he'd been expecting something. And here he was, the shadow's owner.

River hadn't laid eyes on Hobden before, but this had to be him: average height, thinning brownish hair, look of terror as he turned to face this new intrusion even while crushed in an arm-lock by the previous invader, the achiever — except this wasn't an achiever: he was black-clad, wore a balaclava, had a utility belt round his waist, but the ensemble lacked the hi-tech tailoring of the genuine article. Besides, what he held to Hobden's head was a .22: small, and non-Service issue.

And now the gun swung towards River, and its size became insignificant. He held out an arm, as if trying to

194

placate an upset dog. "Shall we put that down?" Astonishing himself with his banality of expression and evenness of tone. Hobden erupted, an unpunctuated gabble — "What's going on who are you why" — and the black-clad man silenced him with a tap on the head, then made an on-the-floor gesture at River. Disconnected thoughts held a confab in River's head. *This isn't an op. Take him down. What makes you sure he's alone?* Their meeting done, his thoughts scattered. River knelt, measuring the distance between his hand and the heavy-looking ashtray on the nearby table. Still the man didn't speak. Arm round Hobden's throat, he swung him towards the front door, gun still levelled at River. Briefly, he released the journalist while opening the door. Cold air rushed in. Grabbing Hobden again he backed out, attention trained on River. Whatever his plan was, it didn't take Sid into account, who was waiting outside. She grabbed Hobden's arm, and River seized the ashtray and leaped forward, intending to club the gunman. Hobden fell to the pavement. River reached the other pair in moments; the third part of a triangle which proved anything but eternal. The gun made a quiet cough. The trio dispersed.

Of them, one fell to the ground, landing perfectly in a puddle which hadn't been there a moment ago. It swarmed, spread, and formed an inky stream to the gutter, hardly disturbed at all by the sounds of flight and fear and grief now gathering round it.

Part Two

Sly Whores

Now that he knew he was going to die, a sense of calm had settled upon Hassan. It was almost surreal, though surreal wasn't quite the word. Transcendental, that was it. He had achieved an inner peace, the like of which he'd never known. When you got down to it, life was a rollercoaster. The details of the excitement escaped him now, but there must have been plenty of it, or this feeling of release wouldn't be so welcome. He wouldn't have to go through any of it again, whatever it had been. Dying seemed a small price to pay.

And if he could have remained in that state he might have cruised through his remaining hours, but every time he reached this point in the argument, when *dying* and *price* made their ugly meanings felt, his mind emptied of peace and calm and swarmed instead with panic. He was nineteen years old. He'd never been on an actual rollercoaster, let alone known life to be one. He'd had little of anything he had a right to expect. Had never stood in a spotlight, unreeling one-liners for an adoring crowd.

Larry, Moe and Curly.

Curly, Larry and Moe.

Who were these people, and why had they chosen him?

Here was the story: Hassan was a student who wanted to be a comedian. But the fact was, he'd probably end up doing something totally usual; utterly office-based. Business Studies, that was Hassan's course. Business fucking Studies. It wasn't entirely true to say that his father had chosen it for him, but it was true that his father had been a lot more supportive of this than he would have been of, say, drama. Hassan would have liked to study drama. But he'd have had to fund it himself, so where had the harm been in going with the flow? That way, he'd had the flat, and the car, and, well, something to fall back on. That was Business Studies: something to fall back on if the career in stand-up crashed and burned.

He wondered now how many people there were, including those not under threat of execution in a damp cellar, who were living their back-up plan; who were office drones or office cleaners, teachers, plumbers, shop assistants, IT mavens, priests and accountants only because rock and roll, football, movies and authordom hadn't panned out. And decided that the answer was everyone. Everyone wanted a life less ordinary. And only a tiny minority ever got it, and even they probably didn't appreciate it much.

So in a way, Hassan was sitting pretty. A life less ordinary was what he now had. Fame was waiting in the wings. Though it was true that he wasn't appreciating it much, except during those transcendental moments of inner peace, when it was clear that the rollercoaster ride was over, and he could let go, let go, let go . . .

Larry, Moe and Curly.

Curly, Larry and Moe.

Who were these people, and why had they chosen him?

The horrible thing was, Hassan thought he knew.

He thought he knew.

In the pub near Slough House, at the same table River and Sid had shared earlier that day, Min Harper and Louisa Guy were drinking: tequila for him, vodka and bull for her. They were both on their third. The first two had been drunk in silence, or what passed for silence in a cityroad pub. In a far corner a TV buzzed, though neither glanced its way for fear of seeing a boy in a cellar; the day's sole subject, which forced its way to the surface at last, like a bubble of air escaping from under a rock in a pond.

"That poor kid."

"You think they'll really do it?"

"Off him?"

Off with his head, both thought, and winced at the unhappy phrasing.

"Sorry."

"But do you think?"

"Yes. Yes, I think they will."

"Me too."

"Because they haven't —"

"— made any demands. They've just said —"

"— they're going to kill him."

Both set their glasses down, the dual ringing sending a brief halo into the air.

The Voice of Albion had gone public that evening, with an announcement on their website that Hassan Ahmed would be executed within thirty hours. *56 deaths on the tube*, its argument ran, = *56 deaths in return*. And there was more: the usual drivel about national identity and a war on the streets. The site was a single page, offering no proof of its claims, and there were thirteen other groups currently streaming the Hassan video, claiming responsibility, but the words Voice of Albion had been snatched by Ho from a Regent's Park memo, so it seemed pretty clear who Five thought were responsible. But what was strange, said Ho, was that the website had first appeared only two weeks ago. And there were few other references to the group on the web.

But a name meant progress.

"Now they know who he is, they'll know where to look."

"They've probably known who he is for ages."

"They probably know a hell of a lot more than they've said."

"Not that they'd tell us, anyway."

"Slough House. For the simple things in life."

Like combing Twitter for coded messages. Like compiling lists of overseas students who missed more than six lectures a term.

They finished their drinks and got another round in.

"Ho's probably up to speed."

"Ho knows everything."

"Thinks he does."

"Did you see his expression when he caught the loop?"

"Like he'd cracked the Enigma code."

"Like that was the important thing, that the film was on a loop."

"And the kid was just pixels."

Then, for the first time, they looked at each other without pretending not to. Drinking had done neither any favours. Louisa had a tendency to flush, which might have been okay if it had meant an even pinkness; but instead she grew mottled and patchy, her skin acquiring the topography of a badly folded map. As for Min, his face had sagged, flaps of skin developing along his jawline, and his ears glowed red to match his irises. All over the city — all over the world — this happened; co-workers ruined their chances in the pub, and forged ahead anyway.

"Lamb must know more."

"More what?"

"More than we do."

"You think he's in the loop?"

"More than the rest of us."

"Not saying much."

"I know his password."

". . . Really?"

"Think so. I think he never —"

"Don't tell me!"

". . . reset it from the default."

"Classic!"

"His password is 'Password'!"

"You sure?"

"It's what Ho reckons."

"And he told you?"

"He needed to tell someone. To prove how clever he is."

For a moment, both examined their glasses. Then their eyes met again.

"Another round?"

"Yeah. Maybe. Or . . ."

"Or?"

"Or maybe back to the office?"

"It's late. There'll be nobody there."

"My point exactly."

"You think we should . . ."

"Check Ho's info?"

"If Lamb knows anything, it'll be on his e-mail."

Both considered this for flaws, and found plenty. Both decided not to raise them.

"If we get caught looking at Lamb's e-mail . . ."

"We won't."

If there was anyone there, there'd be lights in the windows, visible from the road. It wasn't like Slough House was high security.

"You sure there's a point to this?"

"More point than sitting here getting pissed. That's not helping anyone."

"True."

Each waited for the other to make the first move.

In the end, though, they had another drink first.

There had been hospitals before, but not since childhood. One bad year had seen River incarcerated twice; first for a tonsillectomy, then for a broken arm, sustained in a fall from a large oak two fields from his grandparents' house. It hadn't been the first time he'd scaled it, though he'd had trouble getting down on the previous occasions. This time there'd been no trouble. Only gravity. Back home he'd tried not to mention the injury, on account of having promised not to damage himself climbing trees, but at length had been forced to admit that yes, he was struggling to hold his fork. The O.B. told him later that it was only after having made the admission that River had turned white, then whiter, then dropped to the floor.

Lying in the dark now, what he remembered that occasion for was that his mother had come as he lay in hospital. It had been the first time he'd seen her in two years, and she claimed to have arrived back on English soil only that afternoon. "Perhaps at the same moment you had your fall, darling. Don't you think that's what happened? That you sensed my arrival, all those miles away?" Even at nine River had difficulty with this scenario, and hadn't been especially surprised when he later learned that Isobel had been in the country for several months. Be that as it may, she was with him now, unaccompanied by his "new father", and unfazed by River's having told his nurse he was an orphan. In fact, the only thing that galvanized her was her parents' negligence.

"Climbing *trees*? How could they let you do such a thing?"

But evasion of blame was so ingrained to her character, even those around her colluded. River himself wasn't immune. Of the injuries she'd bestowed upon him few had caused as much grief as his name, but even at nine he knew a narrow escape when he saw one. Isobel Cartwright's hippy phase had been superseded by an equally short-lived Teutonic one, and had River been a year younger, he might have been a Wolfgang. He suspected that his grandfather would have balked at that. The O.B. was as adept at destroying true identities as he was at creating false ones.

But long time ago. Water under a bridge. River was a name for water that passed under a bridge. Lying in another hospital, River wondered who he'd have been if born to a different mother; one who hadn't rebelled so thoroughly, if ineffectively, against her middle-class upbringing. He wouldn't have been brought up by his grandparents. Wouldn't have fallen out of a tree, or not that tree. And wouldn't have fallen under the spell of an idea of service; of a life lived outside the humdrum . . . But his mother had drifted in and out of his life like a song. During her longer absences, he forgot the words; when she was around, there was always a new one to add to the list. She was beautiful, vague, solipsistic, childish. Lately, he'd recognized how brittle she'd become. She often imagined she'd raised him herself, and would bristle convincingly when reminded otherwise. Her hell-raising years were not only behind her, they belonged to someone else. Isobel Dunstable — her late marriage had been a satisfactory one, bestowing respectability, wealth and widowhood in quick succession — might never have looked at a hash

206

pipe in anything other than puzzlement. It wasn't only her father who was adept at destroying true identities.

Thinking these familiar thoughts was better than the alternative, which was thinking about other things altogether.

There came a scraping from beyond the locked door; as if somebody was balancing on a chair, steadying themselves with their feet against the opposite wall.

As a boy with a broken arm, River had recognized his surroundings for what they were: hospitals were where light gathered in corners, and curtains performed the functions of walls. Where privacy was rarely granted, and unwanted visitors far more common than the other kind.

He heard footsteps heading down the corridor, towards him.

Slough House too was in darkness. At Regent's Park, even when nothing was happening, there'd be enough people about for a midnight football match: eleven a side, plus linesmen. Here there was only emptiness, and the reek of disappointment. Min Harper, climbing the forlorn staircase, decided that the place resembled nothing more than a front for a mail-order porn empire, and with the thought came the dispiriting sense of being part of an enterprise nobody cared about, where tasks that didn't matter were performed by people who didn't care. For the last two months, Min had been examining congestion charge anomalies: cars clocked entering the zone whose owners had never paid; whose owners, in fact, denied being in the zone on the day in question. And time after time, it broke down to the same boring facts: that those who'd been caught were guilty of everyday life. They were playing away from home, or shifting bootlegged DVDs, or delivering their daughters to abortion clinics well out of their husbands' sight . . . There were prison camps whose inmates spent their days carrying rocks from one end of the yard to the other, and then back. That might be a more fulfilling occupation.

Something shifted further up the stairwell.

"Did you hear that?"

"What?"

"I don't know. A noise."

They halted on the landing. Whatever had made the sound didn't make it again.

Louisa leant closer to Min, and he became aware of the smell of her hair.

"A mouse?"

"Do we have mice?"

"We've probably got rats."

Alcohol thickened the syllables, and slurred the sibilants.

Whatever they'd thought they'd heard didn't happen again. The smell of Louisa's hair, though, continued. Min cleared his throat.

"Shall we?"

"Um . . .?"

"Go up, I mean?"

"Sure. Going down's not an option. I mean —"

Good job it was dark.

But as they set off up the next flight of stairs their hands brushed in the darkness, and their drunk fingers entangled themselves, and then they were kissing, and more than kissing; were clutching at each other in the darkness; each pushing at the other as if anxious to occupy the same space, which turned out to be against the wall in Loy's room, the first they'd come to.

Three minutes passed.

Coming up for breath, their first words were:

"Jesus, I never —"

"Shut up."

They shut up.

Two floors above them, a black-clad figure paused inside Lamb's office.

Outside the door, one of Nick Duffy's crew occupied a plastic chair, tilting it so its back was resting against the wall. Dan Hobbs had been two minutes short of going off-roster when he was dispatched here instead. When an agent got shot, there was no such thing as downtime. Even when it was a slow horse. Even when it was their own stupid fault.

Though short on detail, Hobbs was prepared to accept that it had been their own stupid fault.

Service officers were red-flagged, so as soon as the name was entered on the hospital records, it was pinging its way to Regent's Park. Hobbs had picked it up: since then he'd put out an officer-down alert; broken a few limits getting to the hospital; established the agent's injuries; and taken instruction from Duffy: *Secure whoever's still standing and wait there.* So

Hobbs had, in the only available room: a store cupboard down here among the ghosts.

That had been half an hour ago, and not a peep since, and even as that thought occurred to Hobbs he squinted at his phone once more, and an awkward truth hit him.

He had no signal.

Damn.

A quick trip upstairs. It would take less than a minute. And the sooner he was back in touch with the Park, the less chance anyone would know he'd lost contact to start with.

Then he heard the rubbery squeaks that meant someone was coming down the stairs.

Righting the chair, Hobbs planted his feet on the floor.

This time, there was no doubting it. There'd been a noise, loud enough to distract Louisa and Min from what they were doing. Three minutes later it wouldn't have done, but those were the edges on which outcomes balanced.

"Hear that?"

"I heard it."

"Came from upstairs."

"Lamb's office?"

"Or Catherine's."

They waited, but heard nothing further.

"You think it's Lamb?"

"If it was, there'd be a light on."

They eased apart, zipping up, and moved for the door without noise. Anyone watching might think they'd rehearsed movements like these: stealthy progress through dark territory, with an unknown third party lurking near.

"Weapon?"

"Desk."

It yielded a glass paperweight, which fitted neatly into a fist, and a stapler which would serve as a knuckleduster.

"You sure we want to do this?"

"I'd rather be doing what we just nearly did."

"Yeah, but —"

"But now we've got to do this instead."

Or first, perhaps. Whatever.

And anyone watching wouldn't have guessed either had recently succumbed to drink or lust, because both looked like sober joes as they slipped on to the landing again; Min taking the lead and Louisa watching his hands as she followed, alert for any signals he might drop into the silence that drifted behind him.

The approaching man was overweight and trod heavily, and perhaps had wandered downstairs by mistake; was actually here to get his heart sorted, or have a gastric band fitted. Hobbs ran seven miles daily, rain or shine, and thought being out-of-shape was slow suicide. It meant you'd always come off second best in a physical encounter, which wasn't something that had happened to Hobbs yet.

He prepared himself for a brush with the public at whose service he technically served.

But the man turned out not to be public. He didn't even ask who Hobbs was. It was as if he already knew, and already didn't care.

"Here's a tip," he said. "Mobiles? RaspBerries? Gizmos like that? Not at their best underground."

Hobbs retreated into bland civil-servantese: "Can I help you?"

"Well." The fat man pointed to the locked door. "You could open that."

"You must be lost, sir," Hobbs said. "They'll help you up at reception. With whatever you're after."

The man tilted his head to one side. "Do you know who I am?"

Jesus wept. Hobbs licked his teeth and prepared to unfold himself from his chair. "Don't have that pleasure, sir."

The man bent low and spoke directly into Dan's ear. "Good."

His hands moved.

The stairs seemed steeper after lights out, or maybe they were steeper after an evening in the pub, and a knee-trembler in a dark office. But that thought was broadcast from a different set of experiences. The Louisa who'd come from the pub, the Min who'd just been fumbled with, those skins had been sloughed when they'd heard the intruder. Now they were real people again; the people they'd been before calamity

212

had struck, and exiled them to this damp building on the edge of nowhere important.

No more noises yet. Maybe it had been an unattended accident: a picture dropping off a wall. When the tube rattled past, not many yards away, unanchored objects felt gravity's pull. Min and Louisa might be creeping upstairs, armed with stapler and paperweight, to launch an attack on a moment's slippage.

On the other hand, whoever was up there might have frozen on realizing they weren't alone.

Silent messages passed between the pair:

You okay?

Of course . . .

We trained for this.

So let's go . . .

Up they went.

Whatever had just happened ended with the sound of something being lowered to the floor. This had been preceded by voices, one of which River recognized, so he wasn't surprised when the door opened and a familiar shape appeared. "Jesus on a skateboard." Jackson Lamb was loud as a train. He flicked the light switch. "Get on your feet, man."

Because River was lying on the floor. Cardboard boxes were piled against the walls, their labels indicating that they held rubber gloves; fitted sheets; plastic cups; disposable cutlery; other stuff: he'd lost interest and turned the light out. It was clear, though, that Hobbs had locked him in a store cupboard.

"How long have you been in here?"

River shook his head. Ten minutes? Twenty? Three? Time had happened differently once the key had turned in the lock.

He'd put up no resistance. Getting here had left him drained; had been a nightmare ride through zombie-strewn streets, following a racing ambulance. There was blood all over him. *Head wounds bleed. Head wounds bleed bad.* This was a factoid he'd clung to. Head wounds bleed bad. That Sid Baker was bleeding bad from the head didn't necessarily mean anything critical had happened. Could be a graze. So why had she looked so dead?

He'd watched her strapped to a gurney and rushed along a corridor by medical staff, and hadn't even attempted to come up with a fake identity. A bullet wound meant police, of course, but say what you like about the Service Dogs, their response time was sharp. Hobbs had got here first, and had secured River, pending debriefing.

River suspected that any debriefing that followed the shooting of an agent would be a lengthy and unpleasant process.

"Well, how long were you planning on staying?" Lamb asked. "Get a move on."

Maybe this would be lengthy and unpleasant too.

River got to his feet and followed his boss into the light.

At the top of the stairs, nobody lurked. The paperweight felt comfortable in Min's hand by now; a round smooth heavy presence, not entirely dissimilar to — but he thrust that thought away; stepped into Jackson Lamb's office. The blinds were down. Pinpricks of light poked in from London's night sky; the neon glow that settled on the city like a bubble.

Shapes took on slow substance. Desk, coatstand, filing cabinet, bookshelf. No human form. No waiting stranger.

Behind him, Louisa checked out the cubicle-sized kitchen. Unless whoever had made the noise could fit in a fridge, it was danger-free.

"Catherine's room."

Similar story: desk, shelves, cabinets. But there was a skylight, and a ghostly grey light hovered over Catherine's absence. She'd left her keyboard balanced on top of her monitor, and aligned her folders with the edge of the desk. There were shadows here too, but most of them seemed empty.

"I'm going to turn the light on."

"Okay."

It hurt both their eyes for a second, as their drunkenness re-bloomed.

"There's nobody here."

"Doesn't seem to be."

Doeshn't sheem to be.

In the light, both looked washed out.

They turned back to the other office, where they could now see something leaning against the wall. It was Lamb's corkboard, the one on which he pinned his money-off tokens.

"Do you think —?"

Did they think it had fallen off the wall?

Movement behind them broadcast itself a moment before Min was struck.

Only a moment, but long enough for him to move, so the punch scraped his ear only, throwing him off balance but not to the floor — their assailant was clad in black; wore a balaclava; carried a small gun he wasn't using. He'd sprung from the shadows in Catherine's room; must have been hiding in her cupboard. His second blow caught Louisa in the chest and she gasped in pain.

Min launched himself at the stranger's legs, and the pair of them went crashing down the stairs.

Hobbs was asleep in the plastic chair, or looked asleep. A faint smear of dribble glistened on his chin. River paused to retrieve Service card and car keys from his pocket, then followed.

Upstairs, two policemen were talking to the charge nurse, who was examining a clipboard. Lamb led River past them without a sideways glance as the nurse shook his head and pointed the cops towards the reception desk.

Outside it was dark, and starting to rain again. River's car, which he'd left slantwise in an ambulance space, was gone. He wondered if Sid was gone too. There'd been urgency about the way those doctors, those nurses, had trolleyed her off. Perhaps they'd not heard the same factoid he had. They certainly hadn't said *Nah, head wound. They always look bad.*

"Stay with the programme, Cartwright."

"Where now?"

The words were cotton wool, sucking moisture from his mouth and leaving him tired and sick.

"Anywhere but here."

"My car's gone."

"Shut up."

So now he was tracking Lamb across the short-stay car park; all those vehicles that hadn't expected to be here tonight, and whose owners were inside the building behind him. He shut out the possible injuries that had brought them here, knife fights, random muggings, dicks stuck in vacuum hoses; blanked out too the picture of Sid on an operating table, her head invaded by a bullet. Or had it only plucked at her on its way past? He hadn't been able to tell. There'd been so much blood.

"For fuck's sake, Cartwright."

Two police cars were parked nearby. Neither was occupied.

Lamb drove a boxy-looking Japanese car. River didn't care. He got in, sat back, waited for Lamb to start up. That didn't happen.

River closed his eyes. Then opened them to a rain-flecked windscreen, each drop of water holding a tiny bulb of orange light.

Lamb said, "So you got locked up."

"Pending," River said. "Pending . . . whatever."

"And your ID's flashing lights and blowing whistles from here to Regent's Park. Have you any clue what you're doing?"

"I had to get her here."

"You called the ambulance. It was necessary to follow it?"

"She might have died. Might be dead now, for all I know."

Lamb said, "She's still on the table. Bullet took a chunk out of her head."

River couldn't look at him.

"They say she might live."

Thank Christ for that. He thought about the tussle on the pavement; that sudden sound. *Phut*. And then there'd been blood, and Sid was down, and the blood had been black on the pavement. Robert Hobden was nowhere to be seen. As for the man in black, he was halfway down the road before River had got to his knees, frightened to touch Sid, frightened to move her, unable to assess the damage. It had taken him three goes to ring for an ambulance. His fingers felt like thumbs, his thumbs like bananas.

"On the other hand, she might not. And even if she does, she might end up with the life choices of a carrot. So on the whole, not a great night's work." He reached out and clicked his fingers an inch from River's face. "Wake up. This is important."

River turned to face him. In the dim light, Jackson Lamb resembled something pegged on top of a bonfire. His eyes were madly red, as if already tortured by smoke. His jowls were whiskery. He'd been drinking.

"Who was it?"

They tumbled in a noisy mess of arms and legs to the next landing. Louisa followed in a rush; two bounds bringing her level. Min was on the floor, the man in black draped over him like a duvet. Louisa grabbed, twisted, and encountered less resistance than she might have expected.

Like a beanbag. Like a broken scarecrow.

"Jesus, are you —"

"Where did the gun go? Where did it go?"

The gun was in the corner.

While Min scrambled to his feet, the man in black flopped like a beached pike, like a burst binbag.

"Is he dead?"

He looked dead. He looked like he'd landed on his head, and bent his neck to a stupid angle.

"I hope he's fucking dead."

Min collected the gun, bones clicking as he bent. He'd be aches and pains in the morning. He hadn't taken a dive down a flight of stairs since, well, ever. And it wasn't an experience he planned to repeat soon, except . . .

Except it felt good, for a moment, standing here. A vanquished intruder at his feet, a gun in his hand. Louisa gazing at him, unfeigned admiration in her eyes.

Well, that was stretching it. Louisa was looking at the stranger, not at him.

". . . Is he dead?"

They both hoped he was dead, though neither knew what he was doing here. This was Slough House, and anyone who knew about it knew it wasn't worth raiding. But this guy had turned up armed, in a balaclava.

Armed, but he'd hidden from them.

"No pulse."

"Looks like a broken neck."

Why would a man with a gun hide from a couple armed with a paperweight and a stapler?

"Let's see who the bastard is."

"Who was it?" Lamb asked.

"He was kitted out. Combat gear, balac —"

"Yeah, I guessed. But did you recognize him?"

River said, "I was meant to think he was one of ours. One of the achievers. But there was something not right. Even apart from him being on his own."

"What sort of something?"

"Something — I don't know . . ."

"For fuck's sake, Cartwright —"

"Shut up!" River closed his eyes again, relived those frantic moments. The guy who'd shot Sid was halfway down the road before River had got to his knees . . . It had taken him three goes to ring for an ambulance. No, that wasn't it, it was before then, the something, whatever it was. What was it?

He said, "He never said a word."

Neither did Lamb.

River said, "All the way through it. Not one squeak."

"So?"

River said, "He was worried I'd recognize his voice."

Lamb waited.

River said, "I think it was Jed Moody."

Louisa peeled the balaclava from the man's head.

From Min's vantage point the uncovered face was upside down, but he knew who he was looking at.

"Shit."

"Yeah . . ."

They weren't even supposed to be here.

They were going to have to get their stories straight.

The rain was stopping when Lamb pulled out of the car park. River stared straight ahead, through the m-shape the wipers' last sweep had left, and didn't need to ask where they were headed. They were going to Slough House. Where else?

There was blood on his shirt. There was blood on his mind.

Lamb said, "What the hell did you think you were doing?"

Any debriefing that followed the shooting of an agent would be a lengthy and unpleasant process . . .

He said, "Watching Hobden."

"I got that much. Why?"

"Because he's got something to do with the kid. The one who's —"

"I know which kid you mean. What makes you think that? Because he hangs out with wannabe Nazis?"

River felt his certainties washing away before Lamb's belligerence. He said, "How did you find me?"

A pedestrian crossing brought them to a halt. A hooded troupe of youth dragged itself across the road in front of them. Lamb said, "Like I said, lights and whistles. A Service name pops into the system, cops, hospital, whatever, and you've got morris dancers and fucking whatnot blowing gaskets. That your idea of undercover? You're called *River*, for Christ's sake.

221

There's probably about four of you in the whole of Great Britain."

River said, "And the Park let you know about it?"

"Well, of course not. Do I look like I'm in the loop?"

"So?"

"Slough House may be a backwater, but there's a couple of things we do have." The lights changed. Lamb drove on. "Ho has the people skills of a natterjack toad, but he knows his way round the ether."

The people skills of a natterjack toad. It was like there was a whole other world somewhere, in which Jackson Lamb didn't think that sentence might be used of him.

"I'm having difficulty imagining Ho doing you a favour." Then River added, in fairness, "You or anyone else."

"Oh, it wasn't a favour. I had something he wanted."

"Which was?"

"What does Ho always want? Information. The answer to a question that's driving him buggy."

"What's that?"

"How come he's ended up in Slough House?"

River had wondered that himself, on and off. He hadn't cared much. Still, he'd wondered. "And you told him?"

"No. But I told him the next best thing."

"Which was?"

Lamb's face gave away less than Buster Keaton's. "I told him why I'd ended up there."

River opened his mouth to ask, then closed it.

Lamb used the hand he wasn't driving with to find a cigarette. "You think Hobden's the only right-wing fruitcake in the country? Or was he the only one you could think of at closing time?"

"He's the only one I know of who's had two spooks sicced on him in the past forty-eight hours."

"So you're a spook. Congratulations. I thought you'd failed your assessment."

"Fuck off, Lamb," he said. "I was there. I saw her shot. You know what that's like?"

Lamb turned to study him through half-open eyes, causing River to remember about the hippo being among the world's most dangerous beasts. It was barrel-shaped and clumsy, but if you wanted to piss one off, do it from a helicopter. Not while sharing a car.

"You didn't just see it," he said. "It was down to you. How clever was that?"

"You think I let it happen deliberately?"

"I think you weren't good enough to stop it. And if you're not good enough for that, you're no use to anyone." Lamb changed gear like it was a violent assault. "If it wasn't for you, she'd have been tucked up in bed. Hers or somebody else's. And don't think I haven't noticed the looks you've been giving her." The car growled onwards.

River said, in an unfamiliar voice, "She told me she was a plant."

"A what?"

"That she'd been put in Slough House for a purpose. To keep an eye on me."

"Was that before or after she got shot in the head?"

"You bastard —"

"Don't even bother, Cartwright. That's what she told you, is it? That you're the centre of the universe? Newsflash. Never happened."

For a dizzy moment, River was aware only of a ringing in his ears; of a throbbing in his palm from yesterday's burn. All of it had happened, even Sid's words: *I was put there to keep an eye on you, River. You're not supposed to know about this*. That had happened. The words had been said.

But what they meant was anyone's guess.

The Chinese restaurant, which even when open looked derelict, was definitely shut. Lamb parked opposite, and as they crossed the road River caught a glimmer of light from one of the higher windows.

Probably a reflection from the Barbican towers.

"Why are we here?"

"Somewhere you'd rather be?"

River shrugged.

Lamb said, "We both know you know nothing, Cartwright. But that doesn't mean Regent's Park won't be looking for you." He led the way round the back, to the familiar scarred door. "I won't say this is the absolute last place they'll look, but it won't be top of their list."

Entering, they were met with the sound of newly established silence.

River wasn't sure how they knew this, but both did. The air trembled like a fork in the darkness. Somebody

— some bodies — had recently stopped moving; some bodies were waiting up the stairs.

"Stay," was Lamb's harsh whisper.

And then he was heading up, light as a whisper. How did he do that? It was like watching a tree change shape.

River followed.

Two flights later he caught up, and here was what they'd missed: Jed Moody, a balaclava peeled from his face, dead as a bucket on the landing.

Sitting three and five steps up respectively, Min Harper and Louisa Guy.

Lamb said, "If you had issues with him, I could have spoken to HR. Arranged an intervention." He tapped Moody's shoulder with his foot. "Breaking his neck without going through your line manager, that shit stays on your record."

"We didn't know it was him."

"Not sure that counts as a defence," Lamb said.

"He had a gun."

"Better," Lamb said. He regarded the pair of them. "He used it earlier, if it helps. Shot Sid Baker with it."

"*Sid?*"

"Christ, is she —"

River found his voice. "She's alive."

"Or was twenty minutes ago," Lamb corrected. Bending his knees, he went through Moody's pockets. "When did this happen?"

"Ten minutes ago."

"Maybe fifteen."

"And you were planning on what, waiting for it all to go away? What were you doing here anyway?"

"We'd been over the road."

"In the pub."

"Can't afford a room?" Lamb produced a mobile phone from Moody's pocket. "Where's the gun?"

Harper gestured behind him.

"He look like using it?"

Harper and Guy exchanged glances.

"Let's get one thing straight," Lamb said. "This isn't a court of law. Did he look like using it?"

"He was carrying it."

"He didn't point it exactly."

"You might want to reconsider your position on that," Lamb said, fishing a faded brown envelope from inside Moody's jacket. "Son of a bitch!"

"He was in your office."

"We figured he was on a raid."

Watching the pair of them in contrapuntal gear, River recognized something new going on; a shared conspiracy that hadn't been apparent before. Love or death, he figured. Love in its most banal guise — a quick fumble in the stairwell, or a drunken snog — and death in its usual weeds. One of the two had fused this pair together. And he flashed again on that moment on the pavement outside Hobden's, when whatever had been starting to grow between himself and Sid Baker ended.

Her blood was on his shirt still. Possibly in his hair.

"He had a balaclava on."

"Didn't look like a junkie thief."

"We didn't mean to kill him, though."

"Yeah," said Lamb. "It's all very well being sorry now, isn't it?"

"What's in the envelope?" River asked.

"You still here?"

"He took that from your office, didn't he? What's in it?"

"The blueprints," Lamb said.

"The *what*?"

"The secret plans." Lamb shrugged. "The microfilm. Whatever." He'd found something else: Moody's black-wrapped form hid more pockets than a magician's. "Son of a bitch," he said again, only this time with less venom; almost with admiration.

"What's that?"

For a moment, it seemed Lamb was about to secrete what he'd found in the folds of his overcoat. But he held it up to the light instead: a brief strand of black wire, the length of a straightened paperclip, with a split-lentil head.

"A bug?"

"He bugged your office?"

"Or maybe," River said, "he was on his way to bug your office."

"After the evening he'd had, I doubt tapping my office was top of his list," Lamb said. "No, he was cleaning up. Prior to getting out." He hadn't finished his body-search yet. "Two mobiles? Jed Jed Jed. I'm surprised you had enough friends to carry one."

"Who's he been talking to?"

"Thank God you're here. Would I have thought of that?" A mobile in each hand, Lamb pressed buttons with each thumb; surprisingly dextrous for a self-proclaimed Luddite. "Now that's strange," he said, in a tone indicating that it wasn't. "This one's barely used. Just one incoming call."

River wanted to say "Ring back," and only the cast-iron knowledge that Lamb wanted him to say it too kept his tongue in harness.

Still sitting, Min and Louisa kept their own counsel.

After a moment's thought, Lamb pressed a few more buttons, and raised the mobile to his ear.

It was answered almost immediately.

Lamb said, "I'm afraid he can't come to the phone right now."

And then he said, "We need to talk."

Down a quiet street in Islington — its front doors perched atop flights of stone steps; some with pillars standing sentry; some with Tiffany windows above — Robert Hobden walked, raincoat flapping in the night wind. It was after midnight. Some of the houses were dressed in darkness; from others, light peeped behind thick curtains; and Hobden could imagine the chink of cutlery, and of glasses meeting together in toasts. Halfway down the street, he found the house he was after.

There were lights on. Again, he caught an imaginary murmur from a successful dinner party: by now, they'd be on to the brandy. But that didn't matter: lights or not, he'd still be ringing the bell — leaning on it, in fact, until the door opened. This took less than a minute.

"Yes?"

It was a sleek man speaking, dark hair brushed back from a high forehead. He had piercing brown eyes which were focused on Hobden. Dark suit, white shirt. Butler? Perhaps. It didn't matter.

"Is Mr Judd in?"

"It's very late, sir."

"Funnily enough," Hobden said, "I knew that. Is he in?"

"Who shall I say, sir?"

"Hobden. Robert Hobden."

The door closed.

Hobden turned and faced the street. The houses opposite seemed to tilt towards his gaze; the effect of their height, and the overhead clouds scudding against a velvet backdrop. His heartbeat was curiously steady. Not long ago he'd come as close to death as he'd ever been, and yet a calm had settled upon him. Or maybe he was calm because he'd come close to death, and so was unlikely to do so again tonight. A matter of statistics.

He didn't know for sure the intruder had meant to kill him. It had been confused — one moment he'd been pacing the room, waiting for a phone call that wouldn't come; the next there'd been a black-masked stranger demanding his laptop in an urgent whisper. He must have picked his way through the door. It was all noise and fear, the man waving a gun, and then another intrusion, another stranger, and then somehow they were all outside and there was blood on the pavement and —

Hobden had run. He didn't know who'd been shot, and didn't care. He'd run. How long since he'd done that? Back when he'd had urgent places to be, he'd have taken a taxi. So before long his lungs felt fit to burst, but still he'd pounded away, feet slapping pavement like wide flat fish, the juddering shock reverberating up to his teeth. Round one corner, then another. He'd been living in London's armpit for longer than he cared think about: still, he was lost within minutes. Didn't dare look back. Couldn't tell where his own footfalls stopped and another's might start; two loops of sound interlocking like Olympic circles.

At last, heaving, he'd come to a crumpled halt in a shop doorway where the usual city smells lurked: dirt and spoilt fat and cigarette ends, and always, always, the smell of winos' piss. Only then had he established that nobody was following. There were only the late-night London ghosts, who came out when the citizens were tucked up in bed, and anyone still on the streets was fair game.

"Got a light, mate?"

He'd surprised himself with the ferocity of his reply: "Just fuck off, all right? Just fuck off!"

You could say this for the mad, at night; they recognized the madder. The man had slunk away, and Hobden had recovered his breath — filled his lungs with that obnoxious stew of smells — and moved on.

He couldn't go back to his flat. Not now; maybe never. This was an oddly cheering thought. Wherever he went, he wasn't going back there.

And in fact, there weren't many places he could go. Everyone needs somewhere where the doors will always open. Hobden didn't have one — the doors in his life had slammed shut when his name appeared on that list; when, for the first time ever, he'd shuddered to see his name in the papers, no longer the smoothly *provocative* but the rawly *unacceptable* — but still, still, there were letterboxes he could whisper through. Favours people owed him. Back then, when the storm was raging, Hobden had kept his mouth shut. There were some who thought this meant he valued their survival over his own. None had made the simple connection: that if they'd been made to suffer the same ostracism he endured, their cause would have been set back years.

Nothing to do with racism, whatever the liberal elite pretended. Nothing to do with hate, or repulsion at the sight of difference. Everything to do with character, and the need for national identity to assert itself. Instead of lying down and accepting this unworkable *multiculturalism*; this recipe for disaster . . .

But he hadn't had time to rehearse unanswerable arguments. He'd needed sanctuary. He'd also needed to get his message across: and if Peter Judd wasn't going to answer his phone calls, then Peter Judd was going to have to answer his door.

Though Peter Judd, of course, didn't answer his own door. Certainly not at this time of night, and probably not at any other.

The door opened, and the sleek character reappeared. "Mr Judd is not available."

The absence of *sir* carried its own echo.

But Hobden had no qualms about blocking the door with his foot. "In that case, tell Mr Judd he might have to make himself available first thing in the morning. The red-tops like their front pages laid out by lunchtime. Gives them time to organize the important stuff. You know, girly shots. Gossip columns."

His foot withdrew, and the door closed.

He thought: Who do these people think I am? Do they think I'll lie on my back, waggle all four legs in the air, while they pretend I'm some stray they never invited home?

Maybe two minutes; maybe three. He didn't count. Again, he studied the clouds whipping elsewhere, and the looming roofs opposite threatening to come crashing down.

Next time the door opened, no words were spoken. Mr Sleek simply stepped to one side, his demeanour suggesting he'd drawn the word *grudging* in a post-dinner game of Charades.

Hobden was shown downstairs, past the drawing room, from behind whose closed door came the soft murmur of happiness. He couldn't remember the last time he'd attended a dinner party, though he'd probably been discussed at a few since.

Downstairs was the kitchen, which was about the size of Hobden's flat, and more carefully outfitted: wood and gleaming enamel, with a marble block forming a coffin-sized island in its centre. Pitiless overhead lighting would have shown up streaks of grease or splashes of sauce, but there were none, even now: the dishwasher hummed, and glasses were assembled along one surface, but it all looked like a tidy representation of a party's aftermath in a catalogue dedicated to polite living. From stainless steel hooks on a rail hung shiny pans, each with their sole purpose; one for boiling eggs, another for scrambling them, and so on. A row of olive oil bottles, ordered by region, occupied a shelf. He still had a journalist's eye, Robert Hobden. Depending on who he was profiling, he'd take these things as evidence of middle-class certainty, or mail-ordered props intended to buffer up just such an image. On the other hand, he wasn't writing profiles any more. And if he was, no one would print them.

Sleek stood by the door, pointedly not leaving Hobden alone.

Hobden drifted to the far side of the room; leant against the sink.

He wasn't writing profiles any more, but if he were, and if his current host were his target, he'd be bound to start with the name. Peter Judd. PJ to his friends, and everyone else. Fluffy-haired and youthful at forty-eight, and with a vocabulary peppered with archaic expostulations — Balderdash! Tommy-rot!! Oh my giddy aunt!!! — Peter Judd had long established himself as the unthreatening face of the old-school right, popular enough with the GBP, which thought him an amiable idiot, to make a second living outside Parliament as a rent-a-quote-media-whore-cum-quiz-show-panel-favourite, and to get away with minor peccadilloes like dicking his kids' nanny, robbing the taxman blind, and giving his party leader conniptions with off-script flourishes. ("Damn fine city," he'd remarked on a trip to Paris. "Probably worth defending next time.") Not everyone who'd worked with him thought him a total buffoon, and some who'd witnessed him lose his temper suspected him of political savvy, but by and large PJ seemed happy with the image he'd either fostered or been born with: a loose cannon with a floppy haircut and a bicycle. And here he was now, bursting through the kitchen door with an alacrity that had Mr Sleek making a sharp sideways step to avoid being flattened.

"Robert Hobden!" he cried.

"PJ."

"Robert. Rob — Rob! How are you?"

"I'm not so bad, PJ. Yourself?"

"Oh, of course. Seb, take Robert's coat, would you?"

"I won't stay long —"

"But long enough to remove your coat! That's just dandy, that's just fine." This to Seb, if that was Sleek's name. "You can leave us now." The kitchen door swung closed. PJ's tone didn't alter. "What the fuck are you doing here, you stupid fucking cunt?"

It reminded him of darker days; of missions you might not come back from. He'd always come back from them, obviously, but there were others who hadn't. Whether the difference lay in the mission or the men, there was no way of knowing.

Tonight, he expected to come back. But he already had one body on the floor and another in a hospital bed, a pretty high casualty rate when he wasn't even running an op.

The meet was by the canal, near where the towpath came to an end and the water disappeared inside a long tunnel. Lamb had chosen it because it cut down on directions of approach, and he didn't trust Diana Taverner. For the same reason, he got there first. It was approaching two. A quarter moon was blotted now and then by passing clouds. A house across the water was lit, all three storeys, and he could hear chatter and occasional laughter from smokers in the garden. Some people threw parties midweek. Jackson Lamb kept tabs on his department's body count.

She came from the Angel end, her approach signalled by the tapping of her heels on the path.

"Are you alone?" she asked.

He spread his arms as if to measure the stupidity of her question. As he did so his shirt came untucked, and night air scratched his belly.

She looked beyond him, at the treed slope leading up to the road. Then back at him. "What do you think you're playing at?"

"I lent you an agent," he said. "She's in hospital."

"I know. I'm sorry."

"Lloyd Webber-grade, you said. One step up from sharpening pencils. But now she's got a bullet in her head."

"Lamb," she said. "The job was the other day. Whatever's happened to her since, that's hardly —"

"Don't even bother. She was shot outside Hobden's place. By Jed Moody, intentionally or otherwise. When you're not co-opting my team, you're subverting them. You gave Moody a mobile phone. What else did you give him? An earful of promises? A ticket to his future?"

Taverner said, "Check the rulebook, Lamb. You run Slough House, and God knows, nobody's looking to take that away. But I'm head of ops, which means directing personnel. All personnel. Yours or anyone else's."

Jackson Lamb farted.

"God, you're a vile specimen."

"So I'm told," he said. "Okay, say you're right, and this is none of my business. What do I do about the body on my staircase? Call in the Dogs?"

If he hadn't had it before, he had her attention now.

"Moody?"

"Uh-huh."

"He's dead?"

"The proverbial dodo."

Across the water, the smokers fell upon a joke of unusual hilarity. The canal's surface was ruffled by the wind.

Lamb said, "You wanted to subcontract, you could have chosen more carefully. Jesus, I mean, Jed Moody? Even when he was any good he wasn't any good. And it's a long time since he was any good."

"Who killed him?"

"You want to hear something funny? He tripped over his own feet."

"That'll sound good before Limitations. Though you might want to leave out the bit about it being funny."

Lamb threw back his head and laughed a silent laugh, while leaves' shadows flickered across his wobbling face. He looked like someone Goya might have painted. "Good. Very good. Limitations, yes. So we call in the Dogs? Hell, it's a death. Why don't I call the plod? As it happens, I've a mobile with me." He grinned at her. His teeth, mostly different shapes, shone wet.

"Okay."

"The coroner. His turf, right?"

"You've made your point, Lamb."

He went fumbling in his pockets, and for a horrified moment she thought he was unzipping himself, but he produced a packet of Marlboro instead. He drew one with his teeth, and as an afterthought waved the pack in her direction.

Taverner took one. Always accept hospitality. It forms a bond. Makes you allies.

Of course, whoever had taught her that hadn't been thinking of Jackson Lamb.

He said, "Talk."

"It's good to see you too, PJ."

"Have you lost your cocking mind?"

"You've not been taking my calls."

"Of course I haven't, you're fucking toxic. Did anyone see you arrive?"

"I don't know."

"What kind of prick answer is that?"

"The only prick answer I've got!" Hobden shouted.

The pitch of his voice caused something metallic to ring.

It gave PJ pause, or caused him to appear that it did. "Yes," he said. "Yes. Well. Crikey. I suppose you've got a reason."

"Someone tried to kill me," Hobden said.

"To kill you? Yes, well. Lots of fanatics about. I mean, you're not the most *popular* —"

"This wasn't a fanatic, PJ. It was a spook."

"A spook."

"We're talking assassination."

Judd's lapse into his public persona didn't survive the word. "Oh, for fuck's sake. What was it, a close encounter on a zebra crossing? I've got guests, Hobden. The fucking Minister for Culture's upstairs, and he's got the attention span of a gnat, so I need to —"

238

"He was a spook. They've been following me. He broke into my flat and waved a gun around and — somebody got shot. If you don't believe me, turn the news on. Or on second thoughts, don't — there'll be a D. But call the Home Secretary, he'll know. Blood on the pavement. Outside my flat."

PJ weighed it up: the likelihood of any of this having happened, as against Hobden's appearance in his kitchen. "Okay," he said at length. "But you live at the arse end of nowhere, Robert. I mean, home invasions, they must be weekly events. What makes this different?"

Hobden shook his head. "You're not listening." Then shook his head again: he hadn't laid out the whole story. That business at Max's the other morning; the split coffee. Nothing to it at the time, but since the gunman's appearance Hobden had replayed recent history, and concluded that this evening had been a culmination, not a one-off. When he'd picked up his keys to leave the café, his memory stick had fallen loose and bounced on to the table. It had never done that before. Why hadn't a warning bell rung?

"They tried to take my files. They want to see how much I know."

And now PJ took on a new seriousness; a side the public never got to see. "Your *files*?"

"They didn't get them. They copied my memory stick, but —"

"What the fuck do your files contain, Hobden?"

"— it's a dummy. Just numbers. With any luck they'll think it's a code, waste their time trying to —"

"What. Exactly. Do your files contain?"

Hobden raised his hands to eye-level; examined them a moment or two. They shook. "See that? I could have died. They could have killed me."

"Give me strength." And now Peter Judd started ransacking his kitchen, morally certain there'd be alcohol somewhere, or what was the point of it? A bottle of vodka appeared. Cooking vodka, would that be? Did people cook with vodka? Was PJ muttering any of this aloud, or did his body language shout it while he located a glass and splashed out a generous measure?

"So." Handing the glass to Hobden. "What do your files contain? Names?" He barked the sudden laugh TV audiences liked. "My name wouldn't be there anywhere." Underneath the bark, the hint of bite. "Would it?"

"No names. Nothing like that."

This was good news, but prompted a follow-up. "So what are you on about?"

Hobden said, "Five's running an op. I've known about it for a while. Or not known about it, exactly — known something was going to happen, but not precisely what."

"Oh, for Christ's sake. Start making sense."

"I was at the Frontline. One night last year."

"They still let you in?"

A flash of anger. "I've paid my subs." He finished his vodka, held the glass out for more. "Diana Taverner was there, with one of her leftie journalist pals."

"I've never been sure what disturbs me more," Peter Judd said, filling Hobden's glass. "The fact that MI5 is run by women, or the fact that everybody seems to know this. I mean, didn't it used to be called the secret service?"

Pretty sure he'd heard this riff already, probably on a panel show, Hobden ignored it. "It was the night of the Euro elections, and there'd been BNP gains. Remember that?"

"Well, of course I do."

"And that was the subject of discussion. This hack, Spencer his name is, got rolling drunk, started spewing off the usual nonsense about how the fascists were taking over, and when were Taverner's lot going to start doing something about it. And she said . . ."

Here Hobden screwed his eyes shut while summoning up history.

"Something like yes, that's under control. Or on the agenda. Christ, I don't remember the exact words, but she gave him to understand it was *happening*. That she was setting something up not just against the BNP, but against what she'd call the extreme right. And we all know who that includes."

"She said this in your hearing?"

"They didn't know I was there."

"Second Desk at MI5 announced her intention to sting the BNP, to sting the right, and this happened in a *bar*?"

"They were drunk, okay? Look, it happened. Is happening. Haven't you seen the news?" PJ eyed him coldly. "The kid in the cellar?"

"I know what you're referring to. You're saying that's it? That's a Service op?"

"Well, it's a big bloody coincidence, don't you think? That I'm being hassled the same week it happens, that somebody tries to kill me the same day —"

"If it is," PJ said, "it's the single most cack-handed intelligence operation I've ever heard of, and that includes the Bay of fucking Pigs." He glanced down at the bottle in his hands, then hunted around for a second glass. The nearest candidate was an unrinsed stem, waiting by the sink. He poured a slug into it, and put the bottle down. "Is this why you were calling?"

"What do you think?"

PJ slapped him hard, the noise ricocheting round the kitchen. "Don't talk back to me, you little creep. Remember who's who. You're a one-time journalist whose name stinks from here to Timbuktu. And I'm a member of Her Majesty's loyal cabinet." He examined his wet shirt cuff. "And now you've made me spill my drink."

Hobden, his voice as shaky as a pea in a whistle, said, "You *hit* me!"

"Yes, well. Tempers running high. Oh, for God's sake." He poured more vodka into Hobden's glass. Hobden was a toad, but not an ignorant toad. It had been a mistake to forget that. Still, though: PJ was furious. "You were calling me because you think this this this piece of *theatre* has been organized by MI5 to discredit the right — you've barely finished explaining that you're under surveillance, and you're *calling me*? Have you lost your fucking mind?"

"Somebody had to know. Who was I supposed to call?"

"Not me."

"We've known each other for years —"

"We are not friends, Robert. Don't make that mistake. You always treated me fairly in print, and I respect that, but let's face it, you're a fucking has-been, and it's no longer appropriate to be associated with you. So take it somewhere else."

"Where do you suggest?"

"Well, your chums in the British Patriotic Party spring to mind."

The red weal PJ's hand had left on Hobden's cheek darkened. "Chums? My chums? When that list appeared on the net, who do you think they blamed? Half the death threats I get come from people I supported! As far as they were concerned, if it weren't for me, they'd have been left alone. Because we all know who was responsible for posting that list. The same bunch of leftish criminals who're hassling me now!"

"Maybe so. But I'm still not sure why that means you have to turn up on my doorstep in the middle of the night —"

"Because this has got to be stopped," Hobden said.

Lamb said, "Talk." Then flicked a lighter in front of Taverner's face like a threat.

She leant forward for the flame. Her seventh of the day: drawing smoke into her lungs was growing familiar. She breathed out. Said, "Do you ever wonder why we do what we do?"

"Taverner, it's after two, and my team's smaller than it was yesterday. Let's get on with it, all right?"

"There've been fifteen failed terrorist plots since 7/7, Jackson. That must be true. I read it in the paper."

"Good for us."

"It was on page eleven, below the fold."

Lamb said, "If you wanted to be famous, maybe the secret service wasn't the right path."

"This isn't about me."

Jackson Lamb suspected it was very much about her.

"Our failures get more press than our successes. You of all people should know that. The dodgy dossier? Weapons of mass destruction? Okay, that was Six, but you think anyone cares?" Her words were coming faster now, each leaving its tobacco trace in the air between them. "There was a poll lately. Forty-something per cent of the public think Five had a hand in the death of David Kelly. Forty-something per cent. How do you think that makes me feel?"

Lamb said, "It makes you feel like doing something about it. Let me take a wild guess. You've set up some half-arsed scheme involving a neo-fascist group kidnapping a Muslim kid and threatening to chop his head off on YouTube. Except it's not gunna happen because one of the group is one of your guys. So when Five step in for a last-moment rescue, you'll have all the airplay in the world underlining what a ruthlessly efficient organization it is." He blew smoke. "Close?"

"Half-arsed?"

"Oh, for Christ's sake. We've got one dead and one in intensive care, and that's with you trying to keep this whole thing out of the papers. And in case you hadn't forgotten, they're both mine. Or were."

"I'm sorry about Sid Baker."

"Great."

"It sounds like Moody tripped on his dick, and I'm not taking responsibility for that. But I'm sorry about Baker."

"I'll have that marked on her chart. You know, the one clipped to her bed, which shows when her catheter's changed. Jesus. Did you really think this would work?"

"It still can."

"Crap. The wheels started coming off before you screwed them on. Tell me about Hobden. What makes him a danger?"

"I don't know for sure he is."

"I didn't come here to fence. You had his files swiped and his rubbish collected. Why?"

Briefly, she touched her forehead with the palm of her hand. When she looked back at Lamb, he felt he could almost see through her skin. Veins stretched tight over gleaming bone. Tap her with a fingernail, she'd shatter. She said: "Do you know Dave Spencer?"

"*Guardian* hack?"

"Used to be. Got his cards. But anyway, yes. He and I, we're friends. Does that sound odd? Me, friends with a pinko journalist?"

Nothing sounded odd to Lamb; except, perhaps, that people had friends.

"We were in the Frontline Club the night of the Euro elections. The night the BNP won two seats, remember?"

Lamb nodded.

"We watched the results coming in, and Dave went predictably mental. He's a drinker. Another reason they sacked him. Anyway, he started railing on, as if it was my fault. What about your lot, he kept saying. Isn't it time you took these pipsqueak fascists out of the game?"

"Oh, Jesus," Lamb said.

"I don't know what I told him. Anything to get him to pipe down. But I said stuff, yes. That they were on the agenda. Something like that. Non-specific. Not for attribution."

"And all in Hobden's hearing."

"Well, it's not like I knew he was there! He was lurking. He was low profile."

"Of course he bloody was. He's a fucking pariah." Lamb shook his head. "So you've got a journo with far-right sympathies on the earie for an op against the far right. Who's already riled by having his extremist leanings exposed, and the Service had a hand in that, right? No wonder you wanted to find out how much he knew before kicking your ball into touch. What did his files show?"

"Sod all. Pi, to about half a million places. And you thought we were paranoid."

Lamb just thought he was careful. What Hobden had done, he'd have done too, the way a tourist carries a dummy wallet: a couple of bucks for the local hoods, with the plastic and the travellers' cheques folded into a sock. "So you sent Moody to what, double check? Lift his hard drive?" He paused a beat. "He was carrying a gun."

"For Christ's sake, Lamb, you think I authorized that?"

"At this point, I'm beyond surprising."

246

She said, "He was supposed to take the laptop. He was *supposed* to make it look like a junkie theft."

"We'll add that to Moody's list of career successes, then." Without warning, he spat noisily. Then said, "So now Sid Baker's on a table, having a bullet removed from her head. As for Moody, even he must have realized things were beyond screwed. So he tried to tidy up, which involved removing the bug he'd planted in my office. And trod on his dick in the dark, like you said."

"Was he alone at the time?"

"We're all alone in the end, don't you think? Those final moments?" Jackson Lamb flicked the dying stub of his cigarette into the dark canal. "Either way, it's over. For him and for you. For this whole operation."

"It can still work."

"No it can't. If Hobden was clueless earlier, he isn't now. Oh, and he's on the loose. Did I mention that? Pulling the plug is your only choice."

"Hobden's a joker. The only rags that'll print him have names like *UK Watch*, and their circulation's limited to those already frothing at the mouth."

"I'm not talking about after the event, I'm talking about tonight. These splinter groups, the BPP, the UK Nazis, the other fuckers, they may hate each other's guts, but not half as much as they hate everyone else. Hobden'll get the word out, if he hasn't already. Pull your agent in. Now. Or Moody and Baker won't be tonight's only casualties."

She turned away.

"Taverner?"

"They're a sealed group. There's no input from anywhere else."

"You wish. But look at how you've managed so far. This thing couldn't have fallen apart faster if you'd bought it at Ikea, and you're the professional. You think the jokers your agent's entrapped in this farce have kept their mouths shut? Any minute now, one of them's going to get a call from someone who knows someone who knows Hobden, telling them they've been set up, which means two people are in extreme danger right now. Your agent and this kid." Lamb blinked. "Who's just some unlucky bastard who's the wrong colour, right?"

She didn't reply.

"Oh, for fuck's sake," Lamb said. "How could this get worse?"

"Because it's got to be stopped," Hobden said. "Don't you see?"

"If it's a Service op, obviously it'll be stopped," Peter Judd pointed out. "Five are hardly going to let anyone be beheaded on the internet. The whole point —"

"I know what the whole point is. It's for everyone to forget about bombs on the tube, and all those dawn raids that finish in acquittals. No, we'll have action footage of our brave spooks rescuing some poor brown-skinned boy, and coincidentally painting the right as a bunch of mad murdering bastards into the bargain. That's what I want stopped. What about you? Do you want to let them get away with it?"

"Given their track record, I rather doubt they will. But you still haven't explained why you're coming to me with this."

"Because we both know the tide's turning. The decent people in this country are sick to death of being held hostage by mad liberals in Brussels, and the sooner we take control over our own future, our own borders —"

"Are you seriously lecturing me?"

"It'll happen, and within the lifetime of your government. We both know that. Not this Parliament, but probably the next. By which time we both know where you expect to be living, and it won't be Islington, will it?" Hobden had grown alive again. Eyes bright. Breathing normal. "It'll be Downing Street."

"Yes. Well." The effing and blinding PJ of ten minutes ago — the PJ who'd slapped Hobden — left the room; in his place was the bumbly figure familiar from countless broadcasts and not a few YouTube moments. "Obviously, if called upon to serve, I'll leave my plough."

"And you'll want to take your party further right, but what if that ground's already staked out? And what if one of the occupying groups is mostly famous for attempting a prime-time execution?"

"Now you're being ridiculous. Not even the muckiest rakers of your former profession are going to equate Her Majesty's Government with —"

"Well, they might if they learn of your connection with one of those groups."

And now they'd come to the meat of the matter.

Hobden said, "Don't imagine that the reason I never mentioned it in print was that I thought it a youthful

249

indiscretion. I just never wanted to hear you deny it in public. You're PM material. With you at the helm, this country can be great again. And those of us who believe in strong government don't want to hear you apologizing for the causes you truly espouse."

PJ placed his glass very carefully on the counter. "I've never had any truck with extremism," he said levelly. Now he was Peter Judd, the people's pundit: his tone precisely the one he used on TV when he was about to put someone right while indicating that few people had ever been wronger. "As it happens, I did write a report on the activities of some fringe right groups in the early nineties, in the course of researching which I attended one or two meetings." He leant closer, so Hobden could feel his breath.

"And do you really think you have any credibility?" His voice was velvet. "You'll think the car crash your life has become is a fucking feather bed. Compared to what'll happen next."

"I don't want to cause a scandal. That's the last thing I want. But if I did —"

Slowly, carefully, Hobden drained his own glass.

"But if I did, I don't need credibility. I have something far more useful."

He set his empty glass next to PJ's.

"I have a photograph."

"Oh, for fuck's sake. How could this get worse?"

Taverner said, "It's not simply about improving Five's reputation. There's a war on, Jackson. Even from

Slough House you must have noticed. And we need all the allies we can get."

"Who is he?"

"It's not who he is, it's who his uncle is."

"Oh, Christ," Lamb said. "Don't tell me."

"His mother's brother is Mahmud Gul."

"Jesus wept."

"General Mahmud Gul. Currently Second Desk at Pakistan's Directorate for Inter-Services Intelligence."

"Yes. Thank you. I know who he is. Jesus Christ."

"Think of it as bringing communities together," Taverner said. "When we rescue Hassan, we make a friend. You think we can't use one? In Pakistan's secret service?"

"And have you given the flipside any thought? If this goes wrong, and Christ knows it's not gone right yet, you've assassinated his nephew."

"It's not going to go wrong."

"Your faith would be touching if your stupidity didn't make me retch. Pull the plug. Now."

Another strain of laughter wafted over the canal, but sounded less than genuine; driven by alcohol rather than wit.

She said, "Okay, suppose we do that. Finish it. Tonight." Her eyes momentarily focused on something beyond Lamb's shoulder, then returned to his face. "A day early. Doesn't mean it can't still work."

"When I hear anyone say that," Lamb began, but she spoke over him.

"In fact, it'll work better. Not a last-minute rescue. We get to the kid twenty-four hours before he's due for the chop, and why's that? Because we're good. Because we know what we're doing. Because *you* know what you're doing."

Lamb appeared to choke. "You're out of your mind," he said, once he could talk.

"It works. Why wouldn't it?"

"Well, for a start, there's no papertrail. No investigation. How'm I supposed to have found him, divine inspiration? He was taken in bloody Leeds."

"They brought him here. They're not far away."

"They're in London?"

"They're not far away," she repeated. "As for the papertrail, we'll work up a legend. Hell, we're halfway there already. Hobden's our point of entry. It was your team burned him, took his files."

"Which were a pile of cack," he reminded her.

"Not necessarily. Not once we've decided what they really say."

Enough light fell on Taverner's face for Lamb to see she meant every word. She was probably mad. It wouldn't be the first time the job had done that, and being a woman couldn't help. If she was thinking straight, she'd have noticed the flaw in her reasoning, which was that he, Jackson Lamb, couldn't give a flying fart for whatever she was offering.

Or maybe she had. "Think a minute. About what it could mean."

"I'm thinking there's a body on my staircase."

"He fell on the stairs. An empty bottle's the only prop you'll need." Her whispers were urgent now; they were talking of death, of other people's death. They were also talking of career-ending moments, and maybe of something else. "Redemption."

"Excuse the fuck out of me?"

"Rehabilitation."

"I don't need rehab. I'm happy where I am."

"Then you're the only one. Christ, Jed Moody would have given his left bollock to be let back inside."

"And look where that got him."

"So he proved he was a slow horse. Are the others as bad?"

Lamb pretended to think about it. "Yeah," he said. "Probably."

"It doesn't have to be that way. Do this, and you get to be a hero. Again. So do the boys and girls. Just think, the slow horses back among the thoroughbreds. You don't want to give them that chance?"

"Not especially."

"Okay, so what about the downside? Was Moody really on his lonesome when he broke his neck?" She put her head on one side. "Or did he have company?"

Lamb showed his teeth. "We've covered this. Call in the Dogs. When they've finished tearing you apart, they'll maybe have strength to pick at the rest of us." He yawned a cavernous yawn he didn't bother to conceal. "I'm not bothered either way."

"No matter who gets swatted."

"You said it."

"What if it's Standish?"

Lamb shook his head. "You're tossing darts, seeing what you might hit. Standish isn't involved. She's at home, asleep. I guarantee it."

"I'm not talking about tonight." And this time she had the sense that a dart had landed close. She could tell by Lamb's body language; a relaxation of the muscles around his mouth, a signal designed to indicate absence of care. "Catherine Standish? She came this close to a treason charge. You think that went away?"

His eyes were black in the moonlight. "That's not a can of worms you want to open."

"Do I look like I'm keen? You're right, this evening's out of control. I want it over, quickly and quietly. With someone I trust at the reins. And like it or not, Slough House is part of this now. You'll all get turned over. And poor Catherine . . . Well, she doesn't even know the trouble she was nearly in, does she?"

Lamb surveyed the canal. Lights swayed on its surface, reflections from stray sources. A few houseboats were shrouded in darkness, their cabin roofs home to potted plants, some trailing green fingers as far as the water, and carefully stacked piles of bicycles. Evidence of an alternative lifestyle, or a hidey-hole for alternative weekends. Who cared?

He said, "It was before your time. But you know why I'm at Slough House."

It wasn't a question.

Diana Taverner said, "I've heard three versions."

"The bad one? That's the truth."

"I guessed as much."

He leant forward. "You've been using Slough House as your personal toybox, and that pisses me off. Are we clear on that?"

She gave the dart another push. "You care about them, don't you?"

"No, I think they're a bunch of fucking losers." He came closer. "But they're my losers. Not yours. So I'll do this thing, but with conditions attached. Moody disappears. Baker was a street victim. Anyone who's with me tonight is fireproof. Oh, and you're everlastingly in my debt. Which, you'd better believe, will be reflected in expense sheets evermore."

"We can all come out of this covered in glory," she said, unwisely.

But Lamb rejected the seven or eight probable rejoinders; simply shook his head in mute disbelief, and looked again at the canal's surface where broken shards of light bobbed in quiet disarray.

"I have a photograph," Hobden said. "It shows you throwing a Nazi salute, with your arm round Nicholas Frost. He's forgotten now, of course, but he was a leading light in the National Front at the time. Stabbed to death at a rally a few years later, which is just as well. He was the sort who gave the right a bad name."

A long moment later, PJ said, "That photograph was destroyed."

"I can believe it."

"So destroyed it might be said never to have existed."

"In which case, you have nothing to worry about."

The various PJs who'd so far been present — the urbane, the bumbly, the vicious, the cruel — melded into one, and for a moment the real Peter Judd peered out from the overgrown schoolboy, and what he was

255

doing was what he was always doing: weighing up who he was talking to in terms of the threat he posed, and assessing how that threat might cleanly be dealt with. "Cleanly" meant without repercussion. If the photograph still existed, and was in Hobden's possession, the consequences would be potentially catastrophic. Hobden might be bluffing. But that he even knew of the photo meant PJ's needle had edged into the red.

First, neutralize the consequences.

Deal with the threat later.

He said, "What do you want?"

"I want you to get the word out."

"The word?"

"That this whole set-up, this supposed execution, is a fake. That the Voice of Albion, who've never been more than a bunch of streetfighters, have been infiltrated by the intelligence services. That they've been made the vehicle for a PR exercise, and they're not going to come out of it well." Hobden paused. "I don't care what happens to the idiots. But the damage they're doing to our cause is incalculable."

PJ let that *our* slide past. Our cause. "And I'm to, what? Announce this in the House?"

"Don't tell me you haven't got contacts. The right word from you, in the right ear, will get a lot further than mine will." His voice became urgent. "I wouldn't involve you if I could deal with this myself. But like I said. They're not my *chums*."

"It's probably too late already," PJ said.

"We have to try." Exhausted suddenly, Hobden wiped a hand across his face. "They can say it was a joke that got out of hand. That they never had any intention of spilling blood."

There was commotion outside; voices calling down the stairs. *PJ? Where have you got to, dammit?* And also: *Darling? Where are you?* This last with more than a hint of tetchiness.

"I'll be right up," PJ called. And then: "You'd better go."

"You'll make the call?"

"I'll see to it."

Something in his glare dissuaded Hobden from taking it further.

Lamb left. Taverner watched until his bulky shape merged with the larger shadows, and then for another two minutes before allowing herself to relax. She checked her watch. Two thirty-five.

A quick mental calculation: the deadline — Hassan's deadline — had about twenty-six hours to run.

Ideally, Diana Taverner would have played that string out longer; waited until every TV screen in the land was running a clock before she set the rescue wheels turning. But tonight would have to do. And anyway, the bright spin she'd put on it — that this was not a last-minute rescue, but a controlled, panic-free operation — would work fine. Never any danger. That's what the report would conclude; that Five had everything under wraps from the start. So, come morning, Hassan would be safely home; Taverner's agent would be out from deep cover; and she herself would be accepting congratulations, watching the Service's cachet skyrocket. And as a bonus, there was no chance of Ingrid Tearney getting back from DC in time to steal her glory.

But it was no great comfort that matters now lay in the hands of Jackson Lamb. Lamb was worse than a Service screw-up; he was a loose cannon, who'd wilfully slipped his moorings. When he'd asked if she knew why he was at Slough House, he'd been threatening her; asking if she knew what he'd once done. If things went screwy tonight, Lamb wouldn't leave it to the Dogs to clean things up. He'd wipe the slate himself.

In which case, a contingency plan was advisable.

She fished her mobile out of her pocket; called up a number. It rang five times before being answered. "Taverner," she said. "Sorry to disturb. But I've just had a very strange conversation with Jackson Lamb."

Still talking, she set off down the towpath, and pretty soon was swallowed by the shadows.

It was late, it was late, but the dinner party was still going strong. The odd line of coke was helping. PJ had resolved to let this pass, but would be having words with the guilty parties, strong words, before the week was out. There were jinks you could enjoy in opposition, and higher jinks you could get away with in government, but once inside the cabinet, there were guidelines to be observed. None of the puppies partaking were at PJ's exalted level, of course, but it showed him deep disrespect to imagine that he hadn't noticed.

But they could wait. In the half-hour since Hobden's departure, PJ had been assessing the deeps and shallows of his story, and had decided it was probably true. Even in the webbed-up world, where conspiracy theories spread faster than a blogger's acne, PJ had no difficulty believing that elements within MI5 might have concocted this piece of Grand Guignol, and it even impressed him, a bit. A little less cloak-and-dagger and a bit more reality TV: that was the way to catch the public imagination. And you couldn't get more real than spilling blood.

What he hadn't decided was what his reaction should be. For all Hobden's doom-mongering, PJ felt that the electorate could distinguish between the establishment version of right-wing and the kind cooked up on sink estates. Besides, follow Hobden's reasoning and it made no difference whether the plot succeeded or failed: either way, the far right came out as murderous bastards. And given that PJ didn't care if one, at best, second-generation citizen lived or died, and that he intended one day to be in a position where the strength of the intelligence services was of immediate personal concern to him, the deck was weighted against his lifting a finger.

But then there was the photo. If it existed. Here in the privacy of PJ's head, there was little point pretending it had never done so, but whether it could still be described in such terms was a different matter, one which a serious amount of money, a fair few promises, and one act of violence had theoretically resolved. At this distance there was little chance that a copy survived, but allowing for the possibility that it did, there were few more likely candidates for finding it than Robert Hobden. Even leaving aside his far-right connections, Hobden's career had been as remarkable for its uncovering of political sins as it had been for its smug pomposity, and before his fall from grace, those in power trod round him with care. And the fact that he obviously didn't know everything made it more likely that he wasn't bluffing — if he'd had even an inkling that Nicholas Frost's death at a National Front rally had been other than it seemed, he'd have raised the matter. So assume, PJ thought, that the photo existed; assume Hobden had a copy. Where did that leave matters? Matters meaning PJ?

It left him plastering the cracks. He pushed his chair back, waved an apologetic hand in his wife's direction; mouthed "Telephone" at her. She'd think this was to do with the hostage situation, and it was, of course. It was.

He found Sebastian on the upstairs landing, where he sat looking out at the quiet street. *Factotum* was one of the words used to describe Sebastian; PJ had also heard *major-domo* and even *batman*. That last one was quite good, in fact. Caped crusader. Dark deeds, in the cause of righteousness. Righteousness also meaning PJ.

If the photo existed: well. There were guidelines to be observed at cabinet level, of course, but one of those was the bottom line itself, which simply stated that you did not allow others to hold a blade at your throat.

Those in power had once trod round Robert Hobden with care. These days, rolling right over him was an option. But first, he'd plaster those cracks; get the word out, as Hobden had wanted. PJ did not maintain personal relations with those who dwelt so far beyond the pale, but then, he didn't need to. What's a batman for?

"Seb," he said. "I need you to make some calls."

Jed Moody's body was still on the landing, bleakly lit by a naked bulb. Lamb paid little attention to it on his way up to his office, where he lifted the corkboard from the floor and rehung it on the wall. Then he unlocked a desk drawer and drew out a shoebox. Inside, swaddled in cloth, was a Heckler & Koch. After examining it briefly by the light of the Anglepoise, he slipped it into his overcoat pocket, causing the coat to hang awkwardly. Leaving the shoebox on the desk, and the low lamp burning, he returned downstairs.

"What happened to the gun?" he asked.

"I've got it," River told him.

Lamb held out a meaty hand, and River surrendered the weapon, which promptly disappeared inside Lamb's pocket. Curiously, to River's eye, it seemed to even him up a little.

Lamb glanced down at Moody. "Keep an eye on the place, eh?"

The dead man didn't answer.

Lamb led the way down, lighting a cigarette before they'd reached the street. Outside, its plume of smoke was almost white. "Anyone else got a car here?"

Louisa Guy did.

"Either of you in a state to drive?"

"Yes."

"Then follow me."

"Where to?" River asked.

"You're with me." To the other two, Lamb said, "Roupell Street. Know it?"

"South of the river."

"This time of night?"

Lamb said, "That supposed to be funny?"

"What do we do when we get there?" River asked.

"We rescue Hassan Ahmed," Lamb said. "And we all get to be heroes."

River, Min and Louisa shared a glance.

Lamb said, "Is that all right with you? Or did you have other plans?"

They had no other plans.

Larry, Moe and Curly.

Curly, Larry and Moe.

Who were these people, and why had they taken him?

You think we give a toss who you are?

For long stretches at a time, Hassan believed that he had stopped thinking. That he was all feeling, no thought. But that was wrong: it was more that his thoughts had become feelings, and were now tumbling round his head like butterflies. His thoughts were fluttering things, impossible to pin down. They led to one thing, then to another, and then to a third, which might be the first thing over again, though it was hard to be sure, as by then he'd forgotten what the first thing had been. Whether the root cause of this was fear or hunger or loneliness, he didn't know. What was interesting — and this interested him in the same way he might once have been interested in the activities of an ant — was that he had discovered a talent for time travel. For fractions of a second, he was able to cast himself out of this cellar and into a past in which none of this would ever happen.

For instance, he remembered the first time he'd asked his mother about the man in the photo on her bedside table; this obvious soldier, with fine firm features, and a look in his eye suggesting that he too knew the secret of time travel, and was seeing through the camera and into the future itself; a future in which children yet unborn would gaze at his photograph, and wonder who he was.

"That is your uncle Mahmud," he was told.

Hassan had been five or so at the time.

"Where is he?" he'd asked.

"He's back home. In Pakistan."

But home didn't mean Pakistan to Hassan. Home meant where he lived; it meant the house in which he woke up every day with his parents and brothers and sisters, and also the street on which that house was set, and the town that street was part of, and so on. It confused him that for his mother, the word might mean something else. If words meant different things to different people, how could they be trusted?

And if this man was his uncle, why had Hassan never met him?

"Why doesn't he visit us?"

Because his uncle was a very busy and important man, who had duties that kept him on the other side of the world.

Information supplied early enough becomes hardwired into the brain, and this nugget had not only satisfied Hassan, but seemed to be the only thing worth saying on the subject. When, years later, he had glimpsed what looked like the same man on the BBC news, a figure in a line of men being introduced to the US President, who'd been on one of his welcome-to-my-world tours, it was simply confirmation of what his mother had told him: that his uncle was a very busy and important man.

And then the flicker of history was gone, and Hassan was back in his cellar.

His uncle was a very busy and important man. Too busy and important ever to visit England; that was the story his younger self had been told. The truth, as his father had told him much later, cast a somewhat different light: his uncle had never visited because he did not approve of his sister's marriage; did not approve of their secular life. Though the matter of his busyness and importance remained true: his uncle was a high-ranking officer in the Pakistan military.

Was that busy and important enough, he wondered now? Was that important enough for Larry, Curly and Moe?

You think we give a toss who you are?

That was what they had said, but perhaps they had lied. After all, they had assaulted, drugged and kidnapped him; imprisoned him in a damp cellar; coldly informed him they were going to cut his head off. They had given him a bottle of water and a banana, and nothing else. They were bad people. That they were liars was not beyond possibility. And since busyness and importance easily equated with wealth, maybe this was in reality a kidnapping of the garden variety; that for all their threats and bluster, Moe, Curly and Larry's aim was to screw money from his busy, important uncle, no more. Which made more sense than that they might demand a ransom from his parents, who were busy but not important; comfortable, but not rich. Hassan was almost certain, then, that this must be the case.

You fucking Paki.

Yeah, sure, they said that, but only to keep him scared.

We're going to cut your head off and show it on the web.

But what they meant was: unless your uncle pays the ransom.

Hassan had seen enough movies to know what this meant; the opportunities the police would have to follow the money; the helicopter surveillance. The low-key tracking, followed by a burst of action: shouting and flashing lights. And then the cellar door would open, and a torch-beam light the way down the stairs . . .

He thought: No. Give up. That's not going to happen.

And then thought: But what's the harm in thinking it? How else should he pass the time while waiting for the axe to fall?

And even as these thoughts fought like butterflies in his crowded head, something thumped on the ceiling above him, and voices cried out in anger or surprise — was that violence he heard? He thought it was violence. A brief outburst ending with another thump, while in his head new pictures painted themselves —

A SWAT team had come crashing in

Armed police had stormed the house

His uncle, the soldier, had tracked him down

Any of the above . . .

And Hassan allowed himself to hope.

Traffic was light, mostly taxis and night-buses. London was a twenty-four-hour city, but only if you counted the things nobody wanted to do, like find a way home in the middle of the night, or head out for a cleaning job in the pitch-dark cold of the morning. Watching through the window, River was trying to get his head round what Lamb had told them before they'd piled into separate cars: that there were three kidnappers. That one was a friendly, but it was anybody's guess which, or how he'd react.

"Are they armed?"

"I'm guessing they've got an edged weapon of some sort. They'd look bloody stupid trying to take the kid's head off with a gherkin."

"So why us?" River asked. "Why not a SWAT team? Why not the achievers?"

Lamb didn't answer.

Through the passenger window River saw a figure curled in a shop doorway under a pyramid of cardboard, but it was gone already; not even a memory. River refocused on his own reflection. His hair was shaggy, and a day's worth of beard graced his chin. He couldn't remember the last time he'd been to a barber's. He supposed they'd have shaved Sid's head first thing. Her head must seem tiny without her hair. She'd look like a Hollywood alien.

His reflection dissolved, and came back when he blinked.

It was all part of the same thing. Hobden, Moody, Hassan Ahmed, Sid being shot — it was all part of somebody else's game, whose pieces seemed to have fallen into place for Lamb. It had been Lady Di he'd gone out to meet. He hadn't said so, but who else could it have been? River himself hadn't laid eyes on Diana Taverner since spending two days tailing her, all those months ago. But Lamb, slow horse or not, had middle-of-the-night parleys with her . . .

They passed a stationer's, its familiar logo lit in blue and white, and a connection he'd fumbled for earlier was made.

"It's money, isn't it?" he said.

"What is?"

"In that envelope. The one Moody took from your office. It's money. It's your flight fund."

Lamb raised an eyebrow. "Flight fund? Haven't heard that in a while."

"But that's what it is."

Lamb said, "Oh, right. Your grandfather. That's where you got it from."

He nodded to himself, as if that were a problem solved.

And he was right, of course; that's where River had heard it. *Every joe needs a flight fund*, the O.B. had said. *Couple of grand, couple of hundred, however much it takes. In the straight world, they'd call it fuck-you money. Dammit, I shouldn't have said that. Don't tell your grandmother.*

River could still remember the thrill that had gone through a twelve-year-old boy, hearing that. Not because of the f-word, but because his grandfather could say *Don't tell your grandmother*, and trust him not to do so. It gave them a secret. It made them joes together.

A flight fund was what you needed when you lived on the edge, and might slip off any moment. Something to feather your fall. To give you the means to walk away.

"Yes," Lamb said, surprising River. "It's a flight fund."

"Right."

"Not a fortune, if you're thinking your ship's come in."

"I wasn't."

"Fifteen hundred, a passport, and a key to a box."

"Switzerland?"

"Fuck you Switzerland. A bank in a two-donkey French town, four hours' drive from Paris."

"Four hours," River repeated.

"Why am I telling you this?"

"So you'll have an excuse to kill me?"

"That's probably it."

Lamb didn't look any different, was still a soft fat rude bastard, still dressed like he'd been thrown through a charity shop window, but Jesus, River thought — Lamb was a joe. He kept a flight fund pinned behind his noticeboard, which he plastered with money-off coupons and out-of-date special offer ads nobody ever saw beyond. Misdirection. It was what a joe did, or so the O.B. had always told River: *There's always someone watching. Make sure they're not seeing what they think they are.*

Crossing the Thames, River saw a world of tall glass buildings. They were mostly in darkness, towers of unilluminated windows casting back pinpricks of light they'd found on the streets below or the skies above, but here and there a pane would be starkly lit, and through some there were figures visible, crouched over desks or just standing in rooms, their attention owned by the unknowable. There was always something going on. And it wasn't always possible, from the outside, to understand what it was.

Of course, hope is what gets you in the end.

Worse than the noise had been the silence that followed.

Hassan was holding his breath, as if he were hiding, rather than being hidden. It half-occurred to him that if these bastards knew how English he was, how wary of drawing attention to himself, they'd forget the colour of his skin and embrace him as one of their own . . . But no, these bastards, they'd never forget his skin. Hassan Ahmed hoped that the SWAT team, the armed police, his uncle the soldier, showed these bastards no mercy, now they'd tracked them down.

Larry, Moe and Curly.

Curly, Larry and Moe.

Hassan didn't give a toss who they were either, all right?

But it wasn't his uncle who burst into the cellar a minute later.

"You."

They meant him.

"On your fucking feet."

But Hassan couldn't get up. Gravity had sealed him to the chair. So they had to help him — grab him. Drag him. Rough-handle him on to shaky legs and pull him through the door and up the stairs. Hassan wasn't sure how much noise he made during this. Perhaps he was praying. Because you always found your gods again. For however long he'd been in that cellar, he'd been begging Allah for release; making all the bargains always made in this situation. Perhaps if Hassan had believed in Him, He wouldn't have abandoned Hassan to the fate of dying for being one of His believers. But Hassan wasn't allowed much time to meditate upon this. Mostly he was being manhandled up a narrow flight of stairs, at the top of which waited whatever was going to happen to him next.

He had thought the execution would happen down in that cellar.

But it happened in the kitchen.

The house was on a terrace that had seen better days, most of them pre-war. The upstairs windows were boarded over and those at ground level thickly curtained, with no light showing. A water stain spattered its façade.

Lamb said, in a harsh whisper, "Hands up who hasn't been drinking tonight?"

Min and Louisa exchanged a look.

"Here." Lamb handed River Moody's gun, the .22. "Point it anywhere near me and I'll take it off you."

It was the first time River had been on a public street with a weapon. It should have weighed more.

He said, "You think they're in there?"

Because the house didn't simply look asleep. It looked dead.

"Act as if they are," Lamb said. They'd driven straight past the house; had parked twenty yards down. Min and Louisa had been right behind them; now all four were crouched beside Lamb's vehicle. River glanced at his watch. If Lamb's estimate had been right, they had five minutes before the achievers turned up. Seven, if you wanted to be strictly accurate.

"We're going in?" he asked.

"We're going in," Lamb said. "You and me. You can do the door." This last to Louisa. "There's a jemmy in the boot. And you watch the back." Min. "Anyone comes out, don't let them see you. But don't lose them. All clear?"

All was clear. Months of waiting for a real job to do: they weren't about to pass it up.

"Okay. Don't anyone get shot or anything. It goes on my record."

Louisa fetched the jemmy, and they approached the house in a line; Min walking straight on by, heading round the corner to watch the back. At the door, Louisa slipped the jemmy in at latch height like a born housebreaker. She leant on it hard, and the door splintered open. And then Lamb was moving faster than a fat man should, wielding an H&K in a double-fisted grip. He snapped to the right two steps in, kicked open a door that led to an empty room. "Armed police!" he shouted. River took the stairs in three bounds. It was dark; no tell-tale strips of yellow painting the doors' outlines. He entered the first room fast and low; spun 360, gun outstretched. "Armed police!" Nothing. Just a pair of mattresses on the floor, and an unzipped sleeping bag curled like a sloughed skin. There was a shout from downstairs. He backed out, kicked open the second door: same story. Another shout: Lamb calling his name. The last door was a bathroom. He pulled the light-cord. A green stain blossomed beneath one of the bath taps, and a shirt hung from the shower rail. It was damp. Lamb shouted his name again. River ran downstairs.

Lamb was silhouetted at the end of the hallway, looking at something on the kitchen floor. His gun was in his hand, but his arm hung by his side.

River said, "Upstairs is clear."

Lamb said, "We need to go."

His voice was ghoulish. Warped.

Louisa Guy approached River from behind. She was holding the jemmy in a two-handed grip. "What is it?"

"We need to go. Now."

River moved closer and stepped through the kitchen doorway.

272

The body sprawled across the kitchen floor had once been taller. Now it lay in a pool of gore, around which a fat bluebottle hummed busily.

Behind him, Louisa said, "Oh sweet Jesus."

On the kitchen table sat a head, raggedly removed from its owner.

River turned and pushed past Louisa. He barely made it out before throwing up into the gutter.

They crossed the black river in a blue car, red memories staining their minds. Enough blood staining their cuffs and their shoes to render them bang to rights at a glance, let alone after forensic study.

The one driving said, "Did you have to . . ."

"Yes."

"He was . . ."

"He was what?"

"I just . . ."

"You just what?"

"I just wasn't ready for it."

"Yeah, right."

"I wasn't."

"No, well, he wasn't either, was he? But guess what? Makes no fucking difference. He's just as fucking dead."

He was. He was dead. They'd left his head on the kitchen table.

How much deader could he get?

"Phones. Now."

Dumbly, they fumbled for their mobiles.

"Where's Harper?"

He was arriving at a trot. "What happened?"

"Your phone," Lamb said.

"My phone?"

"Now, damn it!"

Min Harper fished out his mobile phone; added it to the three Lamb was holding; watched in horror as Lamb dropped all four down the storm drain at his feet.

"Okay, go. Fetch Ho, Loy and White. I'll get Standish."

All of this, to River, like a dream sequence; voices booming in and out of focus; the nearest streetlight swimmy. He felt empty-legged, like a wind might knock him over, and didn't want to look back at the house with its still-open door, with its kitchen, with its table on which sat a severed head. If a head could sit. If a head could sit.

"For fuck's sake, Cartwright, don't do this now."

River said, "I've seen him before."

"We've all seen him before," Lamb said.

274

Louisa Guy ran a trembling hand through her hair. Min Harper touched her elbow, and she shook him off.

"He was one of us, Cartwright. He was a slow horse. Now get moving. Get the others. Don't go home."

River glanced at Min and Louisa, and read their expressions accurately. "We don't know where they live."

"Give me strength." He rattled off addresses: Balham, Brixton, Tower Hamlets.

"Then where?"

"Blake's grave. Soon."

They left in separate cars.

A bare minute later, two black vans arrived, and figures piled out.

"A spook."

"But . . ."

"But fuck all. He was a spook. End of."

He made a chopping motion with one hand.

In both their minds, a head fell to the floor.

"I'm . . ."

"You're what?"

"I'm just . . ."

"You're scared."

"You killed him."

"We killed him."

"I didn't even know you were gunna do that."

"Did you think this was a game?"

"But it changes everything."

"You're a nancy. Nothing's changed."

"Nothing's *changed*? We killed a copper —"

"Spy."

"Spy, copper, what's the difference? You think they'll let this lie? You think they'll — what?"

Because Curly had thrown his head back and screamed in mirthless laughter.

Diana Taverner was in her office. It was shortly after three, and the hub was mostly empty; only a couple of the kids hunched over a console, coordinating surveillance of an animal rights group. She'd just put the phone down. The tactical ops squad — "the achievers" — had gone into the house near Waterloo; it was empty, save for a body. They'd cut his head off. The good part, if you could call it that, was that he'd been dead before that happened.

A fingerprint scan was on its way, but she already knew whose the body was. It wasn't Hassan Ahmed's, so it had to be Alan Black's. Her agent. Jackson Lamb and his crew were nowhere. Her earlier worst thoughts, about things going even more wrong, had come to pass. It was as well she'd set a back-up plan in motion.

Echoing that thought, the phone rang. Ingrid Tearney, her boss. They'd spoken earlier; Taverner had called her from the canal. She was somewhere over the Atlantic, nearer New York than London.

"Ingrid," she said.

"I'm hearing rumours. What's going on, Diana?"

"Like I said earlier. It's Jackson Lamb."

"You're sure?"

"It looks like it." She leant forward; rested her forehead on her palm. Commit to the action, and the voice follows. "The body at Waterloo? It's Alan Black's. He used to be one of Lamb's. Quit last year, but maybe he didn't after all. It looks like Lamb's been playing him all along."

"Jesus wept. This cannot be happening."

"Best I can tell, Lamb was running the kidnapping to make a personal score. Or else, God knows, to make the Service look good. Either way, it's shot to hell. His agent's murdered, and the others are gone, Hassan Ahmed with them. And there's no reason on earth they should stick to their deadline now."

"Christ, Diana, this is your watch —"

"Mine? Slough House hardly falls under my jurisdiction, does it? Before we start the recriminations game, let's get that on the record. And face facts. The body's one of Lamb's people. Lamb knew where to go, for Christ's sake."

Ingrid Tearney said, "He was there, then. At Waterloo."

"Yes. I don't know where he is now. But we'll trace him."

"In time?"

"Ingrid, at this stage he knows as much about Hassan Ahmed's whereabouts as we do. His op's blown. We're looking at damage limitation. I know you're shocked. But he's always been a loose cannon. And ever since the Partner business —"

"Careful."

"I don't officially know what happened then, but I've a shrewd idea. And anyone who can do what Lamb did probably thinks he's above scrutiny. I've been worried about him for some time. That's why I put Sid Baker in there."

"And what did she report?"

"That Lamb runs the place like a mad hermit. Sits in his top-floor lair with the blinds drawn. It's not a big surprise he's tipped over the edge, Ingrid."

She was using her name too often. She'd have to watch that.

"What's Baker said about tonight?"

"She's in no position to say anything. She was one of tonight's casualties."

"Hell's teeth. Did I miss the meeting where war was declared?"

"We're mopping up. I've one of Lamb's people downstairs. It won't take long to get cast-iron proof. All we need is something that puts Lamb with Black since Black quit the Service. Let's face it, Jackson Lamb's not the Friends Reunited type."

"You're very keen on playing the judge."

"Well, it's a fucking mess! We've got the body of a rogue agent, in a house where Hassan Ahmed was held. How's that going to play with the boy's uncle? We can swear we've clean hands till the cows come home, he's still going to smell Service involvement. And this is a man HMG hopes is going to come down on the side of the moderates. We've got to clean it up."

"There's a crew there now?"

"Yes. But they're not investigators, and they don't do forensics. If anything's marked clue, they'll pick it up. But otherwise . . ."

"But otherwise they might miss something that would help the cops find Hassan," Tearney finished.

Both fell silent. A blinking light on Taverner's phone told her she had another call. She ignored it. The receiver felt hot, but she gripped it so tight her hand trembled.

"Okay. Bring him in."

"Lamb?"

"Lamb. Let's see what he has to say for himself."

"What about Hassan Ahmed?"

"I thought you'd covered that."

London rules, she thought. London rules. "I'm going to need to hear you say it, Ingrid."

Some decisions, she wanted other people's fingerprints on from the start.

"Oh, Christ. Having Mahmud Gul's nephew killed on our soil is one thing. Having him killed with our connivance is another. Leave him to the cops, and pray they get to him in time. Either way, I don't want Five appearing in their write-ups."

"Lamb's not likely to come quietly."

"He's not an idiot. Get Duffy on to it. And bring the rest of them in too."

"The rest of them?"

"The Slough House crew. The slow horses. Get them off the streets and find out who knew what before any more damage is done. I don't want mud sticking to Five over this. We get enough flak as it is."

"Consider it done. Safe flight."

For a moment, Diana Taverner sat perfectly still, looking through her wall at the kids on the hub. At all the empty spaces which would be filled in a few short hours by more kids, doing more thankless tasks. They'd have been warned about that as soon as they signed up, of course, and would have pretended to believe it, but nobody ever really did, not at first. Each and every one of them secretly expected to be appreciated. It wasn't going to happen. She'd wanted to drop a spectacular victory in their laps. That wasn't going to happen either. But at least she could make sure the crash happened as far off as possible, and only damaged the dead wood.

Then she rang the crew at the Waterloo house. It was a brief, one-sided conversation: "Disappear the body. Clean the house."

Cleaning houses, when you cleaned them properly, required strong agents. Fire was the safest bet.

Then she returned Nick Duffy's call. He was back in Regent's Park, though well below where she sat now. "Which one? . . . Okay. Five minutes."

"Who was he?"

"Black. Alan Black."

River had never met him. He'd quit Slough House months before River's arrival; one of those in whom the fire that had driven him into the Service had been quenched by quotidian drudgery. River had no idea what failure had landed Black in their company. Asking would have been like dredging up ancestral sins; enquiring which wicked uncle interfered with which parlour maid. More than that, it would have required River to care, and he didn't.

So why had Black's face been familiar?

He sat in the back, with Louisa at the wheel; Min Harper next to her. When the streetlights washed across them, their faces became doughy and unloved, but were, at least, attached to their bodies. The acrid taste of vomit stung River's throat. Streets away, the head on the kitchen table leered at him, and probably always would.

Because River had seen that face before. Last time, it too had been attached to its body. For the moment, he couldn't put the parts together again: the head on the man; the man in his memory. It would come, though. River's recall was good. Already it was churning through possibilities, plucking them like balls from the bubbling air in a lottery machine. No winners yet, but give it time.

"You're sure?"

"That it was Black?"

"Yes."

"Yes. I'm sure. Why did that bastard trash our phones?"

"So no one can trace us."

"Thanks again. I knew that. I meant why's he worried about anyone tracing us?"

River worked it out as he spoke. "We're being set up. We were supposed to be rescuing Hassan Ahmed. We find a former agent, dead. This whole Hassan thing, it must be an op. And it's every which way screwed up."

"How did Lamb know where to go?"

"It was Lady Di he went out to meet earlier, yes?"

"And you're saying she told him?"

River said, "I'm saying that's what he's saying."

"Lamb's running an op?"

"I don't know," River said. "Maybe. But then again, if he was . . ."

"If he was, what?"

River stared out of the window. "If he was, I don't think he'd have screwed up like this."

There was silence from the front seats. Min Harper and Louisa Guy were not big fans of Jackson Lamb.

"He's carrying a flight fund," he told them. "If things had gone belly up, he's got the wherewithal to fade away. He'd not be sending us to collect the others . . ."

He was slower than his companions on this particular uptake.

"Yeah, right."

"Which is why we don't have any phones."

"And are running our arses all over London. While he's where?"

River said, "He didn't have to fetch me. From the hospital."

"He did if he wanted to know what was going on."

"Which he would. If he was running an op."

"So what do we do?" River asked. "What he said? Or head to Regent's Park and start spilling beans?"

This was met with silence; the sound of two bodies still fizzing with alcohol, but shocked out of actual drunkenness.

A blue and yellow blur spun by, siren screaming. Maybe heading for the house they'd just left. But River guessed not. River guessed the tidying up of that particular mess would happen quietly.

Then he heard: "I guess, if he's not at Blake's grave, we'll know we've been screwed."

"And if we're gunna be screwed, we might as well all be screwed at once."

"It'll save time."

River felt grateful, though wasn't entirely sure why.

"Okay. So did either of you get those addresses?"

Without taking her eyes from the road, Louisa Guy recited them, note perfect.

"Nice one," said River, impressed.

"Well, if they turn out wrong, that'll be a clue, won't it?"

"We'd better split," he said. "You do Loy and Ho. Drop me here. I'll head back for White."

"You'll manage for transport?"

"Please," River said. The car slowed; stopped. He got out. "See you later."

In a different car, Curly screamed in mirthless laughter.

"What? What's funny?"

"You think they'd have let it lie otherwise? When we chop the Paki's head off?"

"The plan was never to do it."

"Your plan was never to do it," Curly said. "Your plan."

Hassan was in the boot. They'd pulled the hood over his head, and tied his wrists. *If you shout or make a noise, I'll cut your fucking tongue out.*

"How did you know?"

"Know what?" Curly asked.

"That he was a . . . spook."

Curly tapped the breast pocket of his denim jacket, where his mobile nestled. "Got a call, didn't I?"

"You weren't supposed to have a phone."

"Good job I did. Else we'd still be back there with that fucking traitor. Waiting for the SAS."

He wasn't supposed to have a phone, it was true. Mobile phones could be traced: Larry's rule. But before they could trace you via your phone, they had to know it was yours. Otherwise it was only a mobile signal, and everyone had one of those. So he'd bought a pre-pay, and had used it to call Gregory Simmonds, the Voice of Albion, every couple of hours. Because any time Simmonds stopped answering his phone, that meant the cops were on to them.

Curly had encountered Simmonds through the British Patriotic Party's website, where he'd posted messages as Excalibur88, the 88 meaning HH, *Heil Hitler*. This was just after the Lockerbie bomber had been sent home. There'd been scenes on TV of him meeting a hero's welcome: happy flag-waving crowds. Meanwhile the BNP was being taken to court, because it was against the law to have a party only for true Englishmen, and believers' names were being plastered on the internet, an invitation to left-wing thugs to throw bricks through windows, and threaten wives and families.

The issue, Curly posted, was simple. White man dies in a bomb attack? String up a Muslim from a lamppost. Right here, right now. Didn't matter who. It wasn't like the tube bombers had checked out their victims in advance, making sure there weren't kids or nurses on the trains. You string one up and then another, to show them who they were dealing with. Kick me once, I kick you twice. And then jump on your head. That's how you win a war, and this was a war.

So then he'd been contacted by Gregory Simmonds, the Voice of Albion. A short man with tall opinions, Simmonds had made his money in long-haul logistics, what used to be called removals. He'd founded the Voice because he was sick of seeing this once-proud country dragged downhill by scumbag politicians in the pockets of foreign interests — conversation with him was like listening to a party broadcast, but he wasn't all talk. Voice of Albion was about action. There were a couple of other guys Simmonds knew, a plan coming together. Was Curly interested in action?

Curly was. Curly would have liked to be a soldier. Never worked out, so he was mostly unemployed, but he did a weekly off-the-books stint as an exit-coordinator at a club, what used to be called bouncing. This was in Bolton. There were more exciting cities, more exciting lives.

So anyway. Officers stayed behind the lines, but Simmonds was putting the plan together, with help from these other guys, Moe and Larry.

What they had in mind was an internet execution.

Most people would have chickened out hearing that. Most people would have thought Simmonds was out of his mind. But Curly, because he knew Simmonds was expecting him to say something, and he hated doing what he was expected to do, just drank the lager Simmonds had been buying all evening, and waited.

Until Simmonds said: Thing was, they didn't actually have to cut anyone's head off. They just had to make it look like they were going to. Show the world it could be done. That was the point. Show they could do it if they wanted. That if there was a war, it would be fought on both sides. Was Curly in?

Curly thought about it, but not for long. He was in.

The only part he'd had trouble with was the bit about not actually doing it.

And because he didn't know Larry or Moe, which meant he didn't trust them, he'd played stupid in their company and kept in touch with Simmonds behind their back. Which was how he'd got the call forty minutes earlier, the Voice of Albion ringing him for a change, breathy and terrified. *Compromised* was the word he used. It had filtered down through a contact in the BPP. The mission was *compromised*. They should get out. They should disappear.

Simmonds didn't use Larry's name. Didn't have to. If one of them was a spy, it had to be Larry, who'd managed to make every decision sound like his own.

"Which way?"

Rising panic in his voice. Curly kept his own flat: "Just keep driving." They were still south of the river. But not turning back was the main thing.

He could have run when Simmonds' call came through. He could have been down the stairs and out the front. The others didn't know his real name. He could have been part of the nightlife in minutes, miles away.

286

Instead he'd stood and run a finger along the grimy bedroom wall. Adapted himself to the moment; let these new circumstances sink in. And then he'd left the room and walked downstairs and along the hallway into the kitchen.

The axe leant against the wall like a household tool. Wooden handle, red-and-grey blade, like in a cartoon. Curly had plucked it with his left hand in passing; tossed it into his right without breaking stride. Nice weight. Smooth in the hand. Soldiers felt like this, shouldering rifles.

In the kitchen Moe, at the table, half-turned at his approach. Larry was against the sink, can of Coke in hand. Both were same as always: Moe with a black tee-shirt, and that stupid goatee tickling his chin; Larry with his busy eyes and mildly fuzzed head, his rolled-up sleeves, smart jeans, new trainers. Looked like he was playing a role. As if this was a game, *not like we're actually going to cut his head off*: Larry's superior in-charge smile stuck to his jaw. The smile slipped when he saw Curly. Words were spoken:

What

Why

For fuck's sake

They slipped past Curly; unimportant moments, swallowed by the business at hand.

He'd swung the axe in a sweeping motion that almost caught the ceiling, but instead carved a graceful slice from the air before slamming to a halt in his target's back.

The force of the blow sent a shockwave up his arm.

Moe coughed blood and slammed facedown on to the table.

Larry had always done the talking. But Moe had been the thinker.

Now Curly said to Larry, "Not too slowly. Don't draw attention."

Larry, on whose face a superior in-charge smile wasn't likely to reappear soon, upped their speed.

Curly could still feel it in the muscles in his arm. Not the swing of the axe, but the abrupt stop it had come to. He rubbed his elbow, which seemed to give off heat, like a newly extinguished lightbulb.

In the boot of the car, bound and gagged, Hassan clenched his body tight, as if this might hold his life in place.

"Downstairs" at Regent's Park meant different things, depending on the context. *Downstairs* was where records were kept; downstairs was where the car park was. But there was another downstairs, much lower, and downstairs, in this context, took you lower than the building was high. This downstairs wasn't anywhere you wanted to be.

In Central London, there's almost as much city beneath the streets as above. Some of this is publicly available: the underground itself, of course, and certain sites of special interest, the War Rooms and various bomb shelters among them. And then there's everywhere else. Sometimes, names leak into the public domain — Bastion, Rampart, Citadel, Pindar — but they remain off-limits; part of Fortress London, the

288

complex of subterranean passages and tunnels — the "crisis management facilities" — that exist less to defend the capital itself than to protect its systems of government. If the worst happens, whether toxic, nuclear, natural or civil, these are the redoubts from which control will be reasserted. They are fundamental to London's geography, and appear on no A–Z.

And then there are the other, less acknowledged hidden places, like those under Regent's Park.

The elevator ran slowly, and this was deliberate. A long slow descent had a weakening effect on anyone here involuntarily, inducing in those who were conscious a nervous, vulnerable state. Diana Taverner passed the while checking her reflection. For a woman who'd had less than four hours' sleep in the past thirty, she thought she looked pretty good. But then, she thrived on the dangerous edge. Even when life was on a smoother track, she took corners on two wheels: office/gym/office/winebar/office/home was a typical day, and sleep was never high on her agenda. Sleep was ceding control. While you slept, anything might happen.

It might while you were awake, too. Her agent, Alan Black, was dead; killed by the Voice of Albion thugs. Any other operation, and that would be it: the whole house of cards would have folded. There'd be an inquiry. When an agent died, there was a ripple effect. Sometimes the splash was so big, careers were washed away.

But this had been run under Moscow rules, like a deep-cover op on foreign ground. As far as Black's record showed, he'd quit the Service last year, and

Taverner had had only one face-to-face with him since he'd gone under. The Voice of Albion was a below-the-radar bunch of Toytown fascists, consisting, until Black had stirred them up, of one man and his dog. None of the op details — the safe-house address, Black's co-conspirators, the vehicles they'd used — existed anywhere on paper or, God forbid, the ether. And yesterday's report to Limitations had kept the details scanty; a "watching brief" fell far short of surveillance, and Taverner couldn't be blamed if Albion had slipped the leash . . . It was patchy, but Taverner had sealed leakier ops. One watertight report was worth any amount of tradecraft.

The elevator eased to a halt. Diana Taverner stepped into a corridor markedly different from those above ground level; here was exposed brickwork and bare concrete floor, pitted and puddled like a temporary pavement. Water dripped. It was an atmosphere that required careful maintenance. To Taverner's mind, it reeked of cliché, but tests had proved its effectiveness.

Nick Duffy waited, leaning against a door. The door had a peephole, but the cover had been slapped across it.

"Any problems?"

His look answered that, but he said it anyway. "None at all."

"Good. Now fetch the rest."

"The rest?"

"The slow horses. All of them."

He said, "Fine," but didn't move. Instead he said, "I know it's not my place to ask. But what's going on?"

"You're right. It's not your place."

"Right. I'm on it."

He headed for the lift now, but turned when she called. "Nick. I'm sorry. Things have gone arse over tit. You've probably noticed." The vulgarity startled Taverner almost as much as it did Duffy. "This kidnapping business — it's not what it seemed."

"And Slough House is involved?"

She didn't answer.

He said, "Jesus Christ."

"Bring them in. Separately. And Nick — I'm sorry. He was a friend, wasn't he? Jed Moody."

"We worked together."

"Lamb's story is he tripped over his own feet, broke his neck. But . . ."

"But what?"

Taverner said, "It's too soon to say. But take Lamb yourself. And watch him, Nick. He's trickier than he looks."

"I know all about Jackson Lamb," Duffy assured her. "He put one of my men down earlier."

"Then know this too." She hesitated. "If he's involved in this kidnapping, he'll disappear sooner than be brought in. And he's a streetfighter."

Duffy waited.

"I can't give an instruction, Nick. But if people are going to get hurt, I'd rather it was them than us."

"Them and us?"

"Nobody was expecting this. Go. The Queens'll give you their mobile locations. Call in soon."

Duffy caught the lift.

As Diana Taverner tapped the fingerpad to unlock the door he'd been leaning on, she thought briefly of Hassan Ahmed, who had ceased to be a priority. One of two things was going to happen to Hassan. He'd turn up on a street corner, unharmed, or his body would be dumped in a ditch. The latter was more likely. Having killed Black, the Albion crew weren't likely to let Hassan live. In their shoes, Taverner wouldn't wait. But maybe that was just her. She set a high priority on watching her own back.

The fingerpad buzzed. The door unlocked.

She stepped inside, prepared to break a slow horse.

There was silence from the boot. They'd have drugged the kid again, but it was Moe who'd had the chloroform, and if he'd had more, they'd not found it. Moe had been responsible for most things: choosing the target, finding the house, all the website stuff. Larry had thought he was in charge, but it was Moe all the time. Fucking spook.

"We could dump him," Larry said suddenly.

"Where?"

"Anywhere. We could park and walk away."

"And then what?"

". . . Disappear."

Right. But nobody ever disappeared. They just went somewhere else. "Keep driving," Curly told him.

It still powered through his arm, the force of that blow. The blade had half-disappeared in Moe's back — it looked like he'd sprouted an extra limb — and then there was blood everywhere, some of it pounding through Curly's ears. Larry's mouth flapped, and maybe he'd shouted and maybe he hadn't. It was hard to tell. It probably only lasted seconds. Moe coughed what remained of his life on to the kitchen table, and all through Curly's arm the power sang.

But cutting his head off, leaving it there . . . Why had he done that?

Because it was legend.

Outside, rows of shops dawdled past. Even when their names weren't familiar, they were knock-offs of ones that were: Kansas Fried Chicken, JJL Sports. Everywhere was like everywhere else, and this was the world he'd grown up in. Things used to be different. Gregory Simmonds, the Voice of Albion, was very clear on that point. Things used to be different, and if the natural children of these islands were to enjoy their birthright, they had to be that way again.

He checked behind him. There they were on the back seat: the digicam and its tripod; the laptop and all its cables. He wasn't sure how that worked, but it didn't matter. Getting it on film was the main thing. He'd work out how to post it to the web later.

The axe was there too, wrapped in a blanket. In videos he'd seen, they'd used swords; whacking great blades that sliced through bone like butter. Curly had an English axe. Different strokes for different folks.

A giggle escaped him.

"What?"

"Nothing. Keep your eyes on the road."

Legend. In the pubs and on the estates, on the internet, in all the places where people still said what they thought and weren't afraid of being locked up for saying it, they'd be heroes. It would be a life lived in the shadows, one step ahead of the cops. He'd be the conquering hero, Robin Hood, famous for dealing this mighty blow; showing the foreign fanatics that they weren't the only ones who could draw blood, that not all Englishmen were too frightened to fight back. That there was a resistance. That resistance would win.

He looked sideways and recognized the fear Larry was trying to hide. That was okay. All Larry had to do was what he was told, and he'd do that because he wasn't currently capable of independent thought.

If he was, it would have occurred to him that they'd stand a better chance of getting away if there was only one of them doing it.

But Larry kept driving.

This darkness was smaller than the last. Hassan was hooded again, with a handkerchief stuffed in his mouth, his knees tucked up to his chest, and his hands bound. When he flexed them, the cord dug into his wrists. But even if it snapped, what would he do? He was in the boot of a moving car. His captors still had him. *Two* captors, because one was dead. His head had been left on the table in that house.

They'd brought him up from the cellar, into the kitchen, and there it had been, on the table. A human head. It sat in a pool of blood. What else could he say about it? It had been a head, and Hassan had seen films in which severed heads had been displayed, and had laughed at how "unrealistic" they were, without it ever occurring to him that he had no frame of reference for the level of realism achieved. And now he did. And all he could think was that a real severed head was little different from a movie severed head, with one critical difference: it was real. The blood was real. The hair and teeth were real. The whole thing was real. Which meant that what he'd been told, *We're going to cut your head off and show it on the web*, was also real. *Fucking Paki.*

He had wet himself, and the jumpsuit clung to his legs. He wished he could remove it, and dry himself off. Wished he could have a shower, and change, and go to sleep, somewhere which wasn't the boot of a moving car. If he were going to make wishes, perhaps that was the end he should start at. He should wish he were free and safe, and could worry about changing his trousers in his own sweet time.

The comedy voice in his head had fallen silent. There were issues that were not suitable for comedy. This argument had weekly been shot down in flames at the student stand-up society; try putting forward that point of view, and you'd be accused of fascism. Freedom of speech mattered more than notions of taste and propriety. Hassan Ahmed had agreed with that. How could he not? When the moment came, and he took his stand at the mic, it was all going to come out. Daring, edgy stuff. Nothing off-limits. That was the contract between stand-up and audience: they had to know you were baring your soul. Except now Hassan had encountered a severed head on a kitchen table, and had immediately understood that this was not something that could ever be the subject of a joke. And even if it could, it was not a joke that Hassan could make. Because it proved that the people holding him were capable of cutting off heads.

The thumps and jolts and crashings would not stop. The cord binding his wrists would not fray. Hassan would not find himself unleashed, but would lie suffering until the car reached its destination, and then he too would reach his destination. This was his last journey.

296

So even if he could. Even if he could make the best joke ever. Even if he could make the best joke ever, with its subject the decapitation of unwilling humans, this was not a joke Hassan could ever make, because Hassan was never going to make jokes again. Not that he had made that many to begin with. Because if he were to be uncompromisingly harsh on himself — if he were to tell the truth, observing the contract between stand-up and audience — Hassan would have to admit this too: that he had never been particularly funny. He could make jokes, yes. He could ride riffs. He could unreel a comedy thread and wrap it round the usual observation posts: quips about old people shopping, and teenagers texting, and how nobody smiles on buses. But only in his head. He had never been himself in public. And now never would be. Doing so would remain forever on the list of things Hassan had intended to do in his twenties; a list which would never grow longer and never grow shorter, for Hassan's twenties were not going to happen.

Because these people were never going to let him go. Not without killing him first. *We're going to cut your head off and show it on the web. Fucking Paki.*

The car bounced and bashed him, and Hassan Ahmed tried to make himself smaller. In his mind, he escaped in seventy different ways, but his body remained in the boot.

The common wisdom was that car-theft gave you a buzz, but that probably only held true if your evening hadn't already involved blood, firearms and a severed head. The car was a beat-up Austin, taken from a sidestreet, and River guessed its owner's reaction on finding it gone would be a sigh of relief. There were no spare keys in the glove compartment or behind the rearview mirror, but there was a mobile phone in the former; a chunky grey thing that looked like River's own phone's distant ancestor. Hotwiring took him seven minutes, which was probably six minutes fifty over the record. He'd driven back the way they'd come, crossed the river at Blackfriars, then tried to use the phone to call the hospital again, only to find it was pre-pay, and out of credit.

This, at least, gave him a buzz, but not a welcome one. Throwing the phone through the window would have relieved his feelings, but he settled for swearing heavily. Swearing was good. Swearing helped. It kept his mind off the possibility that Sid was dead; kept it, too, from flashing back to the head on the kitchen table, raggedly sawn from its owner.

But why had it been familiar?

He didn't want to dwell on it, but knew he had to . . . The answer was buried within his subconscious and ought to be within his grasp. He stopped swearing. Remembered he was on a mission, and came to a halt at a junction, re-establishing his bearings. He was on Commercial Road; heading for Tower Hamlets, where he'd collect Kay White. Stationary, he was hooted by a car behind, which swung out to pass him. He swore again. Sometimes it was good to have a visible enemy.

Because God knows, River thought bitterly, he was weary of the invisible kind.

Pushing thoughts of severed heads aside, he resumed his journey. Another two minutes, and he found his turning: on the left-hand side was a three-storey brick-built block, its matching window frames and guttering marking it out as association housing. Maybe twenty yards ahead, double-parked outside what could easily be Kay's address, was the car that had hooted him three minutes ago: lights on, engine running. A figure hulked behind the wheel. River reversed into a space, and disconnected the ignition wires. Got out and walked back to the main road. Turned the corner, dropped to one knee and peered back round, just as a man brought Kay White out of her home and loaded her into the waiting car.

She was neither cuffed nor roughly handled. The man was guiding her by the elbow, but it could have been taken as support if you didn't know what you were watching. He settled her into the back seat, and got in after her. The car moved off. The moments during which River could have done anything to stop any of this had been over before he got here, and he wasn't sure what use he'd have made of them anyway. The last time he'd tried an intervention, Sid had wound up lying in the street.

The car reached the next junction, turned, and was gone.

River returned to the Austin, and stole it all over again.

Struan Loy's night had started promisingly. He'd had a date, his first in three years, and had planned it like an attempt at Everest, the base camps being wine bar, Italian restaurant and her place. Base one had proved a tremendous success, inasmuch as she had turned up; base two less impressive, as she'd left halfway through, and base three remained whereabouts unknown. Loy had returned home to an unmade bed and three hours' sleep, interrupted by the arrival of Nick Duffy.

Now he sat blinking in harsh underground light. The room was padded, its walls covered with a black synthetic material which smelled of bleach. A table dead centre had a straight-backed chair on either side, one of them bolted to the floor. This was the one on which Loy had been told to sit.

"So," he said to Diana Taverner. "What's up?"

He was aiming for a carefree delivery, with about as much success as Gordon Brown.

"Why should anything be up, Struan?"

"Because I've been brought here in the middle of the night."

And certainly looked like he'd dressed in the dark, thought Taverner.

"Nick Duffy brought you here because I asked him to," she said. "We're downstairs because I don't want anyone to know you're here. And we're not having this chat because you've done anything wrong. We're having it because I'm reasonably sure you haven't."

She leant just enough on *reasonably* for him to pick it up.

He said, "I'm glad to hear it."

Taverner said nothing.

"Because I'm pretty sure I haven't done anything."

"Pretty sure?"

"A turn of phrase."

She said nothing.

"I mean, I know I haven't done anything."

She said nothing.

"Or not since, you know."

"Not since that e-mail suggesting that your boss and mine, Ingrid Tearney, was an Al Qaeda plant."

He said, "It was the outfit she wore on *Question Time*, you know, that desert-gown thing . . ."

She said nothing.

"It was a joke."

"And we have a sense of humour. Otherwise you'd not have seen the light of day since."

Loy blinked.

She said, "Only kidding."

He nodded uncertainly, as if receiving his first glimpse of how unfunny jokes could be.

Diana Taverner glanced at her watch, not caring he knew it. He only had one chance to climb on board. This wasn't a decision he could mull over, and get back to her in the morning.

"So now you're in Slough House," she said. "How's that working out?"

"Well, you know . . ."

"How's that working out?"

"Not so great."

"But you haven't quit."

"No. Well . . ."

She waited.

"Not sure what I'd do otherwise, to be honest."

"And you're still wondering whether you'll ever be let back upstairs."

"Upstairs?"

"The Park. Do you want to hear something really funny, Struan? Do you want to hear how many people have made the journey back from Slough House to Regent's Park?"

He blinked. He already knew the answer to that. Everyone knew the answer to that.

She told him anyway. "None. It's never happened."

He blinked again.

She said, "Of course, that doesn't mean it never will. Nothing's impossible."

This time he didn't blink. In his eyes, she saw wheels starting to turn; possibilities sliding into place like tabs into slots.

He didn't speak, but he shifted in his chair. Leant forward, as if this was a conversation he was sharing, rather than an interrogation he was subject to.

She said, "Have you noticed anything unusual at Slough House lately?"

"No," he said, with absolute certainty.

She said nothing.

"I don't think so," he added.

She checked her watch again.

"What sort of unusual thing?"

"Activity. Activity above and beyond the normal course of events."

He thought about it. While he was doing so, Diana Taverner reached for her bag, which she'd hung on the back of her chair. From it she produced a black-and-white photograph, three inches by five, which she placed on the table between them. Turned it so it was facing Loy. "Recognize him?"

"It's Alan Black."

"Your former colleague."

"Yes."

"Seen him recently?"

"No."

"You're sure?"

"Yes."

"You haven't seen him lately in Jackson Lamb's company?"

"No."

"Well, that presents us with a problem."

She sat back and waited.

"A problem," he said at last.

"Yes. A problem," she agreed. "Tell me, Struan. How would you like to be part of the solution?"

In Struan Loy's eyes, wheels turned again.

"Should we go round the back?"

"Can we get round the back?"

"There might be an alley."

Min Harper and Louisa Guy were at Ho's place; had pulled into the last available space moments before another car had arrived, slowed, then headed on down the street and parked. The pair watched without speaking while a man emerged.

They were in Balham, a stone's throw from the railway line. Brixton, where they'd stopped for Struan

Loy, had been a washout: he was either not at home or had died in his sleep. Like all the slow horses, Loy lived alone. That seemed a stark statistic, and it was odd that it hadn't occurred to Min Harper before. He didn't know whether Loy was single from choice or circumstance; divorced, separated or what. It seemed unsatisfactory, this ignorance about his colleagues, and he'd thought about raising the subject with Louisa, but she was driving. All the alcohol they'd put away earlier, it seemed a good idea to let her concentrate on that. Come to think of it, there was other stuff they should be discussing, but that too had better wait. From out of nowhere, they were on an op. How had that happened?

"So . . ."

The man they'd been watching slipped out of sight.

"Okay. Let's try it."

Crossing the road, Min felt his jacket bang against his hip. The paperweight. He was still carting the paperweight he'd used earlier, when confronting the masked intruder who turned out to be Jed Moody. He rubbed his thumb along its surface without taking it from his pocket. He hadn't hit Moody with it. Hadn't needed to. They'd taken a tumble, and only Min had got to his feet. He supposed that should go in the account book somewhere, in the opposite column to the one where he'd stepped off a tube train without a disk, and his career had gone whistling away down the dark tunnel.

He hadn't liked Jed Moody, but didn't enjoy knowing he'd been the instrument of his death. He suspected he hadn't got to the bottom of that feeling yet. Everything had happened so swiftly since that he hadn't yet taken it on board.

Leave it for now, he thought. You could coast for a while on that mantra. *Leave it for now.*

"What do you reckon?"

"Looks doable."

They'd found a thin strip of unpaved passage between the backs of one row of houses and those on the next road. It was unlit, overgrown, and neither had a torch, but Ho lived only four houses along. Louisa led the way. The bushes were wet, and hung with cobweb. Underfoot was slick with mud, and they were walking close enough that if either went down, both would. Any other night, it would make for a comedy moment.

"This one?"

"That's what I make it."

Light showed from an upper storey. Ho seemed to have an upstairs conservatory. They climbed the fence, a flimsy wooden construction, and as Min dropped into the paved-over garden, a plank snapped cleanly behind him with a noise like a bullet. He froze, expecting alarms or sirens, but the noise simply disappeared into the dark. No curtains twitched; no voices were raised. Louisa Guy dropped next to him.

For another moment they waited. Min's hand dropped to his pocket again, and his thumb stroked the paperweight's smooth surface. Then the pair advanced on the back door.

As they got closer, Min thought he could hear music.

★ ★ ★

Audible music strained from an upstairs room, and light bled skywards from a skylight. It was what — after four? And Dan Hobbs could hear the music out here in the street.

He thought: I was a neighbour, I'd break the runt's neck. Toss a wheelie bin through his window to grab his attention, and then take him by the neck and squeeze until his eyes pop like grapes.

Dan Hobbs wasn't having the best night of his life.

He leant on the bell.

After his encounter with Jackson Lamb at the hospital, he'd come to on the floor; no obvious bruising, but he felt like he'd been trampled underfoot. The storeroom door hung open. River Cartwright was gone. Hobbs had got to his feet and made his way upstairs, where the first person he'd encountered was the newly arrived Nick Duffy.

And Hobbs learned the hard way that shit travels downwards.

"He was just this fat guy. How was I to know —"

"Remember Sam Chapman? Bad Sam?"

Hobbs did.

"Bad Sam once said he wasn't frightened of anyone except overweight guys with bad breath and ill-fitting shirts. You know why?"

Hobbs didn't.

"Because once in a nun's nightmare, one of them would turn out to be Jackson Lamb. And by the time you'd realized that, you'd lost your lunch, your boots and most of your teeth. Now fuck off back to the Park."

A couple of hours' fuming, and he had new instructions; another slow horse to collect.

"Name's Roderick Ho." Duffy read out the address. "Slough House geek. Think you can handle him on your own?"

Hobbs took a breath. The Service was hierarchical, to put it mildly, but you didn't get to be one of the Dogs by meekly observing the protocols. "In my fucking sleep," he told his boss. "You said yourself, even Sam Chapman couldn't take Lamb, and I didn't know it was him. So give me a break, all right?"

A twelve-second silence followed. Then Duffy said, "You're as much use as an elastic anchor, you know that? But my four-year-old niece could take down Ho, so I'm going to trust you."

Carefully keeping relief from his voice, Hobbs asked, "How hard do I bring him in?"

"C&C."

Dogs' slang for collect-and-comfort. Which meant without worrying onlookers.

"And Dan? Screw this up, and I'll sack your whole family."

He wouldn't. This wouldn't wipe the slate, but would show he was still in the game. And intended to remain there.

And the next time he encountered Jackson Lamb —

But he shook that thought free too. Nothing screwed you up faster than keeping score.

And now he was at Ho's place. He'd have gone in through the back, but the music changed the rules. Ho was awake. Possibly had company. Geeks had social lives. Who knew?

Company or not, nobody was opening the door. He leant on the bell again, and stayed there.

Having been caught once this evening, he'd done his research, or had the Queens of the Database do it for him. Roderick Ho's records had been on his BlackBerry long before he'd got here, and it was clear from the physicals that if Ho hadn't been geek-supreme, he'd have been invalided out to spare everyone's embarrassment. He looked the type to wear a smog-mask on the tube. And if it turned out the records lied, and Ho was Bruce Lee's forgotten cousin, that was fine too. Hobbs knew some moves himself.

Did the music stutter? Something had happened. Without taking his hand from the bell, Hobbs peered through the marbled window. A fuzzy shape was coming to the door.

Roderick Ho hadn't been to bed. Roderick Ho didn't sleep much anyway, but tonight he had business. Tonight, he was paying off a debt.

On his way home he'd picked up two economy-sized bags of tortilla chips, and had dropped both when a twat in a Lexus honked him on a zebra . . . His glasses had slipped off when he'd bent to retrieve them, and the twat in the Lexus honked again, and it was obvious he'd been enjoying this, was simply livening up those dead moments when he'd been forced to wait at a crossing for a *pedestrian*, for fuck's sake. Because the road belonged to car-users. Belonged to SI 123, as his plate had it. Ho retrieved his glasses, gathered up his bags of chips. He'd barely cleared the Lexus's wheelbase when it roared past, and he knew he wasn't even a memory by this point. At best, he was a punchline. *Should have seen the chinky jump.*

That had been then. This was now:

SI 123 was Simon Dean of Colliers Wood, and Ho wasn't up at four because it had taken him that long to discover this, he was up at four because he was taking Simon Dean's life apart piece by piece. Simon Dean was a tele-salesman for a life-assurance company, or that's what he probably still thought he was, though one of his last acts before leaving work, according to the rigorously backed-up e-mail system his company maintained, had been to send a resignation note to his boss, accompanied by a detailed account of Simon's intentions regarding the boss's teenage daughter. Since then, Simon had maxed out his credit cards, cancelled his standing orders, transferred his mortgage to a new lender at a distressingly poor rate, changed his phone number, and sent everyone in his address book a wedding-sized bouquet of flowers accompanied by a coming-out note. He'd donated his savings to the Green Party and embraced Scientology; had sold his Lexus on eBay; and within forty-eight hours would become aware of his status as a registered sex offender, as would everyone else in his postcode. All in all, Simon Dean was not in for the happiest time of his life; but, looking on the bright side, Roderick Ho felt chirpier than he'd done in ages. And his tortilla chips, it turned out, hadn't been much damaged by their fall.

It wasn't surprising that he'd lost track of the time; allowing his CD changer to keep on pumping music. What was surprising was that his online reverie shimmered at all, and that he noticed something vying for his attention. There was someone at the door. They'd possibly been there for a while.

Jesus, thought Ho. Wasn't a man allowed any peace? He hated it when others failed to show consideration. Shutting the music off, he went down to find out who was disturbing him.

Louisa Guy had a headache coming on, maybe caused by her proximity to the dead. Two deaths tonight. Both colleagues, even if Alan Black had lost that role long before he'd lost his head. She'd smelt the blood before stepping into the kitchen; had known she was about to see something disgusting. But she'd assumed it would be the hostage, Hassan. And instead there he was, there was his head, Alan Black. A man she'd not given a thought to since she'd last laid eyes on him. Hadn't given him a thought before then, to be frank.

Seeing him, the air had gone out of her. Everything became slow. But she'd kept her grip — kept her head — hadn't thrown up like Cartwright. She almost wished she had. She wondered what it said about her, that she could see something like that and not throw up . . . Cartwright's unexpected vulnerability made her readjust her opinion of him. Fact was, she'd avoided most of her colleagues, except, lately, Min Harper. Fact was, the same held true for all of them. They'd been thrown together by fate and poor judgement, and had never operated as a team before. It was somewhat ironic that they were just starting to do so now the team was significantly smaller.

And now she was in the dark again, this time in Ho's back garden. She wondered how come Ho had a garden when everyone she knew lived in shoeboxes. But there was no point wondering why bastards prosper. Min at her side, she advanced towards Ho's back door, forcing herself not to grind her teeth as she did so. There were lights on, and she could hear music. Funny how Ho could be careful in some ways and damn stupid in others. The lengths he'd gone to to keep his head below the parapet, and here he was winding the neighbours up with unnecessary noise after dark.

She and Min looked at each other, and shrugged at the same time.

Louisa reached out and banged on Ho's door.

"What?"

Surly guy, scrawnily built, early twenties, wearing a Che tee-shirt and a pair of Hawaiian shorts.

Any of the above was enough to earn him Dan Hobbs's lasting enmity, but worst of all was the fact that he wasn't Roderick Ho.

"I'm looking for Ho," Hobbs said.

"You're looking for *what*?"

"Roderick Ho."

"Your ho's not here, man. It's like four in the morning. You out your fucking mind, ringing people's bells?"

The door swung shut, or would have done, if Hobbs's foot hadn't been in the way. Hobbs was mentally verifying information, and affirming what he knew: that he hadn't screwed up; that this was the address Duffy had given him, confirmed by the Queens of the Database. The surly guy opened the door wide again, his expression suggesting that he was about to remonstrate. It was a cheque he never got to cash. Hobbs punched him once, a short jab in the throat. With a civilian you could phone first, tell them you were about to hit them, and it wouldn't help them any. Hobbs closed the door, stepped over the man, and went looking for Ho.

What felt like a long time ago, back when he was first feeling his way round the Service systems, Roderick Ho had gone into his personnel records and changed his address. If he'd been asked why, he wouldn't have understood the question. He did it for the same reason he never gave his real name when taking out a loyalty card: because you never gave a stranger the inside track. Look at Simon Dean. Bloody vanity plate. He might as well be handing out cards with the word Tosser printed above his bank details. To be fair, any number plate would have worked as well, but why make life easy for the other side? And as far as Roderick Ho was concerned, everybody was the other side until proved otherwise.

So how come Min Harper and Louisa Guy were in his back yard?

". . . What?"

"Do you always play your music this time of night?"

"Neighbours are students. Who cares?" Ho scratched his head. He wore the same clothes he'd worn when he'd left Slough House ten hours previously, though his sweater was now dusted with tortilla crumbs. As for these two, he couldn't remember what they'd been wearing then, but they didn't look like they'd slept since. Ho didn't do well with people, on account of not liking them, but even he could tell this pair were different tonight. For a start, they were a pair. He'd have asked what was up, but he had a more important question first.

"How did you find me?"

"Why? Were you hiding?"

He said it again. "How?"

"Lamb told us."

"Fucking Lamb," said Ho. "I don't like him."

"I'm not sure he likes you. But he sent us to get you."

"So here we are."

Ho shook his head. He was wondering how Lamb had known he'd altered his records, let alone knew where he lived. And with that thought came another, even more disturbing. What Lamb knew about the digital world could be wrapped inside a pixel. There was no way he'd unpeeled Ho's secrets the honourable way: using a computer. Which suggested the horrible possibility that there were other ways of dismantling a life, and that maybe being a digital warrior didn't bestow invulnerability.

But Ho didn't want to live in a world where that was possible. Didn't want to believe it could happen. So he shook his head again, to dislodge the notion and send it fluttering into the night air, which was rapidly becoming the early morning air.

Then said, "I'll get my laptop."

Duffy said, "What?"

"He's not here."

"So where is he?"

Hobbs said, "I don't know."

There was a moment's silence, during which Dan Hobbs could hear the remains of his career blowing like a tumbleweed down the corridors of Regent's Park.

Then Duffy hung up on him.

He had never visited her flat, nor wasted time wondering what it might be like, so was neither surprised nor reassured by its appearance: an art deco block in St John's Wood, its edges rounded off, its windows metal-framed. Orwell had lived nearby, and had probably stolen local details when constructing his fascist future, but this particular block seemed ordinary enough in the early morning, with its shared entrance and its buzzer system that blinked continuously. Only the sign promising CCTV coverage hinted at Big Brother's world, but signs were cheaper than the actual thing. The UK might be the most surveilled society in the world, but that was on the public purse, and building management companies generally preferred the cheaper option of hanging a fake camera. It took Jackson Lamb a minute to get through the lock, which was of more recent vintage than the building, but not by a huge amount. His feet would have clicked on the tiled surface of the lobby if he'd let them. Only one of the doors he passed on the ground floor showed a light underneath.

Lamb took the stairs: quieter, more reliable, than a lift. Such caution was second nature. It was like pulling on an old coat. *Moscow rules*, he'd decided when meeting Diana Taverner by the canal. She was nominally on his side — nominally his boss — but she'd been playing a dirty game, so Moscow rules it was. And now her game was all over the place, scattered like a Scrabble board, so it was London rules instead.

If Moscow rules meant watch your back, London rules meant cover your arse. Moscow rules had been written on the streets, but London rules were devised in the corridors of Westminster, and the short version read: someone always pays. Make sure it isn't you. Nobody knew that better than Jackson Lamb. And nobody played it better than Di Taverner.

On Catherine Standish's floor he paused. There was no sound save a steady electric hum from the lighting. Catherine's was a corner apartment; her door the first he reached. When he pressed his eye to the peephole, no light showed. He took out the metal pick again. He wasn't surprised to find she'd double-locked the door; nor that it was also on its chain. He was about to deal with this third obstacle when, from behind the now inch-open door, she spoke.

"Whoever you are, back off. I'm armed."

He was certain he'd made no noise, but still: Catherine Standish was wound pretty tight. She probably woke when pigeons passed overhead.

"You're not armed," he told her.

There was silence for a moment. Then: "Lamb?"

"Let me in."

"What do you want?"

"Now."

She had never liked him, and he couldn't blame her, but she at least knew when to jump. Sliding the chain back, she let him in, then shut the door, snapping the hall light on in the same movement. She was holding a bottle. Only mineral water, but she could feasibly have done damage with it if he'd been an actual intruder.

Judging by her expression, perhaps he was. "What's going on?"

"Get dressed."

"I *live* here. You can't —"

"Just get dressed."

She looked old in this unexpected light; her greying hair loose over her shoulders. Her nightdress might have come from an illustration in a book of fairy tales. It fell to her ankles, and was buttoned down the front.

Something in his voice changed the context for her. It was still her home, but she was still Service, he was still her boss. If he was here in the middle of the night, things were happening that shouldn't be. She said, "Wait in there," pointing Lamb at an open doorway, and disappeared into her bedroom.

Before discovering it was Lamb chiselling through her front door, Catherine Standish's thoughts had been the obvious ones: that she was being burgled, or targeted for rape. Grabbing the bottle on her bedside table had been an automatic response. And God help her, when she'd seen who it was, she'd wondered if he'd come to proposition her. She'd assumed he was drunk; had wondered if he were mad. Now, hurriedly dressing, she wondered why she hadn't gone for her telephone instead of the bottle; why her first response to this latest scary moment had not been solely fear. The adrenalin that had pumped through her had felt more like a release of tension than panic. As if she'd been waiting for years, and the all-but-silent scrabbling at her lock was simply the second shoe dropping.

The first had been finding Charles Partner's body.

She pulled on the dress she'd laid out for the morning. Tied her hair back, and checked her reflection. *My name is Catherine and I am an alcoholic.* It was rare that she could look at herself without those words uncurling in her mind. *My name is Catherine and I am an alcoholic.* For a long while she'd thought herself a coward. It had taken some time to understand that becoming dry involved bravery, not the least part of which was making that assertion in public. Reaching for a weapon rather than a phone was that same bravery making itself felt. It had taken great effort to rebuild her life, after so many props had been taken away, and if most days it didn't feel like much of a life, it was the only one she had, and she wouldn't surrender it without a fight. The fact that the only weapon in reach had been a bottle could be labelled one of life's little ironies.

My name is Catherine and I am an alcoholic. There was this to say for the AA mantra: you were in no immediate danger of forgetting who or what you were.

Ready to face her monstrous boss, she joined him in the other room. "What's going on?"

318

He'd been standing by her bookshelf, gathering data. "Later. Come on." He was already heading for the door, not looking back. Expecting her to be on his heels.

Maybe clocking him with the bottle would have been the way to go. "It's the middle of the night," she said. "I'm going nowhere until you tell me what's happening."

"You got dressed, didn't you?"

"I what?"

"You got dressed. So you're ready to leave." He had that look she was used to, of expecting her to do stuff simply because he said so. "Can we move?"

"I got dressed because I've no intention of standing in my dressing gown while you invade my space. If you want me to go anywhere, start talking."

"Jesus, you think I was hoping to catch you in your underwear?" He pulled a cigarette from his pocket and stuck it in his mouth. "Shit has hit fan. Big time. Leave now with me, or soon with less friendly people."

"You're not lighting that in here."

"No, I'm lighting it as soon as I get outside, in less than one minute. Stay or come. Your choice."

Catherine stepped aside to let him leave.

She was always aware of Lamb's physical presence. He took up more than his share of space. Sometimes she'd be in the kitchen at Slough House and he'd decide he needed to be there too: before she knew what was happening, she'd be pressed against the wall, trying to stay free of his orbit while he rooted in the fridge for somebody else's food. She didn't think he did this deliberately. He simply didn't care. Or was so used to living in exile inside his own skin that he assumed others would give him room.

Tonight, she was more aware than ever. Partly because Lamb was in her home, smelling of cigarettes, and yesterday's alcohol, and last night's takeaway; wearing clothes that looked like they were melting; taking her measure with his eyes. But there was more to it. Tonight, he gave the impression that someone was riding his coat-tails. He was always secretive, but she'd never seen him look worried before. As if his paranoia was paying off. As if it had found an enemy that wasn't only his past, lurking in a shadow his own bulk threw.

Scooping her keys from a bowl, unhooking her coat from its peg, she grabbed her bag, which was heavier than expected, double-locked the door behind her, and headed downstairs.

He was in the lobby, unlit cigarette in his mouth.

She said, "What sort of trouble? And how come I'm in it?"

"Because you're Slough House. And Slough House is officially in the shit, as of tonight."

Catherine cast her mind briefly through the last few days' activity; found nothing in her memory but the usual list-assembly, the data-sift. "Don't tell me," she said. "Cartwright's blown a fuse, and we all get to burn down with him."

"Not a million miles off," Lamb admitted. He pushed open the door, and went through it first, scanning the parking area. "These the usual cars?"

320

"Like I notice?" she said. Then said, "Yes. They're the usual cars."

This earned her a swift glance. He said, "Baker's been hurt. Moody's dead. There's probably a C&C out on all of us, and I'd rather not spend the next couple of days answering stupid questions underneath Regent's Park."

"Sid's hurt?"

"And Moody's dead."

"How badly hurt?"

"Not as badly hurt as he's dead. Did you hear that bit?"

"Jed Moody was always going to end badly. But I like Sid."

Lamb said, "You're full of surprises, you know that?" and led her out of the building forecourt, with its resident parking and low wall surround and tall green anonymous bushes, and saw the SUV parked on the pavement opposite.

Nick Duffy, noting Lamb's reaction, said, "I hope he's not going to take this the hard way."

"How hard could that be?" asked Webb. James "Spider" Webb: and there was something as inevitable about his comment as there was about the nickname he'd been saddled with. Webb was under thirty, and married to the notion that anyone twenty years older was lucky to have made it through the flood.

Duffy suppressed a sigh. He'd been scratching the bottom of the barrel all night; had been forced to send Dan Hobbs to collect the Slough House geek solo. That had ended well, with Hobbs lamping a citizen. So Ho was missing, and the other slow horses had either dumped their mobiles or were congregating in a sewer under Roupell Street. Meanwhile, Duffy was forced to commandeer non-Dogs like Spider Webb, to make up the numbers.

On the upside, Lady Di had been right. Here was Lamb, come to collect Standish himself. So provided he didn't do anything remarkable, Duffy would chalk at least one success on his side of the ledger.

Answering Webb, he said, "You'd be surprised."

They got out of the SUV, and crossed the road.

Lamb and the woman watched them come. Not a lot of options, Duffy knew: they could have gone back inside, which wouldn't have helped, or they could have made a run for it. But if Lamb had skills underneath his slobbish exterior, speed wasn't among them. Duffy doubted he'd be running anywhere.

Two yards short of the waiting pair, Duffy said, "Busy night."

"Angling for overtime?" Lamb said. "You're talking to the wrong man."

Spider Webb said, "I need to know if either of you are carrying a weapon."

"No," Lamb said, without bothering to look at him.

"I need to check that for myself."

Lamb, still not looking at Webb, said, "Nick, I'm not holding. Not a gun, not a knife, not even an exploding toothbrush. But if your lapdog fancies frisking me, he'd better frisk my colleague first. Because he's not gunna be able to do her with two broken wrists."

"Jesus," Duffy said. "Nobody's frisking anyone. Webb, get in the car. Ms Standish, you're in the front. Jackson, we're in the back."

"And supposing we object?"

"If you were going to object, you'd not have asked the question. Come on. We've all been doing this far too long. Let's get to the Park, shall we?"

It occurred to him later that Lamb had been playing him. Calling him Nick? They'd met, sure, but were hardly buddies. And Duffy was Head Dog, and not easily flattered. But Lamb, unlike Duffy, had seen undercover service, and it was impossible to ignore that. Kids like Webb might see only a burn-out; an older generation remembered what it was that caused the burn-out . . . Jesus Christ, Duffy thought. He must have found it as tricky as winding his watch. But those thoughts came later, back in Regent's Park, by which time Lamb and Standish were long gone.

The four of them got in, and Webb started the car.

Lamb sneezed twice, then sniffed, and — Catherine didn't see; she was looking straight ahead — made a noise like he was wiping his nose on his sleeve. She was glad she wasn't sitting next to him.

Approaching her was a sporadic trickle of traffic; nothing like the stream, then the flood, these streets would see in an hour or two. The city was still dark, but dawn's first whispers could be heard, and the streetlights were losing their grip on the air. She'd spent many mornings, this sort of time, waiting for light to creep into her room. The first few hundred, she'd been trying not to think about drinking. She didn't do that so much any more, and sometimes even slept through till the alarm, but still: the early morning was not unfamiliar to her. It's just that she wasn't usually in a car; not usually under arrest. However it had been phrased, that's what was happening here. She and Lamb were under arrest. Though really, it ought to have been just her, and Lamb should have been somewhere else. Why had he come for her?

Behind her, he said, "Loy, was it?"

Duffy didn't answer.

"I'm guessing Loy. He'd be easiest to turn. It would take Taverner about three minutes."

From the front, next to Webb, Catherine said, "Three minutes to what?"

"To get him to agree to whatever she said. She's rewriting the timeline. She's putting Slough House in the frame."

Duffy said, "This journey's going to pass a lot quicker if we postpone the conversation till we get there."

Catherine said, "Frame for what?"

"For the execution of Hassan Ahmed." Lamb sneezed again. Then said: "Taverner's scorching the earth, but it won't work. It's the cover-up that gets you in the end, Nick. She knows that, but she thinks she's the exception. That's what everybody thinks. And everybody's always wrong."

"Last time I was at the Park, Diana Taverner was in charge. Until that changes, I do what she says."

"That'll sound good before Limitations. Christ, I thought you were Boss Dog. Isn't it your job to make sure nobody goes off reservation?"

Catherine glanced sideways. Webb, Duffy had called the driver. He looked the same age, same type, as River Cartwright, but quicker to ask how high when told to jump. He caught her looking: just a flicker from his eyes, which were mostly on the road ahead. A faint smile curled his lip.

She had barely a glimmer of what was happening here, but there was a certain comfort in knowing whose side she was on.

"Look," Duffy said at last. "All I know is, you're wanted at the Park. That's it. So you're wasting your time trying to find out what's going on."

"I already know what's going on. Taverner's covering her arse. Thing is, she's too busy doing that to worry about Hassan Ahmed. Remember Hassan, Nick?" Duffy didn't reply. "Taverner would sooner he had his head cut off than admit it was her fault. Which is why she wanted Loy, who's no doubt signed off on her version of events by now. And Moody being dead, well, she can paint him any colour she likes. Not as if he's about to contradict her."

Up front, Catherine decided that the streets were starting to look themselves again; places where business was done and people moved freely, instead of skipping from shadow to shadow. Moved as if they belonged here.

Lamb said, "But it's all going to unravel, Nick. The sensible thing to do would be forget about Lady Di's

London rules and concentrate on finding the kid before he gets whacked too. If that's not already happened." He sneezed again. "Jesus, you keep a cat in here or what? Standish, you got tissues in that bag?"

Hoisting the bag in question on to her knees, Catherine unzipped it and took out Lamb's gun, which he'd placed there while she was dressing. The safety catch was clearly marked, and she snicked it off before pointing the gun at her chosen target.

"We all know I'm not going to shoot you dead," she told Webb. "But I'll put a bullet through your foot if I need to. And that'll wipe the smirk off your face, won't it?"

"You two can walk home from here," said Lamb. "If that's all right."

Blake's grave lies half a mile or so from Slough House, in Bunhill Fields cemetery. It's marked by a small headstone, also dedicated to his wife Catherine, and is out in the open, at one end of a paved area lined with benches and sheltered by low trees. The stone doesn't mark the couple's exact resting place, but indicates that their remains are not far off. Next to it is a memorial to Defoe; Bunyan's tomb is yards away. Nonconformists all. Whether that was why Lamb chose it as a meeting place, nobody was prepared to guess, but that was where they gathered all the same.

Having failed to collect Kay White, River arrived alone. He climbed the gates, which were padlocked, and sat on a bench under a tree. Traffic was building up in the background. The city never really slept; it endured white nights and fitful slumbers. Its breakfast was cigarettes, black coffee and aspirin, and it would feel like death warmed up for hours.

A rattling at the gates meant that others were arriving.

Min, Louisa and Roderick Ho strode into view, Ho clutching a laptop. Min and Louisa looked as pale as

River felt, but were walking tall. Things were happening. They weren't on the sidelines any more.

Ho said, "Moody really dead?"

River nodded.

Ho said, "Right," and sat on the bench opposite. He opened his machine, booted up and attached a dongle. Nobody asked what he was doing. If he'd sat and listened, or tried to kickstart a conversation, they'd have asked, but Ho diving into the web was business as usual.

"White?"

River shook his head. "Too late."

"Not —"

"No. Christ, no. She was just being driven away. What about Loy?"

"No sign."

Louisa sat next to River. Min stood. He stretched suddenly; went on to tiptoe, and extended his arms as if crucified.

"It's the Dogs, isn't it?"

"Guess so."

"They think we killed Jed?"

River said, "I think they think we killed Alan Black. How well did you two know him?"

Both shrugged.

"He was around. But not much of a talker."

"Let's face it, there are no big talkers at Slough House."

"He ever say why he quit?"

"Not in my hearing. You never knew him?"

"He was before my time," River said.

"Why would they think we killed him?"

"Because we're being set up," River said. "Is that a car?"

It was. It slowed, parked and the engine died; all of this out of sight, behind the trees lining the cemetery's western edge. River and Louisa got to their feet. Ho, absorbed in his screen, paid no attention. At the far end of the path, there came a clinking sound, and the noise of a bolt being shot.

"It's Lamb," said River.

"He has a key?"

"Well, that would explain why he wanted to meet here."

A moment later Lamb and Catherine Standish appeared.

This was what it had come to: Curly was in a foreign country, undercover, in time of war. His own country, and he was the stranger.

They were driving past a mosque — a fucking mosque. Here in the capital of England. You couldn't make it up.

For years, there'd been warning voices raised, but what good had it done? Sweet FA. Anyone who wants can wander in and take the country: we've given them the jobs, the houses, the money, and if they don't want jobs, we give them money anyway. Welfare state? Don't make us laugh. Whole country's a charity case.

Plus, they were lost. Had no idea where they were. Follow the signs: North. How hard could it be?

But Larry was flaking. Coward was what it was. *We were only supposed to give him a scare.* Yeah, because

329

that's how you fight a war, right? The 7/7 killers didn't open their rucksacks and show their bombs, say *See what we could've done if we felt like it?* They just did it. Because give them this much: they knew they were fighting a war. And you couldn't fight a war without both sides taking part.

He hadn't realized it was a mosque until they were right next to it, but now he could see it properly, it couldn't ever have been anything else. It bulbed into foreign shapes. As if they'd driven off the map, and wound up the last place they wanted to be. Panic clutched him: the thought that the kid would know where they were — would pick up on the smells and sounds — and start kicking at the boot. Curly had a vision of a crowd surrounding the car; rocking it side to side. Pulling the kid free, and then what? Setting fire to them. Dragging them on to the street and stoning them. Fucking medieval, the lot of them. The reason he was doing this in the first place: give them a taste of their own medicine.

He swallowed the panic. The Paki was in the boot. No way could he know where they were.

None of them knew where they were.

"You got any clue where you're trying to get to?"

"You said to get some distance, right? I've been —"

"I didn't mean bring us into bloody India."

The mosque was behind them. The buildings everywhere were concrete, with barred windows. The only hint of green was a Poundshop's metal shutter.

"We need to get out of the city."

330

★ ★ ★

Lamb perched on the rail around Bunyan's tomb, eating a bacon sandwich. In his other hand he held a second sandwich, wrapped in greaseproof paper. The slow horses were gathered round him.

He said, "Black was recruited by Taverner. The kidnapping was a set-up. Only now it's real, so Taverner's looking for scapegoats." He paused to swallow. "That would be us."

"Why?" Min asked.

Catherine said, "Well, it's not like anyone'll miss us."

"And she already had Black signed up," Louisa put in. "That's one slow horse in the frame already."

"And he won't be contradicting anyone soon," Lamb agreed. "For all we know, Taverner has a papertrail in place. Saying Black was working for Slough House, not her. Not the Park."

"She's going to a hell of a lot of trouble," River said. "Okay, so there's two dead, and it doesn't look rosy for the kid, but ops have gone haywire before. Why's she running scared?"

Lamb said, "The name Mahmud Gul mean anything?"

"He's a General," River said automatically. "In the Directorate for Inter-Services Intelligence. The Pakistani secret service."

That earned him a look. "I bet you used to play Top Trumps with grandad. With spooks instead of racing cars."

Ho's laptop was cradled in front of him like an ice-cream seller's tray. "Gul's Joint Intelligence

Department," he read. "Equivalent to our Second Desk."

River was racking his memory for more details. Nothing came to mind that wasn't painted with a broad brush. "He's a bit of a hardliner."

"Aren't they all?"

Ho said, "Back at the turn of the war, it was thought there were elements inside Inter-Services who were alerting Taliban militants to missile strikes. Gul was one of the likely suspects. Nobody was ever charged, but a Park analyst wrote him up as likely to go either way."

"On the other hand, he's always supported the government in public," River said. "And he's usually mentioned when the next Director's being discussed." Which used up all he knew about Gul. "What's he got to do with this?" But before Lamb could answer, he said, "No. Wait. Don't tell me."

"Oh great," Catherine said. "Twenty questions."

Louisa gave her a glance. That comment didn't sound like Catherine. But then, she didn't much look like Catherine. Her nose was red-tipped in the chill, sure, and her cheekbones were tinted the same, but the spark in her eyes was out of the ordinary. Perhaps she was enjoying this adventure. Then Catherine's eyes met hers, and Louisa quickly looked away.

Lamb finished his sandwich, and belched appreciatively. "That was bloody excellent," he said. "Five stars."

"Where's open this time of morning?" Louisa asked.

He waved vaguely in the direction of Old Street. "Twenty-four-hour place. It wasn't far out of the way. Didn't think you'd mind waiting."

"I hate to interrupt," River said. "Hassan Ahmed. He's one of Gul's?"

"He's not an agent."

"Sure?"

Lamb let his breath out slowly.

"Okay, so — oh, Christ." The truth hit River with a thrill. "He's *family*?"

"His sister's son."

"We've — *Taverner's* had Mahmud Gul's nephew kidnapped by fascist thugs? What the hell does she think she's doing?"

"She thinks she's boxing clever. 'Think of it as bringing communities together'," Lamb quoted. "Her words. 'When we rescue Hassan, we make a friend.'"

Min Harper asked, "Are they close?"

Ho was still scrolling through Regent's Park's file on Gul. "Hassan's mother and father met in Karachi, but he was already living here. She came back to England as his bride. She's not been back since, and there's no record of Gul visiting."

Min said, "But he's a spook. You can't rule it out."

Lamb said, "Either way, we can assume he'd object to the kid having his head chopped off on camera." He unwrapped his second sandwich. A smell of warm sausage wafted round.

Trying to ignore it, River said, "So that was the plan? To romance Mahmud Gul by rescuing his nephew from a bunch of fanatics?"

"*Our* fanatics," Lamb said. "That was the important part."

Louisa said, "So he's in our debt. And so, when he gets to be the next Director of Inter-Services Intelligence, more likely to fall our way."

"Brilliant," River said. "But what happens when we don't rescue Hassan? Did that factor into her thinking at all?"

"Apparently not," Lamb said. "And the way it's looking now, in twenty-four hours or so, the British secret service assassinates the nephew of a more-or-less friendly power's secret service Second Desk."

"Only if they stick to their timetable," Catherine said. "And why should they? As far as they know, they're blown."

"So they kill the kid," Min said. "Jesus. Wars have been started for less."

Lamb said, "Which is why Lady Di's going to any lengths necessary to screw the blame on us. If Hassan dies, that's one thing. If Hassan dies, and it gets public that Five was responsible, it goes beyond being a black mark on her CV." A small piece of meat fell, leaving a mayonnaise smear on his trouser leg. "Damn. I hate it when that happens." He stared angrily at the yellow streak for a moment, which wasn't noticeably larger than any other stain on that leg, then looked back up. "Taverner won't be joining us at Slough House. She'll be looking at the inside of a cell. Unless she's black-bagged first."

"Black-bag a Second Desk? How likely is that?"

Jackson Lamb said, "There's probably a precedent. Why not ask grandad? Meanwhile, nobody's looking for Hassan. Taverner's known from the start where he is, and it's not been in her interests that anyone else does, so the cops have been working without Service input. And until Black infiltrated them, the Voice of Albion weren't making waves on anyone's radar."

Ho said, "You don't make wa —"

"Shut up."

"If they're such amateurs, what are their chances?" Catherine asked. "Maybe they'll trip over their own . . ."

"Dicks?"

Louisa said, "She has a point."

"Not really. Being a bunch of bottom feeders has played to their advantage. Nobody noticed them before, so nobody knows where they came from now."

"But Alan Black found them."

"Yeah," Lamb said. "He did, didn't he?"

River was listening and not listening; his brain churning through newly learned facts, adding them to what he already knew, or thought he already knew, or had forgotten he knew. And also, he was starving. Lamb, the bastard, could have brought sandwiches for everyone: any boss, anywhere, would have done that when heading for a pre-breakfast meeting. Always supposing any boss, anywhere, would have called a pre-breakfast meeting in a graveyard . . . River could barely remember when he'd last eaten, last drunk. It had probably been outside Hobden's with Sid, back when she was still upright, instead of laid out on a hospital bed or operating table, or with a sheet drawn over her head. He still didn't know how she was. Hadn't come to terms with what had happened to her, let alone the information that she'd been put in Slough House to keep an eye on him. By Taverner, presumably. So what was that all about?

Lamb was saying something about headless chickens, and River felt a sudden drop in energy; a need for sugar. For something hot.

God, he'd commit murder for a cup of coffee . . .

In the back of his mind, tumblers clicked.

Lamb took a healthy bite from his sausage sandwich. Chewing, he said, "Thing is, Black was a highly trained secret agent the same way you lot are, which means he was a fuck-up. So he'll have made mistakes."

"Thanks," Louisa said.

Min Harper said, "What difference does it make? He's dead. The others'll off Hassan first chance they get, then crawl back wherever they came from."

"If they were going to . . . *off* Hassan first chance they get," Catherine said, "you'd have found his body next to Black's."

Min looked thoughtful, then nodded.

Ho said, "Fuck-up or not, Black got them out of Leeds the night they took him. The traffic CCTV was down for hours."

Lamb said, "Probably Lady Di. But nobody's pulling strings for them now, and they haven't got Black making their decisions. They'll be headless chickens, clinging to whatever's left of the original plan. Which, we can assume, will have been to his blueprint. So." He stared at each of them in turn. All but River Cartwright looked back: River was gazing skyward, as if expecting a helicopter. "You're Alan Black. What would you have done?"

Min said, "Well, for a start . . ."

"Yes?"

"I wouldn't have got involved in such a godawful mess."

"Any other useful input?"

"I never liked him," Ho said.

"Who?"

"Black."

"He had his head cut off a few hours ago," Lamb said. "And left on a table."

"I was only saying."

"Jesus. This the best you can manage?"

River said, "I've just remembered where I saw him."

In every horror film, sooner or later, the corridor scene occurs. The long corridor, with overhead lighting which shuts down section by section — *boom boom boom.* And then you're in the dark.

Which was where Hassan was now.

In the dark.

The last colour he'd known had been the bright red hell of the kitchen, in the centre of which, on the table, Moe's head had sat like a Hallowe'en pumpkin. One in which no light would ever shine. Take more than a candle to put a gleam in those eyes. *Boom boom.* The floor had been a crimson lake; the walls spattered with gore. *We're going to cut your head off and show it on the web*. It had happened before. It would happen to him next.

The lights in his mind were shutting down.

Even without the handkerchief in his mouth, Hassan wouldn't have been able to shout. He had no words left. His body was bones and liquid.

Boom.

Different things made different noises. He'd been underneath the kitchen when they were doing what they did to Moe, but all he'd heard was a confusion of sound, which might have been anything. It was not the noise Hassan would have expected from such an action. The expected noise would have been a thump, followed by a slow rolling.

But these dark thoughts were escaping him now, as the lights in his mind shut down, *boom boom boom*. And then he was Hassan only in the sense that everyone has to be someone, and that was who he was stuck with until the last of his lights went out, *boom boom*.

And then he was luggage.

Boom.

When River had finished, they stood silent for a while. Not far off, a bird chirped. It must have had inside information of the dawn. There was a vari-coloured glow from City Road, and a more subdued glimmer from the other side, all of it strained through branches.

Lamb said, "You're sure?"

River nodded.

"Okay." He looked thoughtful.

Min Harper said, "Doesn't help us with finding Hassan."

"Well, you're the ray of sunshine, aren't you?"

"I'm only saying."

Ho said, "Is anywhere open round here yet? With wi-fi?"

"And breakfast?" Louisa added.

"God," Lamb said. "Can you not think of anything but your stomach?" He swallowed his last chunk of sandwich, and tossed a scrunched-up greaseproof ball at the nearby bin. "There's a kid out there'll die today. A little focus?" He pulled his cigarettes out.

River said, "Taverner can't get away with this."

"Nice to know where your priorities lie," Lamb said.

"I'm not talking about what she did to me. She's behind all this. If we're to save Hassan, we need to squeeze her."

"We?"

"Nobody else is going to do it."

"Kid's dead meat then."

Catherine Standish said, "You could have let the Dogs round us up. You didn't. What was that about?"

"You think I have a sneaking regard for your talents?"

"I think you do nothing without a reason."

"The day I let Regent's Park screw me around's the day I take the pledge," Lamb said. "If the Dogs tried to steal my pencil sharpener, I'd hide it. And I don't have a pencil sharpener."

Ho said, "What's a pencil sharpener?"

"Very funny."

Ho looked puzzled.

"So what's the point?" Louisa asked. "Why are we here?"

Lamb lit his cigarette. For a moment, his face wreathed in smoke, he might have materialized from the tomb he leant against. "Let's not kid ourselves. Dogs'll pick you up before you get your breakfast. But at least you know what's happening. Taverner's got Loy and White, and she'll have turned both of them by now. They'll swear blind whatever story she feeds them is true. And that'll be that this whole mess was planned at Slough House. Meaning me."

"Nice to know where your priorities lie," River said.

"Yeah, well, the difference between us is I've a career to look back on. And I'm not having Taverner piss all over it."

"And that's it?" Min Harper said. "We just hang about for the Dogs to catch up?"

"You have a better plan?"

Louisa said, "Hassan's still out there somewhere. Maybe not far away. We can't sit on our hands and wait for his body to be found."

"I thought you were dying for your breakfast."

"You're trying to wind us up, aren't you?"

"Yeah, that's right. So you discover the heroes inside yourselves." He paused. "Look. I don't normally say this stuff, but I want to tell you something." He took a drag on his cigarette. "You're fucking useless, the lot of you."

They waited for a "but".

"No, I'm serious. If you weren't fuck-ups, you'd still be at Regent's Park. If you're all Hassan Ahmed's got to rely on, I hope the kid's got religion." He dropped his cigarette and ground it into the damp leaves underfoot. "Now, given that Cartwright's the only one with anything useful to offer, he'd better come with me."

"Where to?" River asked.

"To let the air out of Taverner's tyres," Lamb said. "The rest of you can do what you like."

As they headed towards the gates, Lamb half a pace ahead, River said: "You were trying to wind them up, weren't you?"

"No," Lamb told him. "I meant every word."

"Might have the effect of winding them up, though."

"I don't suppose that'll do much harm," Lamb said. "But it's not likely to do a hell of a lot of good." Producing a key, he tossed it to River, who unlocked the gates, let Lamb through, then followed him on to the pavement.

Lamb was already striding over the road, where a large black SUV was parked half on the opposite pavement.

River said, "Where'd you get the car?"

"Official issue," Lamb told him. "You been near Slough House?"

"Not since we all left together."

"So we don't know whether the cleaners have been in."

For a moment, River thought he meant just that: the cleaners. He hadn't been aware Slough House was ever cleaned. Then he remembered Moody. "It's been a few hours. They might have been and gone."

"Or it might still be there." *It*, meaning Jed Moody's body. Lamb started the engine. "Let's find out."

The others watched Lamb and Cartwright disappear between the trees.

Louisa said, "Bastard."

Catherine Standish said, "He told us we're useless because he wants us to prove him wrong."

"No he didn't. He's covering his arse, that's all."

"But supposing he wasn't?" said Catherine.

"What difference would that make?"

"It would mean he wants us to prove him wrong."

"I'm not desperate for his approval."

"Hassan Ahmed might appreciate it, though."

Min said, "Everyone in the country's been looking for Hassan Ahmed for two days. How are we supposed to find him?"

"We know where he was not long ago. Anyway, we're not looking for him," Catherine said. "We're looking for the people who took him."

"There's a difference?"

"You're Alan Black," she said. "That's what he was saying before Cartwright interrupted. So, we're Alan Black. What would we have done?"

Louisa said, "You're right. It gives us an edge."

Ho said, "You think?"

"Why not?"

He shrugged. "I don't remember ever having a conversation with him."

"So how come you didn't like him?"

"He used to open windows."

Catherine said drily, "I can see how upsetting that must have been for you."

Ho removed the dongle from his laptop and powered down. "Anyway, we can't stay here. It's cold and damp. Where's that caff?"

"Old Street."

"Come on, then."

"All of us?"

"Someone has to come. I didn't bring any money. They have wi-fi, you notice?"

Louisa looked at Min, then back at Ho. "You want to try looking for Hassan?"

Ho shrugged. "Whatever."

"Don't tell me you want Lamb's approval."

"Approval?" Ho said. "Fuck, no. I just want to prove the prick wrong."

The car came to a halt, and Hassan's body was bounced against the boot lid. He barely noticed. Further bruising seemed immaterial.

There was, after all, worse to come.

Lamb pulled up by the bus stop opposite Slough House. One of Moody's checkpoints, River recalled; constantly monitored for loiterers. He said, "So. What we doing?"

"See any lights?"

"Third floor."

"Did you leave that on?"

"I don't remember."

"Think."

River thought. It didn't help. "I don't remember. You were there too. Why is it my fault the light was left on?"

"Because I've better things to worry about."

At the windows no shapes appeared; no other lights went on. The cleaners might be inside, removing Jed Moody. Or might have been and gone, and left the light on; or might not have been there at all.

And might turn up in the next few minutes.

Reading River's thoughts, Lamb said, "Only one way to find out."

"We're going in?"

"You are," Lamb told him. "No point us both running the risk."

344

"And supposing I don't get caught? What am I supposed to do?"

Lamb told him.

"So we what, try to work out what we'd do in their position?"

"We work out what Black's back-up plan would have been. If the safe house was blown."

"But Black was the one planning to blow the safe house."

"Yes," said Catherine patiently. "But given that he probably didn't tell them that in advance, they might have wanted to know if there was a back-up plan."

"They killed Black because they discovered he was a spook," Louisa said. "They're hardly likely to trust his plans now."

"True," Min Harper put in. "But on the other hand, they're a bunch of morons."

"How do we know that?"

"Well, they joined a group called Voice of Albion. You want a definition of moron . . ."

"They sussed out Black."

"Yeah, well, he wasn't James Bond."

"This is getting us nowhere," Catherine said.

They were in a café on Old Street: long and narrow with a counter along the window, and tables against a mirrored wall. Coffee had arrived, and breakfasts been ordered. Ho's laptop was open, and that familiar expression was capturing him; the one where the world on his screen became more real, less irritating, than the one around him.

He said, "They might have offed him already. Why stick to the deadline now?"

"For the sake of the exercise," Catherine said, "let's pretend there's a chance of saving his life. Otherwise we might as well go back to bed."

Louisa said, "What about CCTV? I thought the UK had blanket coverage. Especially on the roads."

Ho offered her a pained look. "All other objections aside, we don't know what they're driving."

"So how do we find out?"

They fell silent.

"He's not likely to have used his credit card," Min said at last.

"But there'll be a papertrail."

"A footprint."

"In a black op?"

"Black ops cost. Unless Taverner's funded it out of her own pocket, there'll be —"

"A footprint," Ho repeated. "Not a papertrail."

"Whatever."

"This isn't a black op," Catherine said. "It's off the books. Different animal entirely."

"What's the difference?"

"A black op's officially deniable. One that's off the books never happened."

"So how's the funding work when it's off the books?"

Catherine thought for a moment. "I once heard about an op where a safe house was kitted out. In Walsall, I think. All the utilities, council tax, everything was on standing order. But the house didn't exist. The money went from Budgeting into a property account, which then funded the op."

"Tracking that," Ho said, "would take forever."

"No, but," Louisa said. She turned to Catherine. "That safe house never existed. But we know one that does, don't we?"

"Roupell Street," Min said.

They looked at Ho.

"I'm on it."

Curly said, "We need to get out of the city."

"We should dump the car. Walk away," Larry said.

He'd been bottling this up, Curly could tell. Until the words felt like a winning argument: *This is what we should do, because I just said it was.*

"We killed a spook," he said.

"You killed him."

"He's dead, you were there. You want to argue details?"

"In a court of law —"

"You what? You fucking *what?*"

"Because —"

"You think we'll end up in court, you're more of a twat than those jeans make you look."

Larry said, "What's wrong with them?"

"We killed a spook. You think they'll arrest us?"

"What you saying?"

"They will shoot. Us. Dead. End of. No arrest, no trial, no weaselly words about how you only watched while I cut his head off." Saying the words, he could feel the blood pulse through his cutting arm. It was like

347

having an erection, right to his fingertips. "A pair of bullets each. Bam bam. Double tap."

Larry was shaking.

"So don't even think about court. We're not going to court. Get it?"

Larry gave no response.

"Get it?"

"I get it."

"Good." And now he let Larry off the hook: "But it's not gunna happen anyway. We're not getting caught."

"We had a spy with us. You think —"

"I know he was a spy. That doesn't mean we're gunna get caught. You think we're alone in this? We're not. The people are on our side. You think they're gunna turn their backs on us?"

Larry said, "Maybe not."

"Maybe not. *Maybe* not. If that's all you believe, you should've just sat in the pub, complaining about the country being taken away from us. Another fucking whiner with no balls."

"I'm here. I'm not all noise. You know that."

"Yeah, right." Curly wanted to say more, to explain to Larry what the future held: that they'd be heroes, outlaws, Robin Hoods. Symbols of the struggle against Islam. And when the war started, leaders of the people. But he didn't, because Larry didn't have it in him. Larry thought he was a soldier, but he was just another coward; happy to talk, scared to walk. No point talking to him about a future that was Curly's alone.

Which Larry didn't know yet, but he'd find out soon.

★ ★ ★

But the Roupell Street house led nowhere.

"Civil Service property since the fifties," Ho said, scanning records he'd pulled onscreen. "Treasury first, then something called 'collateral purposes'."

"Safe house," Catherine said.

"And now it's listed under Sales."

"Which means exactly what it sounds like." Catherine shook her head. "There'll be no papertrail. *Footprint*, sorry. All Taverner had to do was check the sales portfolio for an empty property, and use that."

"So they were squatting," Min said.

"Basically."

"They'd have had a shock if a potential buyer turned up."

"In this climate?"

"Okay, that takes us nowhere. So where are we?" Louisa said.

"Twiddling thumbs," Ho said. "The kid's toast."

"Shut up," Catherine snapped.

Ho eyed her warily.

"Get this through your head. Until we know he's dead, we keep looking. We've no idea what their plan is. They might want to keep to the original timetable because it's, I don't know, Hitler's birthday or something. It might matter to them. We might still have time."

Ho opened his mouth as if to reveal when Hitler's birthday was, but thought better of it.

Louisa said, "None of us are giving up."

Their breakfasts arrived: three platefuls of the full English; one mushroom omelette. Ho shifted his laptop on to his knees, then scooped a forkful of beans into his mouth.

"Were you taught to eat?" Louisa said. "Or is it still a learning process?"

Chewing rapidly Ho nodded at her, as if to indicate that a smart reply was but minutes away.

Min said, "Okay, they got the house for free. They'd still need money. For transport if nothing else."

"They might have stolen it."

"With a kidnap victim? Too risky."

"They might have used their own wheels."

"Black was a pro. He'd have wanted fresh."

Catherine agreed.

"And paid with cash," said Min.

"Most likely," agreed Louisa.

"And if they used cash, it's history."

Catherine cut her omelette into uniform slices. The others watched, fascinated.

When she'd finished, she ate two pieces in silence, then took a sip of coffee. She said, "Not necessarily. Black was using a fake name. When you're establishing a cover, one of the first things you go for is a credit card. It's easy to do. And once you've got it, why not use it? It adds verisimilitude."

"Adds what?" Ho said.

Catherine gave him a look.

Min said, "Sounds good, but where does it take us? We don't know what name he was using."

"Didn't Lamb check his pockets? For a wallet?"

"I think he'd have said if he had. On account of it being, you know. A clue."

"Let's step back," Louisa suggested. "You're running an op. What do you need?"

"A legend," Ho said.

"With at least three back-ups."

"Back-ups?"

Catherine said: "Like a reference on a CV. At least two contact numbers, or addresses, where if anyone comes checking, they'll find confirmation you're who you say you are."

"And how's that work when you're off the books?"

"You go freelance."

They thought about it.

"It's getting expensive."

"Slush fund," Louisa said.

"That's all tight as hell since the Miro Weiss business."

Which was when a quarter of a billion pounds, slated for reconstruction work in Iraq, had gone walkabout.

"Okay, how'd you do it on the cheap?"

"Friends."

"Nobody's got friends that good," Ho objected.

"Not in your world," Louisa agreed. "But there must be people owe Taverner a favour. And I mean, what are we talking? You get a phone call from some little England nut, asking if you can vouch for whatever Black was calling himself? Takes two minutes to say yes."

Catherine said, "No. You need a dedicated phone line, and you need to be in character when it rings, 24/7. On the books, this stuff is handled via the Queens. The system tells them, when they get a caller, who they're supposed to be."

Min reminded himself that Catherine Standish had been Charles Partner's Girl Friday. Partner had been before Min's time, but he was pretty much a legend himself.

He said, "Well —" but got no further.

"Oh fuck," Catherine said.

The first time any of them had heard her say that.

"I think I know what they did."

Curly said, "Thought we were heading out of the city."

"I'm trying."

He didn't seem to be. They'd passed another mosque, unless they were going in circles, and it was the same one.

"How big's this fucking place anyway?"

"London?" Larry said. "Pretty big."

Curly glanced across, but he wasn't taking the piss. He looked like he was hanging on by his fingernails, frankly. Like someone a policeman would stop, to check he wasn't going to stroke out at the wheel.

"Thought you were following the signs."

"I thought you were pointing them out to me."

"Is there a map anywhere?" Then answered his own question, pulling open the glovebox, finding nothing but hire-agreement papers and a couple of manuals.

"There's that," Larry said.

"What?"

"That." He pointed.

The penny dropped.

Curly said, "Okay. Now we're getting somewhere."

★ ★ ★

Letting himself through the door, River paused. A dim glow from the third floor reached him like a ghostly presence, but he heard nothing. Which might mean he was alone. Or that anyone else in the building was being very quiet.

Well, he could hang by the back door wondering. Or go up and find out.

He took the first set of stairs slowly, part wary, part weary. His body was feeling the hours it had put in: surges of adrenalin; shocking sights. It took it out of you. *It's not whether you can cope with the things that happen.* The O.B.'s words. *It's whether you cope afterwards, once they've happened. Once they're over.*

But this wasn't over. And he experienced another rush at the thought of what Taverner had done to him.

The second flight came easier; by the time he was on the third he was almost hoping there'd be someone here — one of the cleaners; one of the Dogs. A few hours ago, he'd gone quietly. This time he wouldn't.

But there was nobody there but Jed Moody, cold and dead on the landing.

Passing him, River went up to Lamb's office. A shoebox sat on the desk, as Lamb had promised. River did as instructed, then carried the box downstairs.

Back on Moody's landing, he knelt by the body. He supposed he ought to care that the man was dead, but what he mostly felt was the strangeness of it; that Moody, like River, had been a counter in a boardgame played by other people. Only for Moody, the game was over. Snakes and ladders were one thing. A staircase was deadlier.

He'd had a gun, though, and needn't have been the one removed from the board. If he'd been prepared to use it, maybe River would be crouching next to a dead Min Harper or Louisa Guy, and Moody would have been in the wind, Lamb's flight fund in his pocket.

But Moody hadn't wanted to shoot them, so maybe there was loyalty between slow horses after all. They weren't friends, or hadn't been friendly, before this long night started. But Moody hadn't been able to bring himself to shoot them.

Shoot another one, anyway. Though shooting Sid had been an accident.

For one reason or the other, River allowed Moody another second's peace.

Then he stripped the corpse.

"Legends never die," Catherine said. "They wouldn't be legends otherwise. When a joe's deep cover, long-term, they get the works. Passport, birth certificate, everything. Credit cards, library cards, all the stuff you fill your wallet with."

"Sure."

"We know that."

"And it costs."

Ho rolled his eyes. He'd been involved in more conversation this morning than the past two months, and it was already sounding familiar. "We established that. Your point?"

"They do it on the cheap."

"Thank you, superbrain. So they what, picked up some knock-off ID down the market? Maybe Oxfam —"

"Shut up, Ho."

"Yeah, shut up, Ho. How do you mean on the cheap, Catherine?"

She said, "They use one that already exists. Did Black ever go undercover?"

This was more like it. Now they had guidance.

"Turn left in one hundred yards."

Larry said, "She's that posh bird."

"They're all posh birds."

"You know the one I mean."

"You know something? I don't. I really don't. And I really don't care."

It was five, which meant they'd been lost for an hour, and there was no noise from the boot. Curly wondered if the Paki had fallen asleep, or died: from a heart attack or something. Like cheating the hangman. He wondered what difference it would make if they had to do it with him already dead, and decided: not so much. Moe had been dead, and taking his head off had been a serious business. The world would sit up and take notice, either way.

He laughed, a sudden sharp bark that startled Larry, who veered and nearly clipped a car on the verge . . . Little things mattered. Clip a car, trigger an alarm, get stopped by a policeman up the road: step out of the vehicle, sir, and what's that on the back seat?

And what's that banging from the boot?

But Larry recovered, and there was no sideswipe, no alarm.

"What's so funny?"

Curly had forgotten. But the insight remained; that it only took a moment for things to unravel. One mistake could spoil everything.

So forget the deadline. Find somewhere safe, and just do it.

Do it, film it, fade away.

Ho pulled Black's personnel files, which had been downgraded since he quit, but remained live — in direct opposition to Black's current status, though Ho didn't say this aloud. He hadn't liked Black, but still: they were all slow horses, which seemed to count for something this morning.

"Is it really that simple to check our records?"

"Can you see ours that easily?"

"No," he replied to the first question, and "Yes" to the second. If it was that easy, anyone could do it. But for Ho himself, yes, it was a piece of cake.

"I thought they switched the settings regularly."

"They do."

But since Ho had hacked the security settings rather than the database itself, and left himself a trapdoor, it didn't matter how often they changed the codes. It was like they fitted new locks every month, but left the door hanging open.

He said: "Alan Black. Here we go. He worked embassy surveillance mostly."

"Cushy gig."

"Any undercover?"

"Give me a sec!"

"Sorry."

"Take your time."

"It's just, we got the impression you were hot shit."

Ho glanced up from his laptop to find three pairs of eyes sharing a joke. He said, "Yeah, well. Kind of fuck off, all right?"

But it felt sort of cool, all the same. Almost as if they'd called him Clint.

Catherine said, "As long as you're there. How did he end up in Slough House?"

Ho said, "He shagged the Venezuelan ambassador's wife."

"It says that?"

"It jazzes up the language a bit."

Catherine thought back to Alan Black, who'd lasted six months at Slough House. She didn't have too clear a memory of him, beyond his slow-burn frustration at having been dead-ended, but that was true of all of them, except maybe Struan Loy. And herself, of course. He'd been overweight, average height, average looks — average personality, really. She couldn't picture him as a successful adulterer. On the other hand, he hadn't actually jacked it in; he'd been recruited by Taverner for her deep-cover op. So he'd obviously had something going for him.

Not that it had worked out happily in the end.

"Okay, here it is." Ho looked up. "He was holding paper on the name Dermot Radcliffe. Full-dress cover."

"If he was working surveillance, why'd he need false ID?"

"Surveillance can be up close and personal," Catherine said.

"Yeah, tell that to the Venezuelan ambassador."

Catherine ignored that. "And working the embassy crowd, you'd be expected to have papers. You're on foreign soil, after all."

"Best not to use your own name when you're on the job."

"Are you two going to giggle about this all morning?"

"Sorry."

Ho said, "Okay, we have plastic. We have an account number."

"But are they still live?"

Catherine said, "Like I say, legends don't die. They don't get wiped off the books. If he had any nous, he'd have kept the plastic and all the rest when he left the Park. As a failsafe."

"In case he ever needed to be somebody else, you mean."

"Or needed to remember what it was like being him," Catherine said.

"Let's check out Mr Radcliffe's credit rating, shall we?" Ho said, his fingers busy on his keyboard.

Hassan?

The voice sliced through the dark.

Hassan!

He knew whose it was. He just didn't believe it.

Open your eyes, darling.

He didn't want to.

Hassan was emptying out. The open mic slot in his head had closed down; its spotlight faded to grey. In its place was darkness, and engine noise, and the vibrations of this metal coffin he'd been folded into.

Hassan — open your eyes!

He wasn't sure he could. Choices were made by other people. Hassan Ahmed no longer had will or ability, and was growing smaller by the minute. Soon there'd be nothing of him left. It would be a relief.

But like it or not, he was being dragged back into the light.

Hassan! Open your eyes! Now!

He didn't. He couldn't. He resisted.

But from deep in his darkness, he wondered: *Why is Joanna Lumley talking to me?*

There was something different about Catherine Standish. This was what Louisa Guy decided as she watched Ho swing through the virtual jungle, a Second Life Tarzan. There was something different about all of them, probably, but it was Catherine who'd assumed the leader's role. She'd been the Slough House ghost; shifting papers, tutting about mess, always there but virtually absent. A recovering alcoholic, because this was somehow common knowledge. Something about her spoke of loss; of an element missing. A blown bulb. But it had never before occurred to Louisa to wonder what Catherine must have been like at full wattage. She'd been Charles Partner's PA, hadn't she? Christ, that made her Miss Moneypenny.

Louisa should keep her mind on the job, though. Lamb thought they were useless. If they were, Hassan would die. If they weren't, he might die anyway. The odds weren't good.

But watching Ho, Louisa realized that he wasn't useless, anyway; that he might be a dick, but he knew his way round a keyboard. And as he pilfered information from the ether, then peered up at the three of them through the thick black frames of his glasses, it occurred to Louisa Guy that she wouldn't want him turning his hacker's gaze on to the private corners of her own life and career.

Though of course, he probably already had.

Regent's Park — the building — was lit up: blue spotlights at ground level cast huge ovals across its facade, drawing attention to the fact that important stuff took place inside. Once upon a time, not many people knew what that was. These days, you could download job application forms from a website adorned with its picture.

Jackson Lamb parked the stolen SUV half on the pavement outside, and waited.

It didn't take long. The vehicle was surrounded inside quarter of a minute.

"Could you step out of the car, please, sir?"

There were no weapons in evidence. There didn't need to be.

"Sir?"

Lamb wound the window down. He was looking at a youngish man who evidently knew his way around a gym: taut muscles under a charcoal grey suit. A white cord coiled from his left ear to the suit's lapel.

"Step out of the car, sir," he repeated.

"Fetch your boss, sonny," Lamb said pleasantly, and wound the window back up.

"He hired a car," Ho said.

"You have got to be kidding."

"Straight up. Triple-D Car Hire. Leeds address."

"He's in the field? And he *hired a car*?"

Catherine said, "No. It makes sense."

It was a measure of their changing relationship that they waited for her thoughts.

"He's in the field, sure. But let's not forget, this wasn't an op with a future. The boy was going to be rescued. Black didn't have to worry about covering his tracks."

"So hiring a car was the simplest thing to do."

"Quite."

"Anyone got a phone?" Ho asked.

"Lamb made us trash them."

"There's a payphone by the loos," Catherine said. "What's the number?"

She scribbled it down as he read it off the screen; was heading for the phone a moment later.

"It's barely dawn. A car hire place'll be open?"

"Triple-D gives twenty-four-hour breakdown relief," Ho quoted.

"A kid with a van and a spanner," Min reckoned.

"Tenner says she blows it."

"I'll take that," Louisa said.

"Me too," Min added.

Ho looked alarmed. "What happened since yesterday? Everyone's acting strange."

"Slough House went live," Min told him. "She'll come back with something we can use."

"The lady's got game," Louisa said.

James Webb, whose futile mission in life was to dissuade everyone from calling him Spider, was in his office. After Jackson Lamb had dumped him and Nick Duffy on the pavement — after he'd recovered from the shock of having a middle-aged woman point a gun at him: *I'll put a bullet through your foot. That'll wipe the smirk off your face* — they'd made their way back, Duffy barely speaking. Hey, Webb had wanted to tell him. It wasn't my fault. But here he was anyway, back in his hutch, Duffy having no further use for him.

But then, Webb wasn't one of Duffy's Dogs. He'd come through the graduate channel; done his two years' rotation; attended the seminars, taken the exams. Spent nights on various godforsaken moors, in with harsh weather, and undergone assessment exercises, staging posts on the fast track: arresting a putative suicide bomber outside Tate Modern, and acting as control when River Cartwright had spectacularly failed an exercise of his own. Along the way, he'd been taken under Taverner's wing; which was why he, not Cartwright, was still in Regent's Park.

And unlike River, he'd never wanted to be a field agent. Joes were pieces on the board; Webb's ambition was to be a player at the table. His current role, interviewing graduates — *HR*, River had scoffed — was a step on the road to being the keeper of secrets, and if there was less glam to it than the streetwork, there was also less weather, less chance of finding out how well those interrogation-resistance lessons stood up in the field, and, theoretically, fewer opportunities for middle-aged women to point a gun at him. Suits and joes was an age-old opposition, but the game had changed in the last ten years, and intelligence was a business like any other. There would always be battlegrounds where things got bloody, but at boardroom level, today's intelligence wars were fought the way Coke battled Pepsi. And that was a war Webb felt comfortable waging.

But right now River seemed to be at the centre of events, because it was the slow horses that had everyone uptight tonight. Sid Baker was under the surgeon's knife; somebody else was dead; and there were rumours that Jackson Lamb had orchestrated the kidnapping of that internet kid. Whatever the truth, there was a general air that shit was about to hit the fan. But it was all internal. There was no ministerial presence. Spider would have noticed: when the Minister was in the building, the ripples spread outwards.

But suit or not, Webb felt sidelined. Taverner didn't like him showing up on the hub uninvited — this was the flip-side of being under her wing: she didn't want anyone knowing about it — but he couldn't sit here under the unwavering gaze of files and folders much longer without starting to feel like he, and not River, had failed an important test.

He didn't think he could, anyway. But after reflecting for a moment on whether he minded pissing Lady Di off, he decided he might manage it a little longer.

"How did you do?"

Catherine Standish said, "Dermot Radcliffe hired a Volvo three weeks ago. Family holiday, he said. He wanted plenty of boot space."

Taking this detail in, Louisa felt her heart pound her chest.

"And they just told you that?"

"Why wouldn't they? I'm his sister, desperately trying to reach him. Our mother's in hospital." Catherine sat and picked up her coffee cup. It was cold to the touch. She put it down and recited from memory the car's number plate.

"Of course, we don't know they're using it now."

"They left Roupell Street in a hurry," Min Harper said. "So they either took that car or stole another one. In which case, that car's still nearby, and their new one'll be reported missing soon."

"Can't drive anywhere through London without showing up on CCTV."

"Which would be great if we were at the Trocadero," said Ho. He meant the nerve centre of the city's surveillance systems, with its massed ranks of monitors covering every inch of the capital. "But I've only got a laptop."

"Still," said Catherine. "That might do the trick."

Three pairs of eyes turned her way.

"Triple-D cars come fitted with sat nav," she said.

Joanna Lumley was the saviour of the Gurkhas, who'd been shabbily treated by a succession of British Governments. Joanna Lumley was a formidable woman. The Gurkhas had been denied the right to live in the country they'd served in the war, and Joanna Lumley had deplored this state of affairs. So Joanna Lumley, in one of those quintessentially English turns of event, had turned a Government on its head and bent it to her will. Forcibly charmed, the Government bestowed upon the Gurkhas rights of residence. In return, the Gurkhas worshipped Joanna Lumley as they might a god.

So how was Hassan supposed to ignore her commands?

Hassan. Open your eyes, darling. There's a good boy.

He didn't want to open his eyes.

I'm not going to ask you again.

He opened his eyes.

There was nothing to see, of course. But at least this nothing was actually there, as opposed to the huge unexisting blankness through which he'd been falling a short while ago.

Things hadn't changed. He was still folded into the boot of a car, still hooded, gagged and bound. He was still being thrown about like a pea in a whistle. And he could still hear Joanna Lumley, though she was no longer talking to him; she seemed, rather, to be offering directions to somebody else. *Straight ahead for two hundred yards.* It came to Hassan that he was hearing a sat nav system, programmed with Joanna Lumley's voice. More expensive than the regular version, but there were those who found it worth it.

Joanna Lumley hadn't been talking to Hassan at all.

On the other hand, for the moment at least, Hassan was back in the land of the living.

Nick Duffy said, "Is this a joke?"

"I'm returning your car. I was worried they'd take it out your wages."

"You pulled a gun on me."

"No, I delegated that. And she didn't pull it on you, she pulled it on your boy." Jackson Lamb, who was still in the driving seat, placed a meaty elbow on the rim of its open window, and mock-whispered: "The gun's in my pocket. Case you thought I was getting excited."

"Out of the car."

"You're not having me shot, are you?"

"Not out here, no."

"Good. Only I was wanting a word with Lady Di."

He sat back, and pressed the button that closed the window.

Duffy opened the door, and held a hand out.

Panting with the effort — a piece of drama Duffy wasn't falling for — Lamb levered himself on to the pavement, then produced the weapon from his coat pocket.

For a brief moment, everyone within sight tensed.

Lamb put the gun in Duffy's outstretched hand, then farted loudly. "Sausage sandwich," he said. "I'll be doing that all morning."

Behind him, the taut young man in the charcoal suit slipped behind the wheel of the SUV. So smoothly it might have been choreographed, he swung the car back into the road and drove it round the corner, where it would disappear down the ramp and into one small part of the subterranean world of Regent's Park.

"So," Lamb said, once this was taken care of. "I could murder a coffee. Shall we pop inside?"

"Turn here."

"Here?"

"Am I talking to myself?"

Larry took the exit road. Joanna Lumley objected.

"Change of plan, darling," Curly said, and switched the sat nav off.

"To what?" Larry said.

The turn-off took them on to one of the minor roads skirting Epping Forest. If they'd headed directly north they'd not be within miles of here, but getting lost had its advantages. Curly had never been here, but he knew the name. Everyone knew the name. It was a place of shallow graves; regularly name-checked on true-crime programmes. This was where your gangsters buried their enemies. Or sometimes didn't even bother: just set fire to the car they'd shot them in, then whistled their way home to the concrete jungle. Place had probably seen more deaths than picnics. Plenty of room for another. Two, if necessary.

This road was thickly lined by trees, and the sky disappeared behind a canopy of branches. An approaching car dipped its headlights. Flashing past, its noise reached Curly's ears like something happening under water.

"We're gunna cut to the chase," he said.

A bubble welled inside him, and escaped as a brief giggle.

Larry cast him a sideways glance, but didn't dare open his mouth.

Pissing off Lady Di was not a good career move, and Spider Webb's choices were largely dictated by such demands. But he didn't have to go on to the hub. He could wander downstairs instead. Regent's Park was like any other office block: the guys on the desk were the first to know what was up. So like any suit with an eye to the edge, Spider made a point of being friendly to the guys on the desk.

Leaving his office, he walked down the corridor, through the fire door, and into the stairwell. Here he paused a moment, distracted by movement through the window. Two storeys below, a black SUV was coming down the concrete ramp into the car park beneath the building. One SUV was much like the next, but still: Webb wondered if this was the same one Lamb had hijacked earlier. If it was, Lamb had either been picked up again, or turned himself in. Spider hoped the former, and hoped it had happened roughly. The woman, too. *I'll put a bullet through your foot.* He wasn't forgetting that in a hurry. Mostly for the absolute sincerity of the woman's tone.

The car was gone. No way of seeing from here who'd been driving, which left open the possibility that it had been Lamb himself. Without Park clearance, Lamb shouldn't have made it through the barriers, but Webb had heard myths about Jackson Lamb. Clearance might be something required by other people. In which case, Lamb might be loose in the belly of the building.

It wasn't likely, but it gave Webb all the excuse he needed to go and find out what was happening.

As Catherine Standish watched Roderick Ho perform more virtual acrobatics, another shock of excitement fired through her body. Nothing to do with Ho.

Catherine didn't especially admire technological ability; it was useful when other people had it, because this rendered it unnecessary to have any herself, but she no more regarded it as an aspect of character than she would ownership of a particular make of car.

No: the excitement had been born earlier that morning, when she'd lifted Lamb's gun from her bag, and pointed it at the young man next to her. *I'll put a bullet through your foot if I need to. That'll wipe the smirk off your face.* Sometimes the scary moments happened to other people.

Min Harper had spoken, unless it had been Louisa Guy. She said, "Sorry. I was miles away."

Harper said, "You think we'll trace him in time?"

This was new too. They were looking to her, as if she had answers, or opinions worth listening to. Below the tabletop her right hand curled, as if it were once more wrapped around the handle of a gun. "I think we act as if we're saving his life, not finding his body," she said.

He shared a look with Louisa that she couldn't interpret.

It was growing lighter, and traffic was building outside. There was a flow of custom inside, too; people collecting takeaway coffee and breakfast rolls, or grabbing supper on their way home from the nightshift. Catherine was an early riser, a poor sleeper; none of this was unfamiliar to her. But she was seeing through new eyes this morning. She unclenched her hand. Fighting her addictions had taught her about their power, and she knew she was clinging to an unhealthy memory. But right now it felt good, and she could only hope those shocks of excitement weren't visible to the others.

Ho said, "Now we wait."

Louisa said, "You've got the sat nav system?"

"Sure. They use RoadWise. It's just a matter of hacking the system."

"And how does waiting help?"

"Because I've reached out for someone who's done it already. Quicker than doing it myself." He bent to his laptop again, until his colleagues' silence broke through his self-absorption. "What?"

"Care to elaborate?"

He sighed, but overdid it. "Hacking, there's a community, you know?"

"Like stamp collectors."

"Or trainspotters."

"Or poets."

"A bit," Ho agreed, to general surprise. "Only way more cool. Hackers hack systems for one reason only. They're there. Some people do crosswords or sudoku." His expression made it clear what he thought of that. "We hack. And we share."

"So someone will have hacked, what did you call it? RoadWise?"

"RoadWise. Yeah, sure, if it's there, it's been hacked. And anyone cool enough to hack it'll be in the community." He nodded at his laptop, as if it held global masses. "And they'll be getting back to me any moment." Perhaps he saw doubt in their expressions. "We never sleep," he said.

Catherine said, "There's something I don't get."

Ho waited.

"You're telling us you've got friends?"

"The best kind," Ho said. "The ones you never meet."

His laptop bleeped.

"My ride's here."

Catherine watched as he bent to work. *We act as if we're saving Hassan's life, not finding his body.* It was the only approach they could take.

It would be good, though, if they could hurry up a little.

Time was not on Hassan's side.

The car stopped, and the engine cut out.

For a moment, the silence and stillness were worse than the noise and the motion. Hassan's heart pounded, struggling for release. He wasn't ready, he thought — wasn't ready to put an escape plan into operation, because he didn't have one. And wasn't ready because, well, he wasn't ready. Wasn't ready to be poured out of the boot and told he was going to die. He wasn't ready.

Eyes clamped shut, he tried to summon up Joanna Lumley, but she wouldn't appear. He was on his own.

And then he wasn't, because the boot was opening, and rough hands were hauling him out, dropping him like a sack of vegetables on to cold ground.

Instinctively, the first thing he did he was pull the hood from his head; a clumsy operation with his hands bound, but he managed it. With his head free, Hassan saw the world for what felt like the first time. He was in

372

a forest. The car had come to a halt on a dirt track, and all around stretched trees, with mossed-over stumps lurking like goblins in the hollows. The ground was hard-packed mud, with a covering of dead leaves and twigs. The air tasted like early morning. Light was starting to make its presence felt; etching a fine tracery of bare branches overhead.

His two remaining kidnappers stood over him, so his first view was of their boots. That seemed appropriate. He guessed their boots saw more action than their brains ever did. And this thought liberated Hassan a little. He was cold and bruised and filthy and stank, but he was not in a cellar. And he was not these bastards' dog, ready to roll over on their word. In every way that mattered, he was better than the pair of them.

Then one of the boots was on his shoulder, pressing him down on to the earth. It belonged to the one Hassan called Curly. Way up above his boot, Curly was showing him a thin, cruel smile.

"End of the line," he said.

Taverner said, "I'm glad you've seen sense."

Lamb ignored her, surveying her team instead, who were at their own or each other's workstations, and engrossed in their current tasks, and studying every move he made. Soft light rained on them, and there was a slight buzzing in the air, white noise, which seemed to act as an aural curtain. Even without the glass wall, he doubted whether anyone could have heard their conversation.

Nick Duffy was a different matter, of course. Nick Duffy was with them in Taverner's office. Nick Duffy could hear every word.

If there'd ever been any doubt that Diana Taverner could read minds, she put it to rest then and there. She said, "It's okay, Nick. You can leave us."

He didn't like it, but he went.

"Three sugars, there's a love," Lamb said to his departing back.

Taverner said: "You want the bottom line?"

"Oh, I'm gagging for it, darling."

"Black's body's been found. He used to be one of yours. It's clear he was involved in the kidnapping of Hassan Ahmed. You were seen meeting with him in the early summer, long after he'd quit Slough House. Two of your crew have signed statements to that effect. You want me to continue?"

"It's the only thing keeping me going," Lamb assured her. "These statements. Loy and White, right?"

"They make credible witnesses, and they put Black and you together. That, plus Moody's homicidal outing last night, puts Slough House in a very messy frame. If you want it to go away, we can manage that. But you're going to have to cooperate."

Lamb said, "Homicidal?"

For the briefest of moments, a shadow crossed Taverner's face. She said, "I'm sorry. You hadn't heard."

He smiled, but it wasn't a real smile; just a tightening of the flesh across the face. "Well. That's another loose end clipped off, isn't it?"

"That's how you see your team? 'Loose ends'?"

"But Baker was never on my team, was she? You assigned her to Slough House, but not because she'd slept with the wrong boss. She was a plant. She was watching River Cartwright."

"Your evidence being?"

"Her own words."

"Which she won't be repeating any time soon." Taverner's gaze was steady. She said, "I'll make you an offer, Jackson. Something clean we can all walk away from. Co-sign Loy and White's statements, and that'll be the end of it."

"I don't do subtle. You're going to have to explain why I'd want to do that."

"You're old school, Jackson, and not in a good way. You're out of the loop. I go to Limitations with a sacrificial victim, and outcomes will matter more than proofs. That's how things are done now. If there's a quiet out available, Limitations will sign off on it. They'll even call it a retirement. It's not like you'll lose your pension fund."

Jackson Lamb reached inside his coat, and had the satisfaction of seeing her flinch. Her expression turned to distaste as he scratched his armpit. "Think I might have been bitten at the canal."

She didn't reply.

He withdrew his hand and sniffed his fingers. Then put his hand in his pocket. "So your plan is, I cough to your sins? Or else what?"

"It gets messy."

"It's already messy."

She said, "I'm trying to find a way out that causes the least damage for all of us. Like it or not, Slough House is in the firing line, Jackson. Appearances count. You'll all come under scrutiny. All of you."

He said, "This about Standish again?"

"Did you think I'd forgotten?"

"You know me. Always hoping for the best."

"Charles Partner implicated her in everything. He left an itemized statement of his treachery in which he named her as an accomplice. She was lucky not to be arrested."

Lamb said, "She's a drunk."

"That's not an excuse for treason."

"It wasn't meant to be. It's what made Partner think he could get away with it. Why he kept her on after her breakdown. A dried-out drunk is still a drunk. She was loyal to him so he used her, tried to make out she helped him sell secrets. But no one who saw his, what did you call it? — *itemized statement*, believed it for a second. That was his last-ditch attempt to spread the blame, and it was pure fiction."

"And swiftly covered up."

"Of course it bloody was. Service had enough problems. Partner's crimes were black-ribboned from the off, and half the chinless idiots on Limitations still don't know about them. Drag all that up now, and things'll get messy all right. You sure that's a road you want to go down?"

"Covering up treachery's a crime in itself. This time round, they'll do a full audit." Of the two Diana Taverner was in better shape, and knew it. But then,

Jackson Lamb could climb out of a sauna, wrap himself in brand-new threads, and still come off second best to her on her worst day. "You found her a safe berth once, else she'd have drunk herself to death in a bedsit by now. But you can't save her twice. I'm offering to do that for you." Her eyes shifted from Lamb to the hub behind him. Her team were making little pretence of not studying events in her glass-walled office. She deepened her voice slightly. It's the tone she'd have used if she were trying, God help her, to seduce him. A tone that rarely failed. "Put your hands up to this. It was an honourable attempt to get a good result, and not your fault it went wrong. The public at large will never know. And between these walls, you'll be a hero."

She stopped. She was good at reading people. Lamb was a tricky subject — had taught himself to be illegible — but still, Diana Taverner could see him weighing her words. His eyes suggested he was immersed in calculation; the consequences of a scorched-earth policy, as against the walk-away compromise on the table. And seeing this, she felt as a whaler must feel, watching the first harpoon strike flesh: a single wound, and far from mortal, but enough to guarantee the outcome. All that was left was the waiting. And she continued believing this until Jackson Lamb bent, scooped the metal waste-paper basket from beside her desk, and in a surprisingly graceful near-pirouette, hurled it at the glass wall behind him.

"Got it."

"Got what?"

"What are we looking for?" A flash of the familiar Roderick Ho; an expression of lofty contempt for the analog mind. "The car. Dermot Radcliffe's Volvo."

Min Harper scraped his chair round the table, so he could see the laptop's screen. For a moment he thought Ho was about to block his view; hook an arm around it like the class swot hiding his homework. But he restrained himself, even shifting the laptop slightly so Min could see it.

If he'd been expecting a blinking red light on a stylized streetmap — which he partly was — Min was disappointed. Instead, he was looking at a slightly out-of-focus but recognizable photograph of the tops of a whole bunch of trees. "It's under there?"

"Yes," Ho said. Then said, "Probably."

Catherine Standish said, "Care to elaborate on that?"

"That's where the sat nav system registered to the car Dermot Radcliffe hired from Triple-D Cars three weeks ago was, roughly fifty seconds ago." He looked across the table at Catherine. "There's a slight time lag."

"Thank you."

"And they might have dumped the sat nav, of course. Might have tossed it out of the window hours ago."

Louisa said, "Assuming Black was the brains, they probably wouldn't have thought of that."

"Let's not underestimate them," Catherine said. "Black's dead. They're not. Where's the sat nav now, Roddy?"

Ho coloured slightly, and his finger stroked the keyboard's touchpad. An OS map sprouted on to the screen. Two more taps, and it had magnified twice over.

"Epping Forest," he said.

★ ★ ★

Curly moved his boot away. Hassan pulled the handkerchief from his mouth, and tossed it as far as he was able. Then lay on the ground, sucking mouthfuls of cold damp air. He hadn't realized how empty his lungs were. How foul it had been in that boot, with only his own stink to survive on.

He sat up, every part of his body protesting. Behind Curly stood Larry: taller than Curly, broader too, but somehow less substantial. He was holding what looked like a bundle of sticks. Hassan blinked. The world turned swimmy, then washed back into line. It was a tripod. And that matchbox in his other hand: that would be a camera.

Curly was holding something altogether different.

Hassan drew his knees up, leant forward, and pressed his hands to the cold earth. It felt reassuringly solid, and at the same time coldly alien. What did he know about the outdoors? He knew about city streets and supermarkets. He pushed himself unsteadily on to his feet. I wobble, he thought. I wobble. Here among these trees, which are so very big, I am small, and I hurt, and I wobble. But I'm alive.

He looked at Curly, and said, "This it, is it?" His voice sounded strange, as if he were being played by an actor. Someone who'd never actually heard Hassan speak, but had worked out what he might sound like from a faded photograph.

"Yeah," Curly told him. "This is it."

The axe he was holding looked to Hassan like something from the Middle Ages. But then, it *was* something from the Middle Ages — a smoothly curved length of wood with a dull-grey metal head, sharpened to a killing edge. Used down the centuries, because it rarely went wrong. Sometimes the handle wore thin, and was replaced. Sometimes the blade grew blunt.

Joanna Lumley was long gone. Hassan's inner comedian had not returned to the stage. But when he spoke again his own voice had returned to him, and for the first time in an age, he uttered the precise words he was feeling.

"You fucking coward."

Did Curly flinch? Was he not expecting that?

Curly said, "I'm a soldier."

"You? A soldier? You call this a battlefield? You've tied my hands, dragged me into a forest, and now you're what? Gunna cut my head off? Some fucking soldier."

"It's a holy war," Curly said. "And your lot started it."

"*My lot?* My lot sell soft furnishings." A wind stirred the woods, making a noise like an appreciative audience. Hassan felt blood run through his veins; felt fear build into a bubble in his chest. It might burst at any moment. Or might just float him away. He looked at Larry. "And you, right? You're just gunna stand there and let him do what he wants? Another fucking soldier, right?"

"Shut up."

"Yeah, right. Or what? You'll cut my head off? Fuck the pair of you. You want to film this? Film me now, saying this. You're both cowards and the BN fucking P are a bunch of fucking losers."

"We're not BNP," Curly said.

Hassan threw his head back and laughed.

"What's so funny?"

He said, "You think I care? You think I care who you are? BNP or English Defence League or any other kind of stupid fucking Nazi, you think I care? You're nothing. You're nobodies. You'll spend the rest of your lives in prison, and you know what? You'll still be nobodies."

Larry said, "Right. That's it."

Duffy arrived full-tilt, of course. He'd never been far away. He found a waste-paper basket rolling harmlessly across the carpet, and a glass wall showing no sign that violence had been offered. But Taverner was white-faced, and judging by Jackson Lamb's expression, that counted as a result.

Lamb said, "A handler never burns his own joe. It's the worst treachery of all. That's what Partner was doing, using Standish as a shield. That's what you're doing now. Maybe I am old school. But I'm not watching that happen twice."

Nick Duffy said, "Partner?"

"Enough," Taverner said. Then: "He's been running Slough House like a private army. He's been running *ops*, for Christ's sake. Take him downstairs."

While she was speaking Lamb had found a loose cigarette in his overcoat pocket, and was now trying to straighten it. His expression suggested this was currently his major problem.

Duffy wasn't armed. Didn't need to be. He said, "Okay, Lamb. Put that down, and drop your coat on the floor."

"Okay."

Duffy couldn't help it: he glanced at Taverner. She was glancing right back.

"Something you should know first, mind."

And now they both looked at Lamb.

"The SUV your guy just drove under the building? There's a bomb on the back seat. A big one."

A second passed.

Duffy said, "You're kidding, right?"

"Might not be." Lamb shrugged, then stared at Taverner. "I told you. I don't do subtle."

The desk guys weren't as fond of Spider Webb as he thought, but everyone likes having information. Somebody had parked a Service car on the forecourt, and received the inevitable response: the security drones and a couple of Duffy's boys, not long back from various errands. They'd surrounded the car until Duffy himself appeared.

"Who was it?"

"Jackson Lamb," the older desk guy said.

"You sure?"

"I've worked here twenty years. You get to know Jackson Lamb."

The word *sonny* was all the more eloquent for remaining unspoken.

Lamb had come in under Duffy's steam; was up on the hub. The desk guys' monitors didn't cover what happened there, but he hadn't reappeared.

Spider chewed his lip. Whatever Lamb was up to, it didn't involve the madwoman with the gun; or River, either. He mumbled his thanks to the desk guys, and didn't see the look they shared as he headed back upstairs. On the landing he stopped by the window. Nothing was happening on the street. He blinked. Something was happening on the street. A black van screeched to a halt, and almost before it had stopped moving the back was open, allowing three, four, five black-clad shadows to pour like smoke into the morning. Then they were gone, headed into the underground car park.

The achievers, everyone called them. Spider Webb had always thought it a ridiculous name; a piece of jargon that shouldn't have stuck, but had. They were the SWAT guys, who mostly did extractions and removals; he'd seen them in action, but only on drills. This hadn't struck him as a drill.

He wondered if the building were under attack. But if so, there'd be alarms, and a lot more activity.

Through the window, the same nothing was happening again. Small disturbances only. A wind rearranged the trees over the road; a taxi passed. Nothing.

Webb shook his head; an unnecessarily dramatic gesture, given there was nobody to witness it. Story of his life. The joke was, last time he'd been close to anyone, it had been River Cartwright. Some of the courses they'd been on, you couldn't get through without forming alliances; what people called friendships. More than once, he'd assumed that their futures would run on parallel lines, but something had prevented that, which was Spider's slow-dawning realization that River was better than him at most things; so much so, he didn't have to make a big show of it. Which was the sort of moment on which alliances foundered.

He carried on upstairs. Next flight up, he opened the door to his corridor, and one of the achievers stuck a gun to his temple.

Larry said, "That's it. I'm done. You want to do this, you're on your own."

"You're *going?*"

"It's all fucked up. You can't see that? We were only meant to scare him. Film it. Show them we meant business."

"Scaring them's not business."

"It's enough for me. You killed a spook, man. I'm leaving. Get back to Leeds, maybe just . . ."

Maybe hide under the bed. Maybe get home, and hope it would all go away. Close his eyes tight enough, and none of this would have happened.

"No way," Curly said. "No fucking way are you going anywhere."

Larry dropped the tripod and tossed him the digicam. It landed by Curly's feet. "Still want to film it? Film it yourself."

"And how am I supposed to —"

"I don't care."

Larry turned and started to pick his way along the track.

"Get back here!"

He didn't reply.

"*Larry!* Get fucking back!"

Hassan said, "Soldiers, right. You're soldiers."

"Shut up!"

"Soldiers get shot for deserting, don't they?"

"*Shut your fucking hole!*"

"Or what?" Hassan asked. Inside him, the bubble burst. He'd soiled himself, wet himself, sweated and wept through days of fear. But now he'd come out the other side. He'd done the worst of dying: the knowing it was going to happen, the absolute shame of knowing he'd do anything to avoid it. And now he was watching his murderer's plans crumble. "Show this on the internet, you fucking Nazi. Oh, right, you can't, can you? You've only got one pair of hands."

In pure blind rage, Curly hit him with the axe.

The four sat around the table, their plates now cleared away. Since Catherine had got back from the phone, and the other three had confirmed, in the way of small groups of people everywhere, what they all knew already — that she had called the police, explained who she was, what she knew, and how she knew what she knew — no one had spoken. But Ho had folded his laptop away, and Louisa was leaning forward, her hands cradling her chin, her teeth grinding. Min's lips were pursed in a way that suggested deep thought. And every sudden noise attracted Catherine's attention, as if every rattle of every cup, every dropped spoon, threatened disaster.

Out on Old Street, cars whistled past in bursts dictated by the nearby traffic lights.

Min cleared his throat as if about to speak, but thought better of it.

Ho said, "You know something?"

They didn't.

"I've got my mobile in my pocket." He took it out and placed it on the table, so they could see it for themselves. "All this time, Catherine's trotting off to the callphone in the corner. And I've got my mobile in my pocket."

Catherine looked at Louisa. Louisa looked at Min. Min looked at Catherine. They all looked at Ho.

Min said, "For a communications genius, that was kind of rubbish, wasn't it?"

Then they waited some more.

A man in black — an achiever — appeared on the hub. Under his arm was a cardboard box, which he carried into Diana Taverner's office and placed on her desk. It was ticking loudly.

"I assume that's not a bomb," Taverner said.

He shook his head, removed the box's lid, and put Lamb's office clock on Taverner's blotter. Wooden, friendly-faced, it was out of place in these hi-tech surroundings.

Taverner said, "I didn't think so."

Duffy and Lamb were still there. Out on the hub, the same crews were doing the same things they'd been doing before Lamb's announcement had brought the achievers into play; or at least, were still pretending to do them, though with less plausibility. What was happening behind the glass wall was occupying all of their attention.

Lamb said, "Technically — and I might be wrong about this, but I get a lot of e-mail crap from HR — technically, you should still have evacuated the building."

"Which is what you wanted."

"I mean, if that was an actual bomb, you'd be in a shitload of grief."

Duffy said to Taverner, "If that thing had been ticking on the back seat when my guy drove into the car park, he'd have heard it."

The achiever was already leaving, talking into his throat-mic as he went.

Taverner pointed at Lamb. "You didn't want us out of the building at all. You brought somebody in."

Lamb said, "You still think a cover-up's a possibility? Or is it all falling apart?"

Spider Webb stumbled backwards into his office, tripped on the rug, and sprawled on the floor. River pulled Moody's balaclava from his head and stuffed Moody's gun into the back of his waistband. He thought about punching Spider in the head, but only for a moment. Climbing out of the SUV's boot, putting Lamb's fake bomb on the back seat and making his way up the stairs hadn't taken long, but he didn't have much time to play with. If Lamb had done his bit, the real achievers would be swarming the building soon.

He said, "My assessment report."

Spider said, "Cartwright?"

"You kept a copy. Where is it?"

"That's what this is about?"

"Where is it?"

"Are you out of your fucking mind?"

River bent and grabbed Spider by his shirt collar. "This is not a game." He was armed, he was in Regent's Park, more or less dressed as an achiever. If the real thing arrived, he'd be shot on sight. Thoughts that carried a certain amount of heft. He pulled out Moody's gun again. "Let me put it this way. My assessment report. Where is it?"

Spider said, "You're not going to shoot me."

River slammed the handle of the gun into Spider's jaw, and Spider yelped as a fragment of tooth flew free. "You sure?"

"You bastard —"

"Spider. I'll keep hitting you till you give me what I want. Get it?"

"I haven't got your assessment report, why the hell would I?"

"London rules, remember?" River said. "You said it yourself, the other day. You play London rules. You cover your arse."

Spider spat a mouthful of blood on the fawn-coloured carpet. "How long do you think you've got? Before your brains join my tooth on the floor there?"

River hit him again. "You crashed King's Cross, and we both know it. Blue shirt, white tee, whichever way round it was. It was Taverner put you up to that, because she wanted rid of me. You didn't know why, did you? And didn't care, so long as you got the nice office and meetings with the Minister and a bright shining career. But you knew enough to keep a copy of the report because you're playing London rules, and the last person you trust is the one you just did a favour. So where is it?"

Spider said, "Screw you."

"I won't ask again."

"Shoot me and you'll be dead one minute later. Then you'll never find it, will you?"

"So we agree you've got it."

Footsteps sounded in the corridor, and Spider opened his bloodied mouth to shout. But River clubbed him again, and guaranteed his silence.

Hassan must have blacked out. Who wouldn't have done, struck with an axe? But it had been the blunt end Curly hit him with; a swift vicious jab with the handle, bang in the forehead. Perhaps half a minute ago. Long enough, anyway, for the scene to have shifted: Larry had stalked off down the track, and Curly had chased after him, caught him up; was shouting at him — words floated back on the cold, moss-flavoured air: *stupid chicken bastard . . .*

The axe hung limply in Curly's hand. The pair of them, arguing — well, they were no longer the Three Stooges, obviously. They were Laurel and Hardy. Stan and Ollie. In another fine mess again.

And here was a funny thing. Sometimes a blow to the head can clear away the cobwebs.

This wasn't true, but for a moment Hassan pretended it was, and wondered what he'd do if it were. He would stand up, he decided. So that's what he did.

389

There. That was better.

Wobbly on his legs, he became aware of the enormous space everywhere. Space hemmed in by trees, but without walls, and with a sky overhead. He could see it now. Branches were growing into focus. Somewhere, there'd be a sun. Hassan couldn't remember the last time he'd seen the sun.

He started walking.

The ground was spongy and unfamiliar. Partly this was due to his condition, but mostly it was because he was in a wood. But still, Hassan could walk, he could shuffle; he could almost break into a run. The trick was to look down. To watch where he placed his feet. This sudden view of the ground gave him the illusion that he was moving much faster than he really was.

If he looked back, he would see Curly and Larry breaking off their argument; come lolloping after him, Curly with axe in hand. So he remained focused on the ground instead, on how much space he was covering. He had no idea where he was going. Whether he was moving deeper into the forest, or would break into open land any moment . . . Which didn't seem probable. Everything was too thick, too woody, to surrender itself so swiftly. But those were things Hassan had no control over, while he did, at last, control his own movements. So thinking, he tripped; thrust his hands out before hitting the ground, and couldn't prevent a cry escaping him as a sharp pain seared outwards from his wrists. Which mattered much less than the noise he'd made.

So now he did look round. He'd travelled much less further than he'd thought; maybe half what he'd hoped.

Curly and Larry were about the distance away that Hassan could have thrown a kitchen chair. Both were staring at him.

Hassan could have sworn he heard the grin break out on Curly's face.

The footsteps passed Webb's office in a rush, and River released the breath he'd been holding, along with his grip on Spider's collar. Spider collapsed on to the carpet, incapable of further conversation.

River waited, but there was no more noise. It occurred to him that if it had been the achievers, he'd not have heard a sound: there was more to them than dressing the part. And with that thought an idea occurred, which he wasted two minutes implementing before turning to his search.

The files and folders took up seven shelves, stretching the length of the far wall. There could easily be a hundred on each, and River had maybe three minutes to find the one he wanted, always supposing it was there rather than, say, locked in a desk drawer. So he tried the drawers first, most of which contained junk, and only one of which was locked. River retrieved the key from Spider's pocket, but the locked drawer hid only bank statements and a passport in Spider's name. Dropping the key, River headed for the shelves. A snapshot memory from last year told him he'd submitted his interim exercise report in a black plastic folder, but at least a third of the spines were that same glossy colour, the rest being orange, yellow, green. He pulled a black one at random, to find it labelled in the top right corner: *Ennis*. Assuming this was a surname, he checked the Cs; found a Cartwright who wasn't him; then looked under R, but found no Rivers. Tried A for Assessment, and found a bunch of them, all black, but none of them his.

He took a step back and assessed the wall as a whole. "Spider Spider Spider," he murmured. "London rules . . ." Webb had said it himself: those were the rules he played by. So if Webb had burned River at King's Cross, on Taverner's instructions, he'd have kept evidence of it, to make sure he didn't end up in the line of fire himself. Given Taverner's expertise at throwing former allies to the Dogs, this was wise.

"Spider Spider Spider . . ."

London rules he'd said, but he'd also said something else. As River groped in his memory the door opened, and into the office slipped one of the achievers, a real one, his drawn pistol aimed directly at River's head.

It wasn't a grin. Curly turned when he heard the yelp, and snarled when he saw the kid was on the move. He barked at Larry — a cross between a threat and a prediction — and took off.

Behind him, he knew, Larry would be rooted to the spot. Glad to be left behind; hoping he could vanish.

I'm not doing this. I'm out of here.

No balls. With soldiers like him, the war was lost. Hell, it wasn't even fought. It was all hot air and history.

But Curly was at war. If Larry didn't know which side he was on, that was his lookout. The thing about an axe was, it didn't need reloading.

The Paki was showing his heels again. He ran like a girl, elbows tucked into his sides. Curly, though, was flying. Days of tension, of built-up excitement, and here was the moment at last.

We're gunna cut your head off.

Call it a declaration of war.

Then his right foot landed on something slippery and wet, and for half a beat he might have lost his balance and sprawled on his back, while the axe went flying freely through the air — but it didn't happen, he didn't fall; his body was finely in synch with the natural world, and his left foot firmly in place on solid ground; his hip twisting just enough that his centre of balance held, and now he was moving even faster, and the distance between himself and his prey was disappearing by the second.

He wished the Paki had been looking back to see that. Get some idea of what he was dealing with.

We're gunna cut your head off and show it.

But he was still making tracks, running like a girl. Scared as a mouse. Frightened as a rat.

Curly slowed his pace. This was too good. This was too good to hurry. This was what they meant by thrill of the chase.

We're gunna cut your head off and show it on the web.

Nick Duffy covered his phone with a hand and said, "They've got him."

"Where?"

"Webb's office."

Taverner glanced at Lamb, who shrugged. "If my guys were any good, they'd be your guys."

"Why Webb?" she asked. Then: "Never mind." To Duffy, she said, "Tell them to take whoever it is downstairs. And tell Webb to get up here."

"He's on his way."

"Thank you. Give me a minute, would you?"

Duffy left, talking into his phone.

Taverner said, "Whatever just happened, that was your last chance. Hope you enjoyed your morning, Jackson, because it's the last you'll see for a week. And by the time you're back upstairs, you'll have signed a confession, and anything else I tell you to."

Lamb, sitting facing her, nodded thoughtfully. He seemed to be about to say something important, but all he could manage was, "Mind, your lad Spider doesn't half like a colourful tie."

Behind her, the door opened.

"Of course, my lad River can't do a knot to save his life."

The minutes spent swapping shirts with the unconscious Spider hadn't been wasted after all. River Cartwright, wearing Webb's jacket and tie, closed the door behind him, a black folder tucked under his arm.

Hassan couldn't look back. Could barely look forward. Had to look at the ground, scan it for roots and stones and unsuspected dips; for anything that might grab his ankle and bring him to a sudden end. For dangers at head-height, he trusted his luck.

"Having fun yet, Paki?"

394

Curly, gaining on him.

"Playtime's nearly over."

Hassan tried to speed up, but couldn't. Everything he had to offer, he was already pouring into this one aim: to keep moving. To never stop. To run to the end of the wood, and then beyond; to always be one step ahead of this Nazi thug who wanted to kill him. With an axe.

The thought of the axe should have been a spur, but he had nothing left to give.

A sudden dip in the ground almost threw him, but he survived. A root reached for his ankle, but missed him by an inch. Two escapes in as many seconds, and that was it: his luck ran out. A branch struck him in the face and Hassan staggered from the blow, ran into a tree without enough force to damage himself, but with more than enough to bring him to a halt. His legs didn't quite buckle, nor his body quite fall, but there was nothing left. He couldn't start the engine again. He held on to the tree a moment longer, then turned to face his murderer.

Curly stood on the other side of the dip, panting lightly. A doglike smile was painted across his face, colouring every aspect but his eyes, and he was swinging the axe gently, as if to demonstrate his total control over it. There was no sign of Larry. No sign of the digicam, either; no tripod; nothing. Hassan, though, had the feeling that events were moving to a conclusion regardless. Curly's need to film this horror was paling beside his need to commit it. The axe was all he required now. The axe, and Hassan's participation.

But even knowing that, Hassan had given all he had. He couldn't move another step.

Curly shook his head. "The trouble with you lot," he explained, "is you're just not at home in the woods."

And the trouble with your lot, thought Hassan . . . The trouble with your lot . . . But there was so much wrong with Curly's lot that there was no smart phrase to do it justice. The trouble with Curly's lot was that it contained Curly, and others like him. What more needed saying?

Curly stepped forward, into the dip, and up the other side. He swapped the axe from one hand to the other; made a little lunge with it to tease his victim; then was neatly hooked round the ankle by the root Hassan had avoided, and hammered down flat on his face. Hassan watched, fascinated, as Curly took a mouthful of leaf and mud; was so engrossed by the spectacle that it took him a full second to register that the axe had just landed at his feet.

But even with bound hands, it took him less than a full second to pick it up.

Mistake? I prefer to call it a fiasco.

Spider Webb's words, the other day. They were right up there with *London rules* as far as River was concerned. *I prefer to call it a fiasco.* Thank you, Spider. That would be a clue.

The folder he held was neatly labelled *Fiasco.*

"And this," he said to Taverner, "is why you had Spider burn me."

"Burn you?"

Lamb said, "He's a kid. He gets carried away with the jargon."

"I'm calling Duffy back in."

"Be my guest," Lamb told her. He was fiddling with his bent cigarette again, and seemed at least as interested in it as in whatever River's folder held. But still: River waited until Lamb threw him a barely perceptible nod, before he went on.

He said, "I did my upgrade assessment last winter."

"I remember," Taverner said. "You crashed King's Cross."

"No, you did that. By getting Webb to feed me misinformation, sending me after a plant. A fake fake. Not the real one."

"And why would I do that?"

"Because an earlier part of the assessment was compiling a profile on a public figure," River said. "My designated target was a Shadow Cabinet Minister, but he had a stroke the night before, and was hospitalized. So I covered you instead. I thought that showed initiative, but you know what?" He opened the folder, and removed a pair of photographs he'd taken months ago, the day before the King's Cross assignment. "It showed you in a coffee shop instead. Happy memories?"

He laid them on the desk where they could all see. The pictures had been taken from outside a Starbucks, and showed Diana Taverner at a window seat, drinking from a regular-sized mug. Next to her was a crew-cut man in a dark overcoat. In the first photograph he held a handkerchief to his nose, and could have been anyone. In the second he'd lowered his hand, and was Alan Black.

"He must have been about to go undercover. Was that your last meet?"

Taverner didn't reply. Behind her eyes, Lamb and River could see calculations rolling once again; as if even here, in a glass room, she might still find a way out that neither of them had yet noticed.

Lamb said, "When you found out what Cartwright had done, you took steps. The King's Cross business should have meant game over, he should have been on the street. But because he had a legend in the family, the best you could manage was Slough House, and once the op was running, and the Voice of Albion was in play, you had Sid Baker assigned to us too, just to make sure Cartwright wasn't getting any clever ideas. Which, given grandad, he'd likely be prone to, right?"

On a train of her own, she said, "I told Webb to get rid of the file."

"He's a quick learner too."

"What do you want, Lamb?"

Lamb said, "There's a reason why handlers are always ex-joes. It's because they know what they're doing. You couldn't have fucked this up worse if you were trying."

"You've made your point. What do you want?"

River said, "You know what I want?"

She turned her gaze on him, and he understood a fundamental difference between suits and joes. When a joe looked at you, if he was any good, you'd never notice. But when a suit turned it on, you could feel their glare scorching holes in your intestinal tract.

But still, he was the O.B.'s grandson. "If Hassan Ahmed dies," he said, "there's no hiding place. It all comes out. Not just here in the Park, but out there in the real world. If your idiot plan gets that kid killed, I will crucify you. Publicly."

Taverner made a noise halfway between a snort and a laugh. She said to Lamb, "Are you going to tell him the facts of life, or shall I?"

"You already screwed him," Lamb told her. "Bit late for a theory lesson, I'd have thought. But I'll tell you what I'll do."

She waited.

He said, "If Hassan Ahmed dies, I'll watch Cartwright's back while he does whatever he thinks necessary."

And River learned something else about suits and joes; that when a joe wants to be noticed, he is.

After a while, Taverner said, "What if the boy's rescued?"

Lamb gave her his shark's grin. "That happens, maybe we'll keep it between ourselves. There's bound to be favours we can do each other."

The grin made it clear in which direction the favours would flow.

"We don't know even where he is," she said.

"Well, my crew's on it, so I'd call it sixty-forty he's toast." He looked at River. "What do you reckon?"

River said, "I don't think it's a joking matter."

But he was thinking: fifty-fifty. Absolute tops, he'd give Hassan fifty-fifty of seeing lunchtime.

Curly was moaning, a long low keening sound, and his foot was twisted at a peculiar angle. Perhaps, Hassan thought, it was broken. One broken ankle versus two bound hands — that made for a level playing field. Or would have done, except that Hassan now had an axe.

On the whole, that gave him the edge.

Placing one foot heavily on the fallen Curly's hand, Hassan rested the blade on the fallen Curly's head.

"Give me a reason not to kill you," he said.

Whatever Curly answered was lost in a mouthful of earth and a whimper of pain.

"Give me a reason," Hassan repeated, lifting the axe an inch.

Curly turned his head aside and spat grit and leaf. "Foo's ur."

"I'm supposed to understand that?"

He spat again. "My foot's hurt."

Hassan lowered the axe once more, so the blade touched Curly's temple. He pressed down, and watched Curly's eyes close and his features tighten. He wondered if the fear Curly felt was the same fear he'd felt himself. Since it seemed to have departed him now, he suspected it probably was. And how's that for a joke, he wondered? How would that work with an audience? That the same fear Curly had set loose in Hassan's gut was now burying its snout in his own bowels? But maybe not everyone would get it. Maybe you had to be there.

400

Another push on the axe loosed a trickle of blood down Curly's face.

"Did you say something?"

Curly had made a noise.

"Did you?"

He made another one.

Wrapping his bound hands tightly round the axe handle, Hassan dropped into a crouch. The blade pressed heavily on the side of Curly's head. He said, "Did you have something to say?", and gave equal weight to each syllable.

Curly said, "D—do it."

Or he might have said, "Don't do it."

Hassan waited, his eyes six inches from Curly's. He wished there were some way he could see inside Curly's head; some way he could allow light into Curly's brain in a way that didn't involve brute surgery. But there wasn't. He was sure there wasn't. So he leant a little closer.

"You know what?" Hassan said. "You make me ashamed I'm British."

Then he stood and walked away.

He walked back to the car and then along the track that led to the distant road. He had no idea how far away it was. He didn't care. He was thirsty, hungry and tired, which were all bad things; he was cold and filthy, and that was bad too. But his hands were no longer bound, because he had severed the cord with the blade of the axe; and fear was no longer chewing at his innards, because he'd left it behind in the woods. He was alive, and nobody had rescued him. He was alive because of who he was.

And maybe because Joanna Lumley had come through, too.

He saw no sign of Larry, and that didn't matter. He saw no rabbits, either, nor heard any birds, and his sense of time had long deserted him, but before Hassan reached the road lights bloomed way ahead of him: flashing ovals which painted the trees blue and then blue and then blue. And soon people were rushing towards him in a fever of noise and motion.

"Hassan Ahmed?"

The axe was taken gently away, and arms were holding him up.

"You're Hassan Ahmed?"

It was a simple enough question, and it didn't take him long to find an answer.

"Yes," he told them. "Yes, I am."

And then he added, "I'm alive."

They were very glad to hear it, he learned, as they carried him back to the world.

The roadworks have eased on Aldersgate. Traffic flows freely once more. If our inquisitive bus passenger of earlier acquaintance were to gaze at Slough House today on her way past, she might find its passage too swift for concentrated study, though on a London bus there always remains the possibility of inexplicable delay. But that aside, a glimpse is all that the new dispensation permits; one brief view of a young Chinese man with heavy-framed spectacles behind a monitor, and Slough House is in the past. Whatever used to happen there presumably continues to do so. Whatever haunts its fading paintwork doubtless still abides.

But fresh opportunities have arisen since our voyeur's first journey. She can alight at the bus stop opposite, for instance, and take a seat, and gaze all day at the never-opening front door of Slough House, with no possibility that Jed Moody will emerge to encourage her departure. Such a vigil, though, would offer little in the way of entertainment, and besides, other views await: across the road, up the staircase at Barbican Station, over the pedestrian bridge, a brief sortie along a bricked-walkway, and — weather permitting — she'll find a dry low wall on which to perch, and perhaps light a cigarette, and feast at her leisure on what she can see through the waiting windows.

Which is more than can be seen from bus-level, certainly. For instance, it is now clear that the wobbling ziggurat to one side of the young Chinese man's desk is composed of pizza boxes, and the tin pyramid to the other of Coke cans; and clear, too, that he appears to have sole occupation of this office. There is another desk, but its surface is clear; almost antiseptically so. It's as if a particularly conscientious cleaner has obliterated all traces of the desk's erstwhile occupant; a sterilization which evidently leaves his former colleague undismayed, occupied as he is by whatever is unreeling on his screen.

This thorough decluttering is in marked contrast to the state of the adjoining office, which looks to have been abandoned at a moment's notice. The desktops here are still littered with the usual detritus: diaries open to future events, uncapped pens, an alarm clock, a radio, a small gonk. Stuff which, upon a desk-worker's abrupt departure, would usually find itself swept into the nearest cardboard box and carted home. But here it all remains, suggesting that whichever pair recently shared this office found good reason not to return; being guilty, perhaps, of the kind of offence which has rendered them not only *persona non grata* but in danger of incurring active hostility from above.

Onwards and upwards, though; onwards and upwards. From the Barbican perch, a view of the second floor is offered, and this is busier, or at any rate, more peopled. In one of the offices — for our watcher, the one to the left — a pair of workers sit at the same desk; or rather, one sits at the desk while her companion perches on its edge, both concentrating on a transistor radio. Meanwhile, in the next room — the one whose windows read *W W Henderson, Solicitor and Commissioner for Oaths* — a young man sits alone; a freshly barbered young man of average height; fair-haired, pale-skinned, grey-eyed; with a sharpish nose and a small mole on his upper lip. He sits unmoving, his gaze apparently focused on the desk in the other half of his room. This, like its counterpart in the occupied office downstairs, appears to have been swept clean of personal effects, leaving only the ubiquitous computer and keyboard, a telephone, and a battle-scarred blotter belonging to another era entirely. But closer inspection reveals something else on the desk's surface; an object our watcher recognizes as a hair-slide, or barrette, though whether that word forms part of the young man's vocabulary is open to question. And yet for the moment at least it demands his full attention: an abandoned barrette on a blotter on an unoccupied desk.

So far, so pleasing, from our watcher's point of view, but even from her current vantage point the topmost floor remains inaccessible; the blind drawn over its windows ensuring that whoever haunts this floor does so unobserved. That should be an end of it, then. Our watcher should move along, there being nothing more to see. And yet still she remains, as if she were in possession of some sophisticated piece of surveillance kit that allows her not only to study the people through the windows but to unpeel their actual thoughts, and thus learn that Roderick Ho's constant trawling through the Service's classified databases is a quest for the secret that ever eludes him, this being the nature of the sin for which he's been banished to Slough House — for he is certain that he has committed no crimes that anyone is aware of. And he might be right about this, but the fact remains that he's looking in the wrong place, since the reason for his exile lies not in his doings but simply in his being. For Roderick Ho is disliked by everyone he encounters, a direct result of his own palpable dislike for everyone else, and his expulsion from Regent's Park was the administrative equivalent of the swatting of a fly. And if this explanation ever does occur to Ho, enlightenment will probably have its roots in that moment in the café on Old Street, when Catherine Standish called him Roddy.

Meanwhile, on the next floor up, Min Harper and Louisa Guy share a desk. If Min retains a tendency to pat his pockets, to make sure he hasn't lost anything, it's a habit held in check for the time being; and if Louisa still grinds her teeth at moments of tension, either she is learning to control this, or is currently feeling no stress. And while there remains unfinished business between this pair, what commands their attention right now is the radio, which is informing them of the death of one Robert Hobden in a hit-and-run accident. Hobden, of course, was a fallen star, but that his passing is not un-newsworthy is evidenced by the contribution of Peter Judd, a politician as assuredly in the ascendant as Hobden was in decline. And what Judd has to say is this: that while Hobden's attitudes and beliefs were, of course, utter hogwash, his career had not been without its highlights, and his tragic — yes, that was the word — Hobden's tragic arc should serve as a warning of the inherent dangers of extremism, in whatever flag it draped itself. And as for his own ambitions, yes, since the question had been asked, Peter Judd would, actually, be prepared to, ah, leave his plough if so required and take up greater office for the common weal — an underused term, but one with historical and cultural resonance, if he might be pardoned the digression.

Leaving unexamined the question of whether Guy and Harper are in a forgiving mood, our watcher's attention shifts now to River Cartwright, alone in the office next door. And what River Cartwright is thinking is that rewriting history is the Service's favourite game; a topic he might illustrate from a hundred of the O.B.'s late-night stories, but which is most immediately realized for him in the fact of Sidonie Baker's absence — not merely from the office, but from the records of the hospital in which she supposedly died, which have been so thoroughly sanitized as to offer reassurance as to the hygiene standards of the NHS. Just as she is not here now, so she was never there then. Indeed, River's own memories and those of his colleagues aside, his only absolute proof of her having existed resides in the barrette he found in his car, and which he has placed on her desk. As for proof of her having ceased to exist, he has none. Which allows him to speculate — or perhaps a better word might be pretend — that what he imagined happened to her did not. And he is also thinking that tonight he will catch a train to Tonbridge, and spend time with his grandfather; and perhaps even call his mother. And that tomorrow he will return to Slough House, where daily boredom is perhaps not so absolutely guaranteed as it once was, now that the Second Desk at Regent's Park is effectively in Jackson Lamb's pocket.

And as for Lamb himself — as for Lamb, he remains the shape he ever was, and of much the same temper, and his current position is what it is most mornings: he is reclining in his chair to a degree that threatens its stability and studying his noticeboard, to the back of which is once more pinned the flight fund so briefly in the possession of Jed Moody. The flight fund's existence, of course, is now known to River Cartwright, but Lamb has other secrets, and major among them is this: that all joes go to the well. River would balk at the information, but Lamb knows it to be true: all joes go to the well in the end, slyly whoring themselves for the coin of their choice. Among the late slow horses, for example, Sid Baker wanted to do her duty, Struan Loy and Kay White sought favour, and Jed Moody needed to be back among the action. Lamb has known greater treacheries. After all, Charles Partner — one-time head of Five — sold himself for money.

There is movement behind him, and Catherine Standish enters, bearing a cup of tea. This she deposits on Lamb's desk before departing again, no word having been spoken during the transaction. But Standish, though she doesn't know it, occupies a place in what

Lamb, when he's forced to acknowledge it, thinks of as his conscience, for another lesson he has long absorbed, and one hardly limited to the Intelligence sphere, is that actions have consequences which harm and ensnare others. Once, in exchange for a service, Lamb revealed to Roderick Ho the sin that had left him in Slough House, and his story — that he had been responsible for an agent's death — was, like all the best lies, true, though rendered harmless by the omission of details; that, for instance, it was Charles Partner's death for which he had been responsible, an execution sanctioned by, among others, River Cartwright's grandfather. For this act, Lamb's reward was Slough House. Lamb, then, went to the well for peace and quiet, for a sanctuary in which to indulge his ironic self-disgust, and the killing of his former friend and mentor does not disturb his sleep. But the fact that it was, inevitably, Catherine Standish who found her boss's body has been known to give him pause. Having found bodies in his time, Lamb is aware that such moments leave a scar. He has no intention of attempting to make amends for this, but if it lies within his power to do so, he will prevent further injury to her.

For the time being, though, he is contemplating immediate options. The status quo is the most obvious of these: Slough House is Lamb's kingdom, and recent events have done nothing to change that. And should the unexpected arise, he always has his flight fund. But a third way seems to be suggesting itself; and this is that perhaps he is not as weary as he thought of the world of Regent's Park and its ever-diminishing loyalties.

409

Perhaps he washed his hands of it too soon. Certainly he's had few moments of late to match that in which he watched Diana Taverner realize that he'd outplayed her, and if he can outplay her, he can surely find more worthy enemies. So far, this is idle fancy; something to fill the space between this cup of tea and the next. But who knows? Who knows?

Enough. Our watcher extinguishes, if she was smoking, her cigarette, and checks her watch, if she's wearing one. Then stands and retraces her steps: along the bricked-walkway, over the pedestrian bridge, down the staircase at Barbican Station, and on to Aldersgate. It is threatening rain again, which it always seems to do on this corner. And she has no umbrella. Never mind. If she walks fast enough, she can reach her destination without getting wet.

If another one ever turns up, she might even step on to a bus.

PART ONE

SHOWTIME

I learnt this in prison. Compulsive is when you do something repetitively. Obsessive is when you think about something repetitively.

Course, I learnt some other stuff too. Not as clear-cut. Not as defined.

The day of my release, the governor had me up for a talk.

Bent over his desk, he kept me waiting. His head over papers, a model of industry. He had a bald patch, like Prince Charles. That made me feel good. I concentrated on it. Finally, he looks up, says,

"Mitchell?"

"Yes, sir?"

I could play the game. I was but a cigarette away from freedom. I wasn't going to get reckless. His accent was from up north somewhere. Polished now but still leaking Yorkshire pudding and all that decent shit. Asked,

"You've been with us now for?"

Like he didn't know. I said,

"Three years, sir."

He hmmphed as if he didn't quite believe me. Riffled through my papers, said,

"You turned down early parole."

"I wanted to pay me debt in full, sir."

The screw standing behind me gave a snort. For the first time, the governor looked directly at me. Locked eyes. Then,

"Are you familiar with recidivism?"

"Sir?"

"Repeat offenders, it's like they're obsessed with jail."

I gave a tiny smile, said,

"I think you're confusing obsession with compulsion," and then I explained the difference.

He stamped my papers, said,

"You'll be back."

I was going to say,

"Only in the repeats,"

but felt Arnie in *The Terminator* would be lost on him. At the gate, the screw said,

"Not a bright idea to give him lip."

I held up my right hand, said,

"What else did I have to offer?"

Missed my ride.

What the Yanks say. I stood outside the prison, waiting on my lift. I didn't look back. If that's superstition, then so be it. As I stood on the Caledonian Road, I wondered if I looked like a con, ex-con.

Shifty.

Yeah, and furtive. That too.

I was forty-five years old. Near 5′ 11″ in height, weighed in at 180 pounds. In shape, though. I'd hammered at the gym and could bench-press my share. Broken through the barrier to free up those endorphins. Natural high. Shit, do you ever need that inside. Sweat till you peak and beyond. My hair was white but still plentiful. I had dark eyes, and not just on the outside. A badly broken nose near redeemed by a generous mouth.

Generous!

I love that description. A woman told me so in my twenties. I'd lost her but hung on to the adjective. Salvage what you can.

A van pulled up, sounded the horn. The door opened, and Norton got out. We stood for a moment. Is he my friend?

I dunno, but he was there. He showed up, friend enough. I said,

"Hey."

He grinned, walked over, gave me a hug. Just two guys hugging outside Her Majesty's jail. I hoped the governor was watching.

Norton is Irish and unreadable. Aren't they all? Behind all the talk is a whole other agenda. He had red hair, pasty complexion, the build of a sly greyhound. He said,

"Jaysus, Mitch, how are you?"

"Out."

He took that on board, then slapped my arm, said, "Out . . . that's a good one. I like that . . . Let's go. Prison makes me nervous."

We got in the van and he handed me a bottle of Black Bush. It had a green bow. I said,

"Thanks, Billy."

He looked almost shy, said, "Aw, it's nuttin' . . . for your release . . . the big celebration is tonight . . . and here . . ." He produced a pack of Dunhills. The lush red luxury blend. Said,

"I thought you'd be gasping for a tailor-made."

I had the brown paper parcel they give you on release. As Norton started the engine, I said,

"Hold on a sec." And I slung the parcel.

"What was that?"

"My past." I opened the Bush, took a long, holy swallow. It burned. Wow, did it ever. Offered the bottle to him. He shook his head.

"Naw, not when I'm driving."

Which was rich, him being half in the bag already. He was always this side of special brews. As we headed south he was rabbiting on about the party. I switched off.

Truth is, I was tired of him already.

Norton said, "I'll give you the scenic tour."

"Whatever."

I could feel the whiskey kicking in. It does all sorts of weird shit to me, but mainly it makes me unpredictable. Even I can't forecast how it will break.

We were turning from Marble Arch and, of course, got caught at the lights. A guy appeared at the windshield and began to wipe it with a dirty cloth. Norton yelled,

"These fuckin' squeegees, they're everywhere!"

This guy didn't even make an effort. Two fast wipes that left skid marks on the glass. Then he appeared at my window, said,

"Four quid, matey."

I laughed, rolled the window down, and said,

6

"You need another line of work, pal."

He had long, greasy hair down to his shoulders. His face was thin, and he had the eyes I'd seen a hundred times on the yards. The eyes of the bottom-rung predator. He leant his head back and spat. Norton went,

"Aw Jaysus."

I didn't move, asked,

"You got a tire iron?"

Norton shook his head,

"Mitch, Jesus, no."

I said, "OK."

And got out.

The guy was surprised but didn't back off. I grabbed his arm and broke it over my knee. Got back in the van and the lights changed. Norton revved fast, crying,

"Oh God, Mitch, you crazy bastard. You're out . . . what? Ten minutes . . . and you're at it already. You can't be losing it."

"I didn't lose it, Billy."

"What, you smash the guy's arm, that's not losing it?"

"If I'd lost it, I'd have broken his neck."

Norton gave me an anxious look, said,

"You're kidding . . . right?"

"What do you think?"

Norton said, "I think you'll be surprised at the place I found for you."

"As long as it's near Brixton."

"It's Clapham Common. Since you've been . . . away . . . it's become trendy."

"Oh shit."

"Naw, it's OK . . . Anyway, a writer guy got into heavy schtook to some moneylenders, had to do a runner. Left everything: clothes, books . . . you're set."

"Is Joe still at the Oval?"

"Who?"

"*Big Issue* seller."

"I don't know him."

We were coming up to the Oval. I said,

"He's there. Pull over."

"Mitch . . . you want to buy the *Big Issue* now?"

I got out, walked over. Joe hadn't changed. He was dishevelled, dirty, cheerful.

I said, "Hi, Joe."

"Mitchell . . . Good Lord, I heard you was doing a stretch."

I handed over a fiver, said,

"Give us a copy."

We didn't mention the change. He asked,

"Did they hurt you in there, Mitch?"

8

"Not so's you'd notice."

"Good man. Got a smoke?"

I gave him the pack of Dunhills. He examined them, said,

"Flash."

"Only the best for you, Joe."

"You'll have missed the World Cup."

And a whole lot more besides. I asked,

"How was it?"

"We didn't win it."

"Oh."

"There's always the cricket."

"Yeah, there's always that."

Three years in prison, you lose
time
compassion
and the ability to be surprised.

I was nigh amazed when I saw the flat. The whole ground floor of a two-storey house. And it was beautifully furnished, all soft pastels and wall-to-wall books. Norton stood behind to gauge my reaction.

I said, "Christ."

"Yeah, isn't it something? Come and see more."

He led me into the bedroom. Brass double bed. He threw open the wardrobes, packed full with clothes. Like a sales clerk, Norton said,

"You've got your
Gucci
Armani

Calvin Klein
and other bastards I can't pronounce. Get this, the sizes are medium to large."

"I can do medium."

Back into the living room, Norton opened a drinks cabinet. Full too. Asked,

"Whatcha fancy?"

"A beer."

He opened two bottles, handed me one. I asked,

"No glass?"

"No one drinks outta glasses anymore."

"Oh."

"*Sláinte*, Mitch, and welcome home."

We drank. The beer tasted great. I indicated the place with my bottle, asked,

"Just what kind of a hurry was the guy in to leave all this?"

"A big hurry."

"Won't the loan shark want some of it?"

Norton smiled, said, "I've already had the choice bits."

It took me a minute. Blame the beer. I said,

"You're the moneylender?" Big smile. He was proud, been waiting, said,

"Part of a firm — and we'd like you on board."

"I don't think so, Billy."

He was expansive.

"Hey, I didn't mean right away. Take some time, chill out."

Chill out.

I let it go, said,

"I dunno how to thank you, Billy. It's incredible."

"No worries. We're mates . . . right?"

"Right."

"OK, I gotta go. The party's in The Greyhound at eight. Don't be late."

"I'll be there. Thanks again."

Briony's a basket case. A true, out-and-out nutter. I've known some seriously disturbed women. Shit, I've dated them, but up against Bri they were models of sanity. Bri's husband died five years ago. Not a huge tragedy, as the guy was an asshole. The tragedy is that she doesn't believe he's gone. She keeps seeing him on the street and, worse, chats to him on the phone. Like the genuine crazies, she has moments of lucidity. Times when she appears

rational

coherent

functional

. . . then wallop. She'll blindside you with an act of breathtaking insanity.

Add to this, she has a beguiling charm, sucks you in. She looks like Judy Davis, and especially how Judy Davis appeared with Liam Neeson in the Woody Allen movie. Her hobby is shoplifting. I dunno why she's never been caught, as she does it with a recklessness beyond belief. Bri is my sister. I rang her. She answered on the first ring, asked,

"Frank?"

I sighed. Frank was her husband. I said,

"It's Mitchell."

"Mitch . . . oh Mitch . . . you're out."

"Just today."

"Oh, I'm so happy. I've so much to tell you. Can I make you dinner? Are you hungry? Did they starve you?"

I wanted to laugh or cry.

"No . . . no, I'm fine . . . listen, maybe we could meet tomorrow."

Silence.

"Bri . . . are you still there?"

"You don't want to see me on your first night? Do you hate me?"

Against all my better judgment, I told her about the party. She instantly brightened, said,

"I'll bring Frank."

I wanted to shout, "Yah crazy bitch, get a grip!" I said, "OK."

"Oh Mitch, I'm so excited. I'll bring you a present."

Oh God.

"Whatever."

"Mitch . . . can I ask you something?"

"Ahm . . . sure."

"Did they gang rape you? Did they?"

"Bri, I gotta go, I'll see you later."

"Bye, baby."

I put the phone down. Wow, I felt drained.

I had a sort through the wardrobe. When you've worn denim and a striped shirt for three years, it was like Aladdin's Cave.

First off I got a stack of Tommy Hilfiger out. Put that in a bin liner. All that baggy shit, maybe Oxfam could off-load it. There was a Gucci leather jacket, nicely beat up. I'd be having that. Lots of Hennes white T-shirts: the type Brando immortalized in *On the Waterfront*. The guys in prison would kill for muscular American T-shirts.

No jeans.

No problem.

Gap khaki pants, a half dozen. A blazer from French Connection and sweatshirts from Benetton.

I dunno if that guy had taste, but he sure had money. Well, loan-shark money.

There was a Barbour jacket and a raincoat from London Fog. No shit, but I'd be a con for all seasons. Odd thing was, not a shoe in sight. But was I complaining? Was I fuck. I had a pair of shoes.

Took a hot shower and used three towels to dry off. They'd been swiped from the Holiday Inn so were soft and friendly. What I most wanted was another beer, but I knew I'd better cool it. The evening ahead would be liquid and perhaps lethal. I needed to at least arrive soberish. Took a quick scan of the books, one whole wall devoted to crime writers. Spotted

Elmore Leonard

James Sallis

Charles Willeford

John Harvey

Jim Thompson

Andrew Vachss.

And that was only the first sweep. Phew! I might never go out. Just bury myself in crime.

I put on a T-shirt, khaki pants and the leather jacket. Checked it out in the mirror. No doubt I could pass for a Phil Collins roadie. Thought — "If I'd money, I'd be downright dangerous."

Walking down Clapham Common, a woman smiled at me. I knew it was the jacket. There's a transport caff in Old Town that used to be the business. It was still there. The type of place if it's not on the table, it's not on the menu.

For an ex-con there can be few greater pleasures than to eat alone. Grabbing a booth I luxuriated in just having it to myself. Knew exactly what I'd order.

The carbohydrate nightmare, neon-lit in medical overload. Like this:

two sausages

mess of bacon

fried tomatoes

eggs

black pudding

toast

pot of stewed tea.

Oh yeah. In the booth next to me was an old codger. Eyeing me. He had the face and manner of a "character". His name would be Alfred.

Course, everyone would love him. Alfred would have his own corner in the pub and his own pewter tankard.

He'd be a holy terror to a new barman.

My food arrived, and he said,

"That food, son . . . you know where it comes from?"

Without lifting my head, I said,

"I've a feeling you're going to enlighten me."

That startled him, but not enough to stop him. He said,

"Big fellah like you, you should have a feed of potatoes."

I raised my head, looked at him, said,

"Old fellah like you, you should mind your own business."

Shut him down.

I tried not to wolf the food. Now that I was out, I was going to have to re-adapt. When I finished, I went and paid. On my way out, I stopped by Alfred, said,

"Nice chatting with you."

Walked down to Streatham and into the bank. I wasn't sure how much money I had, as they don't send statements to prison.

What they should do is send bankers there.

I filled out a withdrawal slip and got in line. It was slow, but I knew how to kill time.

The cashier was friendly in that vacant money way. I handed her the slip; she ran it by the computer, said,

"Oh."

I said nothing. She said,

"This is a dormant account."

"Not anymore."

She gave me the look. The leather jacket wasn't cutting any ice. She said,

"I'll have to check."

"You do that."

A man behind me sighed, asked,

"Is this going to take long?"

Gave him a blank smile, answered,

"I've absolutely no idea,"

The cashier returned with a suit. He was Mr Efficiency, said,

"Mr Mitchell, if you could step over to my desk."

I could. I sat and looked at his desk. A sign proclaimed

WE REALLY CARE

He did bank stuff for a bit, then,

"Mr Mitchell, your account has been dormant for three years."

"Is that against the law?"

Ruffled him.

Recovered,

"Oh no . . . it's ahm . . . let's see . . . with interest you have twelve hundred pounds."

I waited. He asked,

"I take it you wish to reactivate the account?"

"No."

"Mr Mitchell, might I suggest a prudent reserve? We have some very attractive offers for the small saver."

"Give me my money."

"Ahm . . . of course . . . you wish to terminate your account?"

"Leave a pound in it . . . 'cos you guys care so much."

I got my cash but no warm handshake or cheerful goodbye.

You have to ask yourself how much it is they *really* care.

Party time. I'd had a nap and woke with a start. My heart was pounding and sweat cascaded down my back. Not because I thought I was still in prison but because I knew I was out. The guys in the joint had cautioned me:

"Nothing's scarier than being out there."

Which I guess is why so many go back.

Aloud I vowed, "The fuck I'm going back."

Did a hundred sits, a hundred presses, and felt the panic ebb.

The kitchen was stocked with provisions.

No porridge, thank Christ.

Had some OJ and bad burnt toast. There was a microwave, and I zapped some coffee. It tasted like shit, which was exactly what I was accustomed to. Did the shower stuff and skipped shaving. Let that three-day beard kick in.

What's the worst that could happen?

I'd look like George Michael's father.

Slapped on a Calvin Klein deodorant. It said on the label, NO ALCOHOL. Gee, no point in having a slug, then.

Sat for a moment and rolled a smoke. Had the craft down. Could do it with one hand. Now, if I could strike a match off my teeth I'd be a total success.

Took a cruise through the music collection. Oddly, for such a state-of-the-art place, the guy hadn't joined the CD revolution. It was your actual albums or cassettes. OK by me.

Put on Trisha Yearwood. A track called "Love Wouldn't Lie To Me."

Listened twice.

I'm from south-east London. We don't use words like "beauty" unless it's cars or soccer. Even then, you better know your company real good.

This song was beautiful. It stirred in me such feeling of

yearning

loss

regret.

Shit, next I'd be missing women I'd never met. Maybe it's a "being in your mid-forties" thing.

I shook myself, time to rock 'n' roll. Put on the Gap khaki pants — very tight in the waist, but hey, if I didn't breathe, I'd be fine. A white T-shirt and the blazer.

Looking sharp.

Like a magnet for every trainee mugger.

The album was still running and Trisha was doing a magic duet with Garth Brooks.

Had to turn it off.

No two ways, music will fuck your head nine ways to Sunday.

What you regard as a small, isolated incident sets off a chain of events you could never have anticipated. You believe you're making choices and all you're doing is slotting in the pieces of a foreordained conclusion.

Deep, huh!

I took the subway to the Oval. The Northern Line was at its usual irritating best. Two bedraggled buskers were massacring "The Streets Of London." I gave them a contribution in the hope they might stop.

They didn't.

As soon as they finished, they began it anew. Coming out at the Oval, Joe was there with *The Big Issue*. I said,

"Wanna go to a party, Joe?"

"This *is* my party, Mitch." Argue that.

Across the road an Aston Martin pulled in at St Mark's Cathedral. A young woman got out. From the trees by the church, two predators materialized. These are not the homeless, they're what Andrew Vachss calls "skels": bottom feeders. They began to hassle her. I debated getting involved. I didn't want to spoil the blazer. Joe said,

"Go on, Mitch."

I crossed the road. They'd the urban ambush going.

One in front doing the verbals, the other behind about to strike.

I shouted,

"Yo, guys."

All three turned. These preds were early twenties, white and nasty.

The first said,

"Whatcha want, wanker?"

The other,

"Yeah, fuck off, bollocks."

Close up I saw one pred was a woman. I said,

"Leave the lady be."

The first pred read the blazer, read me wrong, moved up, said,

"Whatcha gonna do about it, cunt?"

I said,

"This."

And jammed my index finger in his right eye. It's a common manoeuvre in the yard. When it's serious you pop the eyeball.

This wasn't. It hurts like a bastard, though. I moved to the second pred, said,

"I'm going to break your nose."

She ran.

The woman, the would-be victim, just stared at me. I said,

"Not a smart place to park."

I recrossed the road and could hear music from The Greyhound.

Prayed it wasn't "The Streets Of London".

The pub was packed. A banner over the bar proclaimed,

WELCOME HOME MITCH

Norton, in an Armani suit, greeted me warmly, said,
"Here's a Revolver."
"What?"
"It's a cocktail."
"What's in it?"
"What else but Black Bush, two jiggers of Cointreau and ginger ale?"
"Thanks, Billy, but I'll have a pint o' bitter."
Various Grade B villains approached and shook my hand. The A List were seated and expected me to approach them.
I did.
The party was what Dominick Dunne calls "a rat fuck". Too many people. Promises of sundry jobs were made and lotsa "call me" expressions. I spotted Tommy Logan, an up-and-coming drug lord, asked,
"Tommy, can I have a word?"
"Sure, son."
He was half my age. He said,
"You're looking fit."
"But for what, eh?"
We laughed politely at this. I asked,
"I need a favour, Tommy." He moved me to the end of the bar. Out of earshot if not out of reach. I took a deep breath, said,
"I need some gear."

It was Tommy's business not to show what he felt or thought.

He registered near amazement, said,

"I never had you down for the needle."

"It's a one-off, for a friend."

"Jeez, Mitch, that's the hook . . . just once."

Next he'd be giving me a lecture. I cut to the chase, asked,

"Can you do it? I'd need the works too. A hypo . . . like that."

"Sure, I'll have it for you by close of business."

He shook his head, then,

"I like you, Mitch, so all I'm gonna say is take it easy."

"Iris DeMent has a song called 'Easy'."

"Who?"

Briony arrived looking like a radiant bag lady. She was dressed in some kind of designer bin liner. She gave me a huge hug, asked,

"Do you like my dress?"

"Ahm . . ."

"I stole it from Vivienne Westwood's shop."

Before I could reply, she asked,

"Mitch, would you like a Glock?"

"I've already turned down a Revolver."

She looked disappointed, said,

"It's a 9mm."

"Jesus, Bri, you're serious."

She reached in her handbag, saying,

"I'll show you."

I grabbed her hand, pleaded,

"Christsake, don't pull a gun in this crowd . . . I'll get it later, OK?"

"OK, Mitch."

Norton shouted,

"Bri, whatcha drinking?"

"Harvey Wallbanger."

A woman came into the pub. It was the Aston Martin lady. I said to Bri,

"Excuse me."

"Frank will be here later, Mitch."

The late Frank. I approached the woman, said,

"Hello again." She nearly jumped, then got composure, said,

"I never got to thank you."

"Glad to help . . . did you follow me in here?"

"What? Good Lord, no . . . I'm here on a story."

My heart sank.

"You're a journalist?"

"Yes, any gathering of south-east villains is news."

She looked towards the bar. A group of grim men were deep in conversation. They exuded menace. She said,

"That looks like a nasty bunch."

"You're right. They're the police."

She laughed, asked,

"Are you serious?"

"Would you like a drink?"

"Some mineral water . . . I'm Sarah."

"Mitch."

I considered spiking the mineral water, loosen her up a bit. Then decided to just let it play. As she took a sip, she said,

"I believe the party's for a villain who's just out of prison."

"That's me."

"Oh."

I drank some beer, said,

"I'm not a criminal. I'm simply unemployed."

She digested this, then,

"What type of work do you do besides rescuing women?"

26

"You name it, I can do it."

"Handyman, are you?"

She considered, then asked,

"I'd have to check, do you have a phone?"

I gave her the number and asked,

"Aren't you wary of recommending an ex-con?"

"If you get the job, it's you who'd need to be careful."

I laughed, not taking her seriously.

The first in a line of very bad judgements.

Sarah moved away, to do research I guess. Later, Tommy Logan approached, slipped me a package. I said,

"I owe you one, Tommy."

Bri grabbed me, said,

"Mitch, I've just met a divine young man."

"Uh-huh."

She was holding the hand of a punk. Nineteen or twenty years old. He looked like a sick David Beckham, but he had the essential smirk of the wannabe gangster. He said,

"Yo, bro."

Unless you're black, there is truly no answer to this. Except a slap up the side of the head, but I wasn't in the mood. Bri gushed,

"Mitch. I told him you'll take him under your wing."

"I don't think so."

She seemed genuinely surprised.

"You don't like him?"

27

"Bri, I don't know him and I don't want to know him, now give it a rest."

She disappeared into the crowd. I mingled for a while more, then figured I'd had enough. Saw Norton and said,

"Billy, I'm gonna split."

"What . . . already?"

"I'm used to early nights."

"Oh right . . . listen, about the job . . ."

"The moneylending?"

"It's not like you think. You'd only need to come with me once or twice a week."

"Billy . . ."

"No, listen . . . the pad you're in, the clothes — I don't need to tell you there's no free lunches."

So much for any feeble principles. I wanted the flat, the clothes, the life. I asked,

"When?"

"Is Wednesday good? I'll collect you 'round noon."

"Noon?"

"Yeah, our clients aren't early risers. That's why the dumb fucks are always skint."

As Jack Nicholson said in *Terms of Endearment*,

"I was just inches from a clean getaway."

I'd got to the door when Tommy Logan called me, said, "There's a ruckus out back."

"Like I give a shit."

"You should: it's your sister."

I briefly thought of leaving her to it, then spat,

"Fuck."

Headed back there. Past stacked beer crates, empty barrels, into the yard. The punk was against the wall, a deep gash down his cheek. Bri had the Glock in his face. I said,

"Bri . . . Bri, it's Mitch."

She didn't move, said,

"He wanted to put his thing in my mouth."

I moved closer, said,

"I thought the gun was my present."

"It is."

"Well, let's have it, then, eh?"

She stared hard at the punk, then said,

"OK," and handed it to me.

He appeared on the verge of passing out. Sank down to a sitting position, blood streaming from the gash. I bent to him, began to go through his pockets. Bri asked,

"You're robbing him?"

Not that she cared, she was just curious. I said,

"I'm looking for his stash; he's a cokehead, I saw his sniffles earlier."

"You're going to do a line?"

I found the packet, ripped it open. I spread the coke along the gash and it stemmed the blood.

Bri asked,

"What are you doing?"

"It's an anaesthetic."

"How do you know?"

"I celled with a doper."

I stood up, took her arm, said,

"Let's go."

When I got her outside, she asked,

"Wanna go clubbing?"

I hailed a cab, got her in it, said,

"I'll call you tomorrow."

"Mitch, I hope you don't mind that Frank didn't make it."

"No no, I don't mind."

Heading for the tube, I had heroin, a gun and half a bag of coke. Jesus, what more could you ask of a night on London town?

Back at the flat, I kicked off my shoes, opened a beer and collapsed on the sofa. Sat up after a bit and laid down a line of coke, snorted it fast. In no time, I was numb.

Fucking A.

I'd told Bri the truth about celling with a doper. He'd told me about smack, about kissing God. To hit the very stars.

I'd resolved to try it one time on my first night of freedom.

Night after night, he'd relive his first spike. As if all your life you're living in darkness and suddenly you step into the light. You laugh out loud. Your nerves feel like velvet, and your skin glows. And the energy, like you're fucking bionic.

He told me about the downside too. I figured I could hack it.

But not tonight. It didn't feel right. I went into the bedroom and stashed the gear under the sweatshirts. I put the Glock under my mattress. With the coke, I was up, pacing. Went to the bookshelf and picked out James Sallis.

Poetry.

Loss.

Addiction.

Perfect.

About halfway through my stretch, I got a visit from the chaplain. I was lying on my bunk, reading. My cellmate was at an AA meeting. The chaplain had manners, asked,

"Might I come in?"

"Sure."

Any diversion. He sat on the opposite bunk, scanned my line of books. There was

philosophy

literature

thrillers

poetry.

He said, "Your reading is eclectic."

I thought he said electric, answered,

"Whatever gets you wired."

He gave a religious smile, all front, no warmth, said, "No — *eclectic*, it means random."

I liked it, said,

"I like it."

He picked up a volume of poetry, said,

"Rilke, now that's surprising."

I tried to remember the line, tried,

"Everything terrible is something that needs our love." It worked. He was stunned. I pushed, asked,

"The cons here, do you think they need love?"

He went evangelical, said,

"Most of the men here aren't terrible, just . . ."

But he couldn't find an appropriate adjective. I said, "You obviously haven't chowed down with us. Yesterday a guy got knifed in the face for his crème caramel."

"How unfortunate."

"That's one way of putting it."

I sat up, rolled a cig, offered the chaplain.

"No, but thank you."

I was half interested in him, asked,

"Do you drive?"

"Excuse me?"

"A car. I just like to hear about motors."

"No, I ride a bike."

Of course.

He folded his hands on his knees, adapted his face to empathy mode, asked,

"Is anything troubling you?"

I laughed out loud, indicated the world outside the cell, answered,

"Take a wild guess."

"It's good to share."

"Keep your voice down, Padre. That talk could spark a riot."

He stood up, his duty done, said,

"You're an interesting man. Might I visit on another day?"

I lay back on the bunk, said,

"My door is always open."

Course, he never did visit again.

32

Next morning I was listening to Capital Radio when the phone went. Picked it up, said,

"Yeah."

"Mitch? This is Sarah."

"Right. Did you get a story?"

"No, but I might have got you a job."

"Thanks."

"Don't thank me yet. I have an aunt in Holland Park. She lives in a huge house and it's in dire need of repair. The snag is she's a difficult woman and no other workmen will go there anymore. Believe me, she's had an army of them."

"Why will I be different?"

Long pause, then,

"Well, she'll forgive a man anything if he's handsome."

"Oh."

"Do you want to give it a whirl? She'll pay awfully well."

"Sure, why not."

"She lives at The Elms; you can't miss it, just after the beginning of Holland Park, it has an impressive driveway."

"I'll find it."

"I'm sure you will. Do you know anything about the theatre?"

"Not a thing."

"You won't have come across Lillian Palmer, then."

"Never heard of her."

"I don't suppose it matters. Anyway, that's her, my aunt."

"I look forward to meeting her."

"Don't be so sure. Well, good luck."

I decided to chance it, felt I might be on a roll, asked, "Listen, Sarah, do you fancy a drink sometime?"

"I don't think so. I'm not part of the package."

And she hung up.

So much for the roll.

I had no equipment for work but figured I'd make it up as I went along. I know enough cowboys to borrow almost anything.

First off, I'd go and see the place, see what I'd need. If I was to be a handyman, I thought casual clothes would be best. Sweatshirt and jeans should be fine.

As I headed for the tube, I thought, "I've a home, clothes, job offers, and I've only been out twenty-four hours."

Those cons had got it wrong; life on the outside was a breeze.

In Alcoholics Anonymous, they refer to HP. It means higher power. On the street they also refer to HP . . . for homeless person. The connection between both is booze. Alcoholics have to abstain to survive. The homeless depend on it to survive.

34

I dunno what set this off in my head. A legacy of jail is this travelling on a tangent of thought.

Whatever, by the time I snapped out of it I was nearing Holland Park. I got off the tube at Notting Hill and walked up. Found The Elms, no problem. Like Sarah said, there was a huge driveway. Strolled up, looking at the trees that lined the way.

Then the house and I muttered — "Wow."

It was a mansion, no other description would apply. It shouted,

WEALTH.

I moved to the door, made of solid oak. Up close the house looked run-down, shabby even. Lots of work here. I lifted the heavy knocker, gave it a wallop.

The door opened. A butler stood there in full regalia. I couldn't believe it. I thought all the butlers had gone to California or sitcoms or both. He was small and sturdy. In truth, like Oddjob from the Bond movie. I was too taken aback to speak. He asked,

"Yes?"

I gave my name, mentioned Sarah and expected the bum's rush.

He said, "Madam is expecting you. Come this way."
I did.

Into a large hall. He'd have taken my coat if I had one. Led me to a drawing room and said,

"Madam will appear presently."

Then he fucked off.

The room was vast, with Regency furniture. I know that 'cos it looked like no one ever sat on it. Hundreds of framed photographs with a blonde woman in them all. She looked like a laid-back Lauren Bacall with the ferocity. A massive portrait above the fireplace. The blonde again. On the walls were framed posters with "LILLIAN PALMER IN STREETCAR", "SWEET BIRD OF YOUTH", "DESIRE UNDER THE ELMS"

Like that.

Despite the expensive frames they looked old. Heavy drapes covered the windows, and I figured I'd let a little light in.

Pulled them back to reveal bay windows. An overgrown garden stretched all the way back. Without thinking, I began to roll a cig. Lit up. I was staring out the window when a shout nearly put me through it.

"PUT OUT THAT CIGARETTE!"

I turned round to face whoever. A woman brushed past me, screaming,

"How dare you open those drapes? The light will ruin the posters!"

As she covered the windows I got a look. She was dressed in a long black gown. Blonde hair down her back. Then she turned.

Not at all like Bacall. More like John Cassavetes' wife, who I'd seen in *Gloria*.

I'm bad at ages but I reckoned she was an expensive sixty.

Money and care had helped keep the face intact. She had startling blue eyes and used them to scrutinize me, then,

"I presume you're here for an interview. Well? Speak up. What have you to say?"

Her voice was deep, almost coarse. The timbre that cigarettes and whiskey add. Course, arrogance helps too. I said,

"I need an ashtray."

She indicated a large crystal dish. I stubbed out the cig.

It's hard to credit, but the butt threw the room off. In that dish, the lone stub seemed like an affront. I wanted to put it in my pocket. She said,

"You expect to make a good impression by dressing like a runner?"

I said, "You don't have to be nice to me. I want the job."

She stepped forward, and I thought she was going to hit me, then she laughed. A deep down and dirty one. The best kind.

Then she said,

"Sarah mentioned you'd been in jail. What are you, a thief?"

With more edge than I intended, I said,

"I'm not a thief."

"Oh dear, have I hit a nerve? Have I violated some convict code of ethics?"

This was delivered in a dramatic voice. As if she was onstage.

I'd learn that she was never off it. I said,

"I was in a fight, it got out of hand."

Closing the topic, she said,

"There'll be no fighting here."

From out of left field, I felt a flash of desire. I couldn't believe it. My body was responding to her. She

gave a knowing smile, and I didn't want to analyse that.
No way. She said,

"We'll give you a week's trial. Jordan will set your
duties."

She went to the door, stopped, said,

"If you absolutely must steal an item, take that
disgusting ashtray."

And she was gone.

I followed Jordan outside to the garage. More like an
airplane hangar. The first thing I noticed was a car, up
on blocks. I gave a low whistle, asked,

"Is that what I think it is?"

"Yes, it is."

I tried to place his accent, ventured,

"Are you German?"

"Hungarian."

He swept his arm round the garage, said,

"Everything you could possibly need is here."

Tools.

Overalls.

Ladders.

Paint.

I thought that was good, said,

"Good."

He indicated a chart on the wall, said,

"This is your timetable."

"What?"

"Madam likes everything compartmentalised."

It took him awhile to get that last word, but I stayed
on and got his drift, said,

"Piecemeal."
He pointed to the chart, said,
"Please examine it."
I did.

Monday — Painting
Tuesday — Gutters
Wednesday — Roof
Thursday — Windows
Friday — Patio

I pretended to be interested, as if it made any sense.
I said,
"And Saturday, party down."
He ignored that, said,
"You will arrive promptly at seven thirty. You'll partake of a light breakfast. Work will commence at eight sharp. At eleven you will have a tea break, twenty minutes. At one, you'll have lunch for one hour. You will cease work at four sharp."
I wanted to snap off a Hitler salute, shout,
"*Jawohl*, Herr Kommandant."
Instead I asked,
"Does she work now?"
"Madam is resting."
"Jeez, from those posters, she's been resting for thirty years."
"She is awaiting the right vehicle."
I nodded at the Rolls-Royce Silver Ghost, said,
"That should do the job."

Any reply he might have made was lost as a van drove up. On the side was

LEE
BUILDING AND MAINTENANCE

An overweight man climbed out. Took him a while due to the weight he was carrying. He was wearing overalls and a baseball cap. A dirty baseball cap with "LEE" barely decipherable.

He ambled over, nodded to Jordan, looked at me, asked, "Who's the gobshite?"

Jordan said, "Mr Lee, you are no longer employed here. I thought I made that clear."

Lee waved his hand in dismissal, said,

"Lighten up, Jord. The old bat in there doesn't know who's here. I'm not about to let a good thing go."

Jordan sighed, said,

"You have already been replaced, Mr Lee. I must ask that you leave."

Lee laughed, said,

"You run along, Jord . . . git us a cup o' tea, two sugars. I'll sort out this geezer."

Then he moved towards me. Jordan moved faster and delivered two lightning jabs to Lee's stomach. I'd barely time to register it wasn't his fist — open palmed. Lee sank to his knees, groaning, whined,

"Whatcha do that for?"

Jordan stood over him and, with both hands, slammed Lee's ears.

I said,

"That's gotta hurt."

Then Jordan helped Lee to the van, bundled him in. After a few minutes, the engine turned and he drove away slowly. Jordan turned back to me, asked,

"Is Monday suitable to begin?"

"You bet."

I lit a roll-up as I walked down the drive. Got to the gate and looked back. The house seemed dead. I began to head for Notting Hill. Halfway down was Lee's van. He was leaning against it, massaging his stomach. As I drew alongside he said,

"I want a word with you, pal."

"OK."

"I didn't get your name."

"No."

He squared up. I noticed his ears were scarlet. He said,

"You don't want to fuck with me, pal."

"Why not?"

"What are you, a smart-arse?"

"A smart-arse with a job — sorry — with *your* job."

He couldn't decide which way to go, settled for verbal, said,

"If you know what's good for you, pal, you'll stay away."

I made a playful feint to his stomach but didn't actually touch him, said,

"You're gonna have to cut down on them burgers, Lee." I walked away. I could hear him muttering the length of Ladbroke Grove. All in all, I kinda liked old Lee. In the nick, they'd have turned him out in a week.

When I got back to Clapham I could feel the effect Lillian Palmer had had on me. I figured it was time I got laid. Went into a phone booth and scanned the cards on display. Every sexual need was catered for. I decided on the following:

TANYA
RECENTLY ARRIVED FROM SOUTH AMERICA
TWENTY YEARS OLD
BEAUTIFUL, BUSTY, READY TO MEET ALL YOUR DESIRES

Yeah.

I rang and set a time. Yup, she could see me now. The address was in Streatham. As I headed there, I swear I felt nervous.

After three years, you wonder how it's gonna be. Found the building and rang the top bell. Got buzzed in, walked up two flights of stairs. Knocked on the door. A guy in his thirties came out. I said,

"Jeez, I hope you're not Tanya."

"Fifty quid in advance."

I paid, and he asked,

"Need anything else — weed, uppers, downers?"

I shook my head. He stepped aside and I went in. A woman was sitting down, dressed in a slip, stockings and suspenders. She wasn't in her twenties, or busty or beautiful.

She said,

"Would you like a drink?"

Not South American either. I said,

"Sure."

"Scotch?"

"Lovely."

I watched her as she got the drink. A nice bod — I could feel desire returning. Not wild excitement but getting there.

I took the drink, said,

"Cheers." She stood in front of me, said,

"No kinky stuff, no kissing, no bondage."

What could I say? I said,

"No kidding."

I followed her into the bedroom. The radio was playing the Eagles' "Desperado." If "My Way" is the anthem of chauvinists, then "Desperado" is the rationalization of convicts. She handed me a condom as she lay back on the bed.

It was quick.

She indicated the bathroom, said,

"You can clean up in there."

I did.

When I came out she said,

"For another twenty, we could go again."

I said, "I think I've had as much fun as I can handle."

As I left, she said,

"Call again."

Back in Clapham, I went to the Rose and Crown, took a stool at the bar, ordered a pint of bitter. Working on that I rolled a cigarette. A man in his sixties came in and took the stool beside me. I hoped to fuck he wasn't going to be friendly. I fixed my face in the "don't put chat on me" mode. He ordered a large navy rum, said,

"None of that Kiskadee rubbish."

I tuned out. Wanted to engage in some post-coital melancholy.

Then I realized he was talking to me. I said,

"What?"

"Would you believe I was in the middle of an angiogram two months ago?"

"You what?"

"Should have been routine, but an artery the cardio didn't know about got jammed. Just when he's Roto-Rootering another one and —"

I said, "Shut up. I don't wanna hear about it."

He looked wiped, asked,

"Like a drink?"

"I'd like you to bore the arse off someone else."

"Just trying to be friendly."

"I don't do friendly."

Finished my drink and got outta there. When I got outside, a man was standing directly across the road, staring at me. In his thirties, blond hair, a decrepit suit. He looked like he was going to say something, then turned and walked away.

If the traffic hadn't been so heavy I might have gone after him. I thought — "They're coming outta the woodwork today."

The phone was ringing as I got home. Picked it up.

"Mitch?"

"Yeah."

"It's Billy Norton, where've you been — I've been ringing you all morning."

"At a job interview."

"What? You've already got a job."

"Moneylending? That's not a job, it's a virus."

He took a deep breath, said,

"We go tomorrow, like you agreed."

"Yeah."

"Mitch, it's easy, no problem — all you have to do is be my back-up."

"Easy? First I heard that taking money was easy."

He was seriously irritated, tried to rein it, said,

"I'll bring some Red Bull."

"Some what?"

"It's an energy drink. You wash down some amphetamines with it, you're seriously cranked."

"Seriously deranged, too."

"I'll pick you up at noon, OK?"

"I can hardly wait."

Later on, I phoned for a pizza and was waiting for delivery. I was reading Charles Willeford's *Sideswipe* and lamenting there'd be no more of this brilliant series. In prison I'd read one, two books a day. I intended to maintain the habit.

The doorbell went. Opened it. Not the pizza. A well-built man, steel-grey hair, in a dark suit. He asked,

"Mr Mitchell?"

"Yeah."

He produced a warrant card, said,

"I'm Detective Sergeant Bailey — might I have a word?"

"OK."

He followed me in, examining the room as he did, said, "Nice place."

I nodded. He sat down, said,

"We get a daily bulletin on ex-prisoners returning to our manor."

If he expected an answer I didn't have one.

He took out a packet of cigs, didn't offer, lit up, continued,

"I recognized your name, but hey, no address."

"I'm not on parole, I'm a free man."

"Course you are. I gave your friend Norton a buzz, and he was most helpful. So I thought I'd drop by, see how you're settling in."

The doorbell again. This time it was the pizza. Took it and brought the box in, put it on the table. Bailey said,

"Pizza, great. May I?"

"Sure."

He opened the box, went,

"Mmm, and thank Christ, no anchovies . . . how about a nice pot o' tea?"

I went and got it going. He shouted in, his mouth full,

"This *is* good. Best to eat it while it's hot."

When I got back with the tea, he'd gotten through half, said,

"God, I needed that, missed lunch."

He sat back, belched. I asked,

"Was there a particular reason for this visit?"

He poured tea, said,

"I had a look at your file. You did three years for aggravated battery."

"Yeah."

"I was wondering what your plans were now."

"I've got a job."

"By jove! That was quick. Legal, is it?"

"Of course."

He stood up, brushed crumbs off his jacket, said, "Your friend Norton is sailing close to the wind. You'd be wise to avoid him."

I'd had enough of the bonhomie, asked,

"Is that a threat, Sergeant?"

He smiled, said,

"Whoa, watch that temper, boyo. Wouldn't want to have you in trouble again."

I climbed back, said,

"I'm touched by your concern."

"You will be. Call it intuition."

I went back inside, bundled up the pizza and dumped it in the bin. He'd put the butt of the cigarette in the dregs of the tea. I said aloud,

"Fucking pig."

Next morning I was trying to decide what to wear for extortion.

Do you dress up or dress down? Figured I'd play it simple. Jeans and sweatshirt.

Bang on noon, Norton arrived. I got in the van and said,

"Nice day for it."

He was wired to the moon, his foot tapping, fingers drumming on the wheel. As we pulled away, I caught a glimpse of the blond guy in the dead suit, shouted,

"Billy, hold on a mo."

He stopped and I jumped out. The man was gone. I got back in and Norton asked,

"What?"

I shook my head, said,

"It's crazy, but I think I'm being stalked."

"You? Jeez, must be a real nutter to stalk you. Here, have a brewski."

There were stacks of cans of Red Bull. I said,

"Naw, I want to do this cold."

He popped a can, drank deep, went,

"Ah . . . r . . . gh."

I asked,

"Did you drop some speed too?"

"Just a half tab, nothing major."

We were roaring down the Clapham Road. I said, "You're sailing close to the wind."

"What?"

"So a policeman told me."

He stared at me. I said,

"Watch the friggin' road."

He shouted, "You spoke to a copper . . . about me?"

"Yeah, the same fuck who got my address from you."

"Oh."

That shut him down for a bit, then,

"Bailey's a wanker, you don't need to worry about him."

"He's a wanker who knows where I live. That's always worrying."

As we turned into Ashmole Estate, Norton said,

"You've got to lighten up, Mitch; you take things too seriously."

"Right."

"I hate fuckin' nuns."

Norton spat this as a nun scuttled along the footpath.

There's a convent in Ashmole Estate.

I said, "I thought you Irish had religion."

He grunted, answered,

"What we've got is long memories."

"If you don't have religion, you better have a saving grace."

He gave me the look, said,

"Jeez, Mitch, that's bloody deep."

"But not original. The poet Donald Rawley wrote it."

As we pulled up outside a high-rise, he said,

"I hate fuckin' poets."

We got out and Norton slung a sports bag over his shoulder, asked,

"You want somefin'?"

"Naw, like I said, I'll go clean."

"I meant protection . . . like a baseball bat. Poems won't cut it where we're going."

"No . . . what's in the sports bag?"

He gave an evil smile, answered,

"Incentives."

50

* * *

The building had eighteen stories. An intercom system on the front door, but that had been busted to hell. We pushed through and went to the lift.

Norton said, "Keep your fingers crossed."

"What?"

"The lift . . . that it works."

It did.

Covered in graffiti, it smelt of urine and despair. A smell I was familiar with. You don't ever become accustomed.

On the eighteenth, we got out, and Norton said, "Think of it as golf."

"Golf?"

"Yeah, eighteen holes."

We approached a flat and Norton banged on the door. He took out a small red book. The door opened and a child peered out. Norton said,

"Get your mother."

The mother was Indian and nervous. Norton said, "Dues time."

She went back inside and found a bundle of notes, handed them over. Norton checked his book, counted the notes, said,

"You're a little short."

"It's been a terrible week."

He shushed her, said,

"Hey, I could give a rat's ass, but tell you what, you can double up next week."

She agreed far too readily. The three of us knew she'd never have it.

We went down to the seventeenth, and I asked,

"So how's it work? I mean, it seems to me they just get deeper in the hole."

Norton gave a big smile: all speed and no humour, said,

"See, you're a natural — already you've got the gist. Time comes, they hand over the lease."

"And then?"

"Well, don't you worry none. We have removal specialists."

"So lemme guess. You re-rent."

"Bingo. To yuppies who want a view of the cricket ground. We have six units here already."

The next three floors, it was the same sad story. Pathetic women of all nationalities, promising their lives away. On the twelfth, Norton said,

"I've had nothing but grief from these Spanish twits."

When the door opened, he barged inside. A woman was screaming,

"*Nada, nada, nada!*"

Norton looked round, asked,

"Where is he, where's your husband?"

The bedroom door burst open and a man in nothing but bright blue boxer shorts came running out. Brushed by me into the corridor.

Norton was after him like a greyhound, manic smile all over his face.

He was getting off.

He caught the guy at the stairs and jerked the boxer shorts off. With his open hand, he slapped him half a dozen times on the arse.

Then ran him back into the flat. The man was crying, said,

"Take the television."

Norton rooted in his sports bag, took out a claw hammer.

Walked over to the TV and smashed the screen to smithereens.

He said,

"Get me the rent agreement."

They did.

Next floor, he said,

"Time out for a break."

Sweat was pouring off him. He was hyped to heaven, said,

"Don't wait to be asked, Mitch; you can jump in at any stage, help me out."

He popped a can of Bull and a tab of speed, asked,

"Do you wanna get laid?"

"Now?"

"Sure, some of them, they'll do you in lieu of the payment."

"I don't think so. Doesn't anyone call the cops?"

"Get real, you think the cops would come here?"

I rolled a ciggy, lit up, asked,

"The kids . . . doesn't it bother you?"

"So they get to learn early. Toughen 'em up."

He looked with disdain at my roll-up, said,

"You don't have to smoke that shit. You're in a different league now."

I shrugged, said,

"I like 'em."

He took out a pack of Dunhills, luxury blend, got one going, said,

"Can I ask you something?"

"Sure."

He looked round, as if we'd be overheard. The noise in the building was ferocious.

Doors banging

People shouting

Kids wailing and

Rap music underwrit.

"Prison, what was it like?"

I could have said, "Just like this."

But I was thinking of Tom Kakonis, an American crime writer who understood jail perfectly. He wrote:

Call it jungleland, house of mirrors, kingdom of the sociopaths, country of rage, where betrayal is the norm, payback the canon, and mercy never understood or long forgotten. Or, call it a pipe laid across the small of your back, a broom handle up your ass, a shank in your ribs. It means you were utterly alone . . . No one to protect you.

I didn't tell Norton this; instead I said,

"Mostly, it was boring."

"Yeah?"

"No big deal."

He squashed the can when he'd finished drinking, slung it down the stairs. It hit each step. I could hear it rattling down like a scream on B Wing that lasts until the dawn.

On the ninth floor, we hit turbulence. Norton was doing his number on a black woman when her man came striding out. He swung his fist and caught Norton on the side of the head.

Then he came for me. He was big, strong, but that's all he had.

He wasn't dirty.

I was.

I sidestepped his swing and drop-kicked him in the balls. As he went down, I elbowed him to the back of the head.

Got Norton to his feet and he wanted to kick the black man till he bled. I pulled him away, said,

"Maybe we'll call it a day."

He agreed, said,

"Nearly through anyway — from eight down it's a bust." Took the lift the rest of the way. Norton was massaging his head, said,

"I was wrong, what I said about poems."

"Eh?"

"That they're useless. The way you took down that guy, it was fucking poetry."

I headed for the van and Norton said,

"Come on, there's a pub round the corner, I'll buy you a drink."

At the bar, Norton said,

"We're working guys, let's have a couple of boilermakers."

"Whatever."

The barmaid had to be told it was pints with Scotch chasers.

It was lunchtime, and the special was bangers and mash. It smelled good, almost like comfort.

We grabbed a table at the rear and Norton said,

"*Slàinte.*"

"That too."

On the other side of the Scotch we mellowed out. Norton was counting the cash, writing tallies in his red book. He mouthed the figures as he wrote. Next he put a roll together and snapped a rubber band on it. Pushed it across the table, said,

"Your end."

"Jeez, Billy, I didn't do all that much."

"You will, Mitch, trust me."

We were coming round by the Oval when I spotted the blond-haired man. He was going into The Cricketers. I asked Norton to pull up. He said,

"What's happening?"

"I'm going to stalk a stalker."

"That's supposed to make sense?"

"'Course not."

I got out and crossed the road. Then into the pub. The man was at the counter, his back to me. I walked up, gave him a hearty slap on the back, said,

"Guess who?"

He nearly passed out. I noticed he'd a small lager. I gave him a moment to regroup. He said,

"I knew it was a mistake to return."

I took a sip of his drink, said,

"Pure piss."

He looked at the door, and I smiled. He said,

"I'm Anthony Trent."

"You say that like it's supposed to mean something. It don't mean shit to me."

"Oh sorry, of course . . . I lived in the flat before it became your flat."

"And now you want . . . what?"

"If I might just collect some things."

I drank some more of his lager, asked,

"Why'd you leave in such a hurry?"

"I got in over my head to Mr Norton."

"How much is over your head?"

"Ten large."

"So you skipped?"

"Mr Norton has some heavy friends."

He was staring intently at me, and I said,

"What?"

"I believe you're wearing one of my sweatshirts. Don't tumble dry it."

"Well, Anthony, that's a sad story, but it will get sadder if you follow me again."

"Yes . . . of course, I understand. So might I grab some items from the flat?"

I took a moment, then said,

"No chance."

The hooker hadn't helped. I couldn't get Lillian Palmer outta my head. I mean . . . what? I fancied an old bird? Get real.

But deny it as I tried, that knowing smile kept returning. She knew I'd been aroused. Each time I blew it off, the wanting to ravish her came pounding back.

I rang Briony, asked if she'd like to come over for dinner. She asked,

"You're cooking?"

"Sure. How does stir-fry sound?"

"Oh Mitch, I'm vegetarian."

Naturally. "How does vegetarian stir-fry sound?"

"Wonderful, Mitch. Shall I bring wine?"

I thought she said "whine." I gave her the address, and she said,

"Poor Mitch, is it a grungy rooming house?"

"Something like that."

"I'll bring flowers, brighten it up."

A thought hit me, and I asked,

"You won't be stealing this stuff . . . will you?"

Silence.

"Bri?"

"I'll be good, Mitch."

"OK."

"Frank likes me to be good."

"Yeah . . . right . . . see you at eight."

By the time eight rolled round, the apartment seemed downright cozy. Pots on the stove, kitchen smells permeating, the table set. I opened a bottle of wine, poured a glass. It tasted bitter, which was fine. With booze, I had to keep a tight rein. My jail time was a direct result of booze.

When I drink whiskey, I get blackouts. I remember the day clearly. Norton and I had pulled off a caper that netted us three large ones.

Each. I was drinking lights out. Even Norton had said,

"Jeez, Mitch, take it easy."

I didn't.

Come that evening, I remember nothing. The story goes that I got into a barney with some guy. We took it outside.

Norton followed.

He managed to stop me from killing the guy, but only just.

I got three years.

I'm not arguing the toss. Thing is, my hands were clean.

Not even a grazed knuckle. I mentioned it to my brief, who said,

"You used your feet."

Oh.

Men find all sorts of ways to get through the nights in jail.

Be it

hooch

a bitch

glue.

Me, I worked out all day till my body was exhausted. Some men prayed, if quietly. I had my own mantra.

Like this,

"Never mess up an apology with a bloody excuse."

Mostly it worked.

The doorbell went. I opened it to Bri. She was dressed in a black trouser suit, pink sweatshirt. She handed me a huge bouquet of flowers. I said,

"Come in."

When she saw the place, she went,

"Wow . . . this is great."

I poured her some wine, and she sipped, asked,

"Does wine mix with 'ludes?"

"Ahm . . ."

"Cos I wanted to be mellow, not to freak out."

This sounded very promising, if unlikely. She sat down, said,

"I'll move in with you."

"What?"

She laughed out loud. Her laugh was one of the good ones, deep down and only the faintest hint of hysteria. She said,

"Lighten up, Mitch, these are jokes."

"Right."

I went to check on the food, it seemed under control. Bri shouted,

"Sure smells good, Mitch."

I said,

"Should be set in about ten minutes, how'd that be?"

"Lovely."

When I came back, she was arranging the flowers. I sat down, rolled a cig. Bri asked,

"Do I seem different?"

"Ah . . . no . . . you seem . . . fine."

"I've been having therapy."

"That's good, isn't it?"

She put her head down, said,

"I'm not to mention Frank anymore."

I wanted to say, "Thank Christ for that," but what I said was,

"OK."

She did a tour of the flat, went in the bedroom. I could hear the closet doors opening. When she came back she said,

"You sure landed on your feet, Mitch."

"The crust on its uppers."

"What?"

"It's the title of a Derek Raymond book."

"Who?"

"Never mind."

She poured more wine and pointed to the books, said,

"Will you read all those?"

"I plan to."

Then her face looked sad. I said,

"Bri, I want to read them, I like it."

She was shaking her head, said,

"It's a pity."

"What?"

"You won't have time."

"What are you on about, Bri?"

"At the party, a man said you'd be lucky to last six months."

I tried to lighten it.

"I'll read them easy in six months."

It didn't work.

"I don't want you to go back to prison."

I went and put my arm round her, said,

"Hey, come on, I'm not going back."

"Promise?"

"I promise. I have a regular job."

"I don't do so good without you, Mitch."

"Let's eat . . . what do you say?"

The food was good. I'd done garlic bread and garlic mushrooms. She liked them best. I opened more wine, and we chowed down. The stir-fry was limp, but it sneaked along. Bri asked,

"What's your job?"

I told her. When I got to Lillian's name, she said,

"I've heard of her. She was the best Blanche DuBois the West End's ever seen."

Every time I had Briony figured, she'd surprise me. I asked,

"How do you know that?"

"I love the theatre. Will you sleep with her?"

"What? Jeez, Bri, she's older than me."

Bri looked right at me, asked,

"What does she look like?"

"Well, like Gena Rowlands, not bad at all."

"So you will sleep with her?"

For dessert, there was

Greek yogurt

cheesecake

Black Forest gâteau.

I asked, "Which?"

"All of them."

She wasn't kidding.

After, I went to make coffee. Got that squared away and brought it out on a tray. The tray had Lady Di on the front and I knew Bri would like that. She was curled up on the sofa, snoring lightly. I picked her up and carried her to my room, covered her with the duvet. I watched her for a bit, then said,

"Sleep well, precious."

I decided to leave the dishes. I settled on the couch and turned on the TV, keeping the sound low. It was *NYPD Blue*, and Dennis Franz was massacring a hot dog and a perp simultaneously. Turned it off. I wasn't in the mood for cops. Not even Sipowicz.

About half an hour later, the whiskey came creeping along. Seeping and whispering on the edges of my consciousness. Start now, I'd kill a bottle . . . easy. Jumped up, got my jacket and figured I'd walk it off.

Yeah.

What I was thinking was, I'd go see Joe, the *Big Issue* vendor, and shoot the breeze.

At Stockwell, there was a guy holding a placard. He was wearing one of those ankle-length Oz duster coats. They're fine if you've a horse to match. The placard read:

DON'T TUMBLE DRY

As I passed, he gave me a huge, toothless grin. I said, "Good advice."

He said, "Fuck off."

When I got to the Oval, no Joe. A kid of about twenty was in his spot and selling the paper. I asked,

"What's happened to Joe?"

"Something should happen," he said.

I grabbed him by his shirt, heard the buttons pop. I said,

"Don't give me friggin' lip."

"He got hurt."

"What?"

"Straight up, guv, two kids from the Kennington estates done him over."

"Where's he now?"

"St Thomas's. He's poorly."

I let the kid go, said,

"Don't get comfortable, this is Joe's spot."

The kid was looking at his torn shirt, said,

"Yah tore me shirt, yah didn't have to do that."

"Blame Camus."

"Who's he?"

I flagged a cab and had him take me to the hospital. At reception, I had all sorts of grief before I could locate him. He was on Ward 10. That didn't omen well.

When I got up there, a matron barred my way, saying,

"He's not in any condition for visitors."

A passing doctor stopped, asked,

"What's the problem?"

His name tag read "DR R. PATEL".

The matron told him, and he said,

"Oh yes, the *Big Issue* man. All right, Matron, I'll take care of this."

He turned to me, said,

"Of course, if you're a relative . . ."

"A relative?"

"His brother, say."

I looked into his eyes. I almost never see eyes of kindness.

I did now. I said,

"Sure, I'm his brother."

"Joe is not in good shape."

"You mean . . . he might die?"

"I estimate twenty-four hours."

I put out my hand, said,

"Thank you, Doctor."

"You're welcome."

The ward was quiet. Joe's bed was next to the door. So when they take the remains, it doesn't cause a disturbance. I moved to the side of the bed. He looked bad. Both his eyes were blackened, bruises lined his face and his lips were torn. An IV drip was attached to his left arm. I took his right hand in mine.

His eyes opened, he said,

"Mitch."

He tried to smile, said,

"You should see the other guy."

"Did you know them?"

"Yeah, two kids from the estates. They're about fifteen . . . one of them looks like Beckham. Kicks like 'im too. The other one, he's black."

He closed his eyes, said,

"Jeez, this morphine is a rush."

"Good gear, eh?"

"If I'd that at the Oval, I'd get vendor of the month."

"You will, buddy."

He opened his eyes again, said,

"I don't want to die, Mitch."

"Hey, come on."

"Can I ask you something, Mitch?"

"Anything."

"Don't let 'em cremate me. I don't like fire."

He dozed for a bit.

I pulled over a chair but didn't let go of his hand. My mouth was parched, figured it was the wine.

A nurse came by, asked,
"Can I get you something?"
"A tea, please."
When she came back, she said,
"There's only coffee."
"That's fine, thank you."
It tasted like tea with a hint of castor oil. I'd have killed for a cigarette, but I didn't want to leave. The hours dragged by. He'd wake, see I was there and close his eyes.

About five in the morning, he said,
"Mitch?"
"I'm here, buddy."
"I was dreaming of a red rose . . . what's it mean?"
The fuck I knew. I said,
"That spring's coming."
"I like spring."
Later, he said,
"My feet are so cold."
I moved to the end of the bed, put my hands under the blanket.

His feet were like ice.
I began to massage them and said,
"I'll get yah thermal socks, Joe; be just the job for the Oval."
I dunno how long I was doing the massage when I felt a hand on my shoulder. It was the doctor. He said,
"He's gone."
I stopped rubbing his feet.
Thing is, now they felt warm.
The doctor said, "Come to my office."

I did.

He shut the door, said,

"Smoke if you wish."

"Thanks, I will."

He fumbled papers, said,

"The council will take care of the burial."

"You mean cremation."

"That's the usual."

"I don't think so. I'll make the arrangements."

The doctor shook his head, said,

"Is that wise? I mean, a plot in London is as expensive as a parking space and twice as scarce."

"He's from south-east London, that's where he's going to stay."

"Very well. I'll need you to sign some papers."

I finished my cigarette, said,

"I appreciate all your help."

"You're welcome."

We shook hands. When I got outside, I felt bone weary. Hailed a taxi and had him take me to Clapham. The driver checked me in the mirror, said,

"Rough night, mate?"

"You got that right."

A long time later, I came across a poem by Anne Kennedy, titled "Burial Instructions". Among the lines was, "I don't want to be cremated, my clothes sent home in a bag."

The closing lines read:

They say it's Joe
Provides the perpetual rose

But no one knows for certain.
Be sure you put me in the ground
Where I will have a chance to rise.

As I opened my front door, I smelled home baking. Bri
was busy in the kitchen. She shouted,
"Brekky in a moment."
I sank into a chair, beat. I could smell coffee, and it
smelt good. Did it ever. Bri brought in a tray. There was
OJ
coffee
toast
brownies.
Brownies?
She pointed at them, asked,
"Know what those are?"
"Ahm . . ."
"Space cookies. Hash cakes. I learnt how to make
them in Amsterdam. Eat slow — they tend to blow
your mind."
I had some toast, coffee, and considered if I needed
my mind blown. I asked,
"Aren't you having some?"
"Oh no, Mitch, they'd mess with my medication."
I thought, "What the hell."
Took a tentative bite. Sweet. Figured, if nowt else, I'd
get a sugar rush. Bri asked,
"Were you out robbing?"
"What?"
"Well, I know criminals work at night."
"Jeez, Bri, I'm not a villain . . . I have a straight job."

She wasn't buying this, said,

"I don't mind you being a robber as long as you don't get caught."

I had some more space cake. Bri said,

"Didn't you do villain things before prison?"

No denying that.

As a distraction I told her about Joe, even mentioned the rose.

She asked, "Was he a robber too?"

I near lost it, said,

"What's with this 'robber' shit? Could you please stop using that word?"

"Will I come to the funeral with you?"

"Oh . . . sure. That would be good."

"What will I wear, Mitch?"

"Ahm . . . something black, I guess."

She clapped her hands, said,

"Great, I took a Chanel from Selfridges, but I never got to wear it."

Trying to blunt the sarcasm, I said,

"Took!"

"You told me not to use the word 'robbed'."

I wolfed the cake.

The bottom dropped out of my mind.

Jazz.

I could hear jazz. Duke Ellington Orchestra with "Satin Doll".

Shit, where did that come from? I knew I wasn't asleep but wasn't conscious either. I tried to move but felt too languid. Vaguely, I was aware of Briony on the edge of my vision, but blurred. Definitely not important. What was vital was I identify the next tune. Yes, Billie Holiday with "Our Love Is Here To Stay." Then the soundtrack veered and I was Bruce Springsteen with "Darkness On The Edge Of Town." Then I was the amp, blowing fit to bust. I felt everything shutting down. I tried to curl into a ball and then I slept.

Least I think it was sleep.

Early morning. Norton rang. I asked him to find me a burial plot. In reply he said,

"It will cost. Not just money. I need your help."

"Tell me."

"The Brixton run, none of the lads are keen."

"Gee, collecting money there should be a piece of cake."

"Tomorrow evening, Mitch, I'll pick you up."

When Norton picked me up the following evening, he was nervous.

I got in the van, and he said,

"I got the grave, here's who you contact."

Gave me a piece of paper, address on it.

"Thanks, Billy, I appreciate it."

I looked round the van, asked,

"No Red Bull?"

"It's not that kind of gig."

"How so?"

"It can get hairy, there's no buzz in it. We go in, get the cash, split."

Brixton was hopping. The streets thronged with people. Seemed almost carnival. I asked,

"Jeez, will anybody be home?"

He nodded grimly.

"Yeah — the women . . . Saturday evening, the men are strutting and the women are glued to the game shows."

We parked near a high-rise off Coldharbour Lane. Norton handed me a sports bag, said,

"Baseball bat. Now, if it gets heavy, run like fuck. Got it?"

"Sure."

We got out, passed a dumpster and went into the building. The first few flats went OK. Norton collected at two of them, got rent books in the others. Worked down to the second floor. Norton was as jumpy as a cat. I asked,

"What? It's going good, ain't it?"

He kept looking round, said,

"We're not outta here yet."

Coming out of a second-floor flat, Norton in the lead, me walking rear. Standing outside were six black men, dressed in black suits, white shirts, spit-shine black shoes. One stood to the front, the others in military line to his rear.

Norton said,

"Fuck."

I asked, "Not good?"

He shouted,

"Run."

And took off like a bat outta hell. I didn't move. Not from bravado but from the look of these guys, they'd have caught me easy.

I let the bat fall, said,

"I'm not going to need it, right, guys?" The leader gave a small smile. I asked,

"Who are you? Nation of Islam?"

I knew the Nation from prison and, more importantly, I knew don't fuck with them.

My final question was,

"It's gonna hurt, yeah?"

The first blow broke my nose. I could describe the beating as vicious

thorough

brutal.

What it was, was silent. Not a word as they worked me over. Real pros. After they'd finished, they trooped off without a sound. I wanted to shout,

"Is that the best you got?"

But my mouth didn't work. Two of them returned and picked me up, carried me out and threw me in the dumpster. I lost consciousness for a time. Eventually, I managed to crawl out and fall to the ground. I limped as far as the police station and passed out again. Someone stole my watch before the ambulance arrived.

I came to in St Thomas's with Dr Patel standing over me.

Shaking his head, he said,

"What an exciting life you people lead."

God, I felt rough. All my body ached. I asked,

"How bad is it?"

"Your nose is broken, but I think you know that."

I nodded. Big mistake, it hurt like a bastard. He continued,

"Nothing else is broken, but you are covered in bruises. It's almost like whoever did it knew what they were doing. Maximum hurt with minimum breakage."

I asked him to go through my clothes, find the address for Joe's grave. He did. I asked,

"Can you take care of it?"

"Yes, of course."

"When can I get out?"

"You should rest up."

We agreed I could leave in the morning; he'd fit me up with painkillers to get me through the next few days. As I lay there, I realized that Joe was probably still here. At least I was keeping him company. Though not in any fashion I'd have planned.

Sunday morning, on my way home, I had the cab swing by the off-licence. I asked,

"Could you get me a bottle of Irish whiskey?" I figured I could get out of the cab. I wasn't sure I could get back in. He nodded. As I passed over the cash, he said,

"A bus hit you?"

"A black bus."

"Worst kind. Any particular brand of whiskey?"

"Black Bush."

"Good choice."

He was back in jig time, handed over the bottle, said,

"Get some Radox and a steaming bath."

"I will, thanks."

Back home, I moved like an invalid, dropped some painkillers.

Dr Patel had warned, "Don't take alcohol with these."

Yeah, right. I unscrewed the bottle, chugged hard. Whoa-hey, it kicked like a mule. A very bad-tempered mule. I turned on the radio. Tracy Chapman with "Sorry". Fitting. Ran the bath, got it scalding. Had some more Bush.

An hour later, glowing from the bath and drink, I wasn't hurting at all. Found a wool bathrobe and wrapped up in that. It had a monogram, but I couldn't focus. The doorbell went. I shuffled over to open it.

Norton, a sheepish face. He went,

"Jesus, what did they do to you?"

"Their worst."

He looked at the bathrobe but didn't comment, asked,

"Can I come in?"

"Why not."

He glanced at the half-empty bottle, said,

"Partying?"

I ignored that, went in and flopped on the sofa. I said,

"There's beer in the fridge."

"Right, think I will."

He popped a can, sat opposite me, said,

"I'm sorry, Mitch. I thought you were behind me."

"I wasn't."

Now he tried indignation.

"What did I tell you? Didn't I say . . . if it gets hairy, run?"

"I musta forgot."

He drank long, said,

"Don't worry, Mitch, we'll get them, eh?"

I was too mellow to be angry. Leave it to a later date. He dropped a chunk of change on the table, said,

"Least you get paid, OK, buddy?"

"OK."

Trying for friendly, he asked,

"So what's this other job you've got?"

I told him the lot, even down to the fast moves of the butler. He said,

"The old dame, sounds like you got the hots for her."

"Don't be daft."

"Tell me again about the Silver Ghost."

Blame the booze, but I did, told him far too much. Should have seen the glint in his eyes. But like I said, my focus was shot to hell. He said,

"Sounds like loot."

"What?"

"Be worth knocking over."

"Hey."

"No, c'mon, Mitch, like the old days. Bound to be a ton of cash

jewellery

paintings."

I got to my feet. Not very imposing in the dressing gown, said,

"Billy, forget it. Who d'you think the cops'd pull first?"

"Just a thought. I better get going."

At the door, I said,

"I meant what I said, Billy, stay away from it."

"Sure, Mitch, cross my heart and hope to die."

Back to the couch. I eyed the remainder of the Bush. Sleep took me before I reached for the bottle. I was glad of that when I woke on Monday morning. I felt battered and bedraggled but figured I'd at least show up for work.

The phone rang. Dr Patel. He'd made the funeral arrangements and wondered about a service. I said no. Joe would be buried on Tuesday evening. I thanked him, and he hung up.

Wouldn't you know, the tube's on the blink, and eventually I had to take the bus. Yet again, Holland Park seemed another world.

As I got to the front door, Jordan opened it. He eyed me with disapproval, asked,

"Accident?"

"Strenuous workout."

"You can't come in here."

"Excuse me?"

"Tradesman's entrance is round the back."

A look passed between us, we filed it for later.

I went round the back into a kitchen. It looked like the one from *The Servant*. I didn't expect, alas, to find Sarah Miles on the kitchen table. Jordan came in, asked,

"Tea . . . coffee?"

"Coffee's good."

He started to arrange filters, and I asked,

"Like real coffee?"

He gave a tight smile, waved to the sideboard, said,

"There's muesli, cornflakes, toast. As you wish."

I nodded. He turned to face me, said,

"Or perhaps you are more accustomed to porridge."

My turn with the tight smile. I asked,

"You're all the staff, then?"

"Madam requires no one else."

The coffee perked. Sure smelled good. One of the disappointments of life, that coffee never tasted as good as the aroma. Took the cup, tasted it, said,

"Shit, that is good."

He held up a finger, said,

"Madam does not allow swearing in the house."

"She can hear us, can she?"

No answer. I took out two painkillers, swallowed them with the coffee. He asked,

"Are you hurt?"

"Like you care."

He left the kitchen. Returned with some packets, said,

"Dissolve one of these in water; they are quite miraculous."

I had nothing to lose, got a glass, tore one open, added water.

The powder turned pink. I said,

"Pretty colour."

"Madam receives them from Switzerland."

I drank it, tasted sweet but not unpleasant. I said,

"Much as I'd love to chat, I better go to work."

He said, "That's why you're here, isn't it?"

In the garage, I admired the Rolls-Royce again. I'd have given a lot for a spin. Took me a while to put on the overalls. My nose was aching like a bitch. I checked the work chart.

Monday — Painting

Okey-dokey.

The front of the house, windows and shutters, sure could do with a coat. Got the ladders out and began mixing paint.

Half an hour in, I felt relief. The pain that had been continually battering my body ebbed away. I said aloud,

"God bless Switzerland."

One of the most valuable items in prison is a Walkman. That and a bodyguard. You put those headphones on and slip away. It's not a wise thing to do in the yard. You can't afford to be less than 100 per cent vigilant.

As I leant the ladder against the wall, I put on the Walkman.

The tape was Mary Black. Kicked off with "Still Believing", strange prayers in strange places.

Believe it.

Getting into a rhythm of work, I didn't realise I was at a bedroom window. I could see a four-poster bed. Then she walked into view, wearing a silk dressing gown. I thought,

"Whoops, I better get outta here."

I didn't move. She was taking off the robe. Naked as a jay. Her body was in great shape. I was getting hard. Then she began to dress slowly. Black stockings and silk underwear. She looked up, a tiny smile at the corners of her mouth. I moved down the ladder, my mind on fire. Mary Black was doing "Bright Blue Rose", but I couldn't concentrate. Moved the ladder to another window, got going on that.

***

I didn't see her for the rest of the day, but she was lodged in my mind like a burning coal. Come lunchtime, I headed for the kitchen. Sandwiches were neatly laid on the table. A bowl of fruit left beside them. There wasn't a sound in the house. So I ate silently and then went outside for a smoke.

Jordan appeared from the front of the house. I said,

"You don't make a lot of noise."

"No, it's not necessary."

Argue that. I didn't.

I thought, "Fuck him," and concentrated on my cig. He was standing watching me. Then,

"You do good work."

"Glad you're pleased."

More silence. I figured I'd let him do the digging. He asked,

"Do you like it here?"

"What? . . . Oh . . . it's different."

"Would you like to move in?"

"Come again?"

"Not in the main house, but there's a room above the garage, a little Spartan but comfortable. TV and shower, of course."

I stood up, asked,

"Are you serious?"

"It would save you commuting."

I didn't want to close any doors. If the Clapham deal went sour, I'd be glad of an alternative. I said,

"Lemme think about it."

As if he read my mind, he said,

"Perhaps, too, you might get to drive the Silver Ghost."

When I got back to Clapham, the Swiss effect had worn off and I was beat. A BMW was parked outside my place. Tinted windows. The door opened, and Norton got out, said,

"Somebody to meet you."

"Now?"

I couldn't keep the irritation outta my voice. Norton hushed me. I fuckin' love being hushed. He said,

"It's the boss, come to meet you in person."

"Gee whiz."

A large man got out. Wearing a cashmere coat, he had jet black hair, and a pockmarked face and was in his late sixties. An air of casual power. An even larger man got out from the driver's side. Muscle.

Norton said, "Mr Gant, this is Mitch."

He put out his hand, we shook. He said,

"I've heard a lot about you . . . Mitch."

"Mr Gant . . . I've heard absolutely nothing about you."

He looked at Norton, then gave a huge laugh. One of those throw-your-head-back efforts, putting lots of teeth in it. Norton said,

"Shall we go inside?"

I opened my door, led them in. Gant took a measured look round, then said,

"You have no answering machine."

"No."

Gant clicked his fingers at Norton, said,

"Take care of it."

I said, "I'm gonna have a brewski. Get you anything?"

Norton and the minder declined. Gant said he'd join me in a beer. I went and got those, took some pain-killers. Gant asked,

"May I sit down?"

"Sure."

He took off his coat, rolled up his sleeves. Royal Navy tattoo. Drank the beer from the bottle. Just a working stiff.

I started to roll a cig. He asked,

"Could I have one of those?"

I handed him a rolled one, lit him up. He pulled hard on it, said,

"I don't smoke much, but I tell you, that's the biz."

I nodded, figuring we'd get to the point soon. He asked,

"What tobacco you got there?"

"Golden Virginia, what else?"

Again the fingers snapped at Norton.

"Order up a batch for Mitch."

I realized who Gant reminded me of. In Lawrence Block's Matt Scudder series, there's a character called Mick Ballou. A butcher, he disposes of his enemies without mercy. At the same time, he's a working man who likes nothing better than a drink with the boys.

The mistake is to think he's ever one of them.

Gant leant forward, man-to-man stuff, said,

"You did magnificent at Brixton."

I resisted the impulse to touch my broken nose. He continued,

"It takes some balls to stand up to half a dozen guys."

I tried to look modest. Which is difficult with a beat-up face. He said,

"A man like you sends a message. So I'm going to put a high-rise in Peckham under your control."

I looked at Norton, he was impassive. I said,

"I'm very honoured, but I'm still learning the ropes. I'd like to tag along with Billy for a bit, learn some more."

He gave a huge smile, said,

"Capital. But I do like to reward industry. I have a special surprise lined up for you, my boy."

"Oh?"

"Free on Wednesday?"

"Sure."

"Splendid. Billy will pick you up around seven. You won't be disappointed."

He stood up, business concluded. At the door, I asked,

"Ever hear of Mick Ballou?"

"Who?"

"A character in a novel."

"I don't do fiction."

And they were gone.

Tuesday, I was healing gradually. Went to work. I saw neither Jordan nor Lillian. The tradesman's entrance was open and my meals left on the table. I did a good day's work. It was eerie not seeing anybody.

Come lunchtime, I took a stroll down to Notting Hill Gate. I just wanted to see people. Went into the Devonshire and had a half of bitter with a ploughman's lunch. Took a window seat, watching the world. A hippie sat opposite me, wearing a T-shirt that said:

JOHN LIVES
YOKO SUCKS

He was the Portobello Road variety. Long stringy hair, bad teeth. His brain fried in the Sixties, he hadn't touched solid ground since. He had a very battered copy of *Beowulf*.

Gave me the peace sign. Leastways, I took it as such. A pint of Guinness in front of him. He said,

"You're a labourer."

"Shows, huh?"

"The hands, man; good, honest toil."

I figured he'd be a good judge. I nodded. He said,

"Working-class hero, man."

"You think so?"

"Man, John said it all . . . got a smoke?"

Gave him a roll-up, he said,

"Cool."

Time for me to split. I said,

"Stay loose."

"Yo bro, wanna buy a watch?"

"Naw."

"It's a Rolex, man, the real business."

"I'm not into status."

"Me neither, man, but ya gotta try, right?"

I had a lot of replies to that, but what I said was,

"Just . . . *imagine*."

Made his day.

I finished work at four, still not a soul about. I figured:

(a) They trusted me.

(b) They were testing me.

Either way, I stole nowt.

Truth to tell, I sat in the Silver Ghost a bit. Dreamed some crazy dreams. The car smelt of

polished upholstery

oak

old leather

wealth.

As I was walking down the driveway, I turned fast to look at the house. Saw a curtain move in the bedroom window.

That made me smile.

At the Gate I went into Oxfam and found a dark suit. It nearly fit. The volunteer at the register said,

"Oh, that was a lovely find."

"Not really, I was looking for it."

What was lucky was an old Penguin copy of Laurie Lee's *As I Walked Out One Midsummer Morning*.

A guy was selling the *Big Issue* outside Burger King. I got that and said,

"A *Big Issue* vendor is being buried this evening."

"Yeah . . . where?"

"Peckham."

"No can do, mate, too bloody dangerous."

"I think he'd appreciate the effort."

"He's dead, his days of appreciation are over."

I'd been home about twenty minutes, had
   a shower
   a beer
   a painkiller.
Not hurting.

Put on the Oxfam suit. The sleeves were short, the legs too long, but otherwise it fit me like a glove. I got a crisp white Boss shirt from the wardrobe. It fit like a prayer.

Doorbell went.

Briony. She was stunning in a black suit. I said,

"You're stunning."

"I know."

Came in and examined me critically, said,

"You look like an undertaker."

"Thanks, Bri."

She rummaged in her bag, produced a fresh rose, asked,

"Will it do?"

"Perfect."

"Can I have a drink?"

"Sure, whatcha want?"

"Anything lethal, I've only done two 'ludes."

"Black Bush?"

"Lovely."

She clinked her glass against my beer, said,

"To Michael."

"Who?"

"Your friend."

"Joe."

"Are you sure?"

"Trust me, I'm positive."

"OK, to Joe."

We drank. I called a cab, and he came in jig time. A Rasta; the smell of weed in the car was powerful. When I said, "Peckham,"

he said, "Righteous."

The graveyard is at the back of the bus station. Across the road is the bingo hall. I thought Joe would be pleased to hear the call of

FULL HOUSE

The undertaker was waiting. The grave ready, two men standing beside it. No vicar. A man arrived a few minutes later.

"Dr Patel," I said, "good of you to come," and introduced him to Bri. She held his hand longer than expedient. The undertaker asked,

"Any last words?"

I shook my head. He signalled to the men and they lowered the coffin. I threw the *Big Issue* in and Bri dropped the rose. Suddenly, at the gates, a man in full kilt and Scottish regalia appeared — with bagpipes — and began to play "The Lonesome Boatman".

I dunno from beauty, but the piper was beautiful. Bri said,

"A last-minute surprise."

"How did you find him?"

"Outside Selfridges, he does a regular gig."

"Thanks, Bri."

She gave me an enigmatic smile, said,

"Thanks for the doctor."

Uh-oh.

I palmed some money to the diggers. One of them said, "Did you know Rod Stewart used to be a grave-digger?"

How do you reply to that? I asked,

"Do you sing?"

"Not a word, mate."

They had a full and familiar laugh. Then I paid the piper, so to speak.

Dr Patel was deep in conversation with Bri. I said,

"As is usual with a funeral, there's refreshments after. Might I treat you?"

"Yes."

From both.

To get the fuck outta Peckham, we went to The Charlie Chaplin at the Elephant. The best that can be said is . . . it's big.

Bri and the doc took a table, and I went to order.

The barman was a dance short on his card, gushed, "I love the suit."

"It's been in the family for years."

His eyes lit up, thinking, "A player." He said,

"Don't let it go."

"Never happen."

My wit exhausted, I ordered

toasted sandwiches
hot toddies
beer chasers
crisps
nuts.
When he finally brought it all to the table, he exclaimed,

"*Voilà!*"

We dug in. No bullshit from the doc. He downed the hot one, chased it with the beer, bit deep into the toasted. Bri went to feed the jukebox and we were blasted with,

"Hey, if you happen to see the most beautiful girl . . ."

Even I can sing that. I said,

"Doc, you were great to come."

"Please call me Sanji."

"I'll try."

He laughed, then asked,

"Is it terrible to say I'm enjoying myself?"

"It's essential you enjoy yourself."

Bri returned, said,

"That is a happening jukebox." Then she turned to Sanji, asked,

"Were you born in India?"

"Yes. I'm from Goa. Apart from the raves and the hippies, we have the mummified remains of St Francis Xavier."

Bri and I must have looked blank. He asked,

"You're not Catholics?"

"Not even decent atheists."

He chomped on some peanuts, said,

"His body has been preserved, it's regarded as a miracle."

Having no reply, I made none. He continued,

"Someone stole his toe."

"What?"

"Truly. Someone in the world is a devout believer with the toe of St Francis."

I couldn't resist, blame the hot toddy, said,

"Isn't that very Catholic, toeing the line?"

He smiled, but I don't think he was amused. Bri excused herself for the ladies'. Sanji gave me an appraising look, asked,

"Might I see . . . your sister?"

Shit.

"I'd advise against it."

"Nevertheless . . ."

"You will anyway. Sanji, you're a good bloke, I like you a lot, but she's not for you."

"Will you let me try?"

"Can I stop you?"

"No."

Bri came back, and Sanji said he'd order another, asked,

"Same of everything?"

"Why not."

Bri leant over to me, said,

"I love him."

"Jesus."

"No . . . really, Mitch, he's like my soul twin."

Out of anger, trying to get her attention, I said,

"What about Frank?"

And got a look of withering scorn. She said,

"Frank's dead, Mitch. The sooner you face up to it, the better for all of us."

Sanji returned and I felt this was my exit line. I shook his hand and said,

"No doubt I'll be seeing you."

He gave me a concerned look, half medical, half Indian, said,

"I will treat her like a gentleman."

"That's what you think."

As I got to the door, the barman said,

"Yo, party pooper, you can't be leaving already."

"I'm all partied out."

He put his hand on his hip, rolled his eyes, said,

"Mmmm . . . tough guy."

Outside, I hailed a cab and resolved next week I'd buy a car.

When I got back to the flat, I wanted to just crash down and out.

Flicked on the TV. Wouldn't you know, just starting was *Point Blank*.

As Lee Marvin appeared in a suit not unlike my own, I said,

"Now, that's a tough guy."

Wednesday was rained out. I went to work anyway.

Jordan was in the kitchen, gave me a critical look, said,

"Your injuries are healing."

"Think so?"

"They appear so."

Zen or what.

Some drains were blocked, and he asked if I could do anything.

I said, "Sure."

What a bastard. Took me all day to unclog them. Near four, I was spread out, working on an eave chute, dirty water dribbling in my face, when she appeared. Dressed in a red jersey-knit outfit, it was stuck to her curves. She said,

"Now, that's what I like to see, a man on his back."

I finished the bloody job and got to my feet. She came up to about my shoulder. Again with the knowing smirk. I dunno, was it Joe's funeral, my beating, chemistry, or plain lunacy?

But I grabbed her, pulled her against me and kissed her. First she struggled, but then she blended into me. I got my tongue in her mouth and my hands on her arse, was gone. The rain came bucketing down, and she pulled away, said,

"I hope you can finish what you started."

And she was gone.

I stood in the rain, me and a hard-on, and remembered Wednesday night . . . Mr Gant's surprise. Back in the garage, I was peeling off the drenched overalls when Jordan appeared. He said,

"We've gone ahead with the room over the garage. It's all prepared."

"Shit, I dunno."

"There is a shower there, a fresh tracksuit . . . please avail."

I did.

It was a studio-type place:

bed

shower

kitchenette.

And man, bundles of fresh, luxurious towels. As a convict you get a towel per week.

I scalded myself in the shower and, coming out, I noticed a small fridge under the TV packed with beer. I opened a Grolsch and chugged deep.

The bed was freshly made up, and I was sorely tempted. But I had Gant's surprise to come.

The tracksuit was new, black, large size with the logo

COMPLIMENTS OF CLARIDGE'S

Way to go.

On my way out I met Jordan, who said,

"Miss Palmer has expressed a certain . . . *liking* for your . . . work."

"I aim to please."

Blame the Grolsch. He gave a sad smile, said,

"Do aim wisely."

The Northern Line was up to its usual shenanigans, and I didn't get home till seven. Gant's car was parked outside. The door opened and Norton said,

"We're late, get in."

The muscle was driving so it was me and Billy in the back. He asked,

"Where the fuck were you?"

"Hey . . . Billy . . . lighten up. I was at work."

He looked at the tracksuit, said,

"You're with Claridge's?"

"Only in an advisory position."

He was very agitated, a light sheen of perspiration on his forehead. He was lighting one cig from another. I asked,

"What's the surprise?"

He muttered, then said grimly,

"You'll fuckin' see."

We drove to New Cross and stopped outside an old warehouse.

I asked, "Didn't this used to be the meat rack?"

Norton gave me the look. We got out and went inside. Norton said,

"We're in the basement."

"I didn't know it went below ground."

"There's a lot you fuckin' dunno, mate."

Down he went.

It smelt of rot, piss and desolation. I knew the odour. Below were Gant and two other men. They were standing round a man tied to a chair. A black man. A band of silver tape was round his mouth. Blood leaked from it, so I knew they'd broken his teeth. The southeast London signature.

The black man was wearing a Nike sweatshirt, shot through with sweat. He had Gap khakis that were deep stained from where he'd wet himself. Gant was dressed in a Barbour coat, tan cords. The Browning automatic held loosely at his side was almost incidental. He said,

"Ah Mitch, glad you could join us."

The black man's eyes were huge in his head, locked on mine, they were pleading. Gant said,

"As I mentioned, I do appreciate your lone stand against the . . . protectors. So now, I give you one of them as a mark of my gratitude."

I took a deep breath, said,

"He's not one of them."

Gant near exploded, looked to Norton, to the black man, then slowly back to me. His eyes were black stones. He asked,

"How can you tell? Surely they all look the same?"

"Mr Gant, when they beat you with total precision, you remember."

He lashed out with his foot and smashed the black man's knee.

Turned to Norton, said,

"You moron, what did you do — grab the first nigger you saw?"

Norton said nothing.

Gant struggled for control, then shrugged, said,

"Oh well."

And shot the black man in the head.

The shot reverberated in the warehouse, and I swear I heard pigeons in startled flight. Gant said,

"So sorry, Mitch, to have wasted your time."

A thousand thoughts were driving in my skull, but I decided to play poker, said,

"All is not lost, Mr Gant."

He tried to rein in the sarcasm, said,

"Oh really?"

"How would this be? You leave the man in the chair, deliver him as is to the building in Brixton, put a sign on him, let it be."

"A sign?"

"Sure . . . how about:

you borrowed . . .

you pay . . .

back."

A slow smile began on Gant's lips, building to an outright grin. He said,

"Brilliant, I love it. Norton, deliver the goods."

Norton looked extremely pissed off, said,

"Mr Gant, it could be tricky."

And got the look from Gant.

Gant came over, put his arm round my shoulder, said, "Mr Mitchell, I may have underestimated you."

I gave my modest look. Then he stood back, said, "Good Lord, I love the tracksuit."

Thursday morning, I'm heading for work, my nose hurts like a dead horse. I bang refuse to analyse the events of last night.

Pretend as is.

Naturally, there's a queue, and everybody's paying with cheque or card. I don't have a weekly pass cos I'm getting a car soon and soonest.

There's an elderly man in front of me, and he's bewildered by the delay. Finally, we get our tickets and head for the turnstile. As we go through, the old man's wallet slips from his pocket.

A fat wallet.

Seen by me and the ticket collector.

There's the moment, hanging for one glorious suspended second as your instincts ride your beliefs. I bend, pick it up, say,

"Sir, I think you dropped this."

The ticket collector and I lock eyes, then he tips his index finger to his cap. The old man is amazed and delighted.

I brush off his gratitude with a shrug. I know myself pretty good. You lie in a bunk bed, twelve hours of lockdown, you see the depths. If the ticket collector hadn't seen it, I'd have kept it, no danger.

I get on the train, settle into a corner seat, am about to hit my Walkman. I've got Leonard Cohen's "Dance Me To The End Of Love" and "Famous Blue Raincoat". Ready to roll.

The old man sits beside me, says,

"I do so awfully hate to intrude, but I am so terribly grateful."

His accent is even plummier than Margaret Thatchar's when she imposed the poll tax. I nod. Encouraged, he says,

"I must tell you a most remarkable story. Apropos what just happened, it has a certain resonance."

Every chancer in London has a story. I just wish they didn't have to tell them on the train. But here he goes.

"I was required to give a urinary sample!"

Here he paused, to check I understood what urine was, then,

"As I had trouble producing at the hospital, they said I might bring it home."

I tried to look like I was hanging on his every word.

"But dear boy, what does one bring it in?"

I could give a fuck, said,

"How complex."

"So I used a naggin' bottle of Johnnie Walker."

If he was expecting praise, I hadn't got it. He continued,

"En route I stopped at the PO to collect my pension."

"Hmmmhh."

"When I emerged, the bottle was gone. What a hoot, eh?"

We'd come to Embankment, and I had to change for the Circle Line. I said,

"Keep it in your pants, eh?"

He gave a smile, if dubious in its downswing.

100

I spent Friday on the roof; it needed major repair, and I decided to tell Jordan. He said,

"We trust it to see us through another winter."

"Shall I not bother, then?"

He gave me a languid smile, said,

"Fix the most glaring damage, we don't want Madam leaked upon."

I figured I could take that any way I liked. After a day of cosmetic work, I was feeling vertigo. Decided to grab a shower and a brewski. There was no new tracksuit waiting. Thing is, I was a tiny bit disappointed.

My first full week of, if not honest, at least regular work.

Jordan appeared, handed me an envelope, said,

"We presumed you'd prefer cash."

"Good move, Jord."

He didn't go, and I was tempted to say — "Dismissed." What I said was,

"What?"

"Aren't you going to count it?"

"I trust you, pal."

He flicked at a hair on his lapel, said,

"Then you would be making a serious error."

I counted it, went,

"Shit . . . is this for a week or a month?"

He smiled. I wasn't exhilarated, but I was one contented ex-con, said,

"Whatcha say, Jordy, I buy you a large one down at your local."

A beat, then, "I don't fraternize with the help."

I'd hoped for a glimpse of Lillian, but it wasn't to be. On the train, I considered my plan for the weekend. Nice and simple, find the two fucks who'd kicked Joe to death. Eight that evening, I'd finished a curry and was working my way down a six-pack.

The phone rang.

"Yeah?"

"Mr Mitchell . . . it's R. Gant — not disturbing you, am I?"

"No, sir, just relaxing.

"Good man, Mitch . . . might I call you that?"

"Sure."

"No ill feelings about last night?"

"No, sir."

"Might I pose you a question?"

I wondered why he was talking like a gobshite, but it was his dime. I said,

"Shoot."

A pause, then,

"Jolly good, very timely. My question is this: What do you consider to be the most valuable asset?"

"Jeez, I dunno. Probably money . . . sex . . . digital TV."

"It's power, Mitch, and the most powerful tool is information."

"You're onto something, sir."

Like boring the bejaysus outta me. He said,

"I'd like to share some information with you."

"Yes, sir."

"Not over the phone. I've reserved a table for eight at Browns tomorrow evening."

"Browns?"

"In Covent Garden."

"OK."

And he hung up. All the sir-ing had left a bitter taste in my mouth, and I went to rinse it out. For the life of me, I couldn't think of a single thing he could tell me that I would have the slightest interest in.

Saturday morning, I woke with a slight curried hang-over. Nothing too serious, just hold the red peppers. I thought about Browns.

My kind of place.

Normally, they wouldn't let me in, and I wouldn't blame them. We understood our ratings. To them I was a bottom feeder. But it's a rush sometimes, riding on the clout of a Gant, you get to stray.

Meanwhile, I had business. I knew Joe's assailants were teenagers. One wore a Beckham shirt, one was black. So, Saturday afternoon, they'd be kicking ball.

Dress down.

I wore the faded jeans, unwashed sweatshirt — I was cooking. Got the Glock and dry-fired it. No problem. Loaded it fast. Caught a 36 all the way to the Oval tube. If I had to describe how I felt, I'd say

certain

and

cold.

Checked out the Kennington estate, quiet yet. OK. I took a walk up to the Walworth Road and did high-fives with a gang I once ran with. They lured me into the pub and asked what I'd fancy. I said,

"Bottle of Beck's,"

and jig time, four or five bottles at my hand. They knew I was but recent out, asked,

"How was it — stir and all?"

"Better here."

And got the laudatory salutations.

It was a safe pub. Meaning, the guv'nor had done hard time.

Like eighteen and no remission. So you could talk. Jeff, the organizer of the team, asked,

"Need any readies?"

"Naw, I'm in regular employment."

Huge laugh and four more bottles of Beck's. The team did post offices, usually west or north. They weren't greedy and pulled down a nice earner. I'd served my time with them in my early twenties. Jeff asked,

"We're up north next week, Mitch. Wanna tag along?"

I was tempted. It would be two large, no frills, but alas, I was on a different time frame, said,

"Maybe later."

I hadn't touched one beer. It was getting on for two thirty. I said I had to go, and we did the south-east London trip of truly not-felt goodbyes. Outside, for a moment, I wished I could go back.

At the Kennington estate, a furious football game was in progress. I sat on the wall, bided my time. Five-a-side, it was deadly serious. I spotted the black kid right off . . . he was a substitute.

A couple of local residents sat alongside me. I passed along cans of lager, get them talking.

Then I saw him, the Beckham shirt and wild, ferocious talent.

Scored a goal from midfield that was beyond description.

Beside me, a man said,

"Aye, he's been scouted."

"Excuse me?"

"Yon kid, he goes up to Boro at the beginning of the season."

I said with absolute belief,

"He's very talented."

"Aye, lives to play, take away his soccer ball and he's nowt."

The game wound down after that. I waited. Eventually, the spectators drifted away. But not Beckham. He continued to play, dribble, drive, locked in his football dream. The black kid waited, boredom sat large.

Time to rock 'n' roll.

I stood up, stretched, looked round. Deserted. Walking slowly, I approached the Beckham wannabe. He never even saw me. I had the Glock out and pumped both his knees from behind.

Four shots.

Moved straight over to the black kid, whose jaw had literally dropped, stuck the barrel in his mouth, said,

"Not this time, but soon."

Then I walked away. Caught a number 3 bus at the arse end of Kennington Park and was over Lambeth Bridge in two minutes.

As we came up to the Embankment, up into Westminster, I let the Hendrix song play in my head, my body drenched in sweat.

"Hey Joe."

★　★　★

I got home. I was adrenalin city. Alternating 'twixt a high and cold sweats. Kept thinking — "So, to kill someone, you just aim higher."

Jesus. The rush as I replayed shooting Beckham. So fuckin' easy.

The struggle it had been to stop at four shots. I was only gettin' started. Man, I began to understand the seduction of guns.

Talk about pump city.

Checked my watch, two hours to meeting Gant. I'd have to get a grip, mellow down. Rolled a joint, a big one, muttering, "Camberwell carrot." Cracked a beer and slowed the whole show.

Couple of deep blows, I was chilling.

Went in the shower and took it as cold as I could, shouted,

"Fuck . . . I'm deep frozen here!"

Remembered the first week in prison, when I got the "train", Eight or nine guys putting it in you, blood everywhere and thinking, "I'll learn." As I did.

Came out of the shower, shaking water, shaking memories.

Dress to impress. Yeah.

Put on the Gap khakis, a Boss navy sweater and that blazer.

Thought, "Phil Collins lives."

Ready to roll, I'd just finished the joint when the phone went. Picked it up, said,

"Yeah?"

"Mitch, it's Briony."

"Hi, sis."

"Are you OK?"

"What?"

"You sound odd."

Shit, you spent your day shooting young soccer players, you get to sound odd. I said,

"Was there something?"

I couldn't keep the testiness at bay.

"I'm in love, Mitch."

"Good for you."

"You sound angry, Mitch."

"I'm happy for you, Bri, OK?"

"He gave me three orgasms."

Which was triple the information I needed. I said, "Oh."

"Are you angry, Mitch? Angry I've betrayed our race?"

"What?"

"I'd have preferred a Caucasian, but it's karma."

I thought of a thousand put-downs but settled for:

"Be happy, Bri."

"We'll name our first boy after you."

"Thanks, Bri."

"Love yah."

"Like that."

And she hung up.

In all seriousness, after a call like that, how can you possibly believe life has a purpose?

Got to Covent Garden for eight. Browns had a doorman. Before he could start the Nazi spiel, I said,

"Mr Gant is expecting me."

"Go right in, sir."

Inside, it was plush and Regency. At reception, I did the Gant bit again and was told to proceed to the dining room.

Only a few guests and at the window table the man himself.

He stood up to greet me. Dressed in a grey wool suit, he looked like success. Shook my hand warmly, said,

"Glad you could make it. Tell me, there are two Browns in Covent Garden, how did you know which one?"

"The other has no bouncer."

He gave a quiet laugh, asked,

"A drink before dinner?"

Dennis Lehane has a novel titled *A Drink Before the War*.

I said, "Vodka martini."

Figuring I'd get in the swing of things. The waiter came, and Gant ordered two martinis. Gant was in his early forties; the waiter's eyes briefly met mine. It was enough. He had arrogance and contempt finely mixed. Plus, he was an ugly bastard. Prison has its share of them . . . they're the wardens.

Drinks came and we sipped. Gant said,

"I'd like you to organize the collections in
Brixton
    Clapham
        Streatham
           and Kennington."

"I dunno, Mr Gant."

"Call me Rob, eh?"

"OK. Rob."

"You won't have to do door to door anymore. You supervise the teams, make sure they don't skim too much. We all like a little off the top, but no one likes a greedy bugger. Your Mr Norton, now, he's got way too ambitious."

"Rob, he's my mate."

The waiter brought the menus. Rob said,

"I recommend the lemon sole."

"I think I'll have steak."

"Oh."

We ordered that, and Rob asked for two bottles of wine I couldn't pronounce. The waiter repeated them flawlessly so I'd get the point. The food came, and we piled on veg and potatoes. Rob attacked his with relish, said,

"Really, you should have had the fish."

"In jail, you see a lot of fish."

The waiter was pouring the wine as I said it. Let him get the point. Rob asked,

"Hear about the shooting in Kennington today?"

"No. Missed the news."

"Young soccer player shot."

"If you watched Sky Sports, you'd believe they're not shooting half enough of them."

"Get down that way, do you?"

"Kennington . . .? No . . . not my manor really."

He'd finished his grub and was eyeing mine, said,

"You don't eat like a convict."

"Excuse me?"

110

"Protectively."

"Not since I read *Miami Blues*."

He ordered dessert: apple tart with two dollops of ice cream.

I passed. Finally we got to the coffee, and he lit a cigar, said,

"Feel free to smoke."

I wanted the waiter to see me do a roll-up. Made his miserable evening. Rob said,

"Some habits not covered in that book, eh?"

I didn't feel it needed an answer. He said,

"You'll recall I said information was power."

"Yes."

"In return, I'd like something from you . . . interested?"

"Sure."

He stubbed out the cigar, said,

"You did three years for GBH."

"Yeah."

"You were in a blackout."

"Yeah."

"You didn't do it."

"What?"

"Your friend Norton did the beating."

"That's impossible."

"Were your hands marked?"

"No . . . but."

"Norton's were shredded. The barman followed you out, saw the whole thing. You were too out of it to stand up. Norton legged it, and the cops found you — more coffee?"

"Jesus . . . I . . . no."

"A brandy for the shock."

The waiter brought one of those big bubble glasses. You could wash a shirt in it. He left a bottle of Armagnac on the table.

Rob poured generously.

My mind was spinning. I gulped down the brandy. It burned like pain, gave a solid kick to my heart.

Rob said,

"You'll need time to . . . *digest* the information."

"Why are you telling me?"

Rob considered this, then,

"I could say it's because I like you, but I don't think you'd buy that. Norton has become a major problem. Now he's your problem."

"What if I do nothing?"

He spread his hands on the tablecloth, said,

"Then I'd truly be surprised."

I lit another cig and tried to digest all of this. I asked,

"You said you wanted something from me?"

"Yes. Do you feel my revelation was valuable?"

"That's one word for it. So, whatcha want?"

"A Silver Ghost Rolls-Royce."

I laughed out loud.

"You're kidding. I use the bus, mate."

"But you have access to one."

The penny dropped. I said,

"Norton, the fuck, he told you."

Rob smiled. I asked,

"Why don't you steal it yourself? Shit, you know where it is."

He shook an index finger. I fuckin' loved that. He said,

"You're missing the whole point, Mitch. I want you to steal it for me."

"Why on earth?"

"Let's call it a gesture of good faith."

Rob excused himself to go to the gents'. The waiter was over like a shot, sneered,

"Shall I bring the bill, sir?"

"Yeah, and be fucking quick about it."

Rob came back and insisted the meal was on him. I didn't argue.

As we were leaving, he touched my arm, said,

"There's no hurry . . . but shall we say delivery in one month?"

Outside, his car was waiting. He said,

"I'd offer you a lift, but like you said, you're a bus person."

"Rob, I don't think I'll be taking up your job offer."

"Well, then, the rent on your apartment is five hundred a week."

"C'mon, Rob."

"Oh, and the other thing, now that we're outside — it's Mr Gant to you."

With that, he got in the car and was off.

I was going to walk down by Drury Lane but decided I'd had enough theatre for one night.

I moved out of Clapham next day. Packed the essentials:

Gun.

Money.

Dope.

I took the Gucci jacket — well, you'd be mad not to — some sweatshirts and jeans. Left the blazer and dark suit. I didn't plan on any more funerals. A half-dozen crime novels. Was able to fit all that in one bag. Travelling light. Then I just eased on away.

As I walked up the drive in Holland Park, I hoped they'd be home. Went round the tradesman's entrance. Jordan was at the kitchen table, reading the business section of *The Sunday Times*. If he was surprised to see me, he hid it well, asked,

"You're doing some overtime?"

"Actually, I've come to live with you."

He folded the paper neatly, said,

"Madam was right."

"Yeah?"

"She said you'd move in within a week."

He stood up, said,

"Have some coffee, I'll prepare your room."

I sat down, thinking — "Shit, that was easy."

I was rolling a cig when I remembered the no-smoking rule. Lit up anyway. I lived here. When Jordan returned, he looked at the smoke but let it go. He said,

"I believe all you need is there: shower, hot plate, fridge. There isn't a phone so I've lent you a mobile till we get a line in."

I asked, "What's the ground rules?"

"Pardon?"

"C'mon, pal, the dos and don'ts."

He smiled — this guy liked plans — said,

"Very simple. You stay out of the main house unless summoned."

"*Summoned.* I look forward to that."

The summons came quicker than either of us expected. A bell rang, and he said,

"Excuse me."

Ten minutes later he was back, said,

"Madam welcomes you to The Elms and wishes to know if you'd be prepared to drive as part of your duties."

"Sure, do I get to wear a uniform?"

"We don't do uniforms."

I hauled my bag to the garage and went to unpack. The room smelt of air freshener. The phone was on the table. A Rolls-Royce in the garage, a mobile in my hand — welcome to the pleasure dome.

Rang Jeff first, said,

"Jeff, it's Mitch."

"Hi, Mitch, it was good to see you on saturday. Change your mind about the job?"

"No, mate, thanks. What do you know about a villain named Gant?"

"Whoa . . . bad news, a header to boot, your total fuckin' whacko."

"Oh."

"Your mate Billy Norton runs with 'im."

My mate!

"It's a long shot, Jeff, but would you know where he lives?"

"Yeah, I did a piece of work with him, but never again. Trust me, you don't wanna go there, mate."

"All the same, Jeff?"

"Sure, hang on a mo' . . ."

Then, "Nineteen Regal Gardens, Dulwich. He owns the house and most of the street."

"Thanks, Jeff."

"Give 'im a wide berth, mate."

"I'll try."

Next up I rang Bri, gave her my new address and the mobile number. She didn't say anything. I had to ask,

"Bri . . . you there?"

"It's that old girl's address, isn't it?"

"Not like you think, it's work."

"At her age, I'm sure it's very hard work."

And she hung up on me.

Jeez, if Bri wasn't careful, she'd develop a sense of humour.

I was cooking on this mobile. Rang Norton. Sounded like I woke him. I asked,

"Billy, did I wake you?"

"No . . . I . . . was . . . ahm . . . wanking. That you, Mitch?"

"Yeah."

"You're fucked, man."

"Excuse me?"

"Gant has a hard-on for you. Oh . . . and you're fired."

"Gee, Billy, you sound broke up about it."

Deep sigh.

"What's with you, man? I get you the sweetest deal and you shit all over it."

"You're my mate, Billy . . . right?"

"Yeah."

"So lemme tell you, Gant ain't so hot on you either."

"You see . . . you see, Mitch, there you go again, your head's all fucked up."

"Billy, the guy's bad news."

"Mitch . . . you're the bad news. He said you owe him something."

"I owe him jack."

"You better pay it, Mitch, he gets crazy over stuff like that."

"One last thing, Billy. After I did that guy three years ago, how did your hands look?"

Long silence, then,

"You're gone, man, I'm talking to a zero."

And he hung up.

Now I knew it was true. The dirty bastard.

My first year in prison, there was a black queen on the tier above. He'd been turned out his first week and

117

had gone into it wholesale. He was just eighteen and so the legal age for grown-up jail.

He worked at it, trading blow jobs for cosmetics, full anal for lingerie. Every night about eleven thirty he'd begin to sing "Fernando". A slow, crystal-pure version. All blues, all loss.

For the few minutes of the song, the whole shitty institution went deathly quiet. Not a sound. Just this lone achingly raw lyric.

One evening on chow line, he was ahead of me. I said,

"You have a wonderful voice."

He turned, rouge on his cheeks, eyeliner courtesy of boot polish, said,

"Oh, thank you so much. Do you want a blow job?"

"Naw . . . I just wanted to say you've got real talent."

I was already sorry I'd bothered. Any longer with him and I'd be prey again. I went to move off, he said,

"No . . . you can do me for free."

Jesus.

I dunno why, but I gave it a final shot, said,

"Why do you do . . . that stuff?"

"It's my only protection."

Who was I to argue? I moved off, and the next time he greeted me, I said,

"The fuck you talking to?"

A few months later, he was strangled with a pair of panty hose.

I told myself ignoring him was my protection. Sometimes, I half believed it.

118

I stood up, threw the mobile on the bed, said aloud, "Billy-boy, you get to pay for Fernando."

Time was when London was shut on a Sunday. Even the bookies are open now. I headed into Bayswater and joined the Arab world. If anyone was speaking English, I didn't hear them.

To Whiteleys and found what I wanted on the third floor. In the window was a Silver Ghost, flanked by a Lamborghini and a Ferrari. The salesman approached. I said I'd like the Ghost, and he handed it to me. Perfect in every miniature detail. Not cheap either. While the guy was wrapping it, I spotted a DeLorean. The salesman spotted my interest, but I shook my head. I thought — "And they still can't flog one."

Got a small padded envelope and some stamps. Then I addressed the envelope:

ROB GANT

and his home.
I put one stamp on and wrote in glaring capitals:

INSUFFICIENT POSTAGE

Posted it.
Took a walk in Hyde Park and spent an hour being zoomed by rollerbladers. Next time I'd take the Glock. Slow down the speed.

I'd no idea what to plan for Norton, figured I'd let it unfold.

Knowing him, he'd make it happen. Gant too, he'd be coming. I could have left London, but where could I go?

Plus, I didn't want to go.

Also, I'd a fix on Lillian Palmer, and I definitely wanted to see where that went. Where else would I get the shot at driving a Ghost?

I went into a caff and ordered eggs and bacon. The staff was Thai and friendly to the verge of annoyance. The food was good but tasted slightly of peppers. Shit, what did I know? Maybe they were onto something.

PART TWO

FINAL CURTAIN

I had Lillian that same night.

Over

under

sideways

on the floor

over a table

on the bed.

Like that.

When we were through, I said,

"I can't understand how you've problems keeping staff."

About eight that evening, I had been lying on my bed, reading one of the John Sandford "Prey" series.

My mobile went.

It was her. She said,

"I need company."

So I went. Strolled over to the house, all the lights were on. No sign of Jordan. I climbed the stairs. Her bedroom door was ajar, I knocked, heard,

"Enter."

Did I ever.

She was standing by the windows, black silk nightgown.

I walked over and she asked,

"What kept you?"

Let the frenzy begin. I had three years of prison to vent, and she had her own history.

When finally we were sated, she asked,

"Buck's Fizz?"

"I can only pray you're saying 'buck's'."

She was. We got through two bottles of Moët, and I finally got to look round the room. In contrast to the rest of the house, it was spartan. I'd expected hundreds of photos, but not even one. I said,

"How come this room is so . . . empty?"

"One needs an area of simplicity."

"You'd have liked prison."

Then she looked at me, said,

"How the mighty stumble."

I knew this wasn't praise. She asked,

"Do you even know the name of this house?"

"Sure . . . The Elms."

"Its significance?"

"The trees are elms."

"*Desire Under the Elms* . . . Eugene O'Neill."

"Irish, was he?"

She gave a snort of derision.

"My finest role. But I shall yet play Electra."

"You're planning a comeback?"

"Oh yes, I've waited a long time for this. The West End shall hail my return."

"Why now, Lil?"

Her eyes raged, and she tried to slap my face. I caught her wrist, she spat,

"I'm Lillian Palmer, not some bar hussy."

I sat up, said,

"Thanks for the fuck."

She loved that, said,

"Don't go, let me tell you my grand plan."

"I'm sure it's fascinating, but I'm exhausted."

She got up, put on a robe, said,

"They've called me back. Charles Denton's office rang three times."

"You'll no doubt tell me who he is."

"*The* impresario. He's producing two shows right now. I want you to drive me there tomorrow, we'll arrive in style."

She went to the bed and, from underneath, produced a huge volume of papers, said,

"It's my work. I've rewritten *Electra* to make it more modern."

"Nice one."

"I'm giving you the honour of being the first to read it."

Her expression was one of total seriousness. It was her life in those lousy papers. I said,

"I'd be honoured."

And she handed them over like a baby. She said,

"We'll do magnificent things, Michael."

I was on the verge of saying Mitchell, but let it go.

On the way down the stairs, Jordan was gliding up. Not a sound.

We didn't speak, nor did he even look at me.

Back in my room, I cracked a brewski, tried to read her work.

It was gibberish. I couldn't follow one single sequence. I slung it on the bed, said,

"Turkey."

I must have been asleep a few hours when the mobile went.

Jeez, where was the bloody thing . . . found it, muttered,

"Huh."

"Are you finished?"

"What?"

"Were you sleeping?"

"Lillian. No, of course not, I was totally engrossed, lost in it."

I was trying to see the bloody time . . . three fifteen . . . fuck. She said,

"Give me your verdict."

"A masterpiece."

"Isn't it."

"Oh . . . beyond praise."

"Shall I come over, read some now?"

"No . . . no . . . let me just wallow in the magic."

"Good night, *mon cherie*."

"Right."

I've had lots of worry, fear, anxiety in my time, But that I'd *ever* get to see her perform filled me with outright dread.

Next morning I headed for the kitchen. Got some coffee and toast going. Already I had the run of the place. Jordan came in and said,

"There are some suits you'll need for driving."

"You have them already?"

Tight smile and said,

"We try to cover contingencies."

I offered him some coffee. Nope . . . unbending, but he stayed, so I asked,

"Have you heard of Denton?"

"The theatre person?"

I was surprised and said,

"So he does exist?"

"Three times he has phoned for Madam."

"You spoke to him?"

"I *always* answer the phone."

I'm on the second toast when he says,

"In regard to Madam's script, I do hope you haven't become a critic."

Steel in his voice, I said,

"No way, pal, I think it's brilliant."

"Good. I wouldn't like Madam to be upset."

"Don't worry."

"Madam wonders if you're free on Wednesday night."

"Free?"

"For bridge."

"Jesus, I don't play bloody bridge."

He gave a long breath of patience,

"We don't expect you to play, merely to accompany Madam when her friends play."

"Sounds like a gas."

The suits got left on my bed. Three of them in

black

grey

blue.

I checked the brand: Jermyn Street. Half a dozen white shirts.

I went to the garage, and the Silver Ghost was shining, waxed and polished. Jordan was standing alongside. I whistled in true admiration, said,

"You did some job, pal."

"Thank you."

"When did you get the time?"

"Last night when you were reading Madam's script."

"Oh."

"I checked with Mr Denton's office, and they'll expect you at noon at the Old Vic."

I went upstairs to shower and get those exercises done. Gonna need to be fit for Madam. In the shower, I went,

"What the hell?"

I noticed deep bite marks on my chest. The bloody bitch bit me. Bridge that, Jordan.

There were some old mags on top of the closet. No, not porn.

Titles like

GQ

Vanity Fair.

I came across this by Courtney Love:

Fuck all this gender difficulty, fuck all this female experience rage shit.

Now if I could just work this into conversation.

In the nick, I came across an old guy who done fifteen hard in Peru. On release, he was deported, and after one week in London he was arrested for robbery. Got seven years.

Said to me,

"I like English prisons, they're kinda cosy."

"Yeah, tell that to the queen who got strangled."

He wasn't listening, away again on his story. Like this:

"First off they strip you and steal anything you have. Then they'd duck your head in a bucket of cold water, put electric wires on your balls. San Juan de Lurigancho — isn't that a lovely name? It was run by the inmates. Cells were sold by the prison mafia. Shit and mosquitos everywhere. But worst is the silence. Silence meant all-out gang warfare."

I could see his point about cosy.

A knock on my door — Jordan.

"Madam is ready."

He'd brought the car round front. She emerged a few minutes later. Dressed in a white linen suit and a fedora. She looked . . . old. I held the door open for her, then went round to the driver's side.

Now I know why people who drive them are arrogant. The damn car makes you superior. As we cruised outta there, I said,

"All right?"

She never spoke the whole way. I could care. The car had my total focus. Thing is too, how could you ever drive anything else? I mean, if I was to get behind the wheel of a banged-up Volvo, was I going to think — "Yup, this is good"?

It sure pulls attention. From admiration through amazement to contempt. A lot of young drivers try to cut you up, but it would take more than a Japanese town car. I was beginning to believe you'd need someone riding shotgun.

We got to the Old Vic, and I pulled in to the side. I said,

"I'll just go and announce you."

"I'll be waiting."

The doorman, a young kid, never heard of her, said, "Never heard of 'er, mate."

We were arguing when an older man appeared, asked, "What's going on?"

"I've got Lillian Palmer outside, she's expecting to see Mr Denton."

His face lit up,

"Lillian Palmer, my God!"

He went to fetch Denton. The young guy asked,

"What, is she famous, then?"

"We're about to find out."

A man came striding out, a gaggle of assistants in tow. He looked like an ironed George C. Scott. He had no riding boots or megaphone, but it looked as if he did. He said,

"I'm Denton."

I told him my story, and he shouted,

"This sounds like Philips's work, get him. Meanwhile, let's meet Miss Lillian Palmer."

He sure knew how to work her. Escorted her by her arm into the theatre, led her up onto the stage, turned and said,

"Ladies and gentlemen, fellow thespians, I give you the star."

A spotlight was trained on her and people flocked round her.

She was transformed, thirty years just vanished from her face. I was thinking,

"Wow, she must have been something."

Denton must have read my face, answered,

"She was, and a damned fine actress. Is Jordan still around?"

"Yes, he is."

"He was married to her, you know. Hell, at some point, most of us were."

He looked at me, asked,

"Are you drilling there?"

"What?"

"Wouldn't blame you, buddy, she's a class act."

"Did you see her script?"

"At least once a year. Hard to believe it gets worse."

Denton had champagne and canapés delivered, and they had them on the stage . . . Philips was finally found, and yes, he had rung three times. They wanted to rent the Ghost for promotion. Denton said,

"In the end, it's all car commercials."

Lillian wasn't told. They followed us to the car, giving her a wonderful send-off.

She was near delirious with joy, said,

"Did you see . . . did you hear? They loved me! I'm going to regain my place. Pull over someplace. I need you to love me."

I pulled over near the north side of Hyde Park. Got in the back and did her as if I meant it. When I got out after, two park keepers gave me a round of applause.

It was a day of performances.

Thursday, back to the day job. Up on that roof, knocking down stray slates. I'd hear them land on the patio, break like glass. If I were fanciful, I'd say like dreams, but they were only worn slates. Madam was on the phone all day, ordering new clothes, the hairdresser, cooing to her friends. I'd yet to meet any of those but figured "bridge night" would answer that.

Come evening, I was showering and resolving I'd get takeout fish and chips and read Edward Bunker. I was holding the new Pelecanos as a special treat. My phone had been installed and I was settled. Now it rang.

"Mr Mitchell."

"Hi, Doc."

"How did you know?"

"Doc, have a guess at how many Indians are calling me."

"Oh."

"How'd you get the number?"

"Briony did, she's very resourceful."

"That too . . . so was there something?"

"Yes, could I see you? Let me buy you dinner."

"OK."

"Splendid. There's a wonderful Italian place at Notting Hill, named De Vinci's. Shall we, say eight?"

"Italian?"

"You don't like Italian?"

"Well yeah, sure I do, OK. And call me Mitch."

"Right, Mr Mitch."

I'd been kinda banking on them fish and chips, but what the hell. I wore the blue suit and a white shirt. Checked myself in the mirror, said,

"Smokin."

Wouldn't you know — everyone, including the doc, in casual gear.

The place was warm and friendly, and they knew the doc. Good opening. We ordered clams and linguini, then followed with spaghetti bolognese. The bread was crisp and fresh like an idealized childhood. I even liked the wine. I'm mopping up the sauce with that bread, the doc is ordering more wine, and I go,

"What's up, Doc?"

"It's Briony."

"*Quelle surprise.*"

"You speak French?"

"Nope, just that one bit, so I got to ration it. You'd be amazed how often I get to use it with Briony around."

"Can I be honest, Mr Mitch?"

When you hear that, pay the bill and run. I said, "Go for it."

"I love her very much."

"But she's a nutter, right?"

That took him aback but also gave him his cue, said,

"When I was a medical student, I seriously considered a career as a psychologist. I learned about borders."

"You mean like perimeters."

"No."

The waiter came and cleared the debris. It was considerable. They like that, like you to eat. Great people. The doc had pavlova for dessert. I settled for a cappuccino, without the chocolate sprinkle. I hate that shit. The doc said,

"Essentially they split their feelings from their behaviour. The tragedy is, borders never recover. The best you can do is help them coast.

"In the beginning they appear normal, good jobs, but it's a constant tightrope between madness and sanity. Unable to form relationships, never free of a deep rage that leads to self-destruction."

"Her shoplifting?"

"Correct. They live from one disaster to the next. They excel at role-play and have overwhelming feelings of emptiness. They never change."

"Actresses."

"Yes, many borders do well onstage, but then . . ."

I was thinking of Lillian, asked,

"Where's the problem, Doc? Walk away."

He looked down at his dessert, then pushed it from him, said,

"I am besotted with her."

"C'mon, Doc, I'll take you for a drink in an English pub, if we can find one."

I took him to the Sun in Splendour on Portobello. At least it used to be an English pub. Ordered two best bitters and grabbed a table, said,

"Drink up."

He did. Then gave me a long, analytical stare, asked,

135

"How can you be so calm . . . about your sister?"

He meant "cold".

That's OK — I can do manners. I said,

"Doc, I've been in prison. I didn't like it at all. I have a strong instinct it's going to require all my energies not to return. I have to play low-key just to survive. I start to burn and I'm a dead man."

He was horrified.

"But it's a terrible existence, such tight control."

I drained my glass, said,

"Beats prison."

After a bit, we had another round, and midway through, he asked,

"What am I to do?"

"Doc, I don't give advice, and I certainly never take it, but lemme say this. Go for it, have a ball, live like fire, cos truth is, she'll leave you, she always does. Then she'll resurrect Frank and go back to coke and guns and madness."

"How will I live then?"

I touched his shoulder, said,

"Like the rest of us, pal — the best you can."

The next two weeks were calm. I did my work, read my books, serviced the actress.

I hoped when Gant came, I'd be ready. Else I was fucked.

Chris De Burgh song — "Waiting For The Hurricane".

The bridge night proved the dead do return. Three men and a woman. All mummified. You only guessed at them being alive by the cigarettes they smoked.

I didn't play, and no one spoke to me. Except Lillian, who said two things repeatedly:

(1) Another highball, darling.

(2) Clean the ashtrays, darling.

Oh yeah, she gave me a present. A silver cigarette case.

I gave it to a wino at Queensway who shouted,

"The fuck is this?"

Exactly.

The change began with a call from the doc, who said,

"She's gone."

"I'm sorry."

"What will I do?"

"Go back to your life."

"What life?"

Welcome to whinge city.

★ ★ ★

End of the fortnight, I was getting restless. That philosopher who said,

"All of man's problems stem from his inability to sit in a room and do nothing."

He was right.

I went down to Finch's on the Brompton Road. On a whim. I had on the Gucci jacket, so I figure it wasn't entirely haphazard. On the train was a discarded copy of the *South London Press*. I read through as the District Line had its usual trauma. I nearly missed it. A small item at the bottom of the page. A man had been found dead outside a flat in Clapham. The victim of a mugging. I recognized the man's name and the address.

I was wearing his jacket, I had lived in his home.

In Finch's, I ordered a pint of ordinary, took it to a quiet table. Did a roll-up and wondered was it time for whiskey.

After the *South London Press*, after so much, I was sinking into a nine-yard stare. Didn't even realize, just slipped on back there. I learnt it in prison, or rather, it learnt me. Gradually, I realized someone was talking to me. I refocused, noticed I'd neither touched the drink nor lit the cigarette. A woman at the next table was saying,

"Thought we'd lost you there."

I looked at her, like seriously. In her late thirties, she was wearing a suede tan jacket, black T-shirt and faded-to-comfort jeans. Dark hair, pretty face and a heavy scar under her left eye. I said,

"I was thinking."

138

"You were comatose."

Irish accent. The soft vowels always distinguishable. Soothing. I took a hefty swallow of the beer, asked,

"Are you trying to chat me up?"

"I dunno. So far, you've had no chat at all."

She was attractive, no doubt, but I hesitated. She said, "There's a lovely word in Irish, it's *brónach* . . . means sadness but a lot more. Anyway, that's how you looked."

And I still couldn't get my mouth in gear. Here's a fine woman, giving it large, and I'm locked in some awful lethargy.

She said, "Your face is a mess, you know. That broken nose, those bruises, is it sore?"

Finally, I said,

"Would you like a drink?"

"No, I'm grand, thanks."

When in doubt, get ugly. It always worked in prison. I asked,

"How come you're on your own in a shitty, pretentious pub north of the river?"

Got her like a slap in the face. She touched the scar, said, "It's that noticeable?"

Relentless, I said,

"Why don't you get it fixed?"

Further slap. She sat back, said,

"I'm sorry I bothered you."

Now I could talk, said,

"I'm Mitch, how you doing? Bear with me, I've had a bad day."

She smiled. God, a smile of such radiance even the scar folded its tent and went away. She said,

"Go on, then, I'll have a half of Guinness."

"Screw that, have a solid drink."

"What's wicked?"

"Whiskey is always wicked."

I ordered two large. Hot so they'd seem tamer. She said,

"God, that's a lovely drink."

I looked at her, asked,

"Do you always say what you feel?"

"Course, don't you?"

"Practically never."

Her name was Aisling, and once I loosened up, we got on great. I couldn't believe it, I was having me a time. We got out of there, and I had a taxi take us to a club where they play Cajun and serve barbecued ribs to die for. Big buckets of 'em and pitchers of beer. There's no way you can eat them delicately. You get in there, get good and greasy.

She did.

God bless her.

There's a tiny dance floor, and she dragged me on out. The band had a demonic fiddler and we were possessed. Covered in sweat, we retreated to our table and consumed a pitcher, ate more ribs and were in hog heaven.

She grabbed my hand, said, "Kiss me."

I did, and the menu was complete. Then a guest soloist came on and did a down-home slow rendition of

"The Night They Drove Old Dixie Down." We danced slow to that, and I came so close to feeling happy.

I nearly got faint. She said,

"You know, Mitch, you're a lovely kisser."

Jesus wept.

She was brushing her hand along the back of my neck, singing along to the song, and my body was electric. She was feeding me the most treacherous poison of all: hope. She said,

"Tell me, Mitch, tell me this place never closes."

"Would it were so."

Then she opened her eyes, said,

"Tell me something lovely; it doesn't have to be true, just some grand thing I'll always remember."

For then, for the moment, I felt she deserved it, I said,

"You're the loveliest person I ever met."

She hugged me real tight, said,

"That's gorgeous and perfect."

It was also true.

Sometimes the gods relent, even they think — "Enough already, let's let the fucker see what it could have been like. As it is for the blessed."

When the band finished, she said,

"Come back, Mitch, to my awful room in south-east Kensington, and I'll make you Irish coffee."

I did.

We didn't have the coffee, but we did have sweet, gentle lovemaking like I never believed existed. When I was leaving, she asked,

"Won't I see you again?"

"I hope so, I truly do."

Walked home on air. Cajun tunes, her lilting voice, the sheer softness of her body bedazzling my mind. Walking up the drive on Holland Park, I muttered,

"Enough of this, I'm outta here."

On my pillow was what seemed to be a spider. Black and crushed. I approached slowly and then recognized it for what it was. The misshapen remains of the miniature Rolls-Royce I'd sent to Gant.

I finally bought a car. Yup, it was time. An old Volvo, worth another six months and no warranty. It was beat up, but who wasn't? Putting her in gear, I banished all thoughts of Royces from my mind.

Took me three nights of cruising to nail Norton. Eventually, outside Biddy Malone's on the Harrow Road. Off his patch.

I waited, as I'd waited the previous nights. Come closing, out he came. High-fiving with the goodnighters.

All the lagered energy of pissed nothing. He was fumbling with the keys to his car, still laughing when I eased the Glock behind his ear, said,

"Who's down in the zero now, shithead?"

Pushed him into the back seat, put the barrel between his eyebrows, said,

"Threaten me now, arsehole."

Took him a while to recover, then,

"Mitch . . . we can work it out . . . yeah?"

"Leaving tokens on my pillow . . ."

"Look, Mitch, can I sit up, please, get us straight?"

I let him and asked,

"Why didn't you toss the room? Among other goodies you'd have found this."

I pushed the barrel against his nose, continued,

"And I'd now be holding my finger up my arse."

Norton shook his head, said,

"He told me to go in quick, not to touch anything. Especially not to let that fuckin' butler see me. He didn't want the surprise ruined."

"What happened to the previous tenant?"

Norton looked at me, asked,

"Heard about that, did ya?"

"*Read* about it."

"Gant couldn't believe you'd gone. We had the place staked, and then that stupid bastard tries to break in. So Gant lost it, you know what he's like, how he did the nigger."

"Then he's still got a hard-on for me?"

Norton gave a harsh laugh, said,

"More than ever. He's in business sometimes with the Colombians, and he's in awe of their ruthlessness. They kill everybody that belongs to you."

It took a moment to sink in, then I asked,

"My sister?"

He nodded, said,

"Don't make any new friends."

"What about you, Billy?"

"I'm outta it, soon as I can liquefy my assets, I'm gone."

"Aren't you overlooking your present predicament?"

He looked at the gun, at me, said,

"You're not going to shoot me, Mitch."

I considered it. The bastard of it all was I still kinda liked him. He was garbage, but we had a history, most of it bad but it was there. I said,

"You're right, Billy."

I put the gun away and got out of the car. It was just starting to rain. I turned up the collar of my jacket, and Norton got out of the car. We stood for a moment, then he put out his hand, said,

"Let's shake on it, mate."

"Don't push it."

And I walked away.

I was reading Fred Willard's *Down on Ponce*. Right up my street, hard-boiled and hilarious. You've got, like, a guy who describes Atlanta, Georgia, as a city that may be too busy to hate but isn't above taking a little time off to steal.

The phone went. Picked it up, said, "Yeah."

"Mitch, it's Briony."

"Thank Christ, I need to see you."

"I'd like that, Mitch."

"Tomorrow evening, how about I buy you dinner, say that Italian place you like in Camberwell at eight?"

"I'll be on my own, Mitch."

"That's fine."

"I always end up on my own."

"We'll talk about that."

"So you won't bring the old actress."

"No, just you and me."

I hung up, said — "Jesus, she's hard work."

I didn't think I'd be telling her I met someone new. I certainly wouldn't be telling "the old actress". While I'd been reading, my mind was double-tracking. On the book but also on Gant.

I figured I'd try a temporary solution, rang his number. He answered and I said,

"Rob, my man."

Silence, then, "Mitchell."

"None other, how are you, bro?"

"Well, Mitchell, I shall be coming to pay you a visit."

"That's why I called. I want to let you know how I've been spending my various salaries. It cost me a few grand, but I've "engaged" a hitter.

"Here's how it works: You harm me or my sister, he shoots your daughter — what is she now, eleven and doing well at that school in Dulwich, eh? No, there's more. I still had some cash, I could only get a basement deal on your wife. I think it's splendid, how she volunteers for Oxfam those three afternoons. What I got was the "acid sandwich" for her. See, I took your advice, did my research, like you said . . . information is power."

"You're bluffing."

"That's the beauty of it, you have to decide whether I am or not. Our little variation on *Call My Bluff*. Whatcha think?"

"I think, Mitchell, you have no idea who you're threatening."

"All part of the rush."

"Believe me, Mitchell, we'll be meeting."

"Gotta go . . . oh, one last item. The Nation of Islam is keen to chat with you. About the chap you dropped in Brixton . . . in the chair . . ."

I rang off. It would buy me time. He'd check it out and, sooner or later, he'd come after me. By then, I hoped I'd have come up with a plan. Or at least some more ammunition.

Driving to meet Briony the next evening, I decided to park at the Oval. Did that and walked over to see how the new *Big Issue* vendor was doing. The kid was there all right and recognized me right off. I bought a copy and felt him eyeing me. I asked,

"How's it going?"

"You did 'em, didn't yah?"

"What?"

"Them young blokes that done Joe — you done 'em."

"The footballer?"

"Yeah, him who used to wear the Beckham shirt."

"Was he any good?"

"Gifted."

"Well, I'd better be off."

I'd reached my car when the kid shouted,

"You know what I think?"

"Yeah?"

"Fuck 'em."

"Will you keep an eye on the motor?"

"Guaranteed."

I walked down Camberwell New Road. What a shit-hole. Bad pubs and worse vibes. Young guys in those hooded tracksuits cruised continuously. The air was hopping with menace. Like the yard after twelve-hour lockup. Used to be a time, a homeless guy would ask you for a few bob. Now it's demanded. Like this.

A guy clocked me, went by on a first sweep, then back, said,

"Gimme a cigarette."

You've got to give it hard and stay on it. Any shit or apology like "I don't smoke" and they'd carve your tongue out.

I said, "Fuck off."

He did.

Course, if they're cranked, it's a different ball game. There's no rules with a doper. Hurt them fast and keep going. I was deep regretting not driving but all the same, the adrenalin keeps it sharp.

At Camberwell Green, I let out a sigh of relief and went into the restaurant. Briony was already there, working on a glass of wine. She was doing her gothic trip. Dressed in black, white make-up, I said,

"What's this, the banshee look?"

"Do you like it?"

"Awesome."

The owner was an old friend and gave me a high five.

Not an easy gesture for an Italian reared in Peckham. I said,

"Good to see you, Alfons."

"And you, my friend. Shall I order for you both?"

"Great."

Briony poured me some wine, we did the "cheers" bit, drank, and I asked, "So?"

"I had to leave my doctor."

"I heard."

"He gave me his pin number."

"That's why you left?"

She laughed. Thank Christ. The evening wouldn't be total gloom. She said,

"I bought a pup."

I thought she said "pub" and went,

"Jeez, how much money had he?"

"A King Charles Cavalier."

"Oh, a pup."

She looked like a little girl — well, a gothic little girl — said,

"He's a King Charles Cavalier."

"Nice."

"They're very docile, like they're on heavy tranquillizers."

"Lucky dog."

Alfons brought the food.

Like this.

The starters: Fritti Misti Vegetable. A selection of zucchini, eggplant, broccoli. Done in a crispy batter.

Crostino al Prosciutto with thinly sliced ham, covered in melting Parmesan cheese.

It was good to watch Bri eat. She did it with delicacy and concentration. She said,

"I called the dog Bartley-Jack."

"Why?"

She looked like she didn't know, said,

"I dunno."

For the main course, Bri had Cotoletta alla Milanese. A beef dish fried with spice in a breadcrumb batter. Melt-in-the-mouth stuff.

150

I had gnocchi. Small flour dumplings, flavoured with porcini. That's a wild Italian mushroom.

I described all of the above to Bri. She was impressed, said,

"How'd you know all this stuff? You hardly speak English most days."

"My first two weeks in prison, before I learnt anything, all I had to read was an Italian menu. It was pinned on the wall of my cell. I must have read it a thousand times. Then someone nicked it."

"Why?"

"It's jail, it's what they do. Doesn't matter what it is."

We had espresso to finish, the burn-the-roof-of-your-mouth, bitter, real thing. I said,

"Bri, I need you to listen seriously to me."

"Sure."

"Is there some place you can go for a while?"

"Why?"

"I have some business to take care of, and I have to not worry about you."

"No."

"What?"

"I have a pup now, I can't just go."

"Jeez, take the bloody pup with you."

"Not unless you tell me why."

I lit a roll-up, exhaled with a sigh, said,

"There's some people putting pressure on me. They might try to hurt you."

"Hah . . . fuck 'em."

"C'mon, Bri, I'll give you the cash."

"I have tons of money."

"Please, Bri, as a favour to me."

"I might. Why don't you want to know about the doctor?"

"I do really. What happened?"

"He's veggie. A vegan."

"So? Aren't you sometimes that too?"

"I don't like to be told. Anyway, I like villains best, like you."

I gave up. Ordered the bill and paid that. I asked,

"Bri, can I call you a cab?"

"No, I have a bus pass."

"Since when?"

"Like yesterday."

"Take care, hon."

She gave me that smile, promising nothing.

I'd just started back down New Road when a car beeped me.

The window goes down, it's Jeff.

"Mitch, I been looking for you, mate."

"Yeah?"

"Hop in, I'll give you a lift."

"Just to the Oval, I'm parked there."

I get in, and he accelerates. The skels outside just a blur in the speed. He says,

"I need a favour, mate."

"I'll try."

"Monday we go north."

"Yeah?"

"Two of the crew are down. Gerry's gone and broken his leg, Jack's missus is in the hospital."

"Can't you postpone?"

"Last two excursions had to be shelved. It's tough being a villain and a family man."

"And you're asking me what, Jeff?"

"To fill out the crew."

Thing with mates is, you don't make them sweat it.

Yes or no.

I said,

"Yes."

"Oh, cheers, mate. Monday morning at my place . . . eight thirty."

As I got outta the car, he said,

"Be good to have you along, Mitch."

"It's no big thing."

That's what I thought.

As I walked up the Holland Park drive, I noticed the lights were off. Thank Christ, I thought. Having to hop on the actress was about as appealing as a prison breakfast.

I was about to go to my room when I noticed a light in the kitchen. Thought — "Why not?"

Jordan was sitting at the kitchen table in his shirt-sleeves, a stone bottle before him. I said,

"Yo."

He looked up, said, "Join me."

"Okay."

I'd never seen him without a jacket. I could see his arms were brown, heavily muscled. He motioned for me to get a glass.

I did. He tilted the bottle, poured me a full one, said, "It's jenever, Dutch gin."

We clinked glasses, muttered something that sounded like "skol" and drank them off in one toss. By Jesus, did that kick. A moment of grace, then wallop, your stomach was blitzkrieged. My eyes watered. I gasped,

"Phew."

He nodded, said, "Again?"

"Of course."

After I recovered from the double whammy, I began to roll a cig. He said,

"May I have one?"

"Whoa . . . what about the rules?"

"Fuck them."

I handed him one, lit it, said,

"Now you're talking."

He drew deep, not his first time. Here was a guy reared on smoke. I asked,

"How's Madam?"

"Expecting her call to the theatre."

"Jeez! I mean, that ain't going to go down. What then?"

He looked pained. Drunk too, but mainly pained. Said,

"I'll think of something, I always do."

I was feeling the booze, enough to ask,

"What's the deal, why do you stay?"

He seemed amazed, said,

"It's my life."

Didn't elaborate, so I tried more.

"Didn't you used to be her husband?"

My knowing didn't faze him, said,

"I still am."

Then he spread his hands on the table, focused on me.

"Before her I was nothing. She is the beat of my heart."

I figured we were two guys well pissed, so go for it. I asked,

"But . . . doesn't she, you know . . . like, see other guys?"

He spat on the floor, made a sound that went,

"*Ph . . . tt . . . h.*"

Then,

"They are nothing — playthings she discards like rubbish. I am constant."

There was a trace of spittle on his lips, and his eyes were fevered. I considered he might not be playing with a full deck. I eased down, said,

"You sure take care of her."

He waved his hands in dismissal. I downed more gin, asked,

"Ever hear a duet from Garth Brooks and Trisha Yearwood called 'In Another's Eyes?'"

"No."

"Don't listen to music much, eh?"

"There is only Wagner."

I don't think there's a sane reply to this. Leastways, I didn't have it.

Then he did the oddest thing. Stood up, bowed, said,

"I enjoyed our talk, but now I must secure the house."

I got up, not sure should I shake his hand or not. I said,

"Thanks for the drink."

I'd just got to the door when he said,

"Mr Mitchell, if you are ever in trouble, I will be available."

"Oh."

"I am a valuable ally."

As I headed for bed, I didn't doubt that for a minute.

I tried to watch TV for a bit; I was having double vision.

I must have been very drunk, as I thought *Ally McBeal* wasn't bad.

Friday. I figured if I was bank-robbing on Monday, then I better get some R&R.

I phoned Aisling, she said,

"I wasn't expecting to hear from you."

"Why?"

"It's a guy thing. When they say, 'I'll call,' you don't hold your breath."

"OK . . . so, can I take you out?"

"Oh yes, I have a plan."

"Nothing better than a plan."

"Can you pick me up at the Angel tube at eight?"

"Islington?"

"Is that bad?"

"It's north."

"So?"

"No . . . I can do north."

"See you later."

I did a full day's work:
  repaired a door
  cleaned the windows
  whistled some tunes.

Come evening, Jordan laid a wedge of cash on me. He said,
  "Madam would like a word."
  "Sure, listen . . . I need Monday free."
  "Don't make a habit of it."
All the camaraderie of the night before seemed to have evaporated.

But I noticed his eyes were bloodshot. Teach him to guzzle gin.

Madam was waiting in the dining room. She was looking good. The battalion of
  hairdressers
  beauticians
  physiotherapists
had done their work. Her skin and eyes glowed. She was wearing a low-cut cream dress, her skin lightly tanned. Great logo.

I felt stirrings. The body is a bastard, it just does its own thing. Lillian gave the knowing smile, said,
  "You must be all hot and sweaty after your toil."

I gave a noncommittal shrug. She said,

"We're going out this evening, I've booked a table at the Savoy."

"Not me, babe."

"Excuse me?"

"I've got other plans."

"Well, cancel them. It's time I was seen in public."

"Have fun, but I won't be with you."

"How do you expect me to appear unaccompanied? I must have an escort."

"Try the Yellow Pages."

She just couldn't believe I was refusing her, she shouted,

"I will not be denied."

I gave her the hard look, said,

"Jeez, get real, lady," and walked out. I could hear her screaming,

"I didn't dismiss you, come back here!"

Jordan, of course, appeared, and before he could speak, I said,

"She's rehearsing, don't disturb her."

As I showered I thought — "She is one royal pain in the arse."

Little did I know.

After I showered, I cracked a brewski and got dressed. Kept it casual. Sweatshirt and jeans. My nose was still aching, but I could live with it. Gant was hovering on the outskirts of my mind. The mental threads one makes are tenuous and treacherous. I dredged up a line.

Hatred is for wimps, I believe in annihilation.

The gems you learn from children's literature. Ready to go, I picked up the mobile and shoved it in my jeans. The car started on the first turn, and I'd got to the end of the drive when the phone went. I said,
"Yeah?"
It was Lillian, said,
"You are so much more than I had expected but so much less than I had hoped."
And hung up. It was ten after eight by the time I got to the Angel tube. Islington is a bastard in a car. Aisling was waiting. She was dressed in a duffel coat, faded blue jeans. Looked like a radiant student. I opened the door, she jumped in. Leant over and kissed me on the mouth. I said,
"I'm sorry I'm late."
"We'll be sorry if I'm late."
Let that slide and asked,

"Where to?"

She gave me a complicated set of directions and I got lost twice. Finally, she shouted,

"Stop!"

I did.

We were parked outside a pub. She said,

"This is Filthy MacNasty's."

"You've got to be kidding."

"No, that's the name."

"Sounds like it should be in the Bronx."

"I remembered you said you love crime writers. Here they have a crime writer read and they play tracks relevant to his work. Guess who's on this evening?"

I had no idea, said,

"I've no idea."

"James Ellroy."

"No shit . . . that's brilliant!"

Already the place was jammed, but we managed to grab two stools at the corner of the bar. Aisling's face was shining, excitement writ huge. She said,

"I'm buying, what would you like?"

"Pint of Guinness."

She ordered that and a Malibu. The drinks came, and we did the "cheers" bit. I asked,

"What's a Malibu?"

"Rum with coconut."

"Good God."

"Try it."

"I don't think so."

"Ah, go on."

I did, went,

"Jesus, paint off a gate, tastes like cough syrup."
She laughed, squeezed my thigh, said,
"I'm delighted to see you."
I felt great. Jeez, when had I ever felt that? She was gorgeous, funny, smart, and liked me. I had money in my wallet and a promising hard-on. Hog heaven.
Then James Ellroy came on. Big guy and wired. He didn't so much read as give a total performance.
Mesmerizing.
When he took a break, he was mobbed. Aisling said,
"Why don't you have a word?"
"Maybe I'll catch him later."
She gave a wicked smile, said,
"Let me tell you about later. I'm going to lure you to my home, fill a bath with
scents
oil
and
you.
"Open a bottle of wine and soak. Then I'll order a huge pizza and eat you while it's hot. Then while you sleep I'll watch over you."
My phone went.
I had to squeeze through the crowd to find a quiet spot. A guy muttered,
"Fuckin' yuppie."
Me?
Holding the phone close, I said,
"Yeah?"
"Mr Mitchell, it's Jordan."
"Yeah?"

"Miss Palmer has attempted suicide."
Oh shit.
"Is she bad?"
"I'm afraid so."
"What can I do?"
"I believe you should come."
"Aw, shit."
"As you wish."
And he hung up. I said,
fuck
fuck
fuck.
A man said, "He reads better after the break."
I fought my way back, said to Aisling,
"I gotta go."
"Aw, no."
"Listen, I'll drop you off."
"No, you better get moving."
"Will you be OK?"
"Perhaps I'll have a word with James Ellroy."
"I'll make it up to you."
She gave me a sad smile, said,
"We'll see."
As I left, the soundtrack was doing U2 with "Sweetest Thing".
Now if that isn't sticking it to you, I dunno what is.
"Jeez," I thought, "where did that come from?"
Manoeuvring through the Islington traffic I felt bone weary. Took me near two hours to get back to Holland Park.
Into the kitchen and Jordan was there, I asked,

"How is she?"

"The doctor's given her a sedative, but she's awake."

"Should I go up?"

"Please do."

He had nothing further to add, so I went. Up those stairs like a condemned man. Her bedroom was lit by one bedside lamp. In bed, her arms were lying outside the quilt. I could see the bandages on her wrists. No fuckin' chance she'd cover them.

I said, "Lillian."

"Mitch . . . Mitch, that you, darling?"

"Yes."

She made a grand effort to sit up but then sagged back, whispered,

"I'm sorry, Mitch, I didn't want to be any trouble to you."

I wanted to wallop her, said,

"It's OK, you rest now, everything's fine."

"Is she pretty, Mitch, is she young?"

"What?"

"The girl you're seeing."

"There's nobody . . . I was on a boys' night out."

"Promise me, Mitch, promise you'll never leave me."

My mind was shouting, "How the hell did we get to here?" I said,

"I promise."

"Hold my hand, darling."

I did. She gave a deep sigh, said,

"I feel so safe now."

I felt exactly like I did when the judge said,

"Three years."

163

The way to dress for a robbery is comfortable. It's not the occasion to break in a new pair of shoes. Or to have a pair of Y-fronts mangling your balls.

I arrived at Jeff's place early. Two of the old crew were already there. Bert and Mike, as reliable as concrete. The air was thick with cigarette smoke and the aroma of coffee.

The atmosphere was cranked. These guys were pros, but each time the stakes were rising.

A sofa was littered with weapons. Jeff said,

"We've got a new guy."

I didn't like that, said,

"I don't like that."

Jeff put up his hands, said,

"Me neither, but he's got a rep as a wheelman. We don't got a choice."

Jeff's system was simple. Three cars. One for the robbery, then two changes. These motors had been positioned over the weekend. An expert driver was vital. Jeff asked,

"Want some breakfast, Mitch?"

A huge fry-up was simmering alongside a mountain of toast.

There are two schools of thought on a meal before a caper:

164

(1) Pig out for the energy level.

(2) Nowt . . . to hike the adrenalin.

I was with the second, said,

"Coffee'd be good."

I moved over to the couch, selected a 9mm, put it in the waistband of my jeans. Took, too, a pump shotgun.

You rack that fucker, you get everybody's attention. Put on a worn combat jacket, packed the pockets with shells. Tasted my coffee, double loaded, it hit like a fist.

Knock on the door, Jeff opened it carefully. Turned to us, said,

"It's the new guy."

A punk came in. Something very familiar about him. He was dressed like Liam Gallagher before he discovered what a gold credit card implied. He had a long gash down the side of his face. I remembered.

At the party, he'd been out back with Briony, and she'd torn his face before putting the gun in his mouth. He said,

"I know you."

I nodded. He smirked, asked,

"How's that crazy bitch sister of yours?"

Jeff intervened, said,

"Whoa, let's all settle down."

I said to Jeff,

"You'll vouch for him?"

"Guaranteed."

I didn't like it, but it was too late to back out. We got organized and headed off. A transit van was the first leg.

I sat up front with Jeff, the boyos in the back. The punk was mouthing large, but Bert and Mike just ignored him.

Jeff said,

"The target is Newcastle-under-Lyme. The motors are parked at Keele University."

"What's the word?"

"The bank is holding heavy. Maybe twelve thou."

"Nice."

"Let's hope so."

I settled back in my seat, let my mind free-fall.

One night, having serviced the actress, I'd begun to tell her of the range of my reading. I dunno what prompted me to do so, but I was in full flight, listing the different fields I'd read.

When I was done, she said,

"The books of a self-taught man, a working man. We all know how they are,

distressing

egotistic

insistent

raw

striking and ultimately

nauseating."

"You snooty bitch."

She laughed, said,

"Alas, don't blame me, it was Virginia Woolf's analysis of James Joyce. Are you familiar with Virginia?"

"Take a wild guess."

The van lurched, and Jeff said,

"We're at Keele."

We loaded the gear into the waiting car, got into overalls.

Bert would remain with the second car and Mike with the third.

167

It was vital each car be
manned
safe
primed.
The punk got behind the wheel. Jeff beside him and me in back.

As the punk ran through the gears, he said,
"This is a piece of shit."
Jeff said,
"Shut your mouth and drive."
He did.

Twenty minutes later, we rolled into Newcastle. My adrenalin was pumping. Jeff directed the punk to park about twenty yards from the back entrance.

We were out and moving, pulled on ski masks as we hit the entrance. Some firms, they take down a bank, they believe in verbal terror. Go in roaring, screaming obscenities.

Put the fear of God into the punters; I can see the merits.

But Jeff has his own method. He believes a demonstration is worth a thousand words.

So he shot the first customer we encountered.

Shot him in the knees. The guy went down. Jeff loaded his gauge with pellets. Without causing major damage,

they hurt like fuck

look the biz

and scare the bejaysus.

Two minutes, I had staff and customers herded. Jeff went through the bank like a virus, filled two black bags. Then we were outta there.

Running for the car, the great British tradition came into play. Yup, the have-a-go spirit. A guy grabbed me from behind, clamped his arms round me. The punk was gunning the engine. I let my body go slack, then with one move stamped my shoe down on the guy's instep. He let out a roar you'd have heard in Brixton. Mainly, he let me go. I spun round, stuck the shooter in his face, shouted,

"Yah stupid bastard, yah want to get killed, is that it?"

Jeff pulled me off, gritted,

"Let's go, c'mon."

Already I could hear sirens. I backed off and ran to the car.

We tore outta there. Jeff said,

"Jeez, Mitch, I thought you were going to waste him."

"So did I."

The punk was laughing like a hysteric, said,

"You should 'ave, you should 'ave blown him away!"

If he wasn't driving, I'd have given him a fist up the side of his head.

Got to Keele and switched cars. Then a more sedate pace to the third motor. Changed again, and in jig time we were on the highway, lost in a ton of traffic. Once we got to the van, I let out a long breath. Didn't realize I'd been holding it.

In the back, Mike, Bert and the punk were whooping it up; Jeff was driving and reached under his seat. Pulled out a fifth of Cutty Sark, handed it to me. I drank deep, let it burn. He glanced at me, a grin building. I said,

"Piece of cake, eh?"

Back at Jeff's, we began to party. I was drinking Bud and nipping at the Cutty. The punk was doing major damage to a bottle of gin. Jeff and Bert were doing the count.

Mike asked,

"Another Bud, Mitch?"

"Sure."

I was sitting on a kitchen chair, and Mike leant against the table, said,

"You've a hard-on for that kid."

"He's trouble."

"Well, he did OK today."

170

"See his arms, tracks?"

Mike gave a good look, said,

"Doesn't seem like he's using now, his arms aren't swollen."

"Preparation H."

"What?"

"Takes down the swelling."

Mike was truly surprised, said,

"Jeez, Mitch, how do you know that shit?"

"*New Hope for the Dead.*"

"What?"

"By Charles Willeford."

"You've lost me."

"Lost Charles Willeford too, he's dead, and more's the Irish pity."

Jeff raised his hand, said,

"Yo, people, we've got a tally."

We waited. Then,

"Fifteen large."

Loud yahooing. After Jeff took expenses, we got two-seven each. The punk said,

"Party on."

After a time, the guys began to drift away. Jeff said,

"Got a sec, Mitch?"

"Sure."

When they'd gone, he cracked a beer, said,

"Ever heard of a guy named Kerrkovian?"

"Naw."

"Tall, thin fucker, likes to dress in black. Got eyes like marbles, nothing alive there. I think he's one of those Eastern European gangsters."

"Interesting as it is, Jeff, what's it got to do with me?"

"He's been asking about you."

"Oh."

"Watch your back."

"Yeah. Thanks a lot, Jeff."

"You musta pissed someone off big-time."

"I seem to have a talent for it."

I headed for a florist. Ordered up a batch of roses, orchids, tulips. The florist said,

"A mix like that, it's gonna cost."

"Did you hear me bicker?"

"No, but . . ."

Put them in the trunk of the car and headed for Peckham.

Joe's grave was well tended, and a current copy of the *Big Issue*, wrapped in cellophane, rested there. Made me sad.

A man was moving around the cemetery, tidying up. I went over to him, said,

"Hey."

"Hey yourself."

"Did you take care of that grave over there?"

"And what if I did?"

"I just wanted to say thanks."

I peeled off a few notes and he took them fast. Did wonders for his attitude, said,

"A headstone would make all the difference."

"How would one arrange that?"

He took a flask out of his pocket, offered. I shook my head, and he took a swig, said,

"Keeps the chill off."

"I believe you."

Put the flask away, said,

"If you were to go to your regular stonemason, he'd charge you large. I could get it done for half that."

I peeled off more notes, asked,

"Would you?"

"My pleasure. Want an inscription?"

I thought for a bit, said,

" 'He was the issue'."

"That's it?"

"Yes."

"You don't want a poem or anything? I've some hot verses in my shed."

"He didn't do poetry."

"Right, I'll get on it."

He counted the money, said,

"There's too much here."

"No . . . keep the extra."

As I headed off he asked,

"How come you trust me?"

"If you can't trust a guy in a graveyard . . ."

He gave a low chuckle, said,

"The biggest rogues are under your feet."

"Words to live by," I said.

Back at Holland Park I felt the adrenalin leak away, and I longed for a kip. Jordan came out to meet me, said,

"Madam's been asking for you."

"Okay."

"She's not the only one."

"Oh?"

"You had two visitors."

"Together?"

"No, one was a policeman."

"Bailey."

"A bad-mannered individual."

"No argument."

"The other was . . . how do I describe him? . . . In Hungarian, in dialect, there is a word — *Zeitfel*. It means 'a corpse who still walks'."

"Like a zombie."

"Perhaps. It is fuelled by evil, propelled on malice. The Americans have a term: stone killer."

"Was he dressed in black?"

"Yes."

While I digested this, Jordan said,

"As he left, he pointed to the elm."

Jordan nodded to the huge tree to the left of the drive,

"And he said, 'Beware of strange fruit'."

"Billie Holiday."

"Pardon?"

"She sang a song about a lynched man, called 'Strange Fruit'."

Jordan reached in his jacket, took out an envelope, said,

"You also got post."

The handwriting was Briony's. I said,

"Thanks."

I opened Briony's letter. On the front was a sad-looking bear. He held a sign that read:

I'M SAD

Inside was the following:

Oh Mitch,
    You want me to go away. I don't have skeletons in my closet. I put them in other people's.
    Only my little dog loves me.
                    XXX
                    Bri

I guess it would have made more sense if I knew who Isherwood was. Or what his game was.

I lay on the bed and thought about Aisling. I'd really have to call her. Then I replayed the robbery and the moment when the idiot grabbed me from behind. For one moment I had truly wanted to squeeze that trigger.

Had to admit, I'd been amped. I'd gotten off on the rush, and I just hoped I wouldn't want another fix.

Sleep crept up on me and took me mid-thought.

It was late evening when I woke. A vague sense of foreboding hung over me. I made some coffee, got on the other side of that. Rolled a cigarette and smoked it, sitting on the bed. It tasted as old as I was getting. Showered and put on a crisp white shirt, faded jeans. Checked myself in the mirror. Like George Michael's father before the toilet incident.

The phone went, the actress said,

"I've missed you, Mitchell."

"Well, I'm back."

"I've a special surprise for you."

"I'm dressed for it."

"Pardon?"

"I'm on my way."

"You won't be disappointed."

There was an inch of coffee left in my mug, so I searched out the bottle of Scotch, poured in a generous inch. Balance the books. Took it down fast. What it tasted like was more, but I decided to pace it.

Lillian was waiting in the drawing room. Someone had been busy, all the furniture was piled at the back. The carpets rolled back. A high gloss on the wood floor. Centrepiece was a small stage, lit by a single spotlight. I thought, "Oh fuck."

One single chair was placed in front of the stage. Beside it was a bureau with a rake of booze. I sat, checked the bottles and saw a Johnnie Walker. Poured a hefty belt. I was going to need it.

Classical music began to play, the lights went down.

Jordan appeared on the stage, dressed in a black suit, dicky bow. He intoned,

"It is my pleasure to herald the return of Lillian Palmer. This evening, she will recite a short piece from D. H. Lawrence. Her lament for an England already lost."

I was feeling lost myself. Gulped down the Scotch. Jordan bowed and withdrew. If he was expecting applause, he'd be waiting.

No sound of one hand clapping.

Then she appeared. Dressed in some kind of flimsy sari. I could clearly see her boobs. Her head lowered. Slowly she began:

"It is England, my God, it breaks my soul. This England, these shafted windows, the elm trees, the past — the great past, crumbling down, not under the force of the coming birds but under the weight of exhausted leaves. No, I can't bear it. For the winter stretches ahead, where all vision is lost and all memory dies out. I can't bear it, the past, the falling, perishing, crumbling past, so great, so magnificent."

I tuned out. I might even have dozed a bit. Ferocious damage was being done to the Johnnie Walker. Finally, she finished. I stood up unsteadily and shouted,

Bravo.

Magnifique.

Come on, yah Reds.

Next thing I know, I'm on the stage and tearing her clothes off. It was

sweaty

loud

ferocious.

I vaguely recall her sinking her teeth deep in my neck and me roaring,

"Yah fuckin' vampire!"

After, I lay on my back gasping for breath. She said,

"Am I to believe you appreciated my performance?"

Which one?

I curled up, passed out.

Someone was pulling at me, and I was trying to push them away.

Eventually, I sat up. Jordan was standing over me, said,

"There is something you have to see."

"Now?"

I tried to focus on my watch. Took an effort.

Three forty-five.

"Christ," I groaned, "can't it wait?"

"It's of grave urgency. I'll wait for you in the kitchen."

I shook my head. Big mistake. A mother of a headache. Not to mention a churning stomach. As Jordan reached the door, he said,

"It might be an idea to put your clothes on."

Aching, I pulled on my jeans and the balled-up white shirt. Then I threw up.

Jordan was holding a flashlight and looked at me. He nodded and headed out. The night was pitch dark. Jordan headed across the lawn and stopped at the elm tree. Waited for me to catch up. He said,

"Are you prepared?"

"For what?"

He shone a powerful beam up into the branches. Billy Norton was hanging from a thick stem. A black, gaping hole where his groin should have been. I muttered,

"Jesus,"

and was on my knees, retching. Jordan switched off the flashlight.

He asked quietly,

"A friend?"

"Yes."

Then he produced a small flask and a pack of cigarettes. Lit one and handed it to me. Then he took the top off the flask and offered it. I drank full, and he said,

"Brandy and port."

When it hit my stomach it thought about regurgitating but opted the other way, settled. I was able to smoke the cigarette.

I avoided looking at Billy. Jordan asked,

"Did you notice his hand?"

"What? . . . No."

"The fingers on the right are gone, it's a signature."

"A what?"

"Vosnok. East European death squad. Since the gates opened, they're unemployed. London attracts the vermin."

"Kerrkovian!"

Jordan nodded, said,

"I trust this is not a police matter?"

"I'd appreciate that."

We buried him behind the house. It was hard work, least it was for me. A hangover doesn't handle a shovel well. Sweat cascaded down my body. I was in my bare feet, and the soil felt like sludge. Jordan dug with an easy rhythm. I said,

"Looks like you've done this before."

"Many times."

I didn't have the nerve to ask if he meant "in this place". Some things you best let slide. When we'd finished, Jordan asked,

"Will you say words for him?"

Part of me wanted to shout — "Good riddance!" I nodded and said,

"Goodbye . . . Billy."

It seemed enough for Jordan. He headed to the house. I followed. In the kitchen I trailed muddy prints and said,

"Sorry."

He produced some of his sachets of powder and began to mix that healing elixir. My mind went into free-fall.

In the joint, you never gave or received favours. It was fraught with peril. I broke that rule only once. For a guy named Craig. I covered his back when he'd lost focus. After, most days he'd chow down with me. Even offered me his dessert.

His brother was a cop. Not just any filth but a renowned detective who'd put away more child abusers than Andrew Vachss. But finally, the abyss looked back into him. Drunk one night, he'd found himself cruising for a child. Snapping out of it, he'd gone home immediately and shot himself. Only Craig knew the reason for the suicide. To the cops, he remained a hero and had simply "eaten his gun". Then Craig had looked up from his grub and made full eye contact. Convicts never did that unless they'd a knife or pipe to back it up. He said,
   "The point of this story is I avoid zeal. When the gangs go after a chicken hawk here, I abstain."
   I got the point. A frenzy had been building in the prison for some days. It usually culminated in a hunt for a sex offender.
   I said,
   "I hadn't planned on joining the party."
   Holding my gaze, he said,
   "Self-righteousness is very infectious. People get swept along."
   I didn't argue. He was repaying his debt.

Jordan nudged me, handed over a mug, said,

"Drink."

I did.

Jeez, was that the business. Everything near sang, my system felt almost young. He said,

"What will you do about this Kerrkovian?"

"Find him."

"Yes."

I hesitated, but he was prepared to wait. I said,

"Then I'll kill him."

"You'll require assistance."

"It's not your fight."

He folded his arms, said,

"A man comes onto my land, puts a corpse outside my window and you think I'll turn the other cheek?"

"Who'll mind the actress if we're both gone?"

"I'll make provisions."

I stood up, said,

"OK . . . we'll go hunting."

"Have you a weapon?"

"I do . . . do you?"

He gave me a smile. Humour never entered into it.

182

★ ★ ★

I put on the radio to ease me into sleep. Dire Straits were doing their riff, the line about Dixie, laden with threat. I hoped Kerr-fuckin-kovian was tuned.

The next day, Jordan ran a test. Using my car. He said,

"I want you to approach the car with suspicion, the back seat you check carefully."

I did. Tried the door, but it wouldn't open. Looked in the window. All I could see was a crumpled blanket on the floor and empty seats. I tapped on the window, the blanket moved, and Jordan unfolded, emerged. I asked,

"How can you make yourself so small?"

He gave a rueful smile, said,

"Years of servitude."

I asked the obvious.

"How come the door won't open?"

"It's an old car, only the front doors open."

"He'll believe that?"

"He better."

It took us three nights to track him. We'd trawled Clapham, Streatham, Stockwell, Kennington and finally got him at a club in Brixton. I'd brought the Glock. I didn't know what Jordan was packing, but I hoped it was heavy. We parked a ways up the road from the club Kerrkovian had entered.

Jordan said,

"Give me the gun."

"What?"

"He'll frisk you."

"Oh."

"I won't wish you luck, as these matters require only timing and nerve."

"I'll settle for luck."

As I got out, I said,

"See you."

"No, you won't."

The bouncer at the door was a grief merchant and intended to give me large, said,

"Members only."

"How much?"

He gave me the calculating look, went with it, said,

"Twenty-five."

I peeled off the notes, asked,

"Don't I get a card or nuttin?"

"I'll remember you."

"Gee, that's reassuring."

I went in. The place was jammed. A Brixton brew of dreads

     goths

           transvestites

               paddies

        minor villains

    bent cops.

I spotted Kerrkovian sitting at a corner table with the punk. I thought, "Shit."

Moved to them, said,

"Lads."

The punk gave a smirk, said,

"Mitchell."

Kerrkovian was wearing a black suit and looked like a badly fucked Bryan Ferry. He said,

"I hear many things about you."

His accent was pseudo-American. Like he'd watched all the very worst B movies. He had rotten teeth — Eastern Europe not having the best dental plan. He stood up, asked,

"I buy you a brewski?"

"Not right now. I hear you've been looking for me."

"You got it, buddy."

"Well, my car is outside, let's take a ride."

The punk said,

"Get real."

I looked at Kerrkovian, said,

"You wouldn't be afraid to travel with me, would you?"

He smiled, the full frontal of gangrenous molars. I said,

"I'm not packing, you can frisk me."

He did. This was a Brixton club, nobody batted an eye.

The punk said,

"What a wanker."

I asked, "So, are you coming?"

"As long as my new friend comes too."

I shrugged. I went first. As we approached the car, I said,

"The back doors don't work."

The punk moved forward, peered in the back windows, said,

"Nothing there."

I got behind the wheel, the punk beside me and Kerrkovian riding shotgun. The punk said,

"Where did you get this heap of shit?"

As I moved to turn the ignition, Jordan was up, had a wire round Kerrkovian's neck. I smashed my elbow into the punk's face, then crashed his head onto the dash. Kerrkovian thrashed and flailed, but Jordan's knee was pivoted against the seat. What seemed like an hour, Kerrkovian went limp, eyes out of their sockets. I said,

"Jordan . . . *Jordan*, you can let go."

"You can never be too careful with this filth."

"Jesus, he's near decapitated."

Jordan let go. I started up the car and got the fuck outta there. Jordan said,

"Go back to Holland Park."

The front seat was awash with blood. Jordan threw the blanket over them. I asked,

"What about this kid?"

"He can help us dig."

Heavy rain began and helped obscure the bundle on the front seat. Blood was leaking over my shoes and across the brake.

By the time we got to Holland Park, the rain was near torrential. I asked,

"What about the actress?"

"She'll sleep till noon."

"You sure?"

"I made sure. Drive up to the garage."

I did.

We got out and inside. Jordan produced oilskins and said,

"Get the wheelbarrow."

Then we hauled Kerrkovian and the punk into the garage.

The punk was starting to come round. Jordan said,

"Remove everything from their pockets."

From Kerrkovian, I took

a Sig Sauer .45

wallet

cigarettes

stiletto blade and

a piece of paper with a phone number.

It was Gant's.

From the punk, I got

a Browning

thick wad of money

Polo mints

condoms

cocaine.

Jordan filled a bucket of water and threw it over the punk.

He spluttered, choked, then slowly opened his eyes. It must have been nightmarish. Two figures in long waxed coats, the storm and a corpse. He said,

"You broke me nose."

Jordan said, "Stand up, you've work to do."

He got shakily to his feet, whined,

"What's going on?"

Jordan said, "Shut up and you might live."

He shut up.

I asked, "Where are we going to put Kerrkovian?"

"The elm tree, where he placed your friend."

Jordan reached onto a back shelf, produced a bottle of brandy, handed it to me. I drank deep and offered it to the punk.

He was shaking so bad he could hardly hold it. Brandy ran down his front. I said,

"Use both hands."

It made him gag, but he got it down. I passed the bottle to Jordan, who took a small sip. The punk looked to me, said,

"Don't let him kill me, Mr Mitchell."

Mister!

I said, "Course not."

Jordan said, "Help me get the wire out of his throat."

We turned Kerrkovian over, his head was rolling, the teeth had bit clean through his lower lip. The punk went,

"Arg . . . h . . . h,"

and threw up.

The wire had two wooden handles. They looked well worn. I didn't want to think about that. We took a handle each and pulled. It came clear but far from clean. Jordan cleaned it on the dead man's suit. Then he straightened up, cleared his throat and spat on him. He said,

"Lift."

And we threw the body in the barrow. Jordan took the Sig Sauer, hefted it. I said,

"That's the closest thing to a nonjam automatic you'll get."

He pointed it loosely at the punk, said,

"Push that barrow."

The storm had increased. I could feel the rain even through the oilskins. The punk had a tough task pushing the barrow, but eventually we got to the elm tree. Jordan threw a shovel on the ground, said,

"Get digging."

The punk was wiping blood and mucus from his ruined nose, asked,

"By myself?"

"Do it."

The mud made his job a little easier, save he kept slipping.

Jordan handed me a flask, I drank like a demented thing.

Finally, the grave was dug. Jordan leant over the barrow, took a pair of pliers from his coat, cut off Kerrkovian's little finger.

The punk whimpered, and I said,

"Jesus Christ!"

The crack of the bone was like a pistol shot. Then he tilted the barrow, and the body tumbled in. The sound of it hitting was like a splash in hell. Jordan handed me the Sig Sauer.

I said,

"What?"

Jordan looked right into my eyes, said,

"I've noticed your speech is polluted with American-isms so . . . it's your call."

The punk realized what was going down, pleaded,

"Aw God, Mr Mitchell, I won't say nuffink."

I shot him in the forehead. He wavered for a moment, then fell into the hole. Jordan picked up the shovel, began to fill the grave. I didn't move, just stood there, rain teeming down, the Sig hanging loose at my side.

Jordan straightened up, said,

"Let's get a cup of tea."

At the kitchen table, as Jordan made tea, I said,

"Mickey Spillane always had his characters drink whiskey as he couldn't spell cognac."

He didn't answer.

I didn't care.

He put two steaming mugs of tea down and asked,

"A biscuit?"

"Are they Rich Tea?"

"Only Mikado."

"I'll pass, then."

He got a bottle of Glenlivet from under the sink, and I asked,

"What, you have bottles stashed everywhere?"

"Not just bottles."

"Oh."

He unscrewed the cap and dolloped the booze into the tea.

I sipped mine. It tasted like tea with whiskey added.

I rolled a cig and offered it to him. He took it, and I got to work on another. Lit up and we'd a cloud of smoke in jig time. I said,

"Jordan, how'd you get the name? It's not anything to do with basketball . . . is it?"

He sneered, said,
"My father was born on the bank of the Jordan."
"I thought you were Hungarian."
"We moved."
"Did you ever hear the quotation

   'I am filled with coffins
   like an old cemetery'?"

He stubbed out the butt, said,
"It's not over yet."
"I'm afraid you're right."
I stood up, said,
"I have to get some sleep."
"You'll need it."

PART THREE

ACTS CONCLUDING

Jordan sent the severed finger to Gant.

Beautifully wrapped.

Gold box.

Brittle tissue paper.

Red velvet bow.

Said to me, "The moving finger having writ . . ."

I said, "You're one sick fucker."

I got back on track with Aisling. She demurred at first, made me sweat it, then agreed. We met at the Sun in Splendour on Portobello . . . I'd bought new shoes. JP Tod's, the real thing. Those suckers are expensive, but wow, are your feet very grateful.

Tan colour, I was wearing the Gap khakis with them, a cream sweatshirt and the Gucci jacket. Looked good enough to eat.

Aisling was wearing a killer black dress. I said, "Killer dress."

She smiled. Things were looking hopeful. She said, "You're not too bad yourself."

"Do you like the shoes?"

"Bally?"

"No."

"Imitation?"

"Hardly."

"Oh sorry, I forgot you're a man of discernment and taste."

"Isn't that from 'Sympathy For The Devil'?"

"I dunno."

"Before your time, I guess."

She ignored that, asked,

"Where are we going?"

I said, "Fancy dinner?"

"I fancy you, more's the Irish pity."

The thing with the Irish is, they sure can talk, and boy, can they talk well. But what on earth are they talking about?

Fuck knows.

She said,

"Here's a thought, let's rent a vid, order pizza, and you can discover what's under a killer dress."

"Won't it look odd here on the street?"

We went to her place. The minute we got in, she was on me.

Hips grinding, mouth fastened like hope. After we'd done, I gasped,

"What about the pizza?"

Later we watched *Three Colours: Red*. I'm not sure I entirely got it. Aisling cried through most of it. I hate fuckin' subtitles. She asked,

"Did you like it?"

"Loved it."

"Truly, you can say, I won't mind."

In the afterglow, I went way over the top, said,

"I love French films, they have a certain . . . *je ne sais quoi.*"

She bought it

hook

line

. . . and frenched sinker.

Said, "Oh, I am so happy, Mitch, and you speak French."

The one line I had was from the joint. A serial rapist used to scream it when the vigilantes came for him.

Which they did twice weekly. I said,

"Sure."

She sat up, the sheet falling away from her breasts. I'd have spoken bloody Russian. She said,

"This is so cool, it's part of a trilogy; we can watch *Blue* and *White.*"

I nodded, reached for my tobacco and began a roll-up. She watched in fascination. I asked,

"Want one?"

"You're my drug."

Uh . . . huh.

Finally got to the pizza, blitzed in the microwave. As it dripped down my mouth, Aisling asked,

"All appetites satisfied?"

I nodded.

The radio was playing quietly. They'd been good.

Gram Parsons

Cowboy Junkies

till

Phil Collins began massacring "True Colours".

Aisling asked,

"What are you thinking about?"

I know that answer, said,

"You, dear."

She laughed, and I added,

"We don't need a light, your eyes would brighten any room."

"Shite talk."

The radio kicked in with Iris DeMent — "No Time To Cry . . ."

Aisling began to sob. I moved to hold her and she waved me away. Was quiet as the song finished the last haunting melody. She said,

"My dad was an alcoholic. My brother said I lived my childhood like a deer in the headlights of a speeding car. For years the only way I could cope was to move him from the drama to the light entertainment department. When he died roaring from drink, I was glad. At the hospital, they gave me his effects . . . know what they were?"

I had no idea, said,

"I've no idea."

"A Boy Scout belt and rosary beads."

She toyed with a pizza crust, then,

"I threw the beads in the river."

"You kept the belt?"

"It was his estate."

"Jeez, you have a mouth on you, know that?"

She smiled, said,

"You want to hear a crock?"

"A what?"

"A crock of shit."

"Well . . ."

"All you hear nowadays is the New Woman. Doesn't want the traditional things. This woman wants a husband, a home and children."

I kept quiet. Reached for a drink. She said,

"I want you."

Then she leant over, straddled me and began to make love.

I didn't resist. After, she asked,

"Wouldn't I be crazy not to?"

"You would."

I didn't feel crazy. I spent all of the next day with her. Went to Portobello Market, laughed at the junk they were peddling. Drove to the West End and got our photo taken at the Trocadero. Oddly enough, it wasn't a bad snap. Aisling looks young and shining, and me . . . I look like I'm glad she looks like that. I was.

When I got back to Holland Park, it was clocking midnight. The house was dark. I checked on the actress, touched her cheek, she muttered,

"*M . . . m . . .*"

and continued sleeping.

No sign of Jordan.

Went to my room and cracked a brewski. I had that bone weariness that comes from feeling good. Didn't analyse too closely lest I lose it. Did I love Aisling? Sure as shooting, she made me feel like a person I might once have hoped to be.

Drank the brew, it was cold and satisfying. Got my clothes off and climbed into bed. Jesus, I was beat. Stretched my legs. My toes touched something wet and instantly recoiled. Jumped out of the bed, horror building. Tore back the bedclothes. A ball of blood and gore lay there. My eyes could focus, but the mind wouldn't kick. Had to look closer — it was a dog's head. Briony's dog . . . what the fuck was his name . . . Bartley? Bartley-Jack.

Ever hear Dolores Keane sing "Caledonia?"

I did then.

I dunno why.

As I recoiled from the bed of horror, the song pounded in my head.

Madness, I guess.

Then I felt my shoulders gripped and next a hard slap to my face. I said,

"Hey, easy on the slapping."

Jordan said,

"You were shouting, we don't want to wake Madam."

"God forbid that should happen."

He stepped over to the bed, muttered something in Hungarian.

Something the equivalent of "fuck me". I said,

"It's my sister's dog."

"Why are we still here? Let's go."

We got the oilskins and the guns, took my car. Traffic was light and we got across town in about thirty minutes.

Briony lived in a house on the Peckham Road. On a quiet street, just a riot away from the lights.

The house was ablaze with lights. Jordan asked,

"You want front or back?"

"Front."

I kept the Glock in my right-hand pocket. The door was ajar.

I pushed it slowly back. Tiptoed down the hall. Briony was sitting in an armchair, covered in blood. I gasped till I realized it was from the dog, whom she was holding in her lap.

Her eyes were staring, I said,

"Bri?"

"Oh, hello."

I moved into the room, moved near her, asked,

"You OK, hon?"

"Look what they did to my baby."

"Who did?"

"I don't know. When I came home, I found him in my bed. Where is his head, Mitch?"

Jordan stepped into the room. I said,

"Bri, this is my friend Jordan."

"Oh . . . hello, Jordan, would you like tea?"

He shook his head. I said,

"Bri, will you let me hold Bartley-Jack?"

"OK."

I took the mess from her lap. The little dog's body was still warm. That freaked the fuck outta me. Jordan said,

"I'll clean up your sister."

He helped her from the chair and took her by the hand. The phone rang. I picked it up and heard a high-pitched giggle.

I started for the door, and Jordan caught me up, asked,

"Where are you going?"

"It's Gant."

"And?"

"I'm going to kill the fucker."

He turned me round, said,

"Think it through; you want to catch him at a vulnerable time. Has he family?"

"A daughter, school age."

"So, we hit at breakfast."

"After the girl goes to school."

"As you wish."

"How's Briony?"

"She's sleeping, I gave her a sedative."

"What the fuck are you, a mobile pharmacy?"

He smiled. "Among other things."

Jordan went out for about half an hour, returned with a carrier bag, said,

"To help us make it through the night."

"Put a tune to that, you're talking number one with a bullet."

He grimaced. Took out a six-pack of Bud, French bread, ham, tomatoes, pickles, jar of mayo. I asked,

"Where'd you get that shit?"

"This is Peckham."

Argue that.

A few brewskis later, I said,

"I once read:

Winter is cold,
it's supposed to be."

Mid French roll, he asked,

"Which means what?"

"I dunno, seems appropriate."

We formed a plan for hitting Gant's. Rather, we tried various options.

Discarded

modified

arrived at.

Jordan said, "OK. That's good. Now, let's make it look like a drug deal gone sour."

"How?"

He reached in the bag, tossed a

hypo

heroin

and

the works

on the table.

I said, "That's my kit!"

"I know."

I stood up, said,

"You search my room?"

"Daily."

"You fuck, what are you playing at?"

He asked,

"Ever heard of Anthony de Mello? Course not. You've read a handful of mediocre crime books and believe you know life."

He didn't say — "You moron!"

But it hung there.

Oh yeah.

He continued,

"De Mello said ninety per cent of people are asleep. They never wake up. When was the Hungarian Uprising?"

"What is this, a quiz? What do I give a fuck about the Hungarian Uprising?"

"*Voilà*. You don't even know the basic premise of crime writing. *Cherchez la femme*. I grew up watching men who were decent, compassionate people. They had to hunt down and exterminate the child murderers. In so doing, they had to become the beast, turn to stone. They never smiled."

I had no idea where this was going, said,

"I've no idea where this is going."

He produced some pills from the bag, laid them on the arm of the chair, said,

"De Mello tells the story of the Spanish chicken. An eagle's egg falls into a chicken coop. It hatches, and the chickens raise it as their own. The chick learns to pick at the ground, develops like them. One day, he sees a majestic bird fly over. He's told it is the most superb of all creatures. He returns to pecking at the ground, grows old and dies, believing he's a chicken."

I shrugged, said,

"Very deep."

He didn't answer, so I said,

"Lemme tell you about one of the mediocre crime books I've read."

He held up his hand, said,

"You've evidently never heard of the pig."

"What . . . what fuckin' pig?"

"As in . . . don't try to teach a pig to sing. It's a waste of your time, and it only irritates the pig. I apologize for believing you might sing."

Briony cried out, distracting us from where that story might have led us.

She was asleep, but whimpering. I cradled her in my arms and she quietened down. I dozed myself, dreaming of
headless pigs
flying chickens
and
wordless corpses.
Came to as Jordan touched my arm, saying,
"We better go."
He handed me coffee and the pill. I took them. Briony was in a deep sleep and I kissed her forehead. Jordan was watching us, his expression unreadable.

I said, "Only the dead know Brooklyn."

It was a title by Thomas Boyle. Jordan may not have wanted to know about crime novels, but it didn't mean he wasn't going to hear it.

We put on the oilskins, talked quietly about our plan.

The tops of my toes and fingers were tingling. My adrenalin was cranking up a notch. I asked,
"What the fuck's happening to me?"
"You're about to fly."
"What?"
"Let's just say I'm bringing you up to speed."
"Amphetamines?"
"Something like that."
Dawn was breaking. Jordan said,

"I didn't know your sister had a baby."

"She doesn't."

"There's a wardrobe full of baby clothes."

"What? You tossed her room too?"

"Force of habit."

The speed was nipping at my eyes, pushing them wide. Jordan checked his gun, the Sig Sauer. I said,

"You like that number?"

"Nine millimeter, what's not to like?"

We got outside. A street cleaner was leaning against the wall.

Smoke break.

A radio was perched on his cart, ABBA doing "I Have A Dream."

He said, "How-ye, men." Irish.

I said, "Nice bit o' weather."

"Least Sky don't own it yet."

Jordan put the car in gear, and we were outta there. I thought about an interview I'd once read with Charlie Bronson. He said,

> I don't think you ought to have friends unless you're willing to give them time.
> I give time to nobody.

Got to Gant's home in under twenty minutes. Dare I say, I was speeding. It was just on eight. My system was moving into overdrive. Feet and hands twitching, a flood of fuelled ideas toss-tumbling in my head. The street was lined with trees. Jordan said,

"It's a boulevard."

"London's a fuckin' boulevard."

A school bus came slowly down the street. Jordan asked,

"Ever read *Meetings With Remarkable Men*?"

"Desperate men . . . yeah."

He ignored this, eyeing the bus, continued,

"To devour the writings of
> Gurdjieff
>> Ouspensky
>>> Sivananda
>>> Yogananda
>> Blavatsky
> Bailey

. . . Ah . . . and then, to abandon enlightenment, to walk back into darkness."

I was sore tempted to name the Liverpool squad but feared he might shoot me. Gant's front door opened and a woman emerged, holding a young girl's hand. She fussed with the child's schoolbag, fixed her coat, then gave her a hug. The child boarded the bus. The woman watched the bus leave with an expression of loss. Then she went back inside. Jordan said,

"Let's go."

As we walked, he asked,

"Front or back?" I gave a grim smile, bit down and swallowed hard.

What's a sound track for murder? In my head was Leonard Cohen's "Famous Blue Raincoat". As I reached the front door, I muttered about music on Clinton Street. I love that line.

Rang the doorbell.

Chimes!

Worse, it played a tune . . . "Una Paloma Blanca"! I swear to God. Just how long had it been since they'd had a vacation?

She opened the door.

I punched her straight in the face. She went back like a sack of potatoes. I looked round. Half expecting the milkman who'd say — "She didn't pay you either, eh?"

Took hold of her hair, dragged her inside, shut the door. She was out cold. A figure appeared in the hallway. Panicked, I fumbled for my gun. Jordan . . . he shook his head. Then, putting a finger to his lips, he pointed upstairs.

Gant was sitting up in bed, a breakfast tray on his lap. He looked stunned. I said,

"Mornin', all."

He had a coffee cup en route to his mouth. It was frozen mid-air. I walked over, slapped it away. Bounced off the wall.

Jordan was standing by the door. I backhanded Gant and said,

"You wanted to see me, eh? Well, here the fuck I am."

He still hadn't spoken. I grabbed him by the pyjamas, pulled him from the bed. Jordan took a hammer from his coat and began to smash mirrors. Gant said,

"Aw, c'mon."

I took the Glock out, held it loose, asked,

"When you beheaded the dog, did it make you hot?"

"What?"

I lost it and pistol-whipped him till Jordan caught my arm, said,

"He'll lose consciousness."

Coming out of the speed jag, I saw my arms were splattered in blood. Not mine.

Jordan said,

"Time to go."

Gant managed to focus his good eye, said,

"Let's talk a deal."

I shot him in the mouth. Jordan dumped the drug paraphernalia on the bed, then put a bullet in Gant's head. We did a ransack of the house, turned up

twenty grand

a horde of Krugerrands

three handguns

a stash of coke.

Took it all.

As we prepared to leave, the wife began to come round. Jordan kicked her in the head, asked,

"Want to torch it?"

"No, I hate fires."

As we pulled into Peckham, I said,

"Drop me off here, I want to see a friend."

"Are you sure? I mean, you're flying."

"It's a dead friend."

If he had a reply to this, he didn't voice it. He said,

"All this paraphernalia . . ." He indicated the loot.
". . . is yours."

"What?"

"It's yours."

"You're kidding, shit . . . there's the budget for a small country there."

"I don't need money."

"If you insist."

Blame the speed, but I blurted out,

"I think I'm going to get married."

For the first time I saw Jordan give a look of joy. He took my hand, pumped it warmly, said,

"Wonderful, you're thinking right . . . but I'm not sure if Lillian is actually single."

It took me a moment, then I asked,

"Lillian! Who the fuck's talking about Lillian?"

He dropped my hand, his face clouding, asked,

"Somebody else?"

"Sure."

Then I laughed into a blitz of shite talk about Aisling.

Winding down, I said,

"I'll want you at the wedding . . . OK?"

He opened the car door, said,

"Go see your dead friend."

At a florist near the bus depot, I bought a shitpile of flowers. I so overdid that the florist began to get nervous. Till I flashed the cash. I was that demented I wanted to tip the guy. Spin a Kruger in the air, say,

"Have yourself a time."

Having invaded a man's house, punched out his wife, dragged him from his bed, then shot him in the mouth, how was I to set the limits?

Thus, I staggered down to the cemetery with the flowers. A guy leaning against the bingo hall said,

"Me oul' flower."

At the cemetery, the caretaker had placed a white cross on Joe's grave. I said,

"Hey, Joe."

Laid the flowers carefully down. I stood there, up to my eyes in death. I told Joe what had been happening. Then I said,

"I miss you, man."

Back at Holland Park, the speed had evaporated, and I was having a killer downer. I sat on the bed, drank some Scotch, tried to ease the blues. On the bed were the spoils. I said aloud,

"I'm rich, then . . . aren't I . . . fuckin' rich."

The phone rang.

Lillian.

She purred, "How are you, darling?"

"I'm beat is what I am."

"You rest, lover, we'll love later."

"Sure."

"Everything's taken care of now, darling."

"Is it?"

"Oh yes, sleep, my sweet."

I lay on the bed and thought — "What am I missing here?"

I rode the actress as if I meant it. She was surprised at my energy, said,

"Who's been taking their vitamins?"

Sickening myself, I said,

"There's more where that came from."

She hugged me close. I felt post-coital repulsion. I'd made up my mind, one week and I'd walk. Set up home with Aisling and chill. Lillian said,

"Did you see a set of keys on the table?"

"No."

"Go see."

"Now?"

"Please, darling."

I got up, walked naked to the table. A set of shiny keys, picked them up. I could feel Lillian's eyes burn along my body. Went back to the bed, asked,

"These them?"

Her face was glowing, she said,

"They're for a BMW."

"Nice."

"Your BMW."

"What?"

"Took delivery today. I hope you like red."

I hate fucking red, said,

"My favourite."

"Oh darling, it's just the beginning, I'm going to spoil you silly."

"You don't need to do that."

"I want to."

She lay back, and I knew I'd those keys to earn.

I was coming down the stairs as Jordan was coming up. He was holding a silver tray, piled high with letters. I said,

"Bills, eh?"

"Fan mail."

"What?"

"Every day, she hears from her public."

"What makes you so sure they're fan letters?"

"I write them."

The following evening, I was to call at Aisling's place. She'd promised me "an Oirish night".

"What's that?"

"Well, you get to
   drink Black Velvet
     eat Irish stew
       listen to Clannad
    and
   bed a colleen."

"Sounds great."

"It is."

In the afternoon, I went shopping. Time to burn some of the cash. First off to the City. There's a jeweller's tucked right in the centre. Chris Brady, the proprietor, and I go way back. He has an Errol Flynn look. Buckets of charm and graceful movement. He recommends books I should read. When I was almost a citizen, Chris had helped my education. Then I got sidetracked. At first he didn't recognize me, then,

"Mitch?"

"None other."

He came round the counter, gave me a huge hug. Of all the things I am, huggable I ain't. Where I grew up, you touch another man, you lose your arm. He said,

"I'm delighted to see you."

I believed him.

Told him about Aisling and my wedding plan. He said,

"I know exactly what you need."

He disappeared into the back. The radio was playing Midnight Oil and "Beds Are Burning". Catchy tune.

The *Evening Standard* was lying on a chair, early edition. Gant's photo on the front page. I edged the paper round, scanned the story. It was being treated as a drug-related deal.

Chris came back, said,

"This is an Irish wedding ring, known as a heart-in-hand, or Claddagh ring."

I liked it. Caught a glimpse of the price and went,

"Uh-uh."

Chris said,

"Don't worry about that,"
and gave me a 50 per cent reduction.
Time to go, he said,
"Hang on a mo, I have a book for you."
Produced a slim volume. I read the title.

Izzy Baia
by
Kevin Whelan

I asked,
"Any good?"
"Magnificent."
We shook hands, and Chris said, "Listen, come over for a meal some evening. Sandra would love to see you."

I assured him I would. We both smiled at the blatant untruth. Some friends, they don't judge you on the lies you tell.

As I headed out of the city, the ring snug in my pocket, I had a song in my head, Trisha Yearwood with "Hearts In Armor".

It made me sad, but not in any way that worried me.

Next up, I went to Regent Street. I'd promised myself if I ever got flush, I'd buy shoes. Not any shoes, but Weejun. The assistant was better dressed than my bank manager. Same sneer, though. He said,

"How may I help you, sir?"

"You could talk right for a start."

Where do they learn that shit? Is there a school where they grind them in sarcasm and arrogance? I said,

"Pair of Weejun, size ten, tan . . . got it?"

He did.

Put them on and went to shoe heaven.

"Does sir find them satisfactory?"

"Beaut. I'll have two more pairs in black and brown."

The bill was gulp stuff. I gulped. Sneer asked,

"Cash or charge?"

I laid down a wedge, said,

"Take a wild guess."

Then he did the shoe con of:

"Those shoes require careful cleaning."

He began to pile tubes on the counter, I said,

"Naw."

"Sir?"

"You can't beat a spit and a cloth."

"As sir wishes."

I took my packages, said,

"I'll miss you, pal."

He didn't reply.

You gonna shop, you have to take a pit stop. Do the mandatory designer coffee trip. I could do that.

The Seattle Coffee Company. They had coffee nine different ways to Sunday. I ordered a latte. Saying it, you have an instant lisp. The counter assistant was in-your-face fake friendly. Her name tag read DEBI. She asked,

"Like a shot of something in that, sir?"

"Sure; nut a large Scotch in there."

She gave the tolerant smile, said,

"We have

      vanilla

           blackcurrant

              maple."

"Whoa, Debi, just the caffeine."

Plonked myself on the sofa and grabbed a paper. The latte tasted like foam and air. I read about "heshers" — thirteen-year-olds into heavy metal — and "tweakers" — fifteen-year-olds addicted to crystal meth, known as crank or speed. On weekends, they went out with the gang:

"Endlessly cruising the same shopping centres and ghost slot machine arcades."

Getting stoned

drunk

partying

fighting.

Anything to kill the boredom.

The only punctuation was

jail

abortion

suicide.

I put down the paper. The assistant came over, said,

"Would you like a loyalty card?"

"What?"

"Each time you come in, we punch your card, and then, after your tenth visit, you get a free coffee."

"I don't do loyalty."

"I beg your pardon?"

"No offence, Debi, but you're far too young to punch my card."

Outside a guy asked me if I wanted to score some dope. I looked round; no one seemed concerned he was plying his trade in blatant and broad daylight. I asked,

"Do you do loyalty cards?"

Arriving at Aisling's, my heart was pounding. When she opened the door, I went,

"Wow!"

She was wearing one of those sheath dresses. Looked like a slip that shrank. My eyes fell to her cleavage. She said,

"The miracle of Wonderbra."

How could I not say,

"Wunderbar."

Inside, we kissed till she pushed me away, saying,

"Phew . . . I have dinner cooking."

"Me too."

She produced Jameson, said,

"Let us begin, Oirish; would you like a hot one?"

"I'm not even going to pretend I have the obvious reply."

I gave her the book Chris had given me, said,

"I had to search London to get you a Galway author."

She squealed,

"Kevin Whelan! I love him!"

I said, "And . . ."

Produced the box. She took it slowly, opened it carefully, went,

"Oh my God!"

It fit.

The smell of good food cooking wafted from the kitchen. I had a look at a framed poem on the wall. It was by Jeff O'Connell.

It read:

SUFFERING SHIPWRECK
He sought the very moment
when one emotion became its opposite,
As if there he could find the explanation
that might excuse his callous treatment of her.

It gave me an eerie feeling. Like I'd just had my palm read. Aisling asked,

"What do you think?"

"Phew."

"Which means?"

I meant, or think I meant, someone walked on my grave. I asked,

"Where's he from?"

I heard her laugh, then say,

"That's so Irish."

"What?"

"Answer a question with a question."

"Oh."

"He's from Galway, the home of the Claddagh ring. Isn't that odd?"

I thought it was downright spooky.

Keeping the Irish theme, The Fureys were doing "Leaving Nancy," and we'd made hot international love. She asked,

"Do you love me?"

"I'm getting there."

"And will you marry me?"

"I'd say so."

"When?"

"Soon as."

She sat up,

"Oh my God, are you serious?"

"I am."

She ran from the bed and returned with the champagne, said,

"You know, we were to have Black Velvet."

"Yeah?"

In a perfect mimicry of me, she said,

"Screw the Guinness."

I was as near to happy as I'd ever get. That's pretty close.

I tried to do a bad brogue, asked,

"Will you be wanting the wedding to be big?"

"I'll be wanting it to be soon."

Love or its neighbour must have made me selfish or heedless or simply an arsehole. I'm reaching . . . trying to lay off the fact that I didn't check on Briony. Not even a phone call.

Two nights later, I was deep in sleep at Holland Park. It took the phone some ringing to pull me awake. Finally, I grabbed for the phone, muttered,

"What?"

"Mr Mitchell?"

"Yeah."

"It's Dr Patel."

"Who? . . . Oh yeah . . . Jeez, what time is it?"

"Two thirty . . . there's an emergency . . . it's Briony."

I sat up.

"Is she OK?"

"She's apparently taken an overdose."

"Apparently? What are you doing . . . guessing?"

"I'm trying my best, Mr Mitchell."

"Yeah, yeah, I'm on my way."

I thought — "No better time to give my new BMW a run." I also thought that no way could it really be red. Not even Lillian Palmer could pull off a red BMW.

It was. Bright fucking red.

Well, leastways it was night. How much could it show? Glided up towards the lights in Notting Hill

Gate. It was a dream drive. As I waited for the light to change, a blue Mazda cruised up beside me. Packed with brothers, rap streaming. My window was down, and the driver clocked me, said,

"Bro, dat be a righteous colour." I nodded. He reached over, handed me a jay, said, "Rig like dat, yo gots to git down."

I took it, inhaled deep. The light went green, and the driver gunned his engine, said,

"Y'all be cool."

The dope kicked and my vision blurred. I nearly did a cyclist at the Elephant and Castle roundabout. He shouted obscenities, and I answered,

"Be cool, bro."

When I got to St Thomas's, I parked in their doctors' allotted area. A uniform came bundling out, crying,

"Oi!"

"Yes?"

"This is reserved for doctors."

"I'm a doctor."

"Eh?"

"How much are you smoking? Good Lord, man, look at your pallor, when did you have an ECG?"

"I . . ."

"And cut out those burgers, you won't last six months."

I strode past him. Though with the dope, it was more of a mellow sweep.

I met Patel outside the ICU. He didn't shake hands, accused,

"You're stoned!"

"So?"

"Well, it seems inappropriate."

"Is Briony conscious?"

"No."

"So what does it matter a fuck, then?"

I didn't know the rage was there till I tapped into it. The old "kill the messenger syndrome".

He said,

"We pumped her out, she'd ingested seventy-nine paracetamol tablets."

"Counted them, did ya?"

Spittle from me landed on his white coat, my fists were balled. Two seconds and I'd be battering him. He began to back off, asked, "Would you like to see her?"

"Take a wild fuckin' guess."

I had to suit up for ICU:

gown

mask

booties.

I felt like an unneeded extra on *ER*.

Briony looked dead. Pale as the very colour of despair. A respirator was aiding her breathing.

I held her hand and a nurse got me a chair. The nurse said,

"You can talk to her."

"Can she hear me?"

"Perhaps."

"It would be a first."

"Excuse me?"

"She never heard me before."

She died after six. Never made it to the dawn. Later, Patel took me to his office, said,

"Feel free to smoke."

"Thanks."

"I am so very sorry."

"Whatever."

"I had . . . feelings for her . . . I . . ."

"Yo . . . Doc, I don't wanna hear it . . . OK?"

"Of course."

The paperwork done, the doc said,

"You'll want her in the family plot."

I gave a laugh steeped in malice, said,

"The family plot is a shoebox."

"Oh."

He hung his head. I reached in my pocket, took out a heavy wedge, dropped it on the table, said,

"Burn her. Isn't that what you Indians do? Then plonk her ashes on your mantelpiece and you finally get to have her."

I was walking away when he asked,

"What about her little dog?"

"He lost his head, it's a family trait."

At reception a nurse called,

"Mr Mitchell?"

"Yeah?"

"I am so sorry."

"Sure."

"Will you want her raincoat?"

"What?"

"She was wrapped in a coat . . . would you like to take it?"

I gave her a long look, said,

"She was about your build, you keep it."

I turned to go when she said,

"It's Gant."

"What?"

"The coat, it's a Gant, American label — a very expensive brand."

I couldn't get to grips with that, waved her away. Outside, I tried to light a cigarette. My hands were doing a fandango. I threw it away, headed for my car.

Blame the events of the previous days, jeez, the previous weeks, or the dope, the booze, or the shock of Briony's death, or I'm just a dumb motherfucker.

Whatever, I failed to ask two vital questions.

(1) Who found Briony?

(2) Who brought her to the hospital?

No, I was intent on small damage. To lash out at the nearest.

The uniform came striding out. I focused on his shiny pants.

It mirrored the spit in his soul. The miracle of dry cleaning hadn't filtered down to him yet. He folded his arms, didn't speak. Fine, I thought. Fuck you, Jack.

I reached the BMW. Along the front fender, gouged in huge letters, was

I spun round, shouted,

"Call yourself a security guard?"

"Why not? You call yourself a doctor."

Pure white rage coursed through me. What especially galled me was the gouger couldn't spell. I asked,

"And you'll have no idea who did it."

He gave me a toothy smile, said,

"Nope."

Then the anger evaporated. I couldn't be bothered. Got in the car, pulled outta there. I can still see his face, writ in dismay that I just let it go. Felt dismayed myself.

Rest of the day, I drifted like a ghost through pubs in south-east London. I was there

I drank

but never touched base.

Later, at Holland Park, I fell asleep in my clothes. Woke to find the actress giving me a blow job. She stopped, said,

"Don't worry, darling, we're nearly there."

Then, I thought she meant bringing me to climax. As with most everything else, I was hopelessly wrong.

Next morning, I shaved, showered and put on fresh clothes.

Felt fresher if not better. Working through a double hit of nicotine and caffeine, the phone went. I said,

"Yeah?"

"Mitch."

"That you, Jeff?"

"Yeah, listen, — mate, I'm gutted about Bri."

"Thanks."

"Listen, mate, I need to talk with you."

"Okay."

"Eight this evening, the Charlie Chaplin."

"I'll be there."

Put the phone down, thought — "Was there an edge there?"

Then I shrugged it away, not Jeff, no . . . he was my mate. Fuck, he and I went way back.

Outside the house, Jordan was doing the garden. I said,

"No end to your talents, eh."

He looked up, didn't answer. I walked over to the BMW.

The gouge was gone. Jordan said,

"I couldn't allow it."

"You did the repairs yourself?"

"Yes."

"Fuck it, that's brill."

"As always, Mr Mitchell, you overstate the obvious."

My marriage plans required a birth certificate and balls. I'd got one, hoped I had the other. For the meet with Jeff, I put on the Gucci jacket, considered packing heat but decided against. I didn't take the BMW. In southeast London, it would be snapped in a mo. Hailed a cab and told the cabby,

"Charlie Chaplin at the Elephant."

He didn't say anything for a bit, then,

"You know why it's called that?"

"I've a feeling you're going to tell me."

"Cause Charlie was born up the road in Kennington."

I didn't answer lest I encouraged him. Then, undaunted, he asked,

"Know who else lives there?"

"No."

"Greta Scacchi!"

"Gee."

We got there, I paid him, said,

"You ought to be on *Mastermind*."

"Want me to wait?"

"I'll pass."

He handed me a card, said,

"Gimme a bell anytime."

I'd torn it in ribbons before I got to the pub.

Jeff was sitting at the bar, a pint of Guinness in his hand.

I said, "Waiting long?"

"No."

"What's on your mind, Jeff?"

He took a long breath, said,

"That guy, Kerrkovian, he's disappeared."

"Good riddance."

"No argument there, but the kid has gone too."

"Kid?"

"The punk kid, the one you'd a hard-on for."

"So?"

"So, he was hanging with Kerrkovian."

I took a drink, rolled a cig, asked,

"Spit it out."

"Had you anything to do with it?"

"No."

He drained his pint, stood up, said,

"People liked that kid; word is you offed him."

"Bollocks."

"Thing is, Mitch, once you've buried your sister, you'd be advised to stay away from south-east London."

It took a moment to sink in, then I said,

"You're threatening me?"

"I'm delivering a message."

Seemed to me I'd been taking shit from people all day. I said, "Here's a message back."

I swung fast, caught him under the chin. He crashed back against the bar. I turned on my heel, walked straight out.

Not a sign of a cab. I half considered trying to fit the scattered card back together.

＊ ＊ ＊

Next morning, my right hand hurt like a bastard. The knuckles were bruised and swollen. I bathed it and then poured TCP over it.

Stung?

Oh fuck. I dropped the bottle, let my head back and howled like a son of a bitch.

Put on my suit and checked my reflection. Looked like a minor-league mob guy. Bottom feeder and not connected.

Went down to the kitchen, smelt good aromas. Jordan was at the stove, asked,

"Hungry?"

"Like a wolf."

I pulled up a chair and he poured me a scalding hot coffee.

The aroma was so wonderful. I was afraid to taste it. How could it measure up? He put a plate before me. It was eggs over easy, with crispy bacon interwoven. Got a wedge of that with heavily buttered toast, bit down. Ah man, like a childhood you never had. Jordan sat down, dug into his. He ate like a demon, as if he'd a fire that couldn't be fed. He finished fast. I said,

"Jeez, you needed that."

He gave a cold nod. I added,

"You're not a morning type, right?"

"I have a busy schedule."

Stood up, went to a drawer, took out a thick envelope, said,

"You haven't been collecting your wages."

"What?"

"You are still on the payroll."

Then he looked at me, slow, asked,

"Unless you are considering resignation?"

It crossed my mind to tell him I was outta there, in jig time. I said,

"'Course not."

As he cleared the plates, he said,

"Madam and I will be out all day next Friday. Can I rely on you to care for the house?"

"That's what you guys pay me for. What is it, a hot date?"

"Madam is being interviewed by *Hello!* in preparation for her return."

"It's supposed to be unlucky."

"I don't believe in luck."

"Course not . . . do you believe in anything?"

He was surprised, said,

"Madam, I believe only in Madam."

As before, he was telling me exactly how it was. As usual, I wasn't listening properly.

I drove to Kensington High Street. Despite the BMW's colour, I loved that motor. Went and got the registry office squared away. In ten days we'd be married.

To celebrate, I went into Waterstone's and bought Derek Raymond's *The Devil's Home on Leave*.

It fit.

Then to a coffee shop and ordered a large cappuccino, no sprinkle. Got a comfortable seat next to the window and settled in to read.

I put the book down, sipped at the coffee, thought of Briony. As a little girl, she used to say,

"Won't you mind me, Mitch?"

I'd promise with all the empty power and earnestness of a seven-year-old boy.

Got up quickly and left, drove to Aisling.

Derek Raymond said when you dream of rain it's a sign of death. It was raining now. Briony, at twelve years old, crying,

"I'd stand in the snow, with no clothes on, to look at you."

Phew.

Only later did I realize I'd left Derek Raymond in the window on High Street Ken. Maybe he would have liked that, listening to the rain, the rich aroma of fresh brew all round.

I spent the afternoon in bed with Aisling. Later, I asked,

"Was it good?"

"Ish."

"What?"

"Just kidding, it was magic. I just want to lie here, feeling like the cat who got the cream."

The rain lashed down on the roof. I said,

"Good thing we're in."

"Better that we're in each other."

Argue that.

Aisling held her left hand up to the light, said,

"See my ring, how the light bounces off it?"

"Yeah?"

"Notice the very top of the heart?"

I looked. Seemed like a small golden heart. So? I said,

"So?"

"It's chipped."

I sat up.

"You're kidding. I'll have Chris's arse."

"No . . . no, I love it like that. It's perfect that it has a tiny blemish."

"What?"

"The flaw makes it ideal."

I didn't get this, said,

"Is this an Irish thing?"

She laughed out loud, said,

"It's a girl thing."

"Right!"

I took her in my arms, could feel her heart beating against my chest. I was about to say — "I love you."

It was right there, my brain and tongue in sync to deliver the words I had never used, when she said,

"Will you do something for me?"

"I'll give it my best shot."

"Peter Gabriel has a song called 'I Grieve'."

"And?"

"Will you listen to it with me?"

"Like . . . now?"

"Yes."

"OK . . . but . . . are you unhappy?"

"This is the best moment of my life."

"Phew! Let's give Pete a turn, then."

As we listened, she held my hand in both of hers, her face in rapt concentration. I've no beef with Peter Gabriel, in fact I love "Biko", but this just didn't fit. The sadness and pain of his voice and the lyrics made you reach for a lethal Scotch. Finally, it was done, and she turned her face to me, eagerness electric. I said,

"Now, that is an Irish thing."

I got back to Holland Park late on Tuesday night. Watched *South Park* and wouldn't have balked at adopting Kenny.

The actress appeared at my door, asked,

"Can I visit?"

"I'm a little beat, Lillian."

"As in beating your meat?"

Closer than she could imagine. In her left hand was a bottle and two glasses. Held by the neck as they do in the movies.

Scratch that, as they do in *old* movies. She asked,

"Can a girl buy her fellah a drink?"

Jesus!

I said, "Maybe a nightcap."

She handed me the booze, said,

"It's Dom Pérignon."

"Whatever."

I popped the cork pretty good. As is mandatory, most of the champagne went on the floor. People seem to regard that as part of the deal. Some deal.

Lillian was wearing a silver ball gown. I'm not kidding — she told me. I asked,

"Why?"

"I thought a little ballroom dancing would be novel."

"And you hired a band?"

"An orchestra."

I looked at her face, said,

"I can only hope you're kidding."

Sly smile, then, "I don't do kidding."

"What, they're huddled in the hall?"

I indicated my room, added,

"Gonna be a tight squeeze for the guys."

"They're in the ballroom."

I didn't even ask where it was, but thought, "How fuckin' big *is* the house?"

I'd never explored it, and come Friday, when they were *Hello!*-ing, I'd go through it like a dervish. Yeah, shake them branches, see what shook free.

We clinked glasses and I said,

"*Sláinte.*"

She asked, "What is that?"

"Irish."

She shook herself in mock disgust, uttered,

"A nation of buffoons and blarney."

"Gee, how English of you."

She moved closer, said,

"Allow me to French you."

I did.

Her perfume was mothballs in chlorine. Blame the champagne, but I came. Not in a spectacular way due to my exertions with Aisling, more a sad drizzle. Like rain they get in Crete.

Wiping her mouth, she said,

"We need to get lead in that pencil."

I said, "You've exhausted me, there's no way I'll get to the dance."

She bought it, said,

"We'll dance tomorrow, now sleep, my sweet."

When she'd gone, I took a scalding shower, couldn't quite rid myself of her touch. In bed, I tried to think of Aisling, tried not to think of Briony.

Neither worked.

The call came at two o'clock on Wednesday afternoon.
I picked up the phone, identified myself as "Yes" to
"Mr Mitchell?"
It was the police.
"Are you familiar with one Aisling Dwyer?"
"Yes."
"I regret to inform you there's been a tragic
accident."
"What?"
"A piece of paper in her purse listed your name and
number."
"How is she,
              where,
                      when,
                             oh God."
I got the address of the Islington hospital and drove
over.
I don't even remember the series of events. Only that
she was dead, from a hit-and-run on the High Street. A
man had leant over, held her hand until the ambulance
came. Some time later, someone gave me a coffee. It
tasted like the styrofoam cup. Then I was given the
"brown envelope". Her possessions.
It held
money

purse
calling card
watch
no ring.

Must have left it at home. I was surprised she'd taken it off.

At an early hour of Thursday morning, I drove home. Drank lights out.

I surfaced around noon on Friday. Jesus, I was shook. My fingers fandangoed again as I tried to roll a smoke. Sweat cascaded down my forehead, stinging my eyes. I knew a shot of Scotch would shut the works down, but would I stop?

Would I fuck.

Went to my mini fridge, got a brewski. Foster's.

When did I buy that, or worse . . . why?

Never-no-mind.

Popped the ring, drank full. It poured down my chin, drenching my sodden T-shirt. Then, à la Richard Dreyfuss in *Jaws*, I crushed the can, slung it.

Did its mini job, and my system eased. Took a shower, shaved, changed into a white shirt, fresh black jeans. Risked a mirror glance.

Like any seedy waiter.

OK, time to forage.

The house was silent, they really had gone. I avoided Lillian's room. It was already too familiar. Took a time till I located Jordan's. Knew it must be his as the door was locked. Braced myself against the far wall and took a flying kick. Near took it off the hinges.

I entered cautiously — booby traps were a definite possibility.

The room was Spartan, with an army-style cot, spitmade.

I went through the wardrobes first. Half a dozen black suits, black shoes and white shirts. On a top shelf was a shoe box that held a .454 Casull. It is one heavy mother. In every sense not too accurate, but the load it packs would blow a hole in an elephant. I put it gingerly in the waistband above my arse. Three drawers to go. First held spotlessly clean underwear. The second had a pile of old theatre programs, all Lillian, of course. Finally, a storm of socks, put my hand through them. Pulled out a dog collar, said,

"What?"

It had dried blood and a name. Bartley-Jack.

Before I could react, my other hand touched a ring. Held it up to the light, the heart displaying the tiny flaw she so admired. I sank back on the bed, my mind reeling.

I think I must have made a sub-audible noise. It's when people under total stress speak aloud without realizing it. Everybody does it, but some are more prone. I'd never be more prone than then. The sound is below normal hearing range. Years ago, it was called "thoughts in the throat". Course, the higher the stress, the louder the sound. Mine was heard, all right.

A voice said,

"Ah, the penny droppeth!"

Jordan was leaning against the shattered door, his arms folded. It took me a bit to find some voice, but eventually,

"You killed them all . . .
Briony
the dog
Aisling?"

He nodded.

"Christ Almighty . . . *all* of them?"

"Obstacles."

"What!"

"To Lillian."

"You're a fuckin' psycho."

"How trite, how utterly predictable."

I gut-shot him.

They say it's the most intense pain in the world. Slumped in the doorway, he wasn't arguing it. I stepped over him, and he grabbed at my ankle, said,

"Finish it."

"Get fucked —" and I kicked him in the balls. Double his bet.

Lillian was sitting up in bed, a pink shawl on her shoulders.

She gave me a smile, asked,

"What was that commotion, darling?"

"The butler did it."

I lazily raised the gun at her, and she asked in a petulant voice,

"Oh silly, really, how am I supposed to react?"
My turn to smile. I said,
"You're an actress. Try acting scared."